The Lady of Lake Como

A Historical Fiction by Terrance D. Williamson

Dedicated to:
My eternal sons,
My loving daughter,
And my patient wife.

Italian Phrases

If you're not familiar with Italian (which I consider to be the most beautiful language in the world), then you may find it useful to have a reference while reading this book. Don't worry, I've kept the Italian rather simple, but I've used it to provide a sense of realism and place you, the reader, into the setting. Some words will be entirely familiar to the majority, but just in case, here are the Italian phrases:

Grazie mille: Thank you Very Much

Prego: You're welcome

Chi è: Who is it?

Santo cielo: My Goodness

Salve: Hello (formal)

Arrivederci: Goodbye (Formal)

Mio Dio: My God

Midispiace: I'm Sorry

Per favore: Please

Scusi/a: Pardon/Excuse me (formal/informal)

Amica mia: My friend (feminine)

Amico mio: My friend (masculine)

Come stai: How are you? (informal)

Sto bene: I'm good

Ragazzo mio: My Boy

DISCLAIMER: While certain events are taken from Leonarda Cianciulli's life and those associated with her, this is the fictional telling of the historical events that are, in no way, the actual representation of either Leonarda Cianciulli or those associated with her. I would encourage anyone interested in her life, to research and read about the extraordinary events that have been fictionalized in my book.

Inspired by Real Events

Chapter One:
Of Mice and Men

"Patience is bitter, but its fruit is sweet."

Aristotle

Lieutenant Ezio Milanesi sat motionless at his desk in his office, his hands folded tightly across his chest, careful to not emit a single sound. Alone, and in the deathly silence, he listened intently for any sign of movement. Yet the only noise was the ticking of the clock as it reverberated against the brick walls of his dimly lit office, which he felt more resembled a holding cell than a suitable workplace.

With iron bars across the singular window that faced south, Ezio's environment in the police station was an exposition of dreariness. Apart from the hint of the sun that seldom graced his walls, the only other light afforded during the long hours demanded of Ezio was a pale orange lamp situated on the edge of his little desk.

The little desk was unusual in such a large office, but Ezio found it comforting. It was pretentious, he believed, to have a large desk, and certainly unnecessary. All he required to complete his work adequately was a phone, some paper, and a pen. Decorating the desk with Roman busts or large paperweights was quite ridiculous in Ezio's opinion, as he preferred the simple and orderly.

Other than a conceitedly and obligatory large portrait of Benito Mussolini hanging on the wall, the office was entirely barren. Yet even this single image was too much for Ezio to bear, especially with how ridiculous the photograph of Il Duce (as Mussolini was affectionately labeled by his supporters) stood out against the pale grey brick.

The painter had adorned the dictator in a rather flattering ideal by softening his cheeks and chin, giving him a somewhat youthful glow. With the Italian coat of arms underneath Il Duce's portrait, Ezio pondered how he was alone in seeing the irony. Mussolini had positioned himself above the Italian nation and their king, and Ezio stared back into Benito's omniscient gaze with a secret loathing.

Yet the bleak atmosphere and the horrid painting paled in comparison to the pain of hearing the pleasant sounds of Lake Como just outside his office. The sounds of happy children squealing in their delight as they skipped rocks, or the ringing of bells on boats fishing or transporting goods, or the calming crash of waves against the shore, luring him with the promise of relaxation. Ezio often felt like a prisoner hearing the sounds of freedom, never permitted to indulge.

Still, for the last couple of weeks, his latest worries had rather transcended these concerns and now painted them as trivial. Sitting on his desk, staring discontentedly up at him, was the order to arrest a man named Signor Lehner.

The town of Giulino, situated beside Lake Como, was a rather small detachment, and action of any sort in the field of policework was particularly rare, if ever. Ezio's worst cases involved bored teenagers causing trouble, or elderly widows worried about imagined dilemmas that were clearly placeholders for desired human interaction.

But this order, especially given the gravity of the crime, was of exceptional concern to Ezio, and he struggled with the correct course of action. He had intended to arrest Signor Lehner on a previous occasion, but his conscience had stayed his hand, and Ezio did not follow through—especially since Signor Lehner was entirely ignorant of the charge, as he should be.

Signor Lehner's only crime was the accident of his birth. While most Italians cared little for their Fascist counterparts in Germany and their hatred for the Jewish race, the law was clear as to what was required for Jews, especially those of foreign birth. Signor Lehner, unfortunately, had immigrated from Austria, and Ezio's orders were to arrest him for noncompliance.

A squeak sprung from the southwest corner of the office.

Ezio ceased breathing as he stilled his body and waited anxiously for another noise that would reveal his enemy's location. He was certain that he had finally discovered where his adversary was camping and didn't want to miss this opportunity to expel the rodent.

"Get ready," Ezio spoke softly to his cat, Wolfgang, who was sitting sleepily on the edge of a chair next to the desk.

Another squeak.

"Now is your chance!" Ezio whispered harshly to Wolfgang, not wanting to scare the rat into silence.

Yet when Wolfgang showed no interest, Ezio sighed in his frustration and unholstered his pistol as he pointed the weapon into the dark corner. He would kill the vermin by any means necessary.

Drawing a deep breath, he steadied his aim while slowly placing his finger over the trigger, ready to squeeze at the first sign of movement.

"Lieutenant Ezio!" Second Lieutenant Armando burst into the office, his face buried in a newspaper.

Startled, Ezio nearly fired off a round, but with an annoyed huff, he returned the pistol to his holster. Emitting a loud, defiant squeal, the rat took its opportunity and scurried along the wall to the northern side of the building.

"You damned nuisance!" Ezio grabbed a pen from the desk and threw it with all his might at his target, who narrowly escaped.

"The pen is not mightier than the pistol, I see." Armando studied Ezio with peculiarity.

"You're useless." Ezio pointed an angry finger at Wolfgang.

"The rat is back then, is it?" Armando closed the door behind him. "Have you placed Wolfgang on half rations yet?"

"He's down to half a cup of milk." Ezio sat back in his chair as he glared at the cat. "I believe hunger is not his motivation, but never mind that. What is so urgent?"

"The result of the bombings by the Americans last night." Armando slammed the paper down on the desk as he tapped his finger repeatedly and enthusiastically on the article.

"Mio Dio!" Ezio sat upright quickly as he snatched the paper and began reading frantically.

The newspaper displayed a menacing picture of a sky littered with black dots that was set beside another photograph of the resulting devastation. A family was pictured outside their home in shock and grief, where a mother half-heartedly held a brick down by her side. It was likely all that was left of her house, and Ezio's heart broke for her.

"B-42s?" Ezio sighed.

"Si, as far as I can tell." Armando leaned over the desk, and Ezio thought that he appeared nervous.

"We're far away from the danger," Ezio spoke softly to calm the second lieutenant's nerves. "This is the first strike by the Americans in the south. We're far removed from the danger up here in the north. Our men will retaliate in kind."

"I have family in the south. Fortunately, they're all safe."

"How many casualties?" Ezio scratched the stubble on his chin, not entirely sure he was ready to hear the answer. "The paper doesn't say."

"That depends on which truth you would like me to relay?" Armando asked quietly before shooing Wolfgang off the chair and taking his place.

"Dangerous words." Ezio glared at Armando in warning.

"Who's going to arrest me?" Armando chuckled as he leaned back in the chair and put his feet up on the desk. "You and I are the authority here."

"Mussolini's secret police are everywhere," Ezio whispered as he glanced at Wolfgang, who was now settled nicely in a small pocket of sunshine on the floor.

"Are you spying on us?" Armando asked Wolfgang, who simply twitched his tail and looked about the room indifferently.

"I do make light of this, but you really should be cautious." Ezio once more folded his hands across his chest as he resumed his previous position. "And get your feet off my desk!"

"I ask again, which truth would you like to hear?" Armando grew solemn as he complied with setting his feet back on the floor.

Ezio paused for a moment as he studied Armando warily. The second lieutenant had only arrived in Lake Como a few weeks ago as a fresh graduate from the academy, and Ezio surmised that he should tread carefully.

"As Pontus Pilate once asked, 'What is truth?'"

Armando grinned, slightly raising the corner of his mouth, but Ezio thought he caught a hint of disappointment. Still, Armando's viewpoints were vague to Ezio, who wondered if his compatriot intended for good or for ill. Armando, too, Ezio concluded, was likely just as curious, but in this world where even whispers were perilous, it was hard to know who to trust.

Suddenly, Wolfgang's ears perked up, and his little nose bounced as he sniffed in the air. Then, drawing upon some hidden energy, Wolfgang bounded up and moved swiftly toward the two officers.

"Are you only now smelling the fresh meal that has been scurrying by right under your nose?" Ezio scoffed.

"Go away!" Armando waved for Wolfgang to leave them, yet Wolfgang, Ezio noticed, seemed oddly interested in the second lieutenant.

"Looks like he's becoming fond of you." Ezio smirked.

"Well, I'm still not fond of him! Go!" Armando swung with his hand, yet Wolfgang's interest was not swayed.

"Armando…" Ezio squinted at the second lieutenant. "Open your jacket."

"My jacket?" Armando frowned sharply at his superior, although Ezio believed he was merely feigning ignorance.

"What do you have?" Ezio pressed.

"Nothing! What would I have that your cat would be interested in?" Armando frowned at Ezio.

"Armando." Ezio rolled his hand, gesturing at the second lieutenant's jacket.

"Fine! Fine!" Armando growled. "I'll show you."

Slowly, Armando opened his jacket to reveal a brown paper bag. Opening the bag, Armando glanced over his shoulder at the closed door before displaying a red, juicy cut of beef that was seasoned with spices and marinating in herbs of rosemary and thyme.

"Where did you get that?!" Ezio's eyes bulged with a conflicting mixture of indignation and desire.

"I confiscated it." Armando raised his chin as he bravely, or foolishly, defended his actions.

"Mussolini has set very strict rations." Ezio leaned over and snatched the bag from Armando. "You could be thrown in jail for this."

"As I said, you and I are the authority. If you want to place me in chains, I won't refuse." Armando sarcastically held out his hands to Ezio. "Or you can help me dispose of it. Besides, I confiscated it."

"You stole it from someone who is hungry, you mean." Ezio unwrapped the bag again as he inspected the meat, eliciting temptation.

His mouth began to water as his senses were arrested by the delicious smell. It had been years since he had tasted such a prime indulgence, but as quickly as the temptation arose, Ezio wrapped the beef up again.

"My family is hungry, too," Armando spoke softly. "I don't know if I can suffer through any more canned food."

"We're all making sacrifices to see our nation to victory." Ezio's stomach growled. "I've actually grown rather fond of the pickled hot dogs."

"What are you going to do with it?" Armando cleared his throat as he accepted his defeat.

"I'll alert the proper authorities. They will distribute it as they see fit."

"Aren't we the proper authorities?"

"You know who I mean."

"The secret police will just eat it themselves. They don't care about us." Armando shuffled his jaw as he grew annoyed. "They're an immoral brood of vipers."

"I can't control how they behave, but I can control my own actions."

"Ever the puritan." Armando looked at Ezio with slight disdain.

"I'm your commanding officer!" Ezio lost patience with his second lieutenant. "I know I've cultivated a degree of comradery not likely permitted in other stations, but that does not provide you with license to abuse my good graces. I may be a puritan, but I believe that every effort, no matter how small, will make a difference."

"Why is the radio off?" Armando changed the subject as he stood and walked over to the little brown receiver on the corner of the small desk and switched it on.

"How are we to fight both the Americans and the enemies within?" the radio announcer asked with menace. "We must first deal with the Jewish problem in our own land. Then, and only then, will we be able to repel the enemies of glorious Rome! Sons and daughters of Mars, I call upon you to take action in whatever capacity is afforded you. They may be your neighbors, teachers, or friends, but Jews are the adversary of all people. They are responsible for all wars and are responsible for your financial woes. They are rats, they are vermin, and they will remain a plague upon our civilization until they are pulled up by the roots."

That's why the radio is off, Ezio wished to say but held his tongue as he listened to the broadcaster spewing his hate. Again, Ezio glanced at the portrait of Mussolini that was staring back at him as though Il Duce himself was peering into his heart, deciphering his hidden thoughts.

"What's your opinion on the Jewish problem?" Armando asked as he returned to his chair.

Again, Ezio remained wary of the second lieutenant's intentions. Armando had asked innocently enough, and he seemed to be genuinely curious, but Ezio remained suspicious.

A knock came to the door.

Thank goodness! Ezio leaned forward and turned off the radio before shouting, "Chi è?"

The door opened swiftly as Francesca, their receptionist, burst inside while appearing frantic.

While many would find her alarm cause for panic, neither Ezio nor Armando were all that concerned. Francesca's agitation was a permanent mark upon her character, and even with such a small detachment of Giulino, she could scarcely handle the stress.

While it would be expected that one would find such behavior irritating, Ezio didn't despise these qualities in her as she was a constant source of entertainment. She was a breath of fresh air compared to many other receptionists who Ezio had dealt with, that were either bitter at life or just as lazy as Wolfgang. She cared about her work, ensuring that the station's operations were carried out successfully.

"Francesca?" Ezio smiled as he studied her wide, brown eyes staring back at him with dread.

"Uh." Francesca dug into the pocket of her skirt as she retrieved a crumpled piece of paper. "No, that's not it." She grumbled as she dug again into her skirt. "Not that one either."

"How far away is your desk from the office?" Armando asked with a hint of teasing.

"Not far...why?" Francesca watched Armando with worry.

"From the time you took those twenty steps, you forgot what it was you needed to tell the lieutenant?" Armando snickered. "What clouds your mind so? And why would you need to crumple the note in your pockets? Just keep the note in your hand."

"I'm busy thinking of all the ways to keep you two safe!" Francesca barked, not at all pleased with Armando's mockery.

"Keep us safe?" Armando glanced playfully at Ezio.

"You're both rather sensitive." Francesca continued digging through her pockets, desperate to find the correct note.

"Sensitive?" Armando scoffed slightly, but Ezio grinned at how much this bothered the second lieutenant.

"Here it is!" Francesca took a quick breath of relief as she cleared her throat, ready to deliver the message.

"What do you mean sensitive?" Armando held his hand up to stop her as he inched to the edge of his seat.

"Armando!" Ezio threw his hands out in frustration. "Stop proving her point!"

With a huff and a wave of dismissal, Armando sat back in his seat as he crossed his legs and chewed his nails angrily.

"Sensitive," Francesca muttered as she darted her eyes at Armando.

"Drop it!" Ezio grew annoyed as he held up a finger to keep both Armando and Francesca from tearing each other apart. "Francesca, proceed, per favore."

"Signora Setti is here to see you." Francesca refolded the note and shoved it back into her pocket.

"Again?" Ezio frowned.

"That's what you couldn't remember?" Armando scoffed.

"Is this about her sister?" Ezio asked, ignoring Armando.

"She didn't say." Francesca shook her head.

"Send her in." Ezio waved for Francesca to collect Signora Setti.

"Do you need a note to take with you in case you forget?" Armando continued his harassment of the young receptionist, who offered him a challenging glare.

"Also, Captain Cacioppo is attending tomorrow," Francesca spoke swiftly, and both men instantly grew pale.

"Graz—" Ezio choked as his eyes grew wide. "Grazie, Francesca."

"Sensitive." Francesca nodded with a grin of satisfaction as she left to usher Signora Setti in.

"Why would he be coming here?" Armando swallowed. "Is it normal for him to inspect new recruits?"

"He's coming for me." Ezio shifted his jaw as he grew increasingly uncomfortable and glanced at Signor Lehner's arrest order sitting on his desk.

"You?" Armando frowned, but Ezio spotted a noticeable relief wash over him.

"I've delayed Signor Lehner's arrest." Ezio scratched his forehead as he prepared for Armando's barrage.

"Scusa?" Armando asked slowly.

"I couldn't bring myself to take him into custody." Ezio looked sheepishly at Armando. "I was outside his house, cuffs in hand, but something stopped me from knocking on his door."

"He's a Jew!" Armando threw his hands out in frustration at the predicament they were in.

"A fact of which I'm well aware."

"He's also a foreign Jew! An Austrian, for goodness' sake." Armando placed a hand to his head as he grew flustered. "The law is very clear that foreign Jews are to emigrate."

"I know," Ezio sighed. "He served with my father in the Great War, so I have a deep respect for him. I can't justify detaining an innocent man."

"Best case scenario was for you to arrest him and deport him."

"I know."

"Now that he missed his window to emigrate, we'll have to arrest him and send him to a labor camp."

"I know, I know, I know!" Ezio slammed his fist on the desk.

"Listen, you've arrested him a few times already," Armando spoke with a measure of sympathy. "Every time a high-ranking Nazi visits, we bring him in, make him stay a few nights, and then let him return to his life when the Nazi leaves. He's already familiar with this routine. Just let him believe that the Nazis are visiting again."

"That would be unjust." Ezio shook his head in dismissal of the second lieutenant's suggestion.

"You're too lenient." Armando leaned back in his chair. "Now you'll have no choice but to see the full measure of the law carried out. Why did he not comply with the letters demanding his emigration?"

"Would you leave?"

A knock came to the door.

"We'll discuss this later," Ezio spoke softly to Armando as the door opened.

"Lieutenant," Signora Setti brushed rudely by Francesca as she walked briskly into the office.

While Signora Setti was advanced in years, her spirit remained spritely, and she walked with purpose into Ezio's office. With her small purse in hand, a blue and white checkered head scarf, and a tattered coat, Signora Setti sat down across from Ezio with a groan.

"Signora Setti, what can I—"

"You know perfectly well why I'm here!" Signora Setti interrupted, and Ezio caught the look of amusement on Francesca's face when she closed the door as she left, sealing the lieutenant into this cage match, which he was certain not to survive.

"Your sister." Ezio nodded as he folded his hands and leaned forward.

"She's still missing." Signora Setti pressed her finger angrily on the desk, and Ezio felt a cold sweat developing on his brow.

"Signora Setti," Ezio began softly. "We're doing everything within our power."

"Don't patronize me!" Signora Setti looked crossly at him.

"If that's your wish." Ezio grew annoyed. "I'll speak plainly. You showed me the letter from your sister, stating that she was moving to Milan."

"Si, well—"

"And!" Ezio held up a finger as he took a turn interrupting. "You also confirmed that it was her handwriting."

"Still, not one word from her since." Signora Setti tilted her head as she emphasized the peculiarity. "That was three weeks ago."

"Maybe she's settling in?" Armando shrugged.

"Shut up!" Signora Setti scowled severely at Armando, who was surprised at the severity. "I'm speaking with the lieutenant."

"He does make a good point." Ezio threw his lips upside down.

"He's an idiota." Signora Setti's scowl remained affixed to her brow. "I don't value his opinion."

"Signora Setti, I'm disappointed in you for such a harsh judgment of the second lieutenant," Ezio said, attempting to defuse the tension.

"I caught him prowling around the other night," Signora Setti defended her allegation.

"Prowling?" Ezio narrowed his gaze at Armando, hoping for a suitable explanation.

"Patrolling! Pa-troll-ing!" Armando pinched his fingers together as he enunciated the word, and it was clear to Ezio that this was an old argument being rehashed. "I don't prowl! I patrol!"

"So late at night?" Signora Setti shook her head in dismissal of his claim.

"I'm keeping the town safe so that you can sleep peacefully." Armando remained defensive.

"How can I sleep soundly with men like you prowling below my window? You were hoping to steal from a simple old woman, or heaven knows what you were thinking."

"We're straying from the point," Ezio spoke calmly, and both Signora Setti and Armando agreed to an uneasy armistice. "Why don't I reach out to our detachment in Milan and ask if they can check on your sister?"

"You're only thinking of this now?" Signora Setti's frown increased in severity.

"It's important to be good stewards of our police resources, Signora. Especially during these perilous times."

"A good resource would be to use the both of you as cannon fodder." Signora Setti pointed between Ezio and Armando. "Your cat makes a better policeman. Why are young men like you here when you should be fighting the enemy? Leave the police work to old men. They just bombed us, for goodness' sake! You lack experience, so you might as well give your lives for our glorious cause. At least then you would have some purpose."

"You forget, Signora." Ezio tapped his cane beside the desk.

Signora Setti grew silent as she recalled the lieutenant's disability. Still, she was not the sort to apologize, even when so egregiously in error, and remained defiant with her chin held high.

"I'm sure you could serve other purposes in the army." Signora Setti shrugged.

"I tried to enlist. Three times, in fact." Ezio stood and grabbed his cane as he limped toward the door before opening it for Signora Setti, signaling that the conversation was at an end.

"And what's your excuse?" Signora Setti glared at Armando.

"I was ordered to fulfill domestic obligations," Armando replied swiftly, and Ezio gathered that he was prepared for such questioning.

"That means they don't trust you." Signora Setti stood and walked toward the door where Francesca was waiting to usher her back to the foyer. "I don't trust you, either."

"I'll let you know once I hear back from Milan." Ezio closed to door behind Signora Setti and drew a deep breath to calm his nerves.

"I hate her," Armando spoke softly.

"Don't take it to heart. Signora Setti has been awful for as long as I can remember." Ezio limped back to his desk.

"Not her, I meant Francesca." Armando shook his head. "I hate that she is right."

"We're all sensitive to something, I suppose." Ezio sat back down with a huff.

"Still, you have to admit that she's pretty."

"Signora Setti?" Ezio teased as he offered a wry grin.

"You know who I mean." Armando grinned as well. "Is there anything romantic between you and —"

"Goodness, no." Ezio shook his head quickly. "Signora Setti is much too young for me."

Armando rolled his eyes.

"Francesca amuses me, but that is as far as it extends." Ezio ceased his teasing as he provided a genuine response.

"So, there would be no objection to me trying my luck?"

"Francesca might object." Ezio looked apologetically at Armando.

"I think she rather fancies me." Armando raised a cocky eyebrow. "Have you seen the way she looks at me?"

"Have you seen the way she looks at anything?" Ezio chuckled. "Sometimes I'm convinced she was born without eyelids."

"So, Signor Lehner." Armando played with his small mustache as he returned to the previous discussion.

"Right." Ezio ran his tongue along his teeth. "I suppose I can't afford to put that off any longer."

"I'll come with you."

"There's no need." Ezio shook his head as he stood. "I'll take Wolfgang for backup."

Wolfgang meowed.

"He probably has better aim." Armando conceded with a nod. "Do you suppose Signor Lehner will take offense that you're bringing your cat along? It is a rather sensitive undertaking."

"Good point. I'll keep him here to protect you. Why don't you send a telegram to Milan and look into Signora Setti's inquiry?" Ezio walked toward the door.

"You can't be serious!" Armando shot his head back in surprise. "You're actually going to devote police time looking into this matter?"

"If it saves me from another of Signora Setti's assaults, I would send a whole battalion to scour the city, leaving no rock unturned."

"If I were her sister, I don't think I would write back either." Armando shrugged.

"Then let's be thankful on a few accounts that you are not Signora Setti's sister."

A squeak came from the northeast corner of the office, and Ezio's teeth set on edge as he grew annoyed at the pest cowering in the walls.

"That's your job!" Ezio griped at Wolfgang, closing the door behind him.

Chapter Two:
Signor Lehner

"If you must break the law, do it to seize power: in all other cases observe it."

Julius Caesar

"Lieutenant!" Francesca shot her hand up to catch Ezio's attention as he walked by reception on his way out of the station.

"Francesca?" Ezio asked with slight annoyance as the gravity of his task weighed heavily on him.

"I need to write down the mileage for the vehicle." She grabbed a clipboard from her desk and prepared to write on a chart. "How many kilometers are on it?"

"I can't remember." Ezio shook his head grumpily.

"But I need to write it down." Francesca looked back at him with wide eyes as though she were about to be disciplined for her failure to record accurately.

"I'm the only one who drives the vehicle." Ezio shrugged. "There's no point in keeping track."

"Headquarters require the numbers." Francesca tapped the chart.

"How about this? When I get back, you can look at the speedometer yourself."

"I don't know what to look for." She shook her head quickly, and Ezio noticed she was becoming overwhelmed.

"Francesca, amica mia." Ezio glared at her with waning patience. "I need to make an arrest. Do you believe this conversation is more important than an officer of the law carrying out their duty?"

"No." Francesca swallowed, struggling to maintain her composure.

With a grumble under his breath, Ezio turned and shoved the station doors open as he limped to the vehicle. While he felt a touch of shame for his treatment of Francesca, he was also not of the mood to be dealing with her concerns when he was about to unjustly arrest a man.

"This damned leg." Ezio shook his head in annoyance as he struggled to drag it into the vehicle.

"Almost ten years we've been together." Ezio looked at his cane with resentment as he set it on the passenger seat beside him. "I think you'll need to be replaced shortly, though."

Worn and cracked along the handle, Ezio's cane was edging closer to the day where it would no longer function as it was intended. While Ezio despised its purpose, or the concealed reason why it was necessary at all, he couldn't bring himself to part with something that had been with him for nearly a decade.

"Stop delaying," Ezio spoke to himself with irritation as he started the vehicle.

Then, slowly, Ezio left the police station as he drove beside the beautiful Lake Como en route to his spiteful task. The splendor of the scenery was lost on Ezio as he tried to contemplate an alternative to arresting Signor Lehner.

The imposing snow-capped mountains looked down upon him with ominous gazes of disapproval, and Ezio felt as though they were the slumbering guardians of Lake Como. The sun shimmered off the calm water as it promised all the comforts and relaxation that Ezio could ever desire, luring him into forfeiting his assignment. The cool winter air refreshed his lungs, reminding Ezio of how precious life was and how he carried a man's fate in his hands.

Churches, houses, and shops that were hundreds of years old flew by his window as he continued his journey. He wondered about the generations that came before him, and if any of them had ever experienced such cruelty as having to force an innocent man out of his ancestral home. The decaying columns and fragmented statues seemed to scream at him from antiquity, begging him to see reason.

And as if in reply to muffle his conscience, propaganda posters that were plastered on every wall tried to stifle any morsel of mercy he might be feeling.

"Do your duty!" one poster cried in bold white letters on a gloomy black background.

"And you? What do you do for your country?" another poster asked as a heroic soldier clutched a rifle while undeterred by explosions erupting behind him.

I'm not the sort of man to carry out this type of work, Ezio thought as he rounded the corner and Signor Lehner's residence came into view.

Parking the vehicle beside a small pier that was guarded by a stone wall, Ezio studied Signor Lehner's property as he bided his time. He listened to the boats gently bobbing against the pier and recalled the times his father would take him fishing. Life was simpler as a child, and how Ezio wished to climb into one of the boats, sail to the middle of the lake, cast his line, and think upon nothing besides what seasoning to use with his catch.

Looking again at Signor Lehner's residence, Ezio admitted that it was enviable, and his cynicism implored him to wonder if covetousness was playing a factor in Captain Cacioppo's insistence. A mere ten steps from Signor Lehner's door rested the majestic Lake Como, and a simple glance out his window lay the picturesque view of the surrounding mountains. This scenery was the makings of postcards that vacationers often sent home to their loved ones to invoke their jealousy.

At least, that is, when vacationers were still able to travel abroad. The war had changed much, and nations that once had no antipathy toward the other were now ferocious enemies. When he was a boy, Ezio loved when an English or French visitor would stroll along their shores. He recalled the candy they would freely give or the strange way they spoke.

Glancing again at Signor Lehner's residence, Ezio noticed another poster that was plastered on the lamppost in front of the house. It was an odd poster compared to the rest that he had seen, and Ezio found its symbolism not nearly as inspiring as the others.

It was the famous image of the she-wolf suckling the twins Romulus and Remus, yet clutched in the she-wolf's mighty jaw hung a bloodied and limp flag of the United Kingdom. With the American bombing fresh in his mind, Ezio wondered how quickly the tides of war would turn against them, and if such images would be treated with equal disdain should the Allies be successful.

"The law is the law." Ezio turned the vehicle off as he convinced himself of his mission. "I have a duty to uphold it, regardless of my personal feelings on the matter."

Grabbing his cane, Ezio left the vehicle before straightening out his uniform, which, he admitted, was a measure of pride for him. The black trousers were gilded with a bright red stripe down the side of the leg, the black jacket was accompanied by a white cross belt that hung over the left shoulder and right hip, and the black cap was adorned with a silver plume medallion.

Despite the glamor, Ezio would've traded the distinguished uniform for one that wasn't required to carry out such horrific deeds. He imagined if he wore the dark green uniforms of the soldiers in the posters, he would instead carry a measure of pride in his duty. Arresting old, innocent men carried none of the glory sought after during these perilous times, and Ezio began to imagine that Signora Setti was correct in her callous assertion that he should at least be used as cannon fodder.

"Signor Lehner, I regret to inform you..." Ezio practiced what he would say, but the sound of a boat docking at the pier distracted him.

Desperate for anything that would give him reason to abandon his assignment, Ezio decided to inspect and moved to the edge of the stone wall above the pier when he noticed Giuseppe, the soap maker's son, docking his little rowboat. He was a younger man, about eighteen or so, and despite the fact he was tall, lanky, and awkward, Giuseppe was obsessed with his appearance. His hair was neatly combed despite the fact that he had just been on a windy lake, his jacket was clean and unsullied, and even his shoes looked new and brightly polished.

"Lieutenant," a sweet, older voice spoke beside Ezio.

Startled, Ezio turned to find the seamstress, Signora Soavi, approaching him swiftly. She was dressed elaborately, which wasn't unusual, but Ezio found her color scheme rather peculiar. Adorned in a white skirt with a white blouse and white hat, Ezio wondered what event she was attending.

Signora Soavi was a rather affluent woman, the wealthiest person in their little town, in fact, but despite her good fortune, the devotion of a caring husband had remained absent. And now, although she was advanced in years and likely past sixty, Ezio pondered if she was possibly en route to meet a suitor.

"Salve, Signora," Ezio spoke pleasantly to her, although he feared he was inviting a conversation, and he was far from the mood of entertaining trivial discussions.

"Come stai?" Signora Soavi asked with a bright smile, and while the seamstress was often of good cheer, her favorable disposition today seemed to carry extra potency.

"Sto bene, grazie." Ezio looked back at her with slight curiosity for what he feared would transpire next.

Yet instead of the dreaded conversation Ezio expected, Signora Soavi simply stood beside him as she looked out at the lake, where Giuseppe was tying his boat to the dock.

As Ezio watched Giuseppe, he noticed that the young man began to behave rather irregularly. Looking through his jacket pockets as he stood on the dock, Giuseppe suddenly froze before frantically patting down his trousers and every pocket. When he was certain that whatever he was searching for was not on him, Giuseppe jumped back into the boat and tossed aside the canvas before breathing a sigh of relief as he held up a pistol.

What business does he have with a pistol? I should see if he has a proper license, Ezio wondered and was about to confront Giuseppe when Signora Soavi grabbed his arm tightly.

"Almost ten years now since your accident," Signora Soavi spoke softly as she looked at Ezio with sympathy.

"That's right." Ezio cleared his throat as he noticed Giuseppe running up the stairs of the dock and onto the street, where he proceeded to his mother's store at the end of the road.

"Though I imagine it's difficult for you to forget," Signora Soavi glanced down at Ezio's leg.

Biting his tongue from lashing out, Ezio simply nodded as he returned his attention to the lake. He knew that she meant well and wished nothing more than to display her kindness in remembering something Ezio wished to ignore. Still, her casual tone set him on edge, reminding him of the terrible task at hand, which was a mere twenty feet behind him.

"Have you been out fishing lately?" Signora Soavi asked quietly.

"No," Ezio replied swiftly and with more than a hint of frustration.

Nearly ten years had passed since he had last been on the lake. Ezio could scarcely think on the subject and didn't know how he would carry a conversation about the tragic matter.

"Maybe you should," Signora Soavi insisted. "Take my boat. It's the little one next to Giuseppe's."

"That's kind, but I—"

"In fact, I'm giving it to you." Signora Soavi looked at Ezio with soft eyes.

"I..." Ezio didn't know how to respond.

"I'm leaving, you see," Signora Soavi continued. "I'm too old to take that boat out myself anyway. I bought it in the hopes that...well...it doesn't matter now. The important thing is that it belongs to you."

"I can't accept this generosity." Ezio shook his head adamantly, still surprised by the gesture.

"Because you don't understand why?" Signora Soavi pressed.

"Partially." Ezio threw his lips upside down. "But I'm also not going to use it."

"Lieutenant." Signora Soavi stared off into the distance as she grew reflective. "I was given a second chance. What I thought was impossible has now become attainable."

Ezio watched the seamstress for a moment, wondering if she was going to clarify, but when she remained elusive, he asked, "A second chance?"

"It's a secret," she whispered as she placed a finger to her lips. "Soon, you'll understand. Take the boat. Go onto the lake and heal what you never thought could heal. If you don't like it, give the boat to my niece, Paola."

Without another word, Signora Soavi patted Ezio's shoulder and returned in the direction that she had come.

In stunned silence, Ezio questioned if the seamstress was of sound mind as he watched her walk away. Still, her encouragement resounded in his heart, and looking back at the lake, he wondered if he could, possibly, find this healing she was speaking of.

"Signor Lehner, I regret to inform you..." Ezio began to practice again as he turned and approached the house slowly. "No, that's silly. Be honest. He'll understand. I hope. Of course, he won't understand. Why would he? I don't even understand."

With a deep breath to calm himself, Ezio knocked on the door before stepping back and waiting. Yet as he lingered outside the residence, Ezio noticed a woman entering a shop that was just down the street.

It was Signora Cianciulli, Giuseppe's mother, and she seemed, to him, to be rather perturbed. Glancing over her shoulder, yet attempting not to appear obvious, Signora Cianciulli was evidently not wanting to be seen, which Ezio found curious. The store she was entering belonged to her, yet she was concealing something inside her coat that she clearly didn't want anyone to see.

Ezio considered himself to be a rather shrewd judge of character, and he was perceptive of what others were convinced that they had obscured. Signora Cianciulli, Ezio guessed, was involved with something untoward. Yet he was also convinced it was likely petty and not worth further investigation. Rations were strict, after all, and Ezio gave Signora Cianciulli the benefit of the doubt that she was simply smuggling food. Then again, he recalled Giuseppe with the pistol and wondered if he should investigate.

Regardless, Ezio was not afforded a further moment to contemplate the matter as the door to Signor Lehner's house swung open.

Yet instead of the aged man Ezio was expecting to find stood a young nun with enchanting brown eyes, smooth, milky skin, and adorable freckles splattered across her nose and just under her eyes. She was the image of perfection, and Ezio stared back at her in stupefied silence.

"Salve. May I help you?" she asked warily and with a measure of disdain that Ezio was surprised to find in a nun.

"Salve, Sister, I—" Ezio choked on his tongue as all moisture in his mouth had seemingly evaporated. "Mi scusi, I'm looking for Signor Lehner."

"What do you want with him?" The nun crossed her arms defiantly, and Ezio squinted at the peculiar behavior from a woman of the cloth. More peculiar still was her accent. She spoke Italian well, but there were certain inflections that he couldn't quite pin.

"It's a police matter, Sister." Ezio removed his black cap as he addressed her. "I would prefer to keep the matter between Signor Lehner and myself."

"He's here to arrest me," Signor Lehner's voice called from further inside the house.

"Arrest you? For what?" The nun continued in her defiance as she turned to watch Signor Lehner approaching.

"As I stated, Sister, this is between the police and—"

"He's my uncle," she blurted. "I'm permitted to share in this discussion. Or do nuns make you nervous?"

"Normally, they scare me to death," Ezio muttered quietly as he returned the cap to his head, realizing that decorum would not gain him any favorable ground.

"Give me a moment to collect my effects." Signor Lehner appeared in the doorway, leaning on his cane. "Then we can go to the station."

"You're going willingly?" The nun frowned severely at her uncle.

"It's, unfortunately, a regular occurrence." Signor Lehner shrugged. "Whenever the Nazis visit, they lock me up for a night or two, then bring me back unharmed."

"That's unacceptable!" The nun scowled at Ezio.

Signor Lehner chuckled at her temperament. "Sister Faustina, this is the way of the world. Rage against it as much as you'd like, but at least Lieutenant Ezio here isn't forcing me into a labor camp like they do with some of our less fortunate Jewish brothers and sisters."

"Actually," Ezio began slowly, and both Faustina and Signor Lehner watched him warily. "Today, unfortunately, your relocation is more permanent."

"More permanent?" Signor Lehner narrowed his gaze.

"You were notified, in writing, that you were required to emigrate." Ezio cleared his throat. "To date, you have failed to comply."

"And you're here to send me to a labor camp, then?" Signor Lehner tilted his head as he looked at Ezio with an unfavorable gaze.

"I'm here to uphold the law, signore." Ezio swallowed to dismiss the discomfort.

"You can't send my uncle to a labor camp!" Faustina's cheeks grew crimson with rage. "He's more crippled than you are."

"Faustina," Signor Lehner spoke disapprovingly.

"Your uncle was aware of the requirement to emigrate," Ezio defended.

"I didn't believe it would actually come to this." Signor Lehner threw his free hand out in exasperation. "My family has been here for hundreds of years. I immigrated from Austria to take over my aunt's property when I was but a lad, much younger than yourself. I became an Italian citizen. I eat Italian, I drink Italian, I live Italian. I've all but forgotten my mother tongue, and I've replaced it with the language of this land."

"Unfortunately, signore, you're still foreign in the eyes of our government." Ezio chewed the inside of his cheek as he awaited the justifiable beratement.

"I'm just as Italian as you!" Signor Lehner pointed his cane at Ezio's chest before tapping his hand against his hip repeatedly. "I've been suffering with this injury for over twenty years because of my service. I bled for this country in the Great War. Suddenly now, that counts for nothing? I served with your father, if you'll remember."

"I do." Ezio nodded as he stared at the pavement in front of him. "To this day, he still speaks highly of you."

"Are you going to arrest your father as well?" Signor Lehner demanded.

"No, signore." Ezio swallowed.

"Because he's not Jewish?" Signor Lehner tilted his head. "Is that really the only reason you've come to collect me? Or could it be that you want my property? It's a desirable location. Get rid of the old Jew living there, hey? Was that the plan?"

"The plan was to give you as much time as possible to leave the country in good order before it came to this!" Ezio lost his patience and now regretted not bringing Armando for backup. "You were warned, signore, years ago that you needed to relocate. I've withheld executing the law out of respect for you, but that time has elapsed."

"Surely there is some exemption for my uncle?" Faustina asked in a gentler tone. "How can you send him to a labor camp? It will kill him. How can you send a man to his death?"

Ezio looked deep into Faustina's eyes as he weighed his options. She was right, he supposed. Sending Signor Lehner to the labor camp would surely kill him. From what Ezio had heard, the camp guards showed little restraint in exercising brutality, and the thought of subjecting such an honored man to this pain was horrid.

Yet Ezio knew that if he left Signor Lehner alone, both of them would be hung by Captain Cacioppo. If he assisted Signor Lehner in his escape, he would face the noose. There was no solution that Ezio envisioned that didn't end with him swinging from the gallows.

Slowly, Ezio shook his head in regret.

"Is there nothing you can do to help us?" Faustina drew closer to Ezio as she spoke softly.

Frowning, Ezio stared back at Faustina with peculiarity. Her character was so averse to that of a nun, he was beginning to believe that she was concealing her true identity.

"Your niece, you say?" Ezio glanced at Signor Lehner, again curious about her accent.

"My late wife's side, who, as you are aware, is pure Italian," Signor Lehner replied swiftly.

"What if my uncle refuses?" Faustina returned to her defiant demeanor, realizing that her charm had little effect on the lieutenant.

"Then I will return with more men."

"Armando?" Signor Lehner laughed. "I've witnessed that useless twit falling over in a strong wind. How can he contend with me? How pathetic it is that a cripple and a fool are sent to arrest me!"

"If you're wanting my sympathy, you're losing it rapidly." Ezio glared at Signor Lehner for the insult.

"What if..." Faustina looked around briskly to ensure they weren't within earshot of anyone before continuing in a whisper, "What if my uncle disappears?"

"Are you not loyal to your country, Sister?" Ezio narrowed his gaze.

"I'm loyal to its people," she replied quickly and with a hint of menace.

"The law is the law. You must come with me, signore. Pack only what provisions you can carry." Ezio stood back and waved for Signor Lehner to proceed.

"Please." Faustina again drew close to Ezio and took his hand in hers.

As a stranger to affection, Ezio didn't know how to respond but instead stared down at her soft, gentle hand clasping his as he felt a sudden warmth in his chest.

"I know how to get my uncle out of the country. He would be safe, and your conscience would be clear," Faustina continued.

"I'm not a smuggler, Sister, if that's what you're implying." Ezio withdrew his hand and cleared his throat.

"Lugano is only thirty-odd kilometers from here." Faustina pointed in the direction.

"Switzerland?" Ezio scoffed.

"Many Jews, like my uncle, have escaped there. The citizens of Lugano speak Italian. He'll blend in easily."

"You know of this, yet you have not brought this information to the authorities?" Ezio frowned sharply at Faustina. "What order do you belong to?"

"Franciscan," she replied quickly, yet a little too automatically for Ezio's liking.

"Convenient." Ezio squinted as he ran his tongue along his teeth. "Signor Lehner, you have five minutes."

"How can you uphold a law that you know to be unjust?" Faustina pressed.

"It's not my position to interpret the law." Ezio shook his head. "I carry it out."

"Uncle, you can't let—"

"There's no use." Signor Lehner patted his niece's shoulder. "He's only following orders. Men much worse than him will return should I not comply. Only, I will say this, Lieutenant Ezio. I, too, was a soldier. I know what it is to carry out orders that you regret. You can pass off the judgment onto your superiors for a spell, but my face will haunt you for the rest of your life, as does the faces of many who haunt my memories. If I had stayed my hand when my heart compelled me to, I would likely not have had such a long life, but better a short life free of shame than to endure long years of remorse."

Ezio nodded for Signor Lehner to prepare himself as he struggled to disguise how distressed he was by the warning. His heart compelled him, as Signor Lehner stated, to not follow through with his orders, but with Captain Cacioppo attending tomorrow, there was little choice in the matter. If he did not proceed as ordered, it was likely that he would be taken by the secret police, and seldom did anyone return.

"You're not this sort of man." Faustina shook her head slowly as she studied Ezio.

"How do you know what sort of man I am?" Ezio growled before speaking forcefully to Signor Lehner, "Due to your service for our country, I'll afford you the courtesy of not dragging you out of your home in handcuffs. I'll wait by the vehicle for you. If you choose not to come, I'll return with more men. If that does not persuade you, then you will face the wrath of Captain Cacioppo, where I can't predict how he will behave."

Swiftly, Ezio turned and limped toward his vehicle, recognizing that if he spent another minute with Faustina's persuasiveness, his mind would be changed and his life forfeit.

Leaning against the hood of the car, Ezio crossed his arms as he waited angrily for Signor Lehner. He hated the part he was playing in such a despicable and heartless decree, yet his hands were tied in the matter. Still, the old man's words echoed through Ezio's mind as he contemplated the correct course of action, feeling conflicted no matter what outcome he explored.

Again, the poster with the she-wolf caught his eye with her bloodied jowls and the two founders of Rome suckling under her. He couldn't help but feel he had become like this she-wolf: a predator. He had joined the police force to keep the peace and help those in need, but now he found himself as the wolf with blood staining his hands.

"How dare you!" a shout came from down the street, and Ezio spotted Signora Cianciulli standing outside of her shop and shaking her fist at Giuseppe, who was now returning to the pier.

I wonder if she found the gun? Ezio watched the young man speeding away from his mother.

"I can do as I please!" Giuseppe retorted angrily.

"Are you trying to kill your mother?!" Signora Cianciulli placed a hand over her chest.

"I want to do my part!" Giuseppe shrugged aggressively, and at once, Ezio understood the nature of the argument.

It was a well-oiled quarrel between many mothers and sons. It was clear to Ezio that Giuseppe had enlisted, and his mother was irate, which was understandable. Giuseppe had fallen for the propaganda that his service in war was the pinnacle of existence. Glory on the battlefield would bring him everlasting praise and admiration, or so the posters reverberated.

"He's the one you should be arresting," Signor Lehner spoke softly as he approached the vehicle with a small bag thrown over his shoulder, and Ezio breathed a concealed sigh of relief that the old man was complying.

"Pardon?" Ezio asked.

"Giuseppe." Signor Lehner pointed with his cane. "He's not right, in the head, that is."

"He's a little peculiar, sure." Ezio opened the door for Signor Lehner.

"Peculiar?" Signor Lehner huffed. "He's troubled. If you'd seen the things I've seen, you would be more worried about him than an old Jew living in peace. Besides, Signora Cianciulli is a diviner. If anyone is guilty of a sin, it's her."

"They're both odd." Ezio watched the mother and son continuing in their spat.

"Among other things, yes." Signor Lehner grunted as he entered the back of the vehicle before uttering, in a sort of threat, "She's educated in many forms of dark magic."

Entering the vehicle as well, Ezio placed his cane on the passenger seat and was about to turn the key in the ignition when he paused. He knew that regret would follow him forever should he carry out these orders, yet there was no clear substitute.

"We're under attack from the enemy. They're bombing our cities." Signor Lehner huffed. "Yet you're arresting an old man. Shameful. We should be investing our resources adequately. Our country is under grave threat, but you have time to arrest the Jews? Laughable! Enemy of the state, they call me! I bled for this country!"

"If the captain arrives tomorrow and you're still in your house, he will kill you." Ezio grew animated as he looked in the rearview mirror. "I hate this as much as you do, but what I'm offering is mercy. This, believe it or not, is a favor."

"Favor?" Signor Lehner shook his head in dismissal.

"This isn't personal," Ezio spoke after a moment.

"Doesn't change the circumstances."

True, Ezio thought before starting the vehicle, unsure of what else to say. Glancing again in the rearview mirror, Ezio's heart shattered as he caught tears in Signor Lehner's eyes as he looked at his residence. Faustina had remained outside, her hands shaking as she covered her face while trying to maintain her composure.

"You'll—" Signor Lehner choked and tapped his forehead as he struggled to control his emotions. "You'll watch over her? Promise me that much, Ezio, ragazzo mio. Watch over her."

"She's Jewish, isn't she?" Ezio asked softly.

"No, as I said, she's—"

"I can't protect her if you don't tell me the truth." Ezio turned around in his seat as he watched Signor Lehner closely.

"She's my niece." Signor Lehner nodded adamantly, and Ezio sighed in his frustration but understood the old man's reason for lying. He was protecting her, but Ezio had no orders to arrest her. To his knowledge, Captain Cacioppo was not aware of Faustina, and Ezio pondered how he could keep it that way.

"I'll take you to the station for the night. In the morning, you'll be sent for processing."

"The cots there are so uncomfortable," Signor Lehner grumbled.

With one last glance at Faustina, who was still beside herself in dismay, Ezio started the vehicle and began the short journey to the station.

But as Ezio drove, the echo of Signor Lehner's warning resounded in Ezio's heart, and he struggled to think of anything else. *You're simply carrying out the law,* Ezio reminded himself. *I'm not to be partial to which law I obey.* Still, Ezio's conscience wouldn't release him from guilt, and he remained plagued by the cruelty of his duty.

"Watch out!" Signor Lehner shouted, and, snapping back to reality, Ezio swerved, narrowly missing a boy playing with a toy gun in the middle of the street.

Ezio's heart raced as he glanced in the rearview mirror to see the boy's mother offering him a rather unkind gesture before turning her wrath on her son and swatting him generously on the backside.

"Lieutenant?" Signor Lehner asked after a moment, and Ezio detected a measure of hopefulness in his voice. "You seem distracted."

"You mentioned, earlier, about regretting orders..." Ezio asked over his shoulder as he baited the man to divulge.

Signor Lehner stared at his hands as he contemplated before answering, "I fought in the Great War alongside your father. I was an Austrian-born Italian citizen fighting against Austria. The Austro-Hungarian armies were fierce. We often doubled their numbers, but still, they were unshakeable. I was sent out, once, with a few other men to scout for supplies.

"We arrived at a farm that had already been raided by the enemy. The crops were already burnt or destroyed, the animals slain or taken, and the women had been raped. When we arrived, they were preparing supper with the meager supplies they had left. A pot of soup, which was water mixed with some bark, was boiling over a small fire. I suggested that we leave them in peace, seeing as they had nothing to give. My commanding officer was convinced that it was merely a rouse to give the impression that they were impoverished.

"On his orders, we lined up the family outside their house and aimed our weapons with the hopes of garnering a confession. Not a single member of that family wept or begged us for clemency. They simply stood there, vacantly staring down the barrel of our rifles, waiting for the bullets to end their suffering. My commanding officer threatened that he would order us to fire if they didn't advise as to where we could find the hidden supplies.

"To this day, I still remember what it felt like to aim my rifle at that sweet girl." Signor Lehner closed his eyes as he positioned his arms in such a way as though he were holding the weapon. "The father removed his hat, walked slowly toward my commanding officer, and with grace and poise, explained that there were no provisions. My commanding officer again threatened to kill them all. The father replied that my commanding officer must do what he feels is right.

"In a rage, the officer ordered us to fire. At first, the men with me didn't believe him. They, like I, were convinced this was still a ploy to elicit a confession. Yet when the officer gave the order again, and with fury, we knew we must obey. I turned away as I pulled the trigger. I don't know if it was my bullet that killed the sweet girl in front of me, but when I turned back to look, she was dead. If I had refused, I would've been shot. It's days like today where I wish I had done the right thing then and saved myself from years of regret."

Ezio tried to dislodge the heaviness on his shoulders as they arrived at the station. Ezio parked the vehicle and turned it off, yet he remained in the driver's seat, unable to move. Something was nagging at him to ask a burning question, yet Ezio feared the answer.

"Was my father with you?" Ezio turned his head and watched the old man through his peripherals.

"He was the officer," Signor Lehner replied quietly.

Turning away sharply, Ezio scrunched his hand into a fist, furious at the weight of his own conscience.

Then, swiftly as he was able with his leg, Ezio left the vehicle and opened the door for Signor Lehner.

Entering the station with Signor Lehner, Ezio noticed Francesca on the phone, frantically writing down some sort of note that he would likely find crumpled on his desk later.

Guiding the old man to the holding cells, Ezio opened the iron bar door as he ushered Signor Lehner inside, still free of shackles, and helped him organize himself.

It was a small cell, given that it was a small town with a small police detachment. While the cots were, as Signor Lehner put it, uncomfortable, the worst part was the lack of privacy.

There were only two cells in the station, and both were adjacent to each other with iron bars for walls and doors. They were exposed to anyone and everyone who walked down the corridor, and Ezio found this, at times, to be useful. When it came to a drunk who needed to sleep the night off, or a thief comforting a bruised ego, these cells were ideal, but for an old man whose only crime was the accident of his birth, it was an unnecessary humiliation.

"Do you have everything you need?" Ezio asked, although he regretted uttering the question given the severity of Signor Lehner's circumstances.

"Last time you and Armando brought a mattress in for me." Signor Lehner stared at the cot with revulsion.

"Last time Captain Cacioppo wasn't attending." Ezio crossed his arms as he, too, stared at the cot.

"Which camp are they sending me to?" Signor Lehner rubbed the back of his neck as he closed his eyes, still in disbelief at the circumstances.

"Trieste," Ezio replied quickly. "In the northeast."

"I know where Trieste is!" Signor Lehner barked.

"I didn't mean to offend."

"I'm not mad at you, ragazzo mio." Signor Lehner sat on the edge of the cot, which squeaked loudly with the promise of all its discomforts. "You're only following orders."

"Coffee?" Ezio asked after a moment.

"No, grazie." Signor Lehner shook his head. "I don't need another reason to not sleep tonight."

"She's your daughter, isn't she?"

Signor Lehner shot a surprised glance at Ezio, who understood that he had uncovered the truth. It was an old tactic, but still had its uses. Ezio was careful to not ask revealing questions while the individual was guarded, instead, he waited for an opportune time. A simple approach, yet often produced the desired results.

"No, no, she's my —"

"You asked me to protect her." Ezio leaned against the bars. "I need to know the truth."

"What is truth?" Signor Lehner grinned slightly, "Or so a certain Roman once asked a rather famous Jew. Tell me, Ezio, in our little world, are you the pagan and I the Jew? Am I to be crucified for my condemnation of the Romans?"

"Comparing yourself to Christ now, are you?" Ezio curled his lips.

"No, but I can empathize." Signor Lehner offered a little chuckle before his cheer suddenly vanished and he hung his head low.

"I'm not going to arrest her, if that's what concerns you." Ezio limped over to the cot and slowly sat beside the old man as their canes rested between them.

"She's my wife's sister's daughter," Signor Lehner replied while keeping his head low.

"I don't have orders to arrest her," Ezio pressed. "If I can keep her safe, I will, but I need to know the truth. Work off your time in the camp, and then come back home. I'll make sure she stays safe and unknown in the meantime."

A squeak came from the corner of the cell, and Ezio's teeth set on edge as he was reminded of the rodent's presence.

"It's as you have guessed." Signor Lehner lifted his head as he rested his elbows on his knees.

Ezio waited patiently for the old man to continue.

"It's a long story." Signor Lehner picked at a scab on his hand as his lips trembled.

Still, Ezio remained silent. Another trick he had learned through his years of service. An uncomfortable silence is an unbearable torture, and many will divulge much more than they had intended.

"The one sin I don't regret." Signor Lehner raised his eyebrows. "During the Great War, most of us didn't quite know how to react to the new style of fighting. I suppose no war is easy to digest, and the killing of other men is not something one should do with ease, but my grandfather's stories of the Napoleonic wars painted a more graceful and romantic impression of what battle looked like."

Signor Lehner paused, and Ezio gathered that he was growing emotional with the memory.

"The Austro-Hungarian armies were ruthless. They withheld our advance time and time again. I was scared. We all were. The roar and crack of the large guns, the whistling of the bullets over your head, and the screams of agony from those suffering wounds were shocking to our quiet, Catholic existence. Still, I knew I had to do my part. It bothers me knowing that I killed men who were just as frightened as I was. I wasn't killing brutes or hunnish invaders. I was killing boys, about my age, and I never forgave myself for that."

Ezio remained quiet as Signor Lehner took another pause.

"I'm not excusing my behavior, but with that fear in mind, I was convinced that I would not live to see another day. There was a woman in a nearby town, I can't remember the name of it, but she took care of me when I fell ill. She washed me, fed me, and then instructed me in ways of lovemaking that were entirely foreign to me. I abandoned my bonds of marriage and embraced her without a crisis of conscience. Immorality begets immorality, as the saying goes, but I haven't thought of her since, really. Last week, Faustina arrived and knocked on my door, stating that she's my daughter. I laughed at first, but she knew details about me that only her mother could know."

"How did she find you?"

"She didn't mention, but I'm guessing her mother tracked me down some time ago."

The cell returned to silence as both men sat beside each other, neither entirely sure what to say. Ezio, for his part, felt burdened for his charge, and Signor Lehner, Ezio assumed, was still bitter at his situation.

"Will you watch over her?" Signor Lehner asked after a moment. "You're a good boy, Ezio. I know your conscience compels you."

"I doubt she'll want my help." Ezio shrugged.

"You must try." Signor Lehner looked intently into Ezio's eyes.

"I promise." Ezio nodded slightly.

A squeak came again from the corner of the cell.

"Do me a favor." Ezio stood. "If you find that rat, kill it for me."

"I'll never take another life again." Signor Lehner shook his head. "No matter how small."

"That's admirable." Ezio studied the old man with peculiarity. "Then, at least, capture it so that I can kill it."

Chapter Three:
A Wolf in Sheep's Clothing

"Finché c'è vita, c'è speranza.
(As long as there is life there is hope)."

Italian Expression

Briskly, Ezio left the holding cells and rushed back to his office, startling Francesca, who looked up from her desk with eyes wider than usual, wondering what had caused Ezio to become so unnerved.

Bursting into his office, Ezio opened the drawer where he had hidden the beef confiscated by Armando, grabbed the parcel, shoved it in his jacket where he could conceal it, scooped up Wolfgang, and returned quickly back through the station.

"A message for you, Lieutenant!" Francesca stood with a pencil and pen in hand, desperate to deliver a pertinent note.

"It'll have to wait!" Ezio called over his shoulder, and Wolfgang meowed in distress at the upheaval to his routine.

Returning to the vehicle, Ezio gently tossed Wolfgang onto the passenger seat before climbing in and gingerly placing the package of meat into the glove compartment.

"You'll have to try and be charming," Ezio spoke to Wolfgang as he started the vehicle. "We need to convince a nun, if that's even possible. Speaking of which, do you know the difference between a nun and a Nazi?"

Wolfgang meowed.

"That's right, you can negotiate with a Nazi."

Leaving the station, Ezio began the short journey back to Signor Lehner's house, along the scenic view. There was no other place on earth, Ezio was persuaded, that contained so much beauty at sunset. The orange and pink clouds reflected off the still waters, and Ezio held the conviction that even Heaven envied the splendor of Lake Como.

"Whoa! Whoa!" Ezio pressed on the brakes as a man walked casually into the street in front of the vehicle.

It was Luigi, the town drunk, and Ezio wasn't surprised in the least to find that he held a bottle down by his side. Honking the horn in his frustration, Ezio watched with annoyance as Luigi didn't react but continued on his stumbling trajectory into the middle of the road.

"Luigi!" Ezio called as he rolled down the window.

"Lieutenant!" Luigi spun around and held the bottle aloft as though he were greeting an old friend.

"Luigi, get out of the street! Presto!" Ezio waved for him to go back to the sidewalk.

"Luigi!" a woman called from the porch of a nearby house, and Ezio noticed it was Isabella, his wife. "Come back here!"

"Why should I?!" Luigi growled at his wife.

A child began to cry, and Ezio spotted a boy with Isabella, about the age of ten or so, sobbing at the sight of his father yet again in this terrible state.

"You're upsetting him! Come back, I'll make you something to eat." Isabella waved.

"With what food?" Luigi scoffed and took a sip from his bottle. "I couldn't force down another spoonful of that lukewarm water you call soup!"

"Luigi, please," Ezio spoke calmly to the man. "I need to be on my way."

"Tell me, Lieutenant." Luigi leaned on the hood of the vehicle. "Do you know when these rations will end? I'm starving! I have no money for food. Look at my poor boy. Look at how malnourished he is."

"How did you buy this?" Ezio pointed to the bottle, not appreciating Luigi's attempt to elicit sympathy for his neglect.

"This? This was a gift, signore!" Luigi scrunched up his nose at the insult.

A horn honked, and Ezio glanced in the rearview mirror to realize there were a few cars now behind him.

"Luigi, amico mio, you have to get out of the road." Ezio threw his hand out in frustration.

"Please, Lieutenant." Luigi looked at Ezio with tears in his eyes. "I need something to eat."

Glancing quickly at the glove compartment, Ezio knew that the beef hidden could likely feed Luigi's whole family. In contention with the compassion stirring in his heart, Ezio recognized the regrettable reality that Luigi would sell the meat for money or trade it for more alcohol. It was also likely, Ezio convinced himself, that Luigi didn't know how to cook this properly, and it would end up an utter waste.

"Go to the station." Ezio pointed over his shoulder. "Tell them I sent you. They don't have much, but they can feed you, your wife, and your son."

"Grazie, Signore." Luigi suddenly became sober and patted the hood of the vehicle as he bounded toward his house without a shred of inebriation.

With a heavy sigh, Ezio rubbed his eyes in frustration at his own naivety.

A horn honked again behind him, and Ezio offered a stern glare in the rearview mirror before intentionally proceeding at a snail's pace.

Arriving back at Signor Lehner's property late in the evening, Ezio watched the house with hesitancy. He struggled to think of something convincing to say to Faustina, and Ezio expected he would be met with resistance. Still, he had given his word to Signor Lehner, and Ezio was nothing if honorable.

Exiting the vehicle, Ezio was startled by a flock of birds that flew overhead. For a split second, he was convinced that it was a bombing raid by the Americans, and Ezio drew a deep breath to try and steady his nerves.

"Pull it together," Ezio spoke to himself as he walked toward the house, but not before addressing Wolfgang, "I won't be long."

Raising his fist to the door, Ezio was about to knock when he noticed a shadow move across the large kitchen window. Deciding to investigate, Ezio walked slowly over to the window, careful not to crush any flowerpots with his cane.

Looking inside, Ezio spotted Faustina sitting at the kitchen table with a single candle lit. Her veil was resting on the table beside her, and while Ezio agreed it wasn't entirely unusual for a nun to expose her head while alone, her hair seemed rather kept. It had been curled and somewhat styled, which was abnormal for a lady of the cloth.

More peculiar still was her attention to a small, tattered book. Ezio assumed it was a prayer book of sorts, but Faustina seemed to be memorizing it instead of praying.

Regardless, Ezio was stunned by her beauty and almost believed that she was from another world. He studied her hair, which looked gentle and soft, and a warmth spread through his chest as his eyes fell to her lips. Then he looked at her hands, remembering how soft and gentle they were and wished that he could hold them again.

Removing himself from view and shaking away the silly romantic notions, Ezio retreated to the door and offered a generous knock.

No movement came from inside.

Ezio knocked again.

Still, after a moment, there was no answer.

"Sister Faustina," Ezio called through the door. "It's Lieutenant Ezio. May we speak?"

Ezio waited another moment before advising, "I saw you through the window. I know you're inside."

A light shuffle could be heard on the floor near the door, and Faustina asked quietly, "Have you come back to arrest me, too?"

"No, Sister, I'm here on behalf of your uncle."

"Speak, then."

"It's of a sensitive nature," Ezio replied as he noticed the curtains on the neighbor's house open a smidge as a peering eye peeked through.

"I'm alone, Lieutenant. It's not appropriate for me to be with you."

"Is that a requirement of your Franciscan order?" Ezio tested her.

"I...I..." Faustina stumbled.

"It's alright, Faustina, your uncle told me the truth. I don't intend you ill. I'm here to help."

"Why don't we speak in the morning?"

"My superior is attending tomorrow," Ezio leaned against the doorpost as he explained softly. "If you're here when he arrives, you will be discovered and questioned."

No response came from the other side of the door.

"I know what you're assuming," Ezio pressed. "You're under the false impression that you can withstand my superior's questioning, or that you will flee in the middle of the night. My superior is an expert in eliciting the truth, and he has means at his disposal to make the interrogation very distressing. If you flee in the middle of the night and are discovered, you will be detained. Your best chance is with me."

Still, no response.

"I'm certain that you feel as though you can't trust me, but I made a promise to your uncle, and, quite honestly, with the captain arriving tomorrow, you don't have a choice."

Ezio waited another moment for a reply, but when none came, he shook his head in annoyance and began to walk away.

The lock clicked.

Pausing, Ezio turned and watched as the door opened slightly, and Faustina peeked at him through the slit. The light from the setting sun painted her face in a soft orange and purple, and with the white and black of her veil,

Faustina appeared as the very image of innocence concealing desire. His breathing began to labor slightly, the palms of his hands tingled, and his heart began to pound as he watched her with forbidden longing.

While it may have been partially due to his disability, or perhaps his temperament toward the opposite sex, Ezio had failed to engage romantically in the past. Most women were unattainable, or else considered him unattractive, which he accepted as an uneasy truce of sorts. Yet this evening, seeing Faustina again with her light brown eyes against her milky skin, Ezio felt a stirring in his soul he didn't believe possible.

"Sister." Ezio removed his cap.

"You took him away." Faustina looked at Ezio warily. "How can I trust you?"

"I followed the law. Despite my personal feelings for your uncle, I did my duty. I'm a man of my word, and I promised him that I would watch over you until he returns." Ezio looked back at her as his voice resonated with passion.

Faustina didn't reply as she studied Ezio suspiciously, and he believed that she was desperate for assistance.

Looking around with slight annoyance, Ezio wondered how he could convince her. He was tired, hungry, and emotionally stretched thin. He struggled to think about his objective with Faustina, but in the back of his mind, his only thought dwelt on the food in his glove compartment begging to be cooked and consumed.

Then, suddenly, an idea popped into Ezio's head, and he grinned slightly. It was silly, he supposed, but he decided to trust his instincts.

"Here." Ezio held out his cane to Faustina.

"What are you doing?" Faustina frowned.

"Take it." Ezio pressed.

"I don't understand." Faustina opened the door further.

"I'm useless without it." Ezio shrugged. "Walking with the cane is difficult, but without it, I'm rather dreadful at what comes so naturally to others."

Stepping outside of the house, Faustina stood at a distance away from Ezio. Then, slowly, she reached out and took the cane from him before swiftly bringing it back to her side, and Ezio assumed she was wary of some sort of trick.

"What happened to your leg?" Faustina studied him inquisitively.

"Now that…" Ezio paused as he grew nervous to take a step. "That is something I cannot share."

Looking down at the cane, Faustina pressed it against the earth as if to test its durability.

"Careful! Careful!" Ezio held up a hand to stop her. "It's on its last legs, so to speak."

Faustina stopped and inspected the cane as if to confirm he was telling the truth.

"May we speak inside?" Ezio again took notice of the neighbor's peering gaze.

With a nod, Faustina retreated inside and held the door open for him.

"May I have my cane for a moment?" Ezio held out his hand.

"No." Faustina shook her head and left the doorway as she moved further into the house.

"Of course," Ezio sighed as he shuffled toward the door, embarrassed that the neighbor was witnessing his struggle.

After much difficulty, Ezio finally reached the doorway and stood in the small foyer as he measured the distance to the table where Faustina was sitting.

At once, and trying not to be too obvious, Ezio began inspecting the house intently. He noticed the men's boots by the front door, the jackets hung up on the racks, the table where Faustina had been studying the prayer book, the chessboard beside the prayer book, and the fireplace gently crackling.

"Be patient with me." Ezio held up a finger to Faustina as he bent over, preparing himself for the long, humiliating trek.

Shuffling with his bad leg, Ezio hobbled gingerly toward the table.

"For goodness' sake!" Faustina walked over to Ezio and handed him his cane, unable to watch his struggle any longer.

"Grazie." Ezio panted, and the two made their way briskly to the table, where they sat across from each other.

"Give it back." Faustina held her hand out to Ezio once he was seated, and he begrudgingly gave her the cane.

"Why won't you tell me what happened?" Faustina pressed.

"With what?" Ezio frowned.

"With your leg." Faustina gestured to his leg.

"Because I believe you are perceptive. If I tell you a lie, you'll spot it immediately."

"What makes you believe I'm perceptive?" Faustina asked as she grinned slightly.

"You noticed I have a bad leg." Ezio grinned cheekily.

"You're witty."

"Grazie." Ezio smiled proudly.

"Serpents are witty." Faustina's smile faded. "Tricksters are witty."

"Be as shrewd as serpents and as innocent as doves. Is that not what your book preaches?" Ezio pointed to her prayer book.

"If I'm to trust you, I need some sort of collateral." Faustina shook slightly as she spoke, and Ezio understood that she was having difficulty containing her nerves.

"Collateral?" Ezio tilted his head.

"You mentioned that my uncle told you the truth." Ezio nodded.

"Then my life is entirely at your mercy and based solely on a shaky trust. I need something that can turn the tables. Something that requires you to trust me as well."

Ezio thought for a moment before reaching for his pistol. With a slight smirk, he unholstered it and handed it to Faustina.

"What are you doing?" Faustina swallowed as she looked at the weapon nervously.

"Collateral." Ezio threw his lips upside down.

"What will your superiors say when they notice your pistol missing?" Faustina asked Ezio as she stared at the weapon in his hand.

"I'll need it back. But for now, you can hold onto it while I take you to my parents."

"Parents?" Faustina offered a sharp, distrustful glare.

"You'll be safe with them. It's too late now to cross the river, but tomorrow, after my shift, I'll drive you to the convent, where the Franciscans will keep you safe and hidden."

"That's your plan?" Faustina looked at him with incredulity. "I need to leave Italy! Take me to Switzerland!"

"Do you have your papers?" Ezio pressed, still holding the weapon.

"Well…"

"Then I can't take you to Switzerland." Ezio shook his head.

"You must have connections." Faustina leaned forward as she lowered her voice.

"Do you know how to use this?" Ezio encouraged her to take the pistol.

"Point and squeeze." Faustina grabbed the weapon and pointed at an imaginary object on the wall.

"There's a little more to it than that. This is a Beretta 1934 and should be shown its proper respect. You'll have to ensure the safety is off." Ezio pointed where the safety was on the gun.

"Right." Faustina drew a deep breath as she studied the weapon and then stunned Ezio further by removing her veil. Again, her striking features lured him into a briefly stupefied stance as her hair fell to her shoulders.

"The windows are open." Ezio nodded for her to return the veil.

"No one is watching," Faustina growled.

"Someone is always watching." Ezio handed the veil to Faustina as he offered her a warning look, and she complied begrudgingly.

"Your uncle mentioned that you had a plan to obtain documentation." Ezio glanced out the corner of his eye and noticed that the chessboard was set with pieces as if in a game interrupted.

"I didn't want him to worry," Faustina confirmed with a nod as she, too, looked at the chessboard.

"It's a smart lie." Ezio nodded.

"So…do you have any connections that could get me these documents?" Faustina again leaned forward as she held the pistol awkwardly.

"I won't break the law, Sister." Ezio shook his head.

"Even to do the right thing?" Faustina grew disappointed as she already knew the answer. "What's the plan then if you won't take me to Switzerland?"

"As I said, I'll take you to my parents' place. You'll be safe there until tomorrow. Then I'll take you to the convent."

"Are your parents sympathetic to my case?"

"They have no love of Jews." Ezio shook his head in regret. "But they hate Mussolini more. They're communists, and they're rather open about their political leanings. Thankfully we live in a rather remote part of Italy, and I imagine in places like Milan, for example, such antics wouldn't go unpunished. They're also not appreciative of religion, which we can use to our advantage."

"How so?" Faustina turned her head slightly, and Ezio's eyes lingered on her soft jawline.

"Because they won't be able to identify your weak points. We'll need to work on them, though."

"My weak points?" Faustina grew offended. "I was instructed by nuns on how to pray and behave."

"Why were you reading this?" Ezio pointed to the prayer book.

"Memorizing."

"That's what I figured. Don't."

"Don't?" Faustina tilted her head. "I don't understand. Wouldn't knowing the prayers help?"

"Be familiar with them, but don't memorize them. Most men and women of the cloth don't know the prayers by heart. Some do, yes, but most know them through the prayer book. You need to look like a seasoned nun; bitter and annoyed at everyone."

"The nuns I met were rather sweet," Faustina recalled.

"You didn't have the nuns that I did for teachers then." Ezio smirked. "Sister Amelia hated me. Still, we'll have to ensure your fabrication is solid. My parents will sniff out anything even slightly shady."

"Why wouldn't I simply stay here then? Or at least attempt to join the convent tonight? Nuns took me in before, I'm certain the ones across the will also."

"It's too dangerous for you to stay here. The convent is on the other side of the lake, and it's too dark to attempt the crossing now. I'll take you to my parents for the night. Tomorrow, after my shift, I'll take you to the convent."

"Has my uncle been harmed?" Faustina asked with worry.

"His spirit is broken, but his body is unscathed," Ezio replied quickly.

"What proof do you have?" Faustina examined Ezio with a suspicious gaze.

"He told me that you were his daughter." Ezio tilted his head.

"He could've confessed under duress as you tortured him." Faustina eyed the pistol in her hands, and Ezio feared she was becoming frantic.

"I was confident that I could arrest your uncle on my own, but with you, if that was what I intended, I wouldn't be enough to overpower you."

"You have a gun." Faustina shrugged as she looked at the pistol in her hands. "Had, I should say."

"I think we're both aware that I'm not the sort of man to shoot a nun." Ezio raised an eyebrow.

"I know you're the sort of man who would arrest an old cripple because of his birth." Faustina scowled at Ezio.

"Unfortunately for me, I have a conscience," Ezio sighed. "But that doesn't supersede my commitment to the law. You're not known to my superiors, so I will protect you."

"Your parents' place then?" Faustina bit her lip as she began to understand there was no alternative.

"Shall we go?"

"I need some items first." Faustina placed the pistol in the pocket of her skirt.

"I'll wait in the car." Ezio grabbed his cane and began walking towards the door.

"You didn't answer, by the way." Faustina stopped him. "I asked what happened to your leg."

"I'll be in the car," Ezio replied quickly as he left the house and limped toward his vehicle.

Yet as he walked, Ezio spotted Signora Soavi, the woman who had gifted him the boat, entering Signora Cianculli's shop. While it was odd enough, given that it was already evening, Signora Soavi was carrying a suitcase but still dressed in all white. Ezio found it curious what business she would have with the soap maker during this late hour and with a suitcase.

Why would she gift me her boat? Ezio pondered. *And why would she be visiting Signora Cianciulli this late in the evening?*

Regardless, Ezio entered the vehicle after shooing Wolfgang away from his seat.

"Am I doing the right thing?" Ezio asked Wolfgang as he watched Signor Lehner's residence. "I just gave her my pistol and left the house. For all I know, she ran out the back entrance. I think her uncle was telling the truth about her, though. If she's in such a horrid situation, then she really has no choice but to trust me. I should've sent Armando to arrest Signor Lehner. I'm just another stupid man who does stupid things for a beautiful woman with the futile hope she'll fall in love with me."

Yet Ezio breathed a heavy sigh of relief as the door to Signor Lehner's house swung open, and Faustina rushed toward the vehicle with a suitcase by her side.

"I thought some of my aunt's clothes would be suitable," Faustina explained as she stood outside the vehicle. "I never knew her, but we seem to be about the same size."

Ezio remained silent as he waited for Faustina to get in the vehicle, yet she hesitated.

"Why won't you answer about your leg?" Faustina asked as she stared at the pavement.

"It's not pleasant," Ezio replied briskly.

After a moment, Faustina opened the back door, threw her suitcase in, and then walked around the vehicle before entering the passenger side, where Wolfgang meowed in his displeasure for the disturbance.

"I'm going to give you another chance." Faustina retrieved the pistol and held it down low as she pointed it at Ezio.

"Why does it matter?" Ezio shook his head as he raised his hands.

"Keep your hands down." Faustina gestured with her pistol for him to comply as she glanced out the window to see if the neighbor was watching. "I need to know if I can trust you."

"How will you know that?" Ezio slowly put his hands on the steering wheel, gripping tightly as fear overtook him.

"I'm a good judge of character. I'll know if you're lying."

"And if I am, what then?" Ezio glanced down at the pistol, realizing what a foolish mistake he had made.

"Then I use this," Faustina spoke boldly and with none of the trepidation she had displayed earlier.

"The whole town knows the story, you can ask anyone you like." Ezio shook his head as he remained wary, yet Faustian showed no remorse as she waited for him to divulge. "Can we at least drive to my parents' place?"

"Why?"

"It looks suspicious. The two of us, lieutenant and nun, sitting alone in a vehicle during the evening."

"You're not taking me to your parents' house. You're taking me to Switzerland."

Ezio closed his eyes as he imagined that he was moments away from a bullet ripping through his side.

"I can't do that." Ezio looked at her with regret.

"Because you're taking me to the camps, aren't you?"

"Why would I lie?"

"To lure me into a trap." Faustina leaned forward with the pistol, and Ezio's stomach tightened further as he braced for the shot.

"I have not lied once! Not once!" Ezio held up a finger as he struggled to breathe properly.

"Take me to Switzerland!"

"I can't!"

"Spinless rat!" Faustina struck Ezio's head with the pistol, and his ears rang as his eyes grew blurry with stars.

"I'm bleeding." Ezio touched where she had struck and felt the warm blood running down his face.

"Sorry," Faustina spoke with regret. "I didn't mean to strike that hard."

"There's a cloth in there." Ezio pointed to the glove compartment, and Faustina retrieved it quickly for him.

"So, shall we go to my parents' house?" Ezio looked at her with annoyance.

"What happened to your leg?" Faustina pressed.

"I want to get this looked at." Ezio pointed to his head. "I promise you; the condition of my leg is inconsequential to your survival."

"We can't go to Switzerland, then?" Faustina relaxed a little as she was beginning to grasp the gravity of her predicament.

Ezio shook his head, and the vehicle returned to silence as they became locked in a stalemate, with Faustina refusing to trust him and Ezio unable to fulfill her wishes.

"Almost ten years ago," Ezio began softly, and Faustina remained quiet as she waited for him to continue. "I took my father's boat out on the lake. I wasn't paying attention, and I struck a rock. I fell out of the boat, and my leg was pinned between the boat and a rock. I was stranded for hours before someone came to rescue me."

"Why didn't they put your leg in a cast?" Faustina narrowed her gaze.

"My mother was angry with me. She refused to let my father seek the appropriate medical assistance." Ezio glanced away as he felt his shoulders tightening with the memory. "My leg never healed properly."

"And this is the family that will keep me safe?"
Faustina studied him warily.

"As I said, they hate the Fascists. If hiding you hurts
their enemy, they'll gladly keep you safe for the night."

"Alright, then." Faustina handed the pistol back to
Ezio.

"What are you doing?" Ezio frowned.

"I'm going to trust you." Faustina drew a deep breath.
"I don't have any other option. I either trust you wholly
or not at all. My life is in your hands, Lieutenant Ezio, and
I implore you to do the right thing."

Chapter Four:
Famiglia

"How much more grievous are the consequences of anger than the causes of it."

Marcus Aurelius

"This is where your parents live?" Faustina asked with a hint of disappointment as they pulled up to a row of houses.

"Unfortunately," Ezio replied with understanding.

While living next to the beauty of Lake Como would be the envy of anyone, Ezio found the house he grew up in far from ideal. Surrounded on every side by other houses and tall trees, Ezio's parents' property was cut off from almost all natural light. The ancient stone walls and narrow cobblestone streets would, to some, seem rather picturesque and romantic, but Ezio yearned for space and privacy. Without a yard or a square, there was no room to play when he was a child, and the only outdoor portion afforded to the residence was a balcony that faced a neighbor.

"Looks like the whole neighborhood is out tonight." Ezio leaned forward as he glanced up at the balconies that were full of grandparents and parents enjoying coffee or tea and smoking as they watched their kids playing happily in the street below.

"Should we wait until dark?" Faustina asked with a hint of worry. "So many witnesses seeing me enter your parents' house."

"I wouldn't worry about them." Ezio opened the door. "I've known them my whole life. They're practically blood."

"They're not my blood," Faustina muttered as she reluctantly opened her door as well.

"You know," Ezio huffed as he picked up Wolfgang out of the vehicle and held him awkwardly as he limped toward the property. "I wouldn't mind you being so fat if it meant you at least caught a rat or two. I should cut you off of milk altogether."

"Allow me." Faustina took Wolfgang from Ezio and held the cat in her arms like she was swaddling a baby.

Stopping in his tracks, Ezio couldn't believe what he was seeing. Wolfgang, having never met Faustina before, was perfectly contented in her arms, looking like a ball of fluff with his tail swaying and twitching happily.

"What?" Faustina paused when she noticed Ezio lingering.

"I've never..." Ezio was lost for words.

"My cats loved this at the farm." Faustina shrugged.

"You learn something new," Ezio muttered to himself as he resumed his pace.

"Lieutenant!" a friendly call came from an elderly man sitting on the balcony of a house across the street from Ezio's parents' house. He was sitting with his wife as the two enjoyed a cup of tea and some crackers.

"Buonasera, Vitelli." Ezio offered a nod of acknowledgment to his neighbor.

"Who is your friend?" Vitelli's wife asked as she turned her nose up at Faustina.

"This is Sister Faustina," Ezio explained with a smile.

Neither Vitelli nor his wife offered a gesture of greeting but instead looked at the nun with curious and peculiar gazes. While Ezio didn't appreciate their cold welcome, he did understand their distrust of anyone new and decided not to take offense.

"Signore!" a boy called from down the street as a stray ball rolled toward Vitelli's house.

"I told you to keep that damned ball away from my plants!" Vitelli shook his fist at the children.

"Mi scusi!" the boy shouted as he grabbed the ball and swiftly ran away in fear.

"Lively neighborhood." Faustina again grew worried for the exposure.

"Exactly." Ezio grinned. "A den of controlled chaos, really. It's so busy anyone will forget they even saw you."

Arriving at the house, Ezio was about to open the door when he paused and looked at Faustina before advising, "A word of warning."

"Oh?" Faustina frowned as she looked back at him warily.

"My family is…how shall I say this…a bit much."

Yet before Ezio could elaborate further, the door swung open, and a young man, with tears streaming down his face, burst out and ran away down the street, showing no concern for the children's game as, to their great dismay, he disrupted their play.

"Who was that?" Faustina asked with concern.

"I'm not sure." Ezio watched the boy running. "My sister, from time to time, makes the mistake of subjecting her love interests to my parents 'charms'. As I said, they're a bit much."

Walking inside the house, the familiar stench of mold struck Ezio. The property, Ezio felt, had been constructed as a last-minute design to plug in the hole between the other properties. It was inelegant, to say the least, with a strange staircase, with about ten narrow steps, that one immediately met upon entering the house. At the top of the stairs was an awkward conjoining of a kitchen, living room, and a little dining area clumsily squished together.

"Ciao!" Ezio called as he struggled up the stairs, closely followed by Faustina, who was still holding Wolfgang in her arms.

"He was a nice young man!" a young woman shouted.

"My sister," Ezio explained to Faustina.

"He was after one thing only!" a deep voice shouted back.

"My mother," Ezio explained again to Faustina as he watched her countenance morphing into worry.

Arriving at the top of the stairs, Ezio half-expected to be greeted by his family, but instead, he watched with slight embarrassment as his mother, father, and sister huddled around the kitchen sink as they argued.

"I thought he was nice." Ezio's father shrugged as he washed the dishes with a towel over his shoulder while his daughter and wife argued on either side of him.

"That's cause you're a witless oaf! You think everyone is nice!" Ezio's mother slapped the back of his head.

"I don't think you're nice," Ezio's father muttered and braced for another strike.

Saving his father from further abuse, Ezio cleared his throat to alert them to his presence, and both his mother and sister glanced quickly at him before offering a double take at the nun standing beside him with Wolfgang in her arms.

With the unusual silence from the women, Ezio's father knew that something was amiss and ceased the dishes as he, too, spun around and looked dumbfounded.

In an uneasy silence, Ezio's family stared at Ezio and Faustina, who both stared back at the family. Ezio, for his part, expected his family to be welcoming, or at least show a measure of hospitality, but knew that he was possibly expecting a little too much.

"Padre, Madre," Ezio began. "This is Sister Faustina. She will need to stay with us for the night."

The silence clung to Ezio's family, who held their conclusion in reserve as they studied both Ezio and Faustina with heavy incredulity.

That is, until the quiet was disrupted when Ezio's mother burst into a deep laugh. She was a taller woman, almost a foot taller than her husband, and accompanying her intimidating voice was an unfortunately harsh and somehow permanent countenance of disapproval. Personal grooming had long been forsaken as her hair, while covered with a red and white checkered scarf, was unkempt, stubble was growing in small patches on her chin, a mole was thriving under her left eye, and a wide jaw accompanied thick hands and arms, making it unfortunately difficult to distinguish her from her husband.

His father, regrettably for him, was shorter than normal, but apart from the height, he was almost identical in appearance to his wife. With loose suspenders holding up worn and tattered trousers, Ezio's father appeared as poor as his status.

His sister, however, took her vanity with intolerable seriousness. She was considerably younger than Ezio and, without regard, flew headlong into the latest trends. Her lips were painted a bright red, and despite the sanctions, she was still able, somehow, to obtain the makeup, her hair was cut short yet curled, her earrings were large and flashy, and she had a fake pearl neckless that rested just above a dazzling dress which Ezio couldn't fathom how she afforded.

"First woman my brother brings home, and it's a nun." His sister leaned back against the counter as she grinned, realizing that the attention would now entirely be on Ezio.

Again, Ezio's mother laughed while Ezio's father remained in stunned silence.

"Sister Faustina, this is my sister, Vittoria, my father, Lorenzo, and my mother, Ludovica. We are the Milanesi family." Ezio glared at his family for the rudeness.

"Nice to meet you," Faustina spoke softly, clearly intimidated by this cold reception.

"You want food?" Ludovica lit a cigarette as she moved over to the pantry.

"I brought something, actually." Ezio reached into his jacket and retrieved the package of beef.

"What is that?" Lorenzo asked eagerly as Faustina's enchantment over him broke with the promise of real food.

"You won't report me?" Ezio opened it up for his father to see as he came closer to inspect.

"Report you?" Lorenzo laughed liberally and slapped Ezio's back roughly as he took the beef from his son and walked carefully back to the kitchen as though he was carrying something fragile.

"Sit." Ludovica pointed to a rickety table in the dining room that was surrounded by mismatched chairs before she took her accustomed spot.

"Grazie," Faustina spoke softly to Ezio as he held out the chair for her.

"Dai campi, dai prati!" Lorenzo began singing an aria heartily as he turned the stove on, and Ezio smiled brightly, knowing how delighted he had made his father.

"What's your name?" Vittoria asked Faustina as she also sat at the table.

"I told you her name…twice." Ezio frowned at his sister as he pointed to the top of the stairs where they had been only moments ago.

"You didn't!" Vittoria barked back with the special enmity permitted to siblings.

"Twice!" Ezio held up two fingers.

"It's fine." Faustina raised her hand gingerly to ease the tension. "I'm Faustina."

"You mean Sister Faustina." Ludovica took a puff of her cigarette as she squinted suspiciously at the nun.

"Yes, of course." Faustina shook her head quickly at the blunder.

"Ritorno e di pace!" Lorenzo continued singing the aria in his euphoria.

"Where did you get it?" Ludovica asked Ezio as she pointed to the stove.

"It's best not to ask these questions." Ezio looked back at his mother guardedly.

"Grab my medicine." Ludovica pointed to the kitchen.

"Now?" Ezio asked quietly.

"Yes, now!" Ludovica gritted her teeth as her eyes bulged. "I still have to recover from your sister's affront with that scandalous boy she claims to love."

"It's not a claim!" Vittoria crossed her arms as she grew defiant.

"I'm not having the discussion again." Ludovica threw her arm out to indicate the conversation was over. "Grab my medicine!"

With a grunt, Vittoria left the table and returned to the kitchen, where she grabbed an unmarked bottle which she then provided to her mother.

"So, where did you two meet?" Vittoria asked Ezio and Faustina with a scandalous tone as if she was trying to uncover some romance.

"Vittoria..." Ezio rubbed his face in annoyance.

"I'm Signor Lehner's niece," Faustina replied quickly.

"Signor Lehner?" Lorenzo's ears perked up, and Ezio recalled the story of his father's war atrocities.

Yet now, looking at his father happily cooking in the kitchen, singing his favorite arias, and looking as harmless as a butterfly with clipped wings, Ezio struggled to reconcile the two. He didn't imagine that Signor Lehner would fabricate such a horrific story, but then again, the man was desperate to appeal to Ezio's conscience.

"Sì, Signore." Faustina nodded as she folded her hands gently on her lap.

While Faustina's gaze lingered on Lorenzo, Ezio stole a moment to inspect her again. A sudden surge ran through his veins and a compression set in his chest as he studied her soft jawline and smooth, flowing neck.

But out of the corner of his eye, Ezio caught Vittoria sneering at him, and at once, he broke his gaze away from Faustina with a quick scowl at his sister.

"How is the old bastardo?" Lorenzo asked as he returned to cooking.

"Ask your son." Faustina turned to Ezio suddenly.

"What do you mean?" Lorenzo watched Ezio carefully.

"It's a private matter." Ezio shook his head.

"He was arrested." Faustina continued to stare at Ezio.

"Arrested?" Lorenzo threw his head back in surprise. "For what? Planting too many flowers in his yard?"

"For the accident of his birth." Faustina clenched her jaw with rage, and Ezio felt his shoulders tightening with fear.

"Ah..." Lorenzo grew quiet for a moment as he understood the implications. "Forgot he was Jewish."

"Does that mean you, then, are—" Vittoria grew concerned.

"No, I'm from his late wife's side of the family." Faustina spoke with such conviction that Ezio almost believed her as well.

"They won't be searching our house then, will they?" Vittoria turned to her father in a slight panic.

"Don't be stupid." Lorenzo looked back at Vittoria with incredulity.

"It's not stupid!" Vittoria pointed angrily at her brother. "He brought a Jew into our house!"

"She's not a Jew." Ezio tapped the table to try and calm her. "Besides, I'm the authority here. If anyone is going to be searching this property, it will be me. There's nothing to worry about."

"She's related to one!" Vittoria's panic began to envelop her senses.

"By marriage, not blood." Ezio grew annoyed.

"What's to become of him?" Lorenzo asked with concern. "Your uncle, that is."

"They'll send him to a labor camp." Ezio glanced at Faustina, who he noticed was trying to contain her emotions.

"I feel bad for saying he was a bastardo now..." Lorenzo returned to cooking.

"Something's off." Ludovica narrowed her gaze as she took a generous gulp of her 'medicine'.

"Off? How so?" Ezio asked.

"Why would she come with you?" Ludovica peered into Ezio's soul as she asked while her cigarette hung out the side of her mouth. "And her accent is strange."

"The property is being confiscated. She had nowhere to stay, and it was too late to go back to the convent on the other side of the lake. I offered her a place for the night," Ezio replied, happy with how convincing and natural he sounded.

"Where will she sleep?" Vittoria asked as she looked around the small house. "She's not staying in my room, and I doubt she wants to bunk with you given her, well, commitments."

"You live here?" Faustina asked curiously.

"You didn't tell her?" Vittoria smirked.

"Offering a nun a place for the night at my place sounds much more scandalous than offering my parents' residence," Ezio defended as he grew embarrassed.

"And yet here we are." Vittoria leaned back as she took more pleasure than was necessary in her brother's humiliation. "She's very pretty."

"Vittoria!" Ezio grimaced.

"What? She is! Did you convince yourself that you could seduce her away from her oath?" Vittoria giggled.

"Please stop addressing her as if she's not in the room with us." Ezio offered an apologetic glance to Faustina, who, he noticed, refused eye contact.

"You must admit that it is a little convenient." Ludovica took another large sip.

"She can use my room, and I'll sleep on the couch." Ezio grew annoyed. "There! Is everyone satisfied?"

"You're in love." Ludovica leaned forward as she studied the two of them before laughing cruelly and stating. "She doesn't love you, though. Fortunately for her."

"Please." Ezio swallowed as he gauged that his mother was in the infancy of her malevolence.

"Did he tell you what happened to his leg?" Ludovica squinted at Faustina.

Faustina nodded quickly.

"He didn't tell you the truth, though, did he?" Ludovica leaned back and crossed her arms. "Otherwise, you wouldn't be here."

"She doesn't need to hear this." Ezio looked at his mother sternly.

"Hear what?" Faustina asked, concerned that Ezio had omitted pertinent details.

"She's in our house. She's about to eat the food you brought us, about to sleep in your room, use our facilities, and by God, she will know why we are so pitiful." Ludovica scowled at her son. "Look at her, in her holy clothes, judging me for this." She raised the bottle and shook it angrily as the contents spilled onto the table. "She needs to know why I drink, why we live in such poverty, and why you will never find love."

"I'm begging you." Ezio closed his eyes as he knew his attempt was futile.

"Like I begged you to bring them back!" Ludovica screamed, and her deep voice sent shock waves throughout the house.

The table drew silent, and even Lorenzo ceased his singing as they awaited the inevitable.

"They're dead because of you!" Ludovica shouted again as her lips trembled.

No one dared to utter a sound or even breathe for fear of the matriarch's wrath.

"I loved them, too," Ezio spoke quietly.

"Tell her! Tell her the truth! Ask her why her God didn't save them! Ask her why God allowed you to live when they should perish! Ask her!" Ludovica offered a generous shove on Ezio's shoulder as she pushed him toward Faustina.

"Mamma," Vittoria spoke softly and patted Ludovica's hand as she tried to calm her mother.

"Get me another!" Ludovica snapped her fingers before pointing to the kitchen.

"Is that wise?" Vittoria asked quietly but regretted it based on the look Ludovica offered her.

"You lied?" Faustina watched Ezio carefully.

"I only excluded some details." Ezio pinched his lips together as his shoulders tightened.

Faustina waited patiently for Ezio to continue, and again the room drew quiet as Vittoria returned with another bottle for Ludovica.

"My two younger brothers were with me." Ezio closed his eyes. "I was pinned between the rock and the boat and unable to help them when they fell into the water."

"You weren't supposed to take the boat. The lake was too choppy." Ludovica opened the bottle and took another sip. "You're absolutely useless. Now you're a crippled coward, and it serves you right. How fortunate for you that you live in such a small town and they were forced to take you for the police force. The fact they made you lieutenant is an intolerable joke. My two sweet boys were taken from me, and the idiota endures. If God exists, he is cruel indeed."

"Ready!" Lorenzo placed a plate of beef in front of Vittoria and Faustina as he tried to lighten the mood.

"This looks wonderful. Grazie." Faustina looked up at Lorenzo, but Ezio could hear the discomfort in her voice.

"Eat!" Ludovica ordered angrily.

"And for you," Lorenzo spoke cheerfully as he placed a plate in front of Ezio and Ludovica.

"You don't deserve it." Ludovica shoved Ezio's plate off the table, and the beef fell with a juicy and tender splat on the floor.

"Mamma," Vittoria spoke softly as she stood and took her mother's hand in hers. "Let's lie down for a minute."

"I don't need to lie down!" Ludovica withdrew her hand forcefully.

"Then have something to eat." Vittoria nudged the plate toward her mother. "You'll feel better."

"Where did you get this?" Ludovica looked suspiciously at Ezio.

"It was a gift," Ezio lied.

"Gift?" Ludovica remained unconvinced.

"Eat, love." Lorenzo pointed with his knife to her plate as he joined them at the table.

"Have mine," Faustina whispered as she inched her portion toward Ezio.

"No! You eat!" Ludovica shook her head vigorously, refusing to allow Faustina's compassion.

"Sì, Signora." Faustina nodded and began to cut into the beef.

"A nun who doesn't pray?" Ludovica frowned severely at Faustina, who now had a generous portion in her mouth.

Stunned by her error, Faustina glanced at Ezio quickly before offering the fabrication while covering her mouth, "I was advised of your unfavorable view of religion. I thought it best to be respectful and to not overstep."

"Heh." Ludovica endured in her skepticism, and Ezio feared she would soon uncover the truth.

"I'm sure you're rather pleased with the Fascists," Lorenzo spoke casually as he shoved the beef into his mouth.

"I am?" Faustina tilted her head slightly, and Ezio grew concerned that her defiance would rear its head and doom them all.

"Mussolini made Christianity the official religion of Italy." Lorenzo shrugged. "That must have made many among your order thrilled, no? We sacrificed the nation to Fascism, but at least Christianity is made lofty. That must have you pleased."

Faustina paused for a moment before answering, and Ezio watched her with bated breath, praying she would answer cleverly.

"My kingdom is not of this world," Faustina replied with a slight grin. "Isn't that what Christ retorted to Pilate?"

The table remained silent as they waited for her to continue, and Ezio watched her intently as he noticed her contemplating heavily.

"There are two types of religion." Faustina cleared her throat. "One is cruel and unjust as it serves the temporary while seeking the subjective and the mundane. It seeks power and prominence in the world. It appropriates its core values and turns them against the people."

"And the other?" Vittoria asked, which Ezio found odd as she rarely engaged in discussions outside of those that revolved around the handsomest boy or latest gossip.

"The other focuses on the eternal. It seeks to uplift the lowly. It seeks not power, but love. It succors the broken and downtrodden. It operates in the shadows where men cannot praise their good deeds."

"And which are you?" Lorenzo asked as he chewed with his mouth open.

"The first, of course," Faustina jested.

"Ha!" Ludovica slapped the table, amused at Faustina's reply.

Vittoria and Lorenzo also chuckled lightly, and Ezio breathed a quick sigh of relief as the tension lifted a measure.

"Did you see the papers?" Ezio asked his father as he tried to change the subject.

"Did he see the papers?" Ludovica huffed. "That's the only reason he wakes up in the morning!"

"The bombings." Lorenzo shook his head with disapproval as he hovered his head at his plate while continuing to shovel food into his mouth.

A meow came from near Ezio's leg, and he glanced down quickly to find Wolfgang eating his fill of the beef on the floor. Ezio's stomach grumbled loudly as he inhaled the scent of rosemary and thyme, promising his tastebuds with the very pleasure he craved. Yet out of the corner of his eye, Ezio noticed his mother taking immense pleasure in his suffering, and he returned his attention to his father as though his hunger was but a trivial matter.

"We're going to lose this war if they don't shape up," Lorenzo continued as he scooped that last morsel of meat into his mouth and chewed happily.

"How so?" Faustina asked.

"Don't encourage him." Vittoria stood as she grabbed the empty plates and the one on the floor before taking them to the kitchen to start washing the dishes.

"We're fighting a new enemy using old tactics." Lorenzo leaned over and drew close to Faustina as though the two of them were drawing up battle plans. "We're using the same weaponry and strategy that we used in the Great War."

"You fought in the Great War?" Faustina asked as her interest soared, but Ezio wondered if this was some sort of ruse to elicit their favor, blinding them to the truth with affection and familiarity.

"I did. With your uncle, in fact. He was my commanding officer."

Wait! Ezio frowned as he reflected on his conversation with Faustina's father. *Signor Lehner mentioned that my father was the commanding officer. Why would he lie?*

"Was he brave?" Faustina pressed.

"Fearless as a wolf." Lorenzo lowered his gaze as he drove home the point.

"He'll need his courage now," Faustina sighed.

"I wouldn't worry about him, Sister." Lorenzo patted her hand quickly. "He's as tough as steel. Besides, I've heard the work camps here aren't as horrid as the German ones. Terrible stories, if they're true. He'll be fine."

Wolfgang meowed at Ezio's feet.

"Poor thing is probably thirsty." Lorenzo jumped to his feet as he sped back to the kitchen and returned with a little bowl of milk.

Faustina glanced quickly at Ezio, who wondered if she found Lorenzo's care for the cat over his own son rather peculiar.

"Let's lie down, Mamma." Vittoria encouraged Ludovica, who was now appearing rather sleepy.

"I'm not tired." Ludovica slapped Vittoria's hand away.

"We're not going to bed. We're just going to relax on the sofa, alright? I'll put the radio on for you," Vittoria spoke softly with a subtle patronizing tone.

"I don't want to hear the news. Nothing but rotten reports." Ludovica shook her head as she complied and followed Vittoria to the sofa, which was a mere ten steps from the dining table.

"There you go." Vittoria put a blanket over her mother, who was now sprawled out over the sofa.

"Radio!" Ludovica demanded.

"I'm getting it! I'm getting it!" Vittoria griped as she lost her patience.

Turning on the radio, the happy plucking of strings stemmed out in a somewhat familiar tune.

"What song is this?" Ezio asked as he enjoyed the music.

"Of course you don't know." Vittoria snickered. "It's *Mattinata Fiorentina.*"

"Is it new?" Ezio pressed, ignoring his sister's slight against him for his ignorance of popular culture.

"You're such an old man." Vittoria shook her head in annoyance before exiting to the balcony, where she sat in the darkness of the evening and lit a cigarette.

"Hey!" Lorenzo whispered harshly from the kitchen, and Ezio glanced over to see him with a plate of meat. "Is she asleep?"

Ezio looked over at his mother before returning a nod of confirmation to his father, who quickly set the plate in front of him after offering a quick wink.

"Grazie! Grazie mille!" Ezio delved into the food.

Closing his eyes, Ezio couldn't contain the smile that crept across his face as he tasted the perfectly cooked beef that was paired wonderfully with the thyme and rosemary. He couldn't recall the last time he had indulged, and it tasted every bit as delicious as he had imagined.

"Shall we play a match?" Lorenzo asked Ezio as he set a chessboard on the table.

"Faustina plays, actually." Ezio grinned at her. "Challenge her."

"You play?" Lorenzo threw his lips upside down in surprise as he began setting up the board.

"How did you know?" Faustina narrowed her gaze at Ezio.

"The chessboard at your uncle's," Ezio recalled. "You were practicing."

"Hmm." Faustina sat upright as she held out a hand to stop Lorenzo. "I'm not sure I'm in the mood."

"You're worried about your uncle?" Lorenzo tilted his head as he looked at her with sympathy.

Faustina nodded quickly.

"You feel it's a disservice to enjoy yourself while he's in misery?" Lorenzo continued, and Ezio, while he didn't dare to admit it, found his father's concern hurtful. How he wished that his father could talk with him so openly instead of ignoring how Ludovica treats him.

"Si." Faustina swallowed.

"If you were in prison, would you like your uncle to be beside himself with worry?"

"Of course!" Faustina nodded adamantly.

"Fair enough." Lorenzo began picking up the pieces.

"But maybe…" Faustina bit her lip as she looked at the board with longing.

"Maybe a healthy distraction could prove beneficial?" Lorenzo looked at her with hope.

"Alright." Faustina relented, and Ezio caught the excitement in her eyes.

Ezio watched with amusement while he continued to eat as Lorenzo held a black and white piece in each of his hands before mixing and concealing which hand contained which color.

Tapping his left hand, Faustina revealed a white piece, and Lorenzo carefully spun the board around to have the white pieces on her side.

"Time?" Faustina asked.

"Ten minutes?" Lorenzo replied. "I prefer a quick game. We can do thirty if that is more suitable for you?"

"Ten is perfect."

"Good. Your move," Lorenzo spoke with slight condescension, and Ezio imagined this was the first time he had played a member of the opposite sex, no less a nun.

"Classic opening." Lorenzo grew disappointed at Faustina's move of pawn to e4.

While Ezio anticipated that Faustina would have some level of competence in the game, he didn't expect her absolute dominance of Lorenzo. In a flash, Faustina responded to Lorenzo's move of his pawn to e5, with her bishop moving to c4. Lorenzo moved his knight to c6 to attack her pawn; his first error. Without hesitation,

Faustina threw her queen to h5 with a veiled threat on Lorenzo's protected pawn. Then, finally, Lorenzo's fatal move came when he positioned his other knight to attack the queen by placing it on f6.

"Checkmate." Faustina drew a quick inhale of satisfaction as she moved the queen to f7.

Lorenzo's arms flopped down to his side in shock as he stared at the board with disbelief.

"Again!" Lorenzo quickly reset the board.

"After my shift tomorrow, I'll take you to the convent," Ezio spoke to Faustina, who ignored him as she concentrated on the new match.

Finishing his food, Ezio looked about the house as he watched his mother sleeping soundly, his father and Faustina locked into their contest, and Vittoria sitting out on the balcony smoking.

Wiping his mouth with his sleeve, Ezio grabbed his cane and carefully walked over to his sister, paying special attention to avoid the areas on the floor that creaked to ensure his mother continued sleeping.

"Checkmate!" Faustina nearly shouted.

"Arg!" Lorenzo grew annoyed.

Joining his sister, Ezio sat in the chair across from her, and the two endured in silence for a moment as they listened to the sound of the lake, the music from the neighbor's house, and their father's bitter complaining with another loss.

"They seem happy tonight." Ezio gestured to his parents.

"You have no idea." Vittoria shook her head. "Before you came home, Mamma overcooked Papa's food on purpose. Out of spite, he ate the whole meal and asked for seconds."

"I'm glad I had some good food to bring home for them then." Ezio patted his now full belly.

"Would you like one?" Vittoria offered a cigarette to Ezio, who politely declined.

"I heard an odd story about Papa." Ezio glanced at his sister, who looked back at him expectantly. "About his time in the war."

"What was odd about it?" Vittoria frowned as she took a puff.

"I heard he was a commanding officer to Signor Lehner." Ezio shifted his jaw as he recalled. "Yet now, Father says that Signor Lehner was the commanding officer."

"Why would Signor Lehner lie?" Vittoria narrowed her gaze.

"Or did Papa lie?" Ezio glanced at her.

"You can't be serious." Vittoria looked at Ezio with incredulity.

"They both have their reasons, but I can't tell who is lying."

"Ask him." Vittoria shrugged.

"I'm not going to ask Papa if he's lying." Ezio took his turn at being incredulous.

"Then you know it was Signor Lehner." Vittoria stamped her cigarette out in the ashtray.

"I'm not so certain. You see—"

"I really don't care about this anymore." Vittoria shook her head quickly as she raised her hand to stop him.

"Of course not." Ezio scratched the back of his neck.

"I need you to drive me to Signora Cianciulli's tomorrow morning before you go to work." Vittoria retrieved another cigarette.

"And you believe being rude to me is an effective way to elicit my assistance?" Ezio asked with a slight sting in his voice from her dismissal of the previous subject.

"Giuseppe found me some work in Milan." Vittoria continued, undeterred by her brother's feelings.

"Work? What sort of work?" Ezio frowned.

"Nothing indecent." Vittoria sneered at her brother.

"I wasn't assuming anything improper," Ezio defended while being quite surprised by his sister.

"I heard it in your voice. You're not as clever as you think." Vittoria looked at him with condescension.

"And you're not omniscient," Ezio replied swiftly. "You convince yourself of your own opinion, and once it is locked in your head, there is no removing it."

"Mine is the only opinion I need." Vittoria took another puff.

"I was genuinely curious what sort of work he found for you." Ezio calmed a little.

Vittoria didn't reply as she continued smoking her cigarette.

"Well?" Ezio pressed.

"Well, what?"

"What do you mean, what? You know exactly what I'm asking. What sort of work did he find for you?" Ezio growled.

"I'm not certain yet." Vittoria looked away, expecting her brother's heated disapproval.

"You're not certain?" Ezio leaned forward as he tilted his head. "If I wasn't assuming anything indecent before, I certainly am now. What did he say to you?"

"Nothing." Vittoria remained guarded.

"You're so infuriating!" Ezio removed his cap and slapped it against his leg. "Please walk me through the conversation."

"He didn't say anything. His mother told me that her son, Giuseppe, had found some work for me."

"And you just agreed? No questions asked?" Ezio delved further into his disbelief.

"I'm not afforded the luxury of questions," Vittoria replied swiftly. "Even with half of our working force spilling their blood on foreign soil, there's little work for women like me."

"What about marriage?" Ezio softened a little as he understood her perspective.

"Marriage?" Vittoria laughed loudly.

Suddenly, the light from their neighbor's living room turned on and the window opened swiftly as a man poked his head out and shouted, "We're trying to have a peaceful meal! Would you shut up for one night?!"

"Peaceful meal?!" Vittoria stood and leaned over the balcony as she shouted back. "I've seen your kids; I'm doing you a favor by distracting you from having to talk to them!"

"You little wench!" the neighbor shouted back.

"What did you call her?!" Ezio also stood, although not as swiftly as he would've liked with his leg.

"You heard me!" the neighbor replied, although with a little less conviction after only now noticing Ezio. "Every man in town has climbed through that balcony!"

"You're jealous!" Vittoria laughed.

"Keep your diseases!"

"Go back inside or I'll have my brother arrest you!" Vittoria took a generous puff.

"Try and catch me, you cripple!" the neighbor threw out his hands in exasperation.

"Give me your gun!" Vittoria demanded as she reached for his pistol.

"What? No!" Ezio swatted her hand away. "You can't shoot him!"

"No one calls my brother a cripple and lives." Vittoria held her hand out for the weapon as she looked genuinely at Ezio.

"That's very kind, but I'd rather be a free cripple than an imprisoned one." Ezio raised his eyebrows.

Yet before either of them had a chance to respond to the unkind neighbor, the light to the other neighbor's house turned on as an elderly woman poked her head out the window.

"Toni!" the elderly neighbor shouted. "Let them enjoy each other's company! They're not playing music loudly or being raucous. They're simply chatting."

"Just you try and enjoy a meal with a laugh like hers! Sets my teeth on edge!"

"What teeth?!" the elderly woman offered a sarcastic cackle. "I saw you stealing from my flowerbed, by the way. You oaf! Do that again, and I'll start planting grenades instead of roses."

"Who would steal from you?!" the neighbor offered an unkind gesture.

"He's an ass." Vittoria returned to sitting as they allowed the fight to ensue between the neighbors.

"Reminds me of you." Ezio looked at her with a wry smile.

"Shouldn't you be keeping the peace?" Vittoria asked as the elderly neighbor tossed a small pot at the first neighbor.

"Checkmate!" Faustina again cried out.

"This is peaceful." Ezio closed his eyes and leaned back in his chair as the neighbors shouted at each other, his mother snored loudly, his dad grumbled bitterly, his sister retrieved another cigarette, and his mind wandered to Faustina.

He couldn't deny that his heart was drawn to her. He knew that any connection between them would be impossible, given that the government which he serves is actively seeking her people for destruction. Still, he felt something toward her that he had never known, and he allowed the dangerous dream to develop.

Chapter Five:
On Witchcraft

"The measure of a man is what he does with power."

Plato

"How did you sleep?" Vittoria yawned as she climbed into the vehicle the next morning where Ezio was waiting, his face planted into the steering wheel.

"How did I sleep?" Ezio asked sarcastically while he peeled his face off the steering wheel and looked at her with thick, heavy eyelids that seemed sealed together. "How do you think I slept? I spent half the night on the balcony chair listening to mother's snoring, which I'm surprised anyone in town could sleep through, and being struck by wafts from your ashtray. I finally gave up and came to sleep here in the car."

"Ew! You're wearing the same clothes as you did yesterday?" Vittoria distorted her face in disgust.

"It's a uniform. I wear the same clothes every day."

"You don't have one for each day of the week?" Vittoria's eyebrows climbed her brow in shock.

"I don't have to take you anywhere!" Ezio offered a warning look to his sister.

"Sorry." Vittoria grew contrite. "You smell wonderful."

"That's it! Come with me, Wolfgang." Ezio grabbed his cane and his cat, and proceeded to open the door.

"No, wait, please!" Vittoria latched onto her brother. "I'm tired. It came out wrong. I'll buy you an espresso when we're done."

"The type that I like?" Ezio bartered.

"Those are so expensive." Vittoria slouched.

"Then enjoy your walk." Ezio shuffled to leave the vehicle.

"Alright! Fine! I'll get what you want!" Vittoria huffed as she crossed her arms and looked out the window.

Watching his sister for a moment, Ezio returned to a proper position in the vehicle and started it.

In silence, the sort which is privileged to siblings, the two drove back through the town toward Signora Cianciulli's shop. Again, Ezio spotted the posters of dashing Italian soldiers celebrated for their sacrifice, and again he felt the ostracizing of his condition. Though he supposed that war wasn't for him, and if that fateful day on the boat had never happened, Ezio would've likely enlisted and been killed rather shortly afterward in battle. Still, what he would do to have his mother's love again.

"I wonder what it would be like to live in Milan?" Vittoria broke the silence as she stared off into the distance, lost in her fantasy. "I imagine the shops are amazing. The men, too, I suppose, are a considerable upgrade."

"Well, the men in Milan might smell better and have nicer clothes, but men will always be men, my sweet sister." Ezio looked at her apologetically. "I can't protect you if you leave, and Mother can't chase them away, so you'll have to reason with your head and not your heart."

"I don't need protecting." Vittoria looked at her brother with disdain for what she considered to be his patronizing treatment of her. "I can't wait to leave this stupid town and be among cultured people and proper fashion."

"What do our parents think of this?" Ezio glanced at her.

"I'm not sure." Vittoria shrugged.

"You haven't told them?!" Ezio's eyes nearly fell out of his head in panic.

"I'm old enough now to make my own decisions." Vittoria held her nose in the air.

"They still need to know!"

"Why?" Vittoria scoffed.

"They're your parents. They love and care for you and—"

"Oh, please!" Vittoria laughed. "They don't know anything about me. I'm just a parasite to them."

"You know that's not true." Ezio looked at his sister with a measure of sympathy.

"Ever since, well, you know, I've been the girl in the background. Mamma loved those boys more than either you or me." Vittoria cleared her throat, and Ezio understood that she, too, was hurt by their mother's loathing.

"At least tell them where you're going," Ezio spoke softly. Don't make me be the bearer of bad news. Whether you believe it or not, your absence will break them."

Rounding the corner to the shop, Ezio drove beside the pier as he looked into Signor Lehner's house. He wondered how the old man had slept in the cell and if he had been fed properly by Armando.

"Does it feel weird to drive by?" Vittoria asked quietly, guessing Ezio's thoughts.

"Of course not," Ezio lied boldly, not willing to be vulnerable with his sister and advise her how tremendously bothered he was by his role in this ordeal, and especially how it affected Faustina.

"Fine." Vittoria shook her head in annoyance as they arrived at the shop.

"I'm coming in with you." Ezio turned off the vehicle as they parked.

"What? No! I was told to come alone." Vittoria frowned at her brother.

"A young man asked you to come alone to his mother's shop in the early hours of the morning?" Ezio looked at his sister with incredulity. "Mother hates me enough as it is. If anything happens to you on my watch, I might as well tie weights to my legs and let Lake Como take me too."

"I don't want to jeopardize this opportunity." Vittoria jumped out of the car quickly as she ran to the door and knocked loudly, taking advantage of Ezio's delay with his poor leg.

"That's not fair!" Ezio hobbled to catch up to her.

The door to the shop opened swiftly, and Signora Cianciulli stood before them with a curious expression. She seemed, to Ezio, to initially have been relieved to see Vittoria but then immensely disappointed to see Ezio.

"Salve, Signora." Vittoria offered a quick nod of greeting. "Is your son available?"

"You were instructed to come alone," Signora Cianciulli spoke quietly as she stared unwelcomingly at Ezio.

"Unfortunately, my brother insisted on escorting me." Vittoria offered Ezio a cutting glare.

"In any case, the position is no longer available." Signora Cianciulli remained staring at Ezio, and he found her hostility odd.

"Because of my brother?" Vittoria pointed with her thumb at Ezio.

"He has nothing to do with it." Signora Cianciulli shook her head quickly.

"May I ask why, then?" Vittoria swallowed, and Ezio assumed she was desperately trying to suppress her feelings on the matter.

Signora Cianciulli again shook her head as she turned her attention to Vittoria.

"If another position becomes available, you'll notify me?" Vittoria drew a deep breath to calm herself.

Yet the soap maker didn't reply. Instead, she studied both Ezio and Vittoria in an unusual way that made Ezio rather uncomfortable. She seemed, to him, to be examining them as someone examines produce at a market, reviewing its blemishes. She looked at Vittoria's arms and hands before studying her face, and Ezio wondered if this 'work' was laborious in nature, or if he was right to assume impropriety.

"I have something for you." Signora Cianciulli nodded for them to follow her back into the store as she left the doorway.

Yet neither Ezio nor Vittoria moved an inch as they remained standing outside, and Ezio assumed his sister was feeling as strange about the encounter as he was.

"What do we do?" Vittoria whispered out the side of her mouth.

"We probably shouldn't follow her." Ezio glanced at his sister as he recalled the soap maker's peculiar behavior the day before, as well as her argument with Giuseppe. "But something is off, and I'm dying with curiosity."

Entering the store, Ezio was overcome by the potency of the chemicals, and he marveled at Signora Cianciulli's tenacity. Trying to be discreet as he covered his mouth, Ezio looked around the shop at the many different types and packages available. Wrapped in either white or brown bags with strings tied around in bows, the packages were labeled with the different scents available and neatly organized on shelves painted blue.

"Through here." Signora Cianciulli nodded as she walked to the back of the store and opened a door that creaked loudly, and an unsettling feeling dropped into Ezio's gut.

Still, curiosity gnawed at Ezio. It was clear to him that his presence perturbed the soap maker, with a glance at his sister, Ezio pressed onward. Following Signora Cianciulli through the door, Ezio walked into a dark backroom where the product was made. If he had found the potency of the produce in the shop too strong, Ezio could scarcely breathe in this backroom.

Buckets were set aside that were filled with lard and other fats or oils, and in the middle of the room, over a fire pit, was a large kettle that Ezio assumed contained about ten to fifteen gallons of water. Jugs of lye water were set along the wall on top of wooden molds for setting the shape of the soap bars.

Painted a sickly shade of green, the room was dark and unhospitable, the only light afforded them from a small window at the back of the room that allowed for some air circulation.

Yet what Ezio found most unusual in the room was a table beside the large kettle. Two chairs were set about the table on either side, and on the table was a deck of tarot cards as well as some crystals that were strewn about in a pattern that Ezio assumed was intentional.

"Sit." Signora Cianciulli waved to Ezio.

"Me?" Ezio pointed to his chest in surprise.

Signora Cianciulli nodded as she began to put the crystals into a pile and shuffle the cards.

"You mentioned you had something for us?" Ezio asked as he covered his nose in the politest manner possible.

"Sit, and I will show you." Signora Cianciulli glared at Ezio in such a way that he knew she would not relent.

"Alright." Ezio offered another worried glance at his sister as he reluctantly sat across from the soap maker.

Yet instead of reading from the tarot cards or casting some spell with the crystals, she simply stared at Ezio with menace, making him curious as to how he had offended her so severely.

"Why are you here?" she finally asked.

"I was escorting my sister," Ezio replied cautiously.

"Do you believe in fate, Ezio?" Signora Cianciulli leaned forward as she stared at him, and Ezio felt as though she was peering into his soul.

"Fate?" Ezio asked, intrigued by the question.

"Fate." Signora Cianciulli clenched her jaw in annoyance.

Ezio paused for a moment as he looked back at her, judging this soap maker and diviner's intentions.

"No." Ezio shook his head. "No, I don't believe in fate."

"Why not?" she asked harshly, as if his response was offensive.

"I would rather not discuss this here." Ezio glanced out the corner of his eye as he grew acutely aware of his sister's presence.

"Leave us!" Signora Cianciulli waved at Vittoria and gestured to the door.

"Pardon?" Vittoria asked with indignation.

"He won't talk with you here!" Signora Cianciulli grew animated.

"Perhaps another time." Ezio stood as he began to leave. "I should be getting to the station."

"Fate has brought you to me, Lieutenant." Signora Cianciulli latched onto Ezio's forearm with a tight grip.

"Please let go of me," Ezio spoke politely as he tried to remain calm, but something about her demeanor unnerved him.

"I know you're curious." Signora Cianciulli complied and let go of Ezio before offering the enticing statement, "I know about the nun."

Ezio's heart fell into his stomach at the mention of Faustina, and he was intrigued by how much she knew. Still, something else, he felt, was drawing him to this soap maker. He didn't believe in divination, or in the spiritual world working in the unseen realm. His experiences with life had made him doubt the existence of anyone or anything divine, yet as he sat across from this woman, he felt a compulsion resting on his shoulders. Something within him agreed that, quite possibly, fate had led him to her door, and he decided to explore this unknown avenue.

"Go to the car." Ezio nodded at his sister for her to leave.

"Don't take too long." Vittoria rolled her eyes as she stormed out of the room.

"Why don't you believe in fate?" Signora Cianciulli again latched onto Ezio's hand, who noticed that her skin was coarse and unkind from years of dealing with chemicals.

"It's not easy to discuss." Ezio swallowed.

"Tell me!" Signora Cianciulli pleaded, and Ezio squinted as he studied her, wondering why on earth this was so important to her.

"If fate exists, then my brothers were meant to die that day I took them out on the lake. How can that be? How can fate design such an existence? How can fate determine that they should perish and I should live as a cripple? To this day, my mother hates me." Ezio felt a lump in his throat as he divulged what was within his heart.

Signora Cianciulli let go of Ezio's hand as she leaned back in her chair and watched him with a softer expression.

"My mother hated me." Signora Cianciulli looked intently into Ezio's eyes. "With her dying breath, she put a curse on me."

Ezio tilted his head slightly as he waited for her to continue. He still wasn't sure where this was headed, but he felt a release within him that he hadn't felt in years. Besides, he needed to uncover what she knew about Faustina, hoping to elicit some information through his complicity.

"Your mother doesn't hate you." She looked at Ezio with a sympathy he wished to experience from Ludovica. "She's wounded and scared. Every time she sees you, she sees your brothers, and that is a hard reality to accept."

"How can I make her see me, then?" Ezio asked, although he found it curious that he would divulge with this diviner.

Yet Signora Cianciulli was quite possibly the first person to truly understand him. If he explained himself to

Vittoria or to Faustina, or even to his co-workers, they could sympathize with him to an extent, but this soap maker understood Ezio on a level no one else could possibly imagine. With Signora Cianciulli, Ezio wondered if he could finally have an avenue to release these emotions and thoughts that were locked inside of him.

"Lieutenant," she began as she stared at the crystals, which were now spread out on the table. "Fate, whether you believe in it or not, has brought you to my door today. I need your help. In return, I can assist you with your mother and the nun."

"What sort of help?" Ezio grew wary of her intentions and recalled Giuseppe with the pistol, wondering if she was about to ask him to turn a blind eye to her son's dealings.

"Before I make this request, you need to understand my story. Many mothers, I'm sure, have asked this of you, or possibly others, but my case, above all, is worth the appeal." Signora Cianciulli again leaned forward and clasped her hands together. "So, I will share something with you that I have never told another soul."

"Of course, Signora." Ezio threw his lips upside down.

"Leonarda, please."

"Leonarda." Ezio nodded.

"I share this with you" — Leonarda paused as she studied her hands — "because you alone, I believe, know a measure of what I have experienced with respect to the absence of a mother's love. My mother, you see, was from a wealthy family, yet she was ignorant to the ways of the world. Her comprehension of existence was still very much trapped within the domain of fairytales."

Ezio waited for her to continue, wondering where this tale was going.

"Her ignorance, unfortunately, mixed with arrogance, and she was convinced that nothing wrong could possibly befall her. She was wealthy, beautiful, and her life carried all the promise of a wondrous existence. That is, until she met my father. He fancied her, but his status and economic position were not suitable to my mother's conceited view of herself. One night, after my mother had attended a dance, she was walking home alone. My father was waiting nearby in some bushes and ambushed her before dragging her back into the bush, where he raped her. She was too young to understand what he was doing, still ignorant to the ways of men, but that didn't matter to my father.

"She returned home that evening, ashamed but unable to tell a soul what occurred. A few months later, when she began to show, her parents grew suspicious. Under coercion, she shared her horrific experience. My grandparents were outraged at how she could allow such a thing to happen." Leonarda laughed ironically at the absurdity of their indignation. "So, my mother's family called upon my father's family, and they organized a meeting. They shared what had transpired between my father and mother, leaving no detail uncovered, and then demanded that my father marry my mother. My mother, of course, was irate. The last person on this earth she wanted to marry was my father, but the families, for the sake of propriety, nullified her protest. The idea of a bastard child was unthinkable, so she was forced to marry and essentially cut off from her parents' wealth and stature.

"She hated my father. She was supposed to marry someone wealthy, prestigious, and decent, or so she convinced herself. Instead, she was encumbered with me as an unwanted child and a drunk who beat and raped her regularly. Without the ability to overpower him physically, she turned her rage onto someone who couldn't lash back at her.

"I was the cause of all her sorrows, or so she repeatedly told me. She beat me, daily, and berated me for everything I did. There was no good within me, according to her. I was the product of her husband's lust, the demise of her proud name, and subjected to all the bitterness she carried in her heart.

"She was a witch as well, you see, and she often pronounced curses over me and my father. Even on her deathbed, she cursed me, and I've had to contend with the effects of her witchcraft ever since. Because of her spell, only four of my fourteen children have survived."

Ezio drew a deep breath as he absorbed her recounting and found himself in the odd position of feeling blessed to have Ludovica as a mother. She was cruel, yes, but Leonarda's mother was wicked to the extent that he began to feel nauseous.

"I promise you this, Ezio. I will not lose another child." Leonarda swelled with passion as she stared intently at Ezio. "My Giuseppe, my favorite and most foolish child, has enlisted. Fate has brought you to me for this very reason."

"I'm not following." Ezio shook his head.

"He wants to be of service, fine, I understand that, but let him be of service with the police force, not the army."

"Leonarda," Ezio began with compassion, "I think you've made the error of inflating my position. I have no jurisdiction over such matters."

"I thought you might refuse." Leonarda clicked her teeth as she pondered before uttering, and in a sort of threatening tone, "I know about the nun."

Ezio looked back at her with a furrowed brow as he tried to gauge her sincerity.

When Ezio didn't reply, Leonarda continued, "I know that she's not a nun. You're a smart man, Ezio. I believe you know this as well. If she was with Signor Lehner, then there's no doubt she's a Jew."

"That's why I returned to arrest her," Ezio lied.

"If you had such orders, you would've taken her with Signor Lehner." Leonarda unraveled his fabrication.

"You intend to turn her in then?" Ezio asked, realizing it was pointless to feign ignorance.

"If you help me with Giuseppe, I'll turn a blind eye. I'll even cast spells of protection." She pointed to the crystals in front of her.

"And if I can't help you?" Ezio looked at her apologetically.

"Then I can't help what information is delivered to your superiors." Leonarda lowered her gaze.

"I can make some inquiries on your behalf." Ezio continued, feeling sorry for the soap maker. "Did you make requisition with Giuseppe's superior?"

"Of course I did!" Leonarda growled. "Daily, I write to them. They don't care about a mother's grief. Their concern is churning out more meat for the grinder, and my son will not be among them."

"If the superiors won't listen to you, I don't think they'll listen to me." Ezio looked at her apologetically, hoping she would understand.

"Then you need to make Giuseppe see reason and abandon this cause. Convince him to join your police force."

"I can't promise you that I'll have much success. Still, for the sake of your son, would you condemn an innocent woman, and myself, to death by turning the nun in?"

"There's a law, Lieutenant." Leonarda picked up the crystals in her hand and held them almost lovingly. "A law which supersedes the one which you have sworn to uphold."

"And what law might that be?"

"The law of equivalent exchange." Leonarda watched Ezio's reaction. "If I give you over to death, my son's life will be spared."

Ezio tried to contain his fear when he realized that Leonarda was not bluffing. Still, a part of Ezio understood her position. Her motivation wasn't from a menacing viewpoint, but rather, from compassion and love for her son. Then again, Ezio began to consider compassion in an unfavorable lens. Because of the love Leonarda bore her son, she was willing to sacrifice both Ezio and Faustina.

"You must understand, Lieutenant Milanesi," Leonarda began as she looked intensely into Ezio's eyes. "Because of my father's lust, which led to my mother's hatred of me, I buried ten of my fourteen children. They were ten souls that his world didn't deserve to have. But now the curse stops. I won't allow my mother's evilness to take another one of my children. I won't permit her another single soul."

A chill ran down Ezio's spine as she spoke with passion and conviction.

"What I tell you is not idly offered," she continued. "Today, you'll be awarded the opportunity only a few have experienced. You'll understand that the influence of the spirits is real and beyond doubt. I'm going to provide you undeniable proof that my powers are real. Today you're going to have to make a choice."

"A choice?" Ezio held his conclusion in reserve.

"You will be forced to contend with a decision which will forever alter the course of your life." Leonarda narrowed her gaze as she looked at Ezio as though she were able to view the unseen world.

"What sort of decision?" Ezio asked.

"That I can't see." Leonarda continued to study Ezio. "But there is a man dressed in black asking you to do something that you cannot fathom."

"Generic answers won't sway me, Leonarda." Ezio grabbed his cane and stood as his patience wore thin. "I should check on my sister."

"When my prediction comes true, today, you will return." Leonarda nodded to the door for him to leave. "Remember the law of equivalent exchange, Lieutenant. What you need, you must give. Whatever it is you desire cannot be fashioned from nothing, but if you need to obtain your ambition, you must give something of greater or equal value. Help my Giuseppe, keep him with me, and I'll make sure the Jew stays a secret."

"Equivalent exchange." Ezio nodded as he pretended to not be bothered by the diviner's predictions.

He still didn't believe in the spiritual world, or fate for that matter, but he did believe in Leonarda's love for her son and understood she would not hesitate to turn Ezio and Faustina in if it meant Giuseppe could be spared the war.

"What did she want?" Vittoria asked as Ezio returned to the vehicle.

"That's private." Ezio prepared to leave as Wolfgang meowed and jumped onto his lap.

"You know that Mother sees her." Vittoria chewed her nails.

"And?" Ezio shrugged.

"She'll just tell Mamma everything you told her and then make it seem like she's received the information for the 'other side'. She's a fraud." Vittoria lit a cigarette.

"I hope so." Ezio looked back at the shop to find that Leonarda was looking out the window at them and recalled her warning of a terrible decision that he would have to make. "By God, I hope you're right."

Chapter Six:
The Black March

"Only the dead have seen the end of war."

Plato

"What's all this?" Ezio asked grumpily as he entered his office to find that his small, quaint desk had been replaced with a massive, solid oak desk.

With intricate designs carved down the sides, two busts of Julius Caesar on each end, and preposterously large gladius paperweights on top of a set of documents, the desk looked entirely out of place in the plain, grey brick office.

"Do you like it?" Armando offered a pompous smile as he sat behind the desk with his feet hanging over the edge of the chair while eating an apple.

"That's what I was trying to tell you about yesterday!" Francesca caught up to him while out of breath, and Wolfgang jumped out of Ezio's arms.

"You didn't tell me about the desk." Ezio pointed. "I would've remembered."

"Yes, when you came back to the station last night, I said there was a message for you, but you said it would have to wait," Francesca defended herself.

"You came back last night?" Armando asked with a mouthful of apple.

"Never mind that." Ezio waved to dismiss Armando. "What's this doing in my office?"

"Captain Cacioppo's orders." Francesca dug through her pocket to try and find the note.

"He promoted me." Armando stood and looked down his nose at Ezio as he awaited a warm congratulations.

"God help us all if that is true." Ezio rolled his eyes.

"I appreciate the vote of confidence." Armando's cheer faded, and Ezio realized he had offended the second lieutenant.

"Ah, here it is." Francesca unfolded the note. "The captain would like his personal desk to be installed in the office until further notice."

"His desk?" Ezio frowned. "You mean he plans to be here for some time?"

"It doesn't say." Francesca looked again at her note.

"You're the one who wrote the note." Ezio grew annoyed as he grabbed the paper out of her hands. "You should know the details as well."

"I write down what they tell me." Francesca snatched the note back from him. "My emotional state isn't so fragile that I need constant reassurance through prodding questions. They tell me that his desk is going to be brought to our station and to let the movers in. If I ask for further details, they get upset and mention that it's not my place to know. I pass along the information to you, and then you get upset that I don't take more information. Either way, I'm upsetting someone. You're all so fragile."

"Regardless, this is what we're dealing with at the moment. We will make do. Have either of you checked on Signor Lehner this morning?" Ezio glanced between Francesca and Armando, who both looked at each other with worry that they had erred.

"I thought that was her job." Armando pointed at Francesca.

"My job?!" Francesca threw a hand to her chest. "Do I look like an officer?"

"I stayed the night with him!" Armando gestured to himself. "You can at least check in with him this morning."

"You're fortunate that I did, but I wanted to see the look on your face when you realized you forgot." Francesca pointed wildly at Armando. "I also want it on record that I'm constantly going above and beyond my duty because of your laziness."

"I was with him all night!" Armando threw his hands out in frustration.

"Enough!" Ezio shouted as he placed a hand to his forehead, unable to contend with either of them at this early morning hour and with such little sleep the previous night.

"I appreciate you feeding him," Armando spoke quietly to Francesca as he released his gratitude reluctantly.

"When is the captain expected to arrive?" Ezio asked as he sat behind the large desk, feeling rather miniature and outlandish.

"At any moment." Francesca glanced at the clock.

"Then it would be prudent to have you at the reception desk when he arrives. We don't want to upset him with any hint of unprofessionalism." Ezio glanced at Armando, who, he assumed, was feeling the same sense of dread.

"Why are you so worried about him?" Francesca leaned against the doorpost. "He's only a captain. That's one rank higher than you."

"When we have such a small detachment, even the slightest hierarchical advantage demands respect." Ezio nodded for Francesca to return to her post.

"You've met him before, then?" Armando asked as he threw his apple core into the garbage.

"Once." Ezio raised his eyebrows as he looked again at the large desk in astonishment. "He presided over my graduation from the Carabinieri Officer School. He instructed a few classes and was as pompous then as he still appears to be."

"Oh, before I forget." Armando dug into his pocket as he retrieved a crumpled-up note.

"Copying Francesca's habit?" Ezio chuckled at the second lieutenant.

"What?" Armando frowned in confusion.

"It's not important." Ezio waved for him to continue. "What's your note?"

"Signora Setti. I checked in with Milan's detachment. They went to the address she provided, but the only person residing there is an old gentleman who has never heard of the name Setti before."

"Really?" Ezio frowned as his curiosity soared.

"Which made me wonder." Armando paused as he tapped his chin.

"Go on." Ezio rolled his hand, annoyed with the lingering.

"As I see it, there are two possibilities. Either Signora Setti's sister lied to her about her whereabouts...or..."

"Or?"

"Or there is foul play," Armando spoke softly, realizing the gravity of such a statement.

"Who would want to harm an old lady?" Ezio scoffed.

"We've both met Signora Setti." Armando shrugged. "I imagine her sister held a similar temperament."

"She's unpleasant, sure, but that isn't motive for murder."

"If it's unpleasant long enough..." Armando raised an eyebrow, and Ezio at once thought of Leonarda's recounting of her own mother's hatred.

A knock came to the door, and at once Armando and Ezio stood at attention.

"It's just me," Francesca spoke through the door.

"What is it?" Ezio groaned in his irritation.

"There's a young woman here to see you." Francesca opened the door and poked her head inside.

"A young woman?" Ezio's heart leaped briefly as he thought of Faustina. "Did she provide a name?"

"No, but she's a relative of Signora Soavi. She claims she's missing."

"Soavi?" Ezio frowned as he recalled seeing her entering Signora Cianciulli's shop the evening prior and her gifting of the boat. "Send her in."

"Right away." Francesca closed the door again.

"Is that name familiar?" Armando peered at Ezio.

"She's the town's seamstress. Rather successful, I might add." Ezio bit his lip as he pondered. "I saw her entering Signora Cianciulli's shop late last night."

"Really?"

"I have a sense that Signora Cianciulli helps women find work that may not be...how shall I say this...honest."

"Are you suggesting what I think you're suggesting?" Armando's face contorted with disgust.

"Signora Cianciulli's son tried to recruit my sister for some mysterious work. When I showed up with her this morning, the position was suddenly no longer available."

"Interesting." Armando hummed in thought.

"Lieutenant Ezio," Francesca spoke politely as she returned with a young woman who entered the office sheepishly.

Modestly dressed, Ezio assumed this young woman had a strong religious influence in her life and wished that his own sister would follow suit.

"Salve," Ezio greeted the young woman but then grew acutely aware of the enormous desk and felt a touch of shame. "Please have a seat."

"I'll check on Signor Lehner." Armando excused himself.

"How can I help?" Ezio sat behind the large desk but felt like a child at their father's desk when he couldn't quite find a comfortable position to rest his elbows.

Abandoning the seat and trying to reclaim a measure of dignity, Ezio elected to stand instead and leaned on his cane beside the desk.

"My aunt, Signora Soavi, I believe she's in trouble," the young woman began timidly.

"Trouble? What sort of trouble?"

"She's a hopeless romantic, you see." The young woman cleared her throat, feeling uncomfortable with the discussion. "She received news that a gentleman had grown affectionate toward her, and she was supposed to meet him in Milan."

"Do you know who this gentleman is?" Ezio asked.

"She didn't even know." The young woman raised her eyebrows.

"What's your name, Signorina?"

"Paola."

"Paola, did your aunt mention anything else? Was there an address? Did she see anyone else before she left?"

"Nothing." Paola again looked at him sheepishly for the little information that she had. "She professed often, and publicly, that she would still find true love. She's nearly sixty years of age, but she believed with all her heart that love would still find her."

"And you're not convinced that she found this love?" Ezio recalled the seamstress dressed in white and her peculiar behavior the previous day.

"It's too convenient." Paola bounced her eyes around, and Ezio assumed she was struggling to piece together a mental puzzle. "She's wealthy as well, you see."

"A marriage of false pretenses, then?" Ezio threw his lips upside down. "Unfortunately, Paola, that is not a matter that the police can intervene with. I'm not at liberty to stop your aunt from marrying or otherwise engaging with anyone. It may be a better use of your time to seek legal counsel."

"That's not entirely why I'm here."

"Oh?"

"She was supposed to call when she arrived last night. I'm afraid something terrible has happened to her." Paola looked at Ezio with wide, scared eyes.

"I can make another call into Milan, but—"

"Another call?" Paola frowned.

"A different matter." Ezio waved to dismiss her concerns. "But I would need some information. A name, an address, a phone number. Anything you have would assist me. I can't simply call the detachment and ask them to search the whole city."

"I understand," Paola sighed in her disappointment.

"If you can't find any new information by tomorrow, then return to the station." Ezio patted her back before moving to open the door for her to leave.

"Tomorrow may be too late, Lieutenant," Paola spoke softly over her shoulder as she left the office.

With a hidden sigh of frustration, Ezio closed the door behind her while holding onto the handle a little tighter than necessary.

"What does she expect me to do?" Ezio asked Wolfgang grumpily. "No address and no name for this mystery gentleman? She'd be better off imploring Leonarda's spirit guides."

Wolfgang meowed as he brushed against Ezio's leg.

"Was it wrong that I didn't mention I saw her aunt at Leonarda's shop yesterday?" Ezio tapped his chin in thought. "Or that her aunt gifted me her boat?"

Wolfgang meowed again.

"I'll have to look into that later." Ezio walked over to the desk and began opening the drawers in search of a pen and paper.

"Empty. This ginormous desk is useless." Ezio threw his free hand onto his hip before looking down at the widening cracks on his cane and spoke to it like a friend, "I should take some wood from the desk for you, don't you think? You'd be sturdy then, I'm certain."

Wolfgang jumped onto the desk and sat near the edge as he made himself comfortable and twitched his tail.

"Why did you like Faustina so much?" Ezio squinted at his cat as he remembered their interaction the evening prior. "I hope she's alright at my parents' all by herself."

Studying Wolfgang for a few more seconds, Ezio moved closer to his cat and extended his hand towards him, wondering if he would jump into his arms as he had with Faustina. With indifference, Wolfgang merely stared at the plain brick walls while ignoring Ezio altogether.

"Come here." Ezio grabbed Wolfgang and, while balancing himself with his cane, tried to single-handedly hold his cat in his arms like he was swaddling a plump baby.

"Lieutenant?" a voice asked behind Ezio, and his heart sank into his stomach.

Slowly turning to face the door, with a cat hanging angrily from his arm, Ezio locked eyes with Captain Cacioppo.

The captain was a thicker man with an imposing air that magnified his stature. He had a wide jaw with a broad chin, and he wore thin, round glasses that pinched at the nose without the need to hang on the ears. His ample shoulders pulled his uniform tight across his chest as he stood tall and proud.

Adorned in a tall cap with a large, silver eagle sown onto the front, a dark grey cape that hung over his left arm, entirely for vanity's sake, and shiny leather gloves, the captain embodied the sort of egotistical soldier who had never seen a moment of action.

"Signore!" Ezio offered the Fascist salute as Wolfgang fell to the ground.

"At ease." The captain closed the door behind him and walked toward Ezio, who immediately detected hints of diesel and tobacco smoke.

"Grazie, Signore." Ezio held his free hand behind his back.

"You keep cats?" the captain asked with a touch of dissatisfaction, and Ezio feared a harsh rebuke.

Yet as if on cue, a squeak came from the southwest corner of the office, and the captain turned toward the noise to inspect.

"Out of necessity, Signore," Ezio explained.

"So I see." The captain returned his attention to Ezio as his disappointment swelled.

Then, looking at Wolfgang, who was now perched happily on the chair beside the desk, the captain sighed at the cat's failure to act.

"That will need to be dealt with." The captain removed his gloves before sitting down behind the large desk, which Ezio was disheartened to find suited his stature perfectly.

The captain drew a deep breath and grinned slightly as he ran his hand along the desk as though he was being reunited with an old friend.

"What do you think?" Captain Cacioppo asked quietly as he bent over and laid his cheek on the desk, but Ezio wasn't entirely certain if the captain was addressing him or the desk.

"I asked you a question, Lieutenant." The captain looked up in annoyance.

"It's…large," Ezio replied, caught off guard by the captain's unconventional behavior.

"It's perfect." The captain sat upright quickly and spread his arms out slightly as he looked commandingly at Ezio.

Ezio nodded in his false agreement as the room delved into an awkward silence. Another squeak came from the corner, and Ezio squeezed his eyes shut briskly before looking at Wolfgang in frustration for his indifference.

"Do you know why I'm here, Lieutenant?" The captain asked as he squinted.

"I have my suspicions, Signore." Ezio swallowed.

"Suspicions?" Captain Cacioppo mocked as he stood and threw his hands behind his back before walking around the desk and stopping in front of the portrait of Mussolini. "I was there, Lieutenant. I was there when we marched on Rome. A sea of Blackshirts descended upon the Eternal City in a glorious throng, and we seized power. Not a single shot was fired, yet we were all willing to lay down our lives for him. We took the first steps to making Rome an empire again."

"Il Duce was absent from the march, if I remember correctly?" Ezio asked rhetorically, though he regretted voicing his opinion.

"What's your point?" Captain Cacioppo turned to look at Ezio with disdain for even suggesting cowardice.

"No point, Signore. Just an observation." Ezio played with his cane as he tried to appear casual.

Another squeak came from the corner of the room, and Ezio feared his superior's patience was already dissipating.

"I'm here, Lieutenant Ezio" — the captain moved slowly over to the corner of the office where the squeak had come from — "to pull the rotten trees up by the roots, to lure the rats out of hiding, and to make Lake Como safe again."

Safe again? Ezio pondered the odd statement.

"There is an enemy that lurks within." Captain Cacioppo slowly knelt and carefully placed his hands on the cement floor as he searched for an opening in the wall. "They walk among us as though they share our humanity, but our eyes have been opened to their degeneracy. We must be patient, waiting ever so carefully for them to crawl out into the open, and then we will strike."

With the captain kneeling on the floor, Ezio found himself in the unusual position of rooting for the rat. The rodent had been a thorn in Ezio's side for some time, but seeing Captain Cacioppo disgrace himself in this posture and comparing this animal to men like Signor Lehner and women like Faustina made his blood boil.

"There is another rat I need to deal with first." Captain Cacioppo stood and brushed off his knees. "Take me to the man you arrested yesterday."

"As you wish." Ezio drew a deep breath as he led the captain to the holding cells, where his spirit was lifted when he found Armando talking happily with Signor Lehner.

Yet as soon as Armando spotted the captain, he withdrew from his cheer and saluted in the Fascist fashion. Signor Lehner also offered the Roman salute as he stood proudly, and Ezio assumed the old man was emphasizing his military history to try and elicit some familiarity for a more favorable treatment.

Slowly, and with menace, Captain Cacioppo stood close to the cell bars and stared in at Signor Lehner as though he was inspecting a specimen in a cage, and not a human.

"At ease, Signor Lehner." Captain Cacioppo removed his hat as he addressed the old man with a measure of respect which surprised Ezio.

"Signore." Signor Lehner dropped his hands to his side but still stood tall.

"I am Captain Cacioppo." The captain threw his hat under his arm.

Signor Lehner nodded swiftly in greeting, clinging to his militaristic background, but quickly glanced at Ezio for reassurance.

"Have you been treated properly?" the captain held his chin high as he asked, and it seemed to Ezio that he was more so interested in the way in which Signor Lehner responded than if he had actually been treated well.

"They're honorable men." Signor Lehner gestured to both Ezio and Armando. "They've treated me with respect."

"You've eaten?" The captain continued his interrogation.

"I have."

"Good." Captain Cacioppo turned his back to Signor Lehner as he then did something Ezio found rather peculiar.

Leaning his head against the bars, Captain Cacioppo closed his eyes and drew a deep breath as though he were burdened with some unbearable weight that he could no longer tolerate.

"Come close." Captain Cacioppo suddenly opened his eyes and spun back toward Signor Lehner.

Again, with a nervous glance of reassurance to both Ezio and Armando, Signor Lehner complied as he timidly walked closer to the captain.

"Closer." The captain waved gently, and Signor Lehner complied.

Captivating Ezio further, the captain began to inspect Signor Lehner intently. His eyes scanned the old man's forehead, then his nose, his cheeks, his lips, and finally landed upon his eyes.

"I'm losing my eyesight." Captain Cacioppo swallowed, and Ezio offered a double take as he examined the captain. "The name for the disease is something I've given up trying to pronounce, or even understand. At first, I reacted as anyone might expect. I was rather angry at the fact that very shortly, I will no longer be able to see my children, or my beautiful wife, or the majesty of this country. My only hope is that I may see my granddaughter. She's due any day now." Captain Cacioppo offered a bittersweet smile. "I could lose my sight altogether at any moment. Could be a week, two months, or possibly even a few years, but there is no question that I will soon be blind."

"I imagine that is difficult to deal with." Signor Lehner looked at the captain sympathetically, yet Ezio detected that he was nervous.

"But then, after some reflection, I've found that it is a gift. Because now, when I look at someone, I truly look at them. Your face, Signor Lehner, is no longer a passing, brief interaction. In you, I see your years of service, the days spent in heartache, the moments of joy, the bitterness of grief; the passage of your life is written in your face. A face, I might add, which may very well be one of the last faces I'll ever look upon. And you know what's interesting?"

Signor Lehner shook his head slowly.

"I've come to understand something about you Jews." The captain placed a finger to his lips as he contemplated. "You look identical to us, but you're not, are you?"

Signor Lehner's jaw tightened, and Ezio recognized that he was becoming agitated.

"The lines on your face are also filled with deceit, contempt, hatred for your country, and a loathing of all that is good. You are a disease, and your position of privilege is at an end."

"Privilege?" Signor Lehner shook his head in astonishment at the incredulous slander. "With all due respect, Captain, I'm the one behind bars. I bled for this country while you parade around in haughty authority without ever having to put your life in danger. If you, after looking at me in this cell, truly believe that I'm privileged, then I would say, Captain, that you are already blind."

"Lieutenant," Captain Cacioppo spoke casually to Ezio before gesturing that he was finished speaking with Signor Lehner.

Leading the captain back down the hallway toward the office, Ezio glanced over his shoulder and offered an apologetic and heartfelt sorry to Signor Lehner, who, he noticed, seemed to be rather terrified.

"Can I let you in on a secret?" the captain asked as they returned to the office.

"Of course." Ezio cleared his throat.

"Before I do so…" The captain rested his cap on the desk neatly. "I need to know why you delayed his arrest?"

Ezio drew a sharp breath as he feared the inevitability of the question and cleared his throat before replying, "I will be honest with you, Signore."

"I can't imagine why you would be dishonest." The captain sat on the edge of his desk as he folded his arms.

"Signor Lehner served with my father in the Great War." Ezio ran his tongue along his teeth as he tried to summon his courage. "I have deep respect for those who served our country."

"A wolf in sheep's clothing, dear lieutenant." The captain looked patronizingly at Ezio. "His race seeks to undermine the whole of humanity. Italy comes first. Above family, friends, and certainly, above Jews. Don't you agree?"

"Certainly," Ezio lied boldly and felt his tongue turning to ash inside his mouth for such a horrendous acknowledgment.

"You know, at first, I was rather cross with you for not arresting him, but now I'm actually quite pleased with the delay as it has afforded us a wondrous opportunity." The captain stood and walked over to the small window.

"Opportunity?" Ezio held his conclusion in reserve.

"I trust that you'll keep what I'm about to tell you confidential?" The captain glanced over his shoulder. "Only a select few are privy to this information."

"You can trust me, signore," Ezio again lied.

"The Nazis are doing something rather extraordinary in their newly conquered lands." The captain returned to looking out the window. "They're once and for all dealing with the Jewish problem."

"How so?" Ezio asked as the hair stood on the back of his neck, fearing the next words that Captain Cacioppo would emit.

"Eradication." The captain grew a small yet hideous smile in the corner of his mouth. "They've set up camps which are poised as labor camps, but their intention is far more righteous."

Righteous?! Ezio nearly shouted but kept his mouth shut and instead asked, "How does this apply to Signor Lehner?"

"There's a particular camp in Poland." The captain returned to sitting behind his desk. "Auschwitz, the Germans call it. We're sending Signor Lehner to the Nazis as part of, how shall I say this, an experiment."

"Experiment?" Ezio's heart pounded in his chest as he now wished he had never arrested the old man.

"If it's successful, I will be promoted to run a camp here, in Italy, which means, of course, that you, too, will be promoted to my current position. This endeavor benefits everyone. See to it that Signor Lehner is delivered to the camp in Trieste. From there, he will be sent to the Nazis, and we will rid ourselves of this plague."

The rat squeaked from the corner of the room, and the captain gritted his teeth with annoyance.

"You may be asking yourself, Lieutenant, why so much attention is being brought to one Jew, but as you can see, even one rat can be a pestilence." The captain studied the corner of the office as he tried to locate the rodent.

"I'll see to it that he's delivered to the camp." Ezio saluted and was about to leave when the captain snapped his fingers.

"Signore?" Ezio asked, fearing that the captain would add another horrific order.

"I'm feeling rather famished after traveling, and I'm in the mood for some good home cooking." The captain looked hopefully at him while hinting at an invite.

Faustina! Ezio panicked. *I promised that I would take her to the convent after my shift. I can't bring this monster back to the house when I promised to keep her safe.*

"I would be honored to have you dine with my family, but unfortunately, Captain, my parents are unwell. I'll—"

"You're a terrible liar, Lieutenant." The captain interrupted. "I know how intimidating it can be to have a superior visit your home. After your task with Signor Lehner, return to the station to drive me to your place for supper. We must celebrate our glorious endeavor!"

Chapter Seven:
The Decision

"Fascism is a religion. The twentieth century will be known in history as the century of Fascism."

Benito Mussolini

Swiftly, as his heart pounded in his chest, Ezio returned to the holding cells where Armando and Signor Lehner were still conversing.

"Lieutenant?" Armando asked with concern after noticing Ezio's distress. "Is everything alright?"

Ezio didn't reply as he looked at Signor Lehner while weighing his options carefully. If he placed Signor Lehner on a train to Trieste, he would be sending him to certain death. If he assisted Signor Lehner to freedom, he would be aiding an enemy of the state, and his life would likely be forfeit.

"Ezio, ragazzo mio?" Signor Lehner asked warily.

"Armando, give me a minute with him." Ezio nodded for the second lieutenant to leave.

"Alright." Armando offered a concerned look at Ezio. "I'll be at reception if you need me."

"Don't flirt with Francesca while the captain is here."

"I'm not flirting," Armando replied grumpily.

"He's a good lad." Signor Lehner watched Armando walking away.

"God knows we could use a few more like him." Ezio again studied Signor Lehner with apprehension.

"I know that look." Signor Lehner stared back at Ezio in such a way as to signify he was accepting his fate. "You've been given orders which you don't agree with."

"Why did you lie?" Ezio held onto the bar with his free hand as he watched Signor Lehner closely.

"Lie?"

"About my father." Ezio shuffled his jaw. "You mentioned he was your officer. When I asked him about your time together, he advised that you were the officer. Why would you lie?"

"I suppose I was afraid." Signor Lehner glanced down at his hands as he played with them nervously.

"You were rather convincing." Ezio drew a deep breath.

"I'm not sure if that's a compliment." Signor Lehner chuckled nervously.

"Do you think you can lie again?" Ezio closed his eyes, realizing that he was sealing his fate.

"I don't understand." Signor Lehner frowned.

"You have your passport?" Ezio gestured to the old man's bag.

"I do." Signor Lehner narrowed his gaze.

Pausing once more to weigh his options, Ezio deliberated intently on his course of action. Either way, Ezio knew that at this point in time, and with this very minute standing before Signor Lehner, his life had forever been changed.

"You'll be forced to contend with a decision that will forever alter the course of your life." Ezio recalled the warning from Leonarda, and a chill ran down his spine as he felt something entirely foreign to him. He was not a spiritual person by nature, but in this moment, Ezio couldn't deny that he felt the presence of something otherworldly. But whether this force was malicious or benevolent, he couldn't tell.

"Ezio?" Signor Lehner placed a gentle hand on the lieutenant's arm.

"I know what I have to do, Signore, but I don't know how to do it." Ezio looked back at him with trepidation.

"What were your orders?" Signor Lehner whispered as he glanced down the hallway to make sure they were alone.

"My orders are to send you to Trieste. It's a concentration camp near the Kingdom of Yugoslavia." Ezio paused, not sure if he could properly relay the rest of the information.

"I thought that already was the plan?" Signor Lehner grew confused.

"From Trieste —" Ezio paused as he collected himself — "you're to be sent to a camp in Poland."

The color in Signor Lehner's face disappeared as he looked back at Ezio with wide, panicked eyes.

"You have to help me, ragazzo!" Signor Lehner demanded as his panic overtook him, understanding what a camp in Poland signified.

"I want to!" Ezio whispered harshly back at him. "I'll take you to Switzerland, but I don't know how to cover up my tracks. What do I tell the captain when he asks why you never arrived in Trieste?"

"You'll think of something!" Signor Lehner's desperation overtook him, and he latched onto Ezio's collar. "You can't hand me over to the Nazis!"

Ezio shook his head as he stared at his feet, clueless as to how to proceed.

"You must have some idea?" Signor Lehner calmed a little as he let go of Ezio.

"If we do this, we have to go now. There is no time for delay." Ezio squeezed his eyes shut as he relented to his conscience.

"I'm ready!" Signor Lehner moved over to the cell door.

Still, Ezio remained in place. His feet felt frozen to the concrete. He knew that if he simply walked away and ordered someone else to take the old man to Trieste, he would have his promotion and he could carry on with his life.

Ezio comprehended that where he stood, in this very spot before the holding cell, would be the last moment that he knew peace. The second he stepped away and unlocked the door for Signor Lehner would be the second his life delved into chaos.

Yet as if in reminder to Leonarda's divination, a small voice echoed her words in the back of his mind, and Ezio knew he had to help Signor Lehner.

"Ezio?" Signor Lehner asked calmly, although with a slightly shaky voice. "This is the right thing, ragazzo mio. Follow your conscience."

"You were the officer who ordered that family to be killed?" Ezio studied Signor Lehner closely, hoping for any justification to simply walk away.

Signor Lehner sighed deeply and rested his head against the cell bars. He didn't reply to Ezio, but in his demeanor, Ezio knew the truth.

"Why, then, should I save you?" Ezio moved closer to Signor Lehner.

"No man steps in the same river twice," Signor Lehner quoted Heraclitus.

"For it's not the same river, and he's not the same man," Ezio completed the quote.

"I'm not that man anymore, Ezio. I know I don't deserve to be saved, and I've lived a life of regret for my actions, but that's not why they're sending me to the Nazis, and you know it." Signor Lehner pointed at Ezio.

Ezio didn't reply as he turned his face to Heaven and stared at the pale gray ceiling as he felt his life hanging in the balance.

"For the sake of my daughter, please," Signor Lehner pleaded.

"I used to consider you a good man." Ezio looked at Signor Lehner in an unflattering lens. "You've shown your cowardice by hiding behind your daughter."

Signor Lehner closed his eyes as he shook his head in regret as he, too, knew that to use her was craven.

"Do as you must, then." Signor Lehner looked at Ezio with compassionate eyes. "Promise me that you'll watch over her?"

"Dammit!" Ezio seethed with rage as he grabbed the keys from his pocket and unlocked the door for the old man.

"Switzerland or Poland?" Signor Lehner asked with concern dominating his voice.

"I haven't decided yet," Ezio replied as he led Signor Lehner by the arm toward the main door of the station.

Yet as they approached the reception desk, Ezio noticed that Wolfgang was basking in the attention of Francesca and Armando, who were teasing him with a ball on the end of string.

"Why is Wolfgang out here?" Ezio grew cross. "It's unprofessional."

"Captain Cacioppo refused to let Wolfgang stay in his office," Francesca explained.

"Come along, then." Ezio let go of Signor Lehner and grabbed Wolfgang. "Francesca, can you send a message to my parents?"

"Sure, what's the message?" Francesca retrieved a pen and paper.

"Tell them that Captain Cacioppo is coming for supper and that it would be preferable if only the immediate family was present." It was imperative that Faustina was absent from the property when the captain arrived. "Make sure you emphasize the immediate family."

"They still don't have a phone then?" Armando leaned against the desk.

"They trust phones about as much as I trust you," Ezio growled. "Make yourself busy before the captain punishes me for your laziness."

"Sì, Signore." Armando's cheeks flushed red with embarrassment at the chastisement in front of Francesca.

Regardless, the second lieutenant's feelings were of little concern to Ezio as he led Signor Lehner out of the station and to the vehicle.

Sitting behind the wheel, Ezio placed the keys to the ignition when he paused, still unsure if his dereliction of duty was morally right. Glancing down at Wolfgang on the passenger seat, Ezio prayed that something or someone would send him a sign.

And as if in answer to Ezio's half-prayer, Wolfgang immediately left the comfort of his seat and jumped into the back of the vehicle, where he curled up on Signor Lehner's lap.

"Ciao, my little friend," Signor Lehner spoke softly to the cat, who began purring.

Starting the vehicle, Ezio pulled out of the station and drove towards the road where he again paused. The road to his left led to Switzerland while the right led to the Como police station where he would hand over Signor Lehner for transportation to Trieste and then, ultimately, death.

Glancing in the rearview mirror, Ezio locked eyes with Signor Lehner, who, he noticed, seemed rather petrified.

With a sigh, Ezio turned left, forever sealing his fate.

In nervous silence, Ezio and Signor Lehner drove along the highway with the watchful Alps and toward the Swiss border, both terrified of failure. Their lives hung in the balance should their true intentions be discovered.

Ezio, for his part, was frantically thinking of a believable fabrication with which he could deliver to the Swiss border guards. Yet fear was holding his mind captive, and he struggled to maintain a singular thought that wasn't interrupted by the feeling of a rope being tightly wound around his neck.

As they grew closer to the border, Ezio noticed that it was beginning to snow softly. Falling to the earth like gentle balls of fluff, the snow melted as soon as it touched the pavement or the vehicle, and Ezio felt a sense of calm wash over him. It was odd, he thought, to feel so at peace under such precarious circumstances, but he embraced this feeling while it lasted.

"Does Armando know?" Signor Lehner broke the silence.

"I'm not certain I can trust him, to be honest," Ezio replied.

"Me neither." Signor Lehner shook his head as he petted Wolfgang.

"Your daughter stayed with my parents last night." Ezio glanced in the rearview mirror. "I'll take her to the convent as soon as I can."

"I appreciate that, ragazzo mio." Relief washed over Signor Lehner's face. "The Fascists raided her house in Austria. Her mother was killed, and all her documents were lost or destroyed, but she was able to sneak into Italy to try and find me. She ran away with nothing except for what she was wearing. A group of nuns came across her and took her in. Without documentation, she's stuck in Italy, but she's working on something, or so she tells me."

The vehicle returned to silence as the setting sun cast shadows across the majestic Swiss Alps. Ezio prayed that Signor Lehner would indeed find refuge behind their protective peaks and that, by some miracle, he would escape this war unscathed.

Tricking the guards would be difficult, but Ezio's rank provided some degree of immunity, and he didn't perceive too much difficulty with the neutral Swiss soldiers. The captain, however, was a different story entirely. Captain Cacioppo was cunning, and he would not be easily duped. Ezio would have to combine all his resources to thwart any suspicion.

"Shit!" Ezio's shoulders tightened when they arrived near the border to find that a checkpoint had been established.

"What's wrong?" Signor Lehner grew concerned.

"They set up a checkpoint." Ezio began to panic. "Word must've gotten out that Jews were escaping to Switzerland. They'll question you."

"Who set up the checkpoint?" Signor Lehner leaned forward to get a better view.

"Aplini. They're a branch of Italian mountain specialists."

"Have they seen us yet?" Signor Lehner leaned forward in his seat.

"I don't think so," Ezio whispered as he studied the guards who were smoking while talking and laughing with each other. What was most concerning to Ezio, however, were the empty bottles lying on the ground. Their inebriation could play in his favor, or, more likely, their lack of proper judgment could lead to violence.

"I'll get out here." Signor Lehner moved to open the door.

"What? Why?" Ezio whispered harshly.

"They haven't seen you yet. I will try and cross the border with my papers. You must return to watch over my daughter."

"Come back to town with me. I'll hide you in my house."

"That's no way to live, Ezio. I'm an old man now. My only options are peace and security or death."

"Surely hiding is better than death!"

Regardless, the option had been stripped from them as a whistle from one of the guards caught Ezio's attention, and he spotted them waving the vehicle forward.

"Don't speak unless spoken to." Ezio drove slowly toward the crossing.

"I have an idea," Signor Lehner spoke hesitantly.

"Just follow my lead!" Ezio griped.

"Promise me that you'll watch my daughter," Signor Lehner spoke sternly.

Ezio didn't reply as he was busy searching his jacket for his identification.

"Promise me!" Signor Lehner nearly shouted.

"I promise! I promise!" Ezio waved to dismiss him.

Slowly coming to a stop at the checkpoint, Ezio rolled down the window as the vehicle was soon surrounded by the guards who were now inspecting them intently.

There were three guards in total, and by their behavior, Ezio supposed that only two of them were approaching drunkenness while the third guard seemed to still be sober. Ezio unlatched the holster for the pistol by his hip, preparing for violence should the need arise. He calculated that his best odds of survival were to take out the sober guard first and let the two intoxicated guards' indulgence play against them.

Further increasing his chances of success, Ezio noticed that these men were quite skinny. The strict rations had clearly taken a toll on their health, and they were close to being famished.

"Salve. Buonasera, Lieutenant. Where are you going?" one of the guards asked slowly as he peered into the vehicle, and Wolfgang meowed.

"Buonasera. We're headed to Lugano." Ezio pointed in the direction of the town, which was a mere few kilometers away.

"Lugano?" the guard asked with a hint of surprise, then looked to his fellow guards to gauge their reaction. "What business do you have in Switzerland?"

"My business is my own," Ezio replied swiftly as he attempted to appear relaxed.

"Your own?" The guard again glanced at his comrades.

"As lieutenant of —"

"Lieutenant of what?" the guard interrupted.

"Carabinieri." Ezio pointed to the stripes on his shoulder.

"Exactly." The guard stood tall as he stared down at Ezio. "We're Alpini. You have no authority over us."

"If you're Alpini, then you're aware of Captain Cacioppo."

"I am." The guard nodded as he continued to study Ezio warily.

"The captain has sent me with special orders to travel to Lugano for a highly sensitive mission."

"Is that right?" The guard remained unconvinced.

"If you want to explain to the captain why you upheld me, you're welcome to do so, but if you're aware of him, then you're also likely familiar with his temper," Ezio pressed.

"What sort of mission?" the guard asked, and Ezio sensed he was somewhat concerned.

"As I advised, it's highly sensitive." Ezio gripped the steering wheel tightly as he hovered his other hand near his pistol.

"Who is your passenger?" the guard pointed to signor Lehner.

"That's not your concern."

"No?" the guard scoffed.

Ezio shook his head quickly.

"Let's see your papers." The guard waved for Signor Lehner to provide his documentation, and he complied quickly.

With an exasperated huff, the guard took the documents, yet before he read through them, he dug out a cigarette from his pocket and put it to his lips. Throwing Signor Lehner's papers under his arm, the guard retrieved a box of matches and tried to light one but struggled significantly.

"Allow me." Ezio grabbed a lighter from his pocket and gestured for the guard to lean down.

Ezio nearly gagged on the stench of the alcohol as the guard leaned in, and wondered if he should take the opportunity to strike against them. In such a vulnerable position, Ezio had the upper hand. He could quickly dispose of this drunk soldier before turning his weapon on the sober one. It was risky, perhaps too risky, and Ezio decided to stay his hand.

"Grazie." The guard took a puff and stood upright as he began looking through Signor Lehner's papers, entirely unaware of how close he had come to meeting his end at Ezio's hand.

Glancing in the rearview mirror, Ezio took note of Signor Lehner's calm demeanor. With a nod to the old man, Ezio encouraged him to stay the course.

"Mario, come here." The guard nodded for his compatriot to come inspect the documents as well.

Ezio watched with his hand still over his pistol as the guard made his way around the vehicle. The guard walked slowly as his gaze remained fixated on both Ezio and Signor Lehner, not trusting either of them.

"A Jew?" the other guard asked in surprise as he leaned over and stared into the vehicle at signor Lehner, who Ezio noticed was now beginning to perspire. "Not a very Jewish name. Is this a doctored passport?"

"I'm taking him for processing," Ezio lied. "I can vouch for the authenticity of his name."

"You seem nervous?" the other guard asked as he narrowed his gaze at Ezio.

"The thrill of the hunt." Ezio grinned slightly to ease the tension.

"Hmm." The guard returned to studying the documents. "Why are you taking this route?"

"Pardon?" Ezio asked, pretending not to hear the question.

"Most Jews are processed in Trieste." The guard pointed behind them. "You're going in the wrong direction."

"As I advised, it's a highly sensitive mission from Captain Cacioppo."

"Listen." The first guard knelt beside the vehicle, and Ezio noticed that they had made a fatal error in their lack of judgment. All three guards were now lined up instead of spread out around the vehicle. Three quick squeezes of the trigger, and Ezio could take them out with relative ease. "We know what you're trying to do."

"I'm following orders." Ezio shrugged as he moved to take his pistol out of the holster.

"We both know that's not true." The guard took another puff of his cigarette, and Ezio felt his heart pounding in his chest. "There's a reason we've been stationed here."

"What are you implying?" Ezio feigned innocence.

"I'm implying that we may be able to come to an arrangement." The guard threw his lips upside down as he baited Ezio.

"Arrangement?" Ezio breathed a sigh of relief, knowing that there would be no need for violence.

"An arrangement." The guard took another puff of his cigarette as he waited for Ezio to bribe him.

Ezio looked at each man carefully before asking, "How much?"

"No, no, no." The man shook his head quickly. "You misunderstand me. We have no use for money. What can we buy up here that will bring us any pleasure? Besides, the money isn't that bad."

"You're hungry?" Ezio raised an eyebrow.

"Are you hungry, Mario?" the guard called over his shoulder.

"I'll turn this gun on myself if I have to eat another tin of mackerel," Mario grumbled.

"I do hope you're not proposing that we eat your cat?" the guard chuckled.

"I don't have any food on me, but I know where I can obtain some prime beef, seasoned with delicious herbs." Ezio recalled the rare experience of the meal he ate yesterday.

"That's not how this works." The guard grew annoyed. "We don't work on promises."

"If money, or a man's word won't suffice, then what?" Ezio asked, wondering if violence would be required after all.

"We'll take the cat and the Jew." Mario countered.

"What do you want with either of them?" Ezio chuckled, believing the guard to be jesting.

Yet when the guards didn't reply and instead stared back at Ezio with hardened expressions, Ezio realized they were serious.

"As it happens, we're heading into Lugano as soon as our relief arrives. We'll take him with us." The guard pointed in the direction of town. "Mario here is desperate for some good company. We talk too much, you see, and he prefers quiet fellowship. Your cat will suffice."

"When is the change of guard?" Ezio asked, feeling that the demand was curious at best.

"A few hours." The guard glanced at his watch.

"He's an elderly man." Ezio shook his head. "He won't survive the cold for that long."

"Then I'll tell you what's going to happen." The guard looked down at his feet as he grew menacing. "We'll arrest you for smuggling an enemy of the state. Then, we'll take your cat and cook it in front of you as we wait for Mussolini's secret police to collect you. Or, you can give us the cat and the Jew, and you can leave. Simple as that."

Ezio deliberated as he knew that the guards' intentions with Signor Lehner were likely cruel. His conscience wouldn't permit leaving Signor Lehner to such pitiless creatures. Again, Ezio hovered his hand over his pistol. His heart pounded in his chest as he took deep breaths to calm his body and ensure his aim would be exact. He couldn't afford to miss a single shot.

"They'll kill me," Signor Lehner whispered harshly as he placed a firm hand on Ezio's shoulder.

"I know!" Ezio whispered back.

But then something happened that Ezio couldn't quite explain. A moment of an infinitesimal break in the passage of time set upon Ezio, and the world about him stood still. He looked at the guards with their tattered uniforms, frostbitten fingers, and sores on their faces from malnutrition. He looked behind him at Signor Lehner, who was holding on tightly to his little bag of clothes, and watching the guards with wide eyes, Ezio realized that he had made a grave error.

This was a moment, he understood, that would forever alter the course of his life. Leonarda's prediction rang true in his head, and a deeply unsettling feeling formed a pit in his stomach as he grew bitter to the guards' malevolence.

"Do you believe in fate, Ezio?" Signor Lehner asked calmly, snapping Ezio back to reality, and he recalled Leonarda asking him the same question earlier that morning.

Ezio watched Signor Lehner in the rearview mirror and felt as though his arms had turned to lead. Not necessarily from fear, but it felt to him like someone was almost holding his arms down by his sides or that some weights were placed upon him, signifying that he was not in control of what was about to happen.

"I think this is how I pay for my crimes. A fitting end, I suppose. I ordered that family to be shot like animals. Now I will be shot by these animals. Still, if you agree to their terms, then they'll let you go." Signor Lehner began to shiver, and Ezio knew he was terrified.

"I can't agree to this!" Ezio shook his head adamantly.

"If they take me, they'll let you go." Signor Lehner moved to open the door. "Watch over my daughter."

"I can't allow this." Ezio reached for the old man, but he had already moved to the door.

"Neither of us have a choice." Signor Lehner opened the door. "If you act rashly, you won't be around to watch Faustina. Please, promise me that you'll watch her."

"I promise." Ezio nodded as a lump grew in his throat.

"We accept your terms," Signor Lehner spoke to the guards as he stepped out of the vehicle.

"And the cat?" Mario asked coldly as he waved for Ezio to hand over his pet.

"I'll inform Captain Cacioppo that you delivered Signor Lehner to Lugano." Ezio maintained his fabrication as he refused to hand over Wolfgang.

"The cat." The guard leaned over as he held his arms out.

"It's just a cat. There are dozens around here, I'm sure." Ezio gestured to the surrounding hills. "It has no value."

"It has value to you," the guard spoke knowingly.

Slowly, Ezio picked up Wolfgang, realizing he would not be able to barter out of this arrangement, and reluctantly handed him to the guard. Wolfgang meowed with fright as his eyes flew wide and he looked around in terror at this transfer.

"Goodbye, old friend." Ezio's eyes welled.

"Arrivederci." The guard waved for Ezio to turn the vehicle around and leave as he struggled to hold Wolfgang, who was stretching out his legs and trying to back out of his arms.

With one last look at Signor Lehner, Ezio reversed the vehicle before turning back in the direction of Giulino. Watching in the rearview mirror, Ezio's stomach churned as he pleaded with God that these men would act justly. He watched as the guards rifled through Signor Lehner's belongings, and Ezio hoped their cruelty ended with robbery.

Wolfgang, although perturbed, was at least starting to calm down, but Ezio's heart was being wrenched out of his chest for leaving behind his companion.

Ezio watched for as long as he could in the rearview mirror as he slowly drove away until the vehicle rounded a bend, and the checkpoint was hidden behind hills and trees.

Pulling over to the side, Ezio killed the engine as he debated his course of action. With his bad leg, it would be impossible to sneak up on the guards, even while they were inebriated. He thought about rushing to the station to put a call in to Lugano, but knew that he likely didn't have enough time and had no clue what he would say.

I should've drawn upon my courage and taken action while I had the chance, Ezio thought. *What am I thinking? If only I —*

A shot rang out.

The echo rushed throughout the hills and mountains, scattering the birds and sending a chill down Ezio's spine.

For a moment, Ezio was unable to think. He couldn't bear the brutality, the malice, the evilness. He couldn't understand how they could kill Signor Lehner. He simply sat in his vehicle as the snow continued to fall gently, ignorant to the life that had just been taken.

"Dammit!" Ezio slammed his fist against the steering wheel. "Dammit! Dammit! Dammit!"

Growling in his anger, Ezio planted his face into his hands as he felt an unbearable sense of rage at the injustice.

"I killed him." Ezio rubbed his eyes as his guilt soared. "If I had just followed orders and arrested him weeks ago, we would've never come this way. Not to mention I've doomed myself. These guards will turn me in the moment they get the chance. How can I protect his daughter now?"

I'm sorry, Wolfgang! Ezio's lips trembled as he imagined his cat was still with him, purring against his leg. *I didn't have a choice!*

"You're right," Ezio spoke aloud to Wolfgang's fabricated meow. "I didn't see them shoot Signor Lehner. They could've fired off a shot to threaten him, but I can't go back now. I'll find his daughter a way out of Italy before I'm discovered. When the guards' shift change arrives, they'll likely report me. If they were telling the truth, this means I likely only have a few hours. I didn't see a telephone at the checkpoint, so they'll have to deliver the news in person. I failed Signor Lehner, but I won't fail his daughter. I hope my parents received and understood the message from Francesca."

Chapter Eight:
Fools and Kings

"The line separating good and evil passes not through states, nor between classes, nor between political parties either -- but right through every human heart -- and through all human hearts. This line shifts. Inside us, it oscillates with the years. And even within hearts overwhelmed by evil, one small bridgehead of good is retained."

Aleksandr Solzhenitsyn

Returning to the station, Ezio tried to contain his shock but felt as though he was scarcely in control of his own movements. He merely continued on a track that predetermined where his feet would take him, unable to deviate from the path he was set upon.

Walking into the building, Ezio spotted Armando still at reception with Francesca and noticed that she was clearly not interested in the second lieutenant's pursuits.

"Oh, Lieutenant, what are the kilometers?" Francesca grabbed her clipboard.

"I don't know," Ezio replied softly.

"Ezio." Francesca's shoulders dropped in disappointment.

A man was just executed without remorse, and your greatest concern is the mileage on the vehicle? Ezio thought but bit his tongue from lashing out. He needed to convince them that nothing was out of the ordinary, and that his task had not bothered him in the slightest, if they were even aware of what he had been delegated.

"Armando, check on the kilometers." Ezio nodded for the second lieutenant to follow through.

"All you need to do is quickly look at the speedometer before you leave the vehicle." Armando shrugged his annoyance for the menial chore.

Regardless, Ezio paid them no further attention as he limped toward his office to collect the captain for supper. He didn't know how he would stomach eating anything or how he would be able to compose himself for an entire evening.

Like a beast without thought, Ezio plunged ahead and opened the door to the office to find the captain sitting behind the desk while smoking a pipe and listening to the radio. The news was reporting on the Italian front in Africa, but Ezio could hardly make out a word that was being uttered as his mind was locked on the sound of the horrible shot.

"It's done, then?" Captain Cacioppo asked quietly.

Ezio nodded, but the smell of the tobacco and the dreadful memory of Signor Lehner's passing caused Ezio to nearly vomit.

"Why do you look so gloom?" Captain Cacioppo tilted his head.

"As I said, Signore, I carry deep respect for the man." Ezio cleared his throat as he sat in the chair beside the desk. He had thought about lying but knew that the captain would detect any deception, and instead played upon the truth.

"You still think he's human, don't you?" Captain Cacioppo leaned forward and pointed with his pipe at Ezio. "Free yourself of such a charge, Lieutenant. He's no more human than the rat infesting your office."

Then, as if they had been discussing something trivial, and not a man's life, Captain Cacioppo opened a newspaper and began browsing it casually.

It was then that a dark and terrible thought entered Ezio's mind. His hand hovered over his pistol as he glared at his captain secretively. Ezio knew his own life was already forfeited by his assisting Signor Lehner, and it was merely a matter of time before his actions were discovered.

He imagined what it would be like to unload his weapon on the unsuspecting captain. Men like him didn't deserve to live, especially in such comfort while they freely gave others over to death without any conflict of conscience.

Yet before Ezio could contemplate further, a knock came to the door.

"Enter," Captain Cacioppo called out as he remained glued to an article.

"Mail for you, Signore." Francesca opened the door and walked into the office with a letter in her hand.

Without further acknowledgment, the captain continued to read the paper as though Francesca did not exist.

"Would you like the letter on your desk, Signore?" Francesca cleared her throat.

Still, the captain refused to reply.

Unsure of the proper etiquette, Francesca placed the letter on the desk in front of the captain, offered an awkward curtsey, and left the two men alone in the office.

In silence, as the clock ticked patiently and the radio announcer advised of the latest casualties from the recent bombings, the captain continued reading while Ezio imagined executing his superior in rather unkind methods.

"Do you want to know the secret to authority?" the captain asked after a moment while still reading.

Ezio didn't reply as he waited for the captain to continue.

"Never be moved by what someone tells you or by any request they make." The captain finally set down the paper and searched through the desk drawers before retrieving a letter opener. "When the young woman brought me the letter, did you notice that I didn't even budge?"

"I did." Ezio nodded slowly, still contemplating his violent intentions.

"Don't respond to people. It makes them uncomfortable." Captain Cacioppo bounced the letter opener in his hand before swiftly slicing the envelope open.

With the swift motion, Ezio was at once reminded of the shot that killed Signor Lehner, and he was forced to press his eyes shut to rid himself of the thought.

"Mio Dio. My prayers have been answered." Captain Cacioppo leaned back in the chair as he held a photograph in his hands and then spoke with a trembling lip, "I'm a grandfather. My eyes have beheld the beauty of a granddaughter. Before my sight left me forever, I have been permitted to see her."

Surprised by the display of emotion from such a contemptible person, Ezio frowned as he studied the captain with peculiarity.

"Look." The captain held the photograph out for Ezio, who took it gingerly and examined the picture of a baby girl sleeping in a basinet.

"Beautiful." Ezio handed the photograph back.

"Isabella, they named her." Captain Cacioppo chocked and his hands shook as he studied the picture. "She's the very definition of perfection. This is the reason for existence, Ezio. Life, or rather, the continuation of it, is the highest ambition. You feel it in moments like this. Are you married?"

"I'm not, Signore, no." Ezio bit his lip as he grew uncomfortable, bracing for the inevitable follow-up.

"Not for lack of trying, I'm sure." The captain looked down his nose at Ezio.

"It's complicated." Ezio cleared his throat.

"In any case, let's celebrate." The captain stood with a large grin plastered across his face. "Tonight, in the home of the Milanesi family, we will toast to our anticipated promotions and to the wondrous news of my granddaughter's arrival."

"Now?" Ezio glanced at his watch, hoping to delay him slightly to give Faustina as much time as possible to vacate the premises.

"Of course, now!" The captain rubbed his hands together eagerly. "I've heard good news of your father's cooking!"

"You have?" Ezio frowned. "I was unaware of his renown."

"Well, I suggested, initially, that I should dine with Armando, but he lavished praises upon your father's culinary skills."

Did he now? Ezio squeezed his hands into fists.

"So, what do you say?" Captain Cacioppo threw his hands out wide.

"Let's eat." Ezio offered a false grin as he struggled to stand.

"Excellent." Captain Cacioppo clapped quickly as he grabbed his cape and hat, and the two began their trek out of the station where, again, Ezio spotted Armando still with Francesca.

"Signore, an urgent message from the border." Francesca held her hand up to stop the captain, and Ezio's heart fell into his stomach.

Fortunately for Ezio, the captain stayed true to his advice from earlier and ignored her altogether as he threw the door to the station open while walking briskly toward the vehicle.

"How did you know which vehicle was mine?" Ezio asked as his suspicion soared while he waited anxiously for the captain to respond.

"I saw you driving earlier," the captain replied swiftly as he waited by the rear passenger door for Ezio to open it for him.

"You did?" Ezio asked slowly as he opened the door, wondering where he could've possibly seen him.

"There's nothing, Lieutenant." The captain paused by the door as he looked sternly at Ezio. "Nothing that happens of which I'm not aware. Whatever secret you think you own now belongs to me. There is no rendezvous, no secret path, and no hidden way that you have taken which I have not seen."

"Signore." Ezio swallowed as he felt the intimidation of this imposing man standing a good foot taller than him.

"Now, let's celebrate." The captain returned to sudden cheer and patted Ezio's arm as he climbed into the back of the vehicle.

Grudgingly, though careful not to show it, Ezio started the vehicle, and they began their brief journey to his parents' house.

"Actually, Lieutenant, let's take a quick detour." The captain leaned forward when Ezio came to the fork in the road, and he wondered if his superior was aware of the direction that he took Signor Lehner.

"Detour?" Ezio asked while trying to mask his nervousness.

"Take me to Signor Lehner's property. I want to see where he was living."

Glancing in the rearview mirror at the captain, Ezio tried to gauge his motives but then glanced away as he turned toward Signor Lehner's old property.

Driving along the road adjacent to the lake, Ezio tried to ignore the large posters demanding everything of him for the sake of his country. Looking out the window at the boats bobbing happily and gently on the water, Ezio wished that he could climb into one and forget his troubles. Even though he had not set foot in a boat since that fateful day nearly ten years ago, Ezio longed for the isolation. He was certain that he would die shortly and regretted not overcoming his fear of Lake Como. How he mourned the days not spent on the peaceful waters.

"Stop!" the captain demanded, startling Ezio, and he slammed on the brakes, narrowly avoiding Luigi, who was again in the middle of the road with a bottle in hand.

"Luigi!" Ezio rolled down the window and shouted at the man to get out of the way.

"Scusi, Lieutenant." Luigi offered a limp Fascist salute.

"I'm not falling for that routine again." Ezio waved for him to move. "I have an important passenger with me as well."

"Wolfgang has been upgraded to important passenger now, has he?" Luigi snickered, and Ezio's voice was stolen from him as he was unable to respond. He simply looked back at Luigi with heartbreak written across his face as he recalled how his companion was taken by the border guard.

"Allow me, Lieutenant." The captain left the vehicle, which Ezio found surprising, and he, too, followed the captain, worried that he was going to behave rashly with the drunk.

"Luigi, is it?" The captain asked politely, and Ezio noticed that Luigi was entirely stupefied by the presence of a man of rank.

"Sì, Signore." Luigi swallowed.

"You look hungry, Luigi. Are you hungry, amico mio?" The captain asked gently, but Ezio struggled to determine if he was genuine or if this was some cruel ploy.

"Desperately." Luigi removed his cap and squeezed it tight against his chest as he looked back at the captain with hope.

"I assume you have a family?" The captain examined Luigi closely.

"Sì." Luigi nodded quickly and then pointed at his house behind the captain, where his family was watching.

"Ah, I see. Their names?"

"That's my wife, Isabella."

"Isabella," the captain spoke warmly as he looked back at Luigi, almost with tears in his eyes. "That's my granddaughter's name."

"And my son, Antonio." Luigi pointed to the young boy beside his mother.

"It breaks my heart to see you so hungry." Captain Cacioppo tilted his head. "I would like to remedy that."

"We would be forever grateful." Luigi looked back at the captain with sad eyes.

"What is your trade?" the captain asked.

"I was a painter before the war." Luigi shrugged. "No one buys my art anymore."

"Do you have any in your house?" The captain grew excited.

"Sì, Signore." Luigi's eyes flew wide with anticipation.

"Bring me one. I'll buy it." The captain waved for Luigi to go fetch a painting.

"Grazie, Signore! Grazie mille!" Luigi ran back to his house and past his wife without explanation for his sudden good cheer.

"You know him?" the captain asked quietly as he crossed his arms and leaned against the vehicle.

"All too well." Ezio also leaned against the vehicle as they waited for Luigi.

"You mentioned this was his routine?" The captain looked at Ezio for an explanation.

"He gets drunk, or sometimes pretends to be inebriated, so that he will be arrested and given food in jail," Ezio replied.

"Did you know him before the war?" The captain asked as he cracked his knuckles.

"Si. I've known him my whole life."

"Did he sell many paintings?"

"I didn't know he was a painter."

"Then you never knew him." The captain studied Ezio.

"Signore!" Luigi shouted while running out of the house with a canvas wrapped in a white sheet.

"Let's see it." The captain ordered with eagerness.

"It's my favorite piece." Luigi panted and looked somewhat nervous as he slowly removed the white sheet.

Ezio, while he had been skeptical of the drunkard's artistic depth and skill and was initially anticipating something rather juvenile, but he was astonished to witness such a moving painting.

A field of blue flaxes stretched over rolling hills, appearing as waves rising and falling with the ocean. In the middle of this flower sea was a single tree with its branches stretching out like a cloud in the heavens. Under this tree was a woman with dark hair, brown eyes, smooth skin, and an enchanting smile.

It was peaceful, calm, and Ezio felt as though he had in the days of his youth and ignorance when all that mattered was setting out on the lake with his brothers to catch fish or swim. In this painting, Ezio found a home, and also felt sorrow for his neglect of Luigi's gifts.

"I'm amazed. Truly, I am." The captain took the painting in his hands and held it at a distance as he reviewed it in detail.

"I'm glad you like it." Luigi let out a nervous chuckle as his shoulders relaxed.

"Lieutenant?" The captain turned to Ezio.

"Signore?" Ezio asked, feeling caught off guard.

"Do you like it?"

"Oh, sì, sì." Ezio cleared his throat.

"It's settled." The captain handed the painting to Ezio before reaching into his jacket and retrieving a stack of folded bills which he then handed to Luigi.

"This is too much!" Luigi held his hands up, refusing to accept the captain's generosity.

"Nonsense." The captain forced the money into Luigi's hand. "It's yours. By some food for yourself and your family."

"Grazie, Signore!" Luigi's eyes welled. "Grazie mille! Grazie mille, Signore!"

"We have business to attend to." The captain returned his attention to Ezio, who opened the door for his superior before placing the painting in the back as Luigi sped happily to his family.

Entering the vehicle, Ezio wasn't entirely certain what to make of this experience. Captain Cacioppo had sentenced Signor Lehner to death without any crisis of conscience and was seemingly without empathy of any sort. Yet now, instead of turning his nose up at Luigi, as Ezio had done previously, Captain Cacioppo gave him more money than he considered reasonable.

"Do you believe that was a mistake, Lieutenant?" Captain Cacioppo asked as he stared out the window at Luigi's residence.

"He might spend it on alcohol." Ezio shrugged, not wanting to relinquish his admiration of the charitable spirit.

"What is alcohol?" the captain asked.

"Pardon?" Ezio frowned, wondering what the captain meant.

"There's a reason we Italians call it *la scusa di Dio*, or God's apology." The captain crossed his legs as he looked at Ezio in the rearview mirror. "Wine is God's way of apologizing for making us conscious, because to be conscious is to understand suffering, and who can tolerate suffering for long? Alcohol, like any vice, is a way to suppress consciousness. I've removed the suffering from their lives, or at least a portion of it. The need for suppression no longer exists."

Ezio contemplated Captain Cacioppo's observation and felt it prudent to take his words into consideration.

"Signor Lehner's?" Ezio asked after a moment.

"Another time, perhaps." The captain patted his belly. "My hunger cannot wait another minute."

With a nod, Ezio started the vehicle, and they began the short journey back to his house. Yet as they drove, Ezio could scarcely think about anything besides the painting. He wanted to experience that surrealism again and remove himself far from this heartless world. Far from an existence where old men were executed for the accident of their birth, and far from a life of endless sorrow and tragedy.

"This is the place?" the captain asked when they arrived, and Ezio caught the disappointment in his voice.

"It tends to have that effect on people." Ezio opened the door for the captain. "But don't worry, I assure you the charm is not lost on its inhabitants."

"Bring the painting." The captain pointed to the back of the vehicle.

"The painting?" Ezio grew confused.

"It's a gift for your parents." The captain smiled at Ezio, who was, again, shocked by the captain's generosity.

"Another visitor?" Vitelli shouted from his balcony as Ezio and Captain Cacioppo walked to the door.

"Buonasera Vitelli," Ezio called up to him cheerfully with the painting under his arm. "This is Captain Cacioppo."

"Signore." Vitelli saluted as he struggled to raise his arm above his head.

"At ease." Captain Cacioppo saluted the old man.

"What brings you to our little town, Captain?" Vitelli asked with a slight smile, and Ezio sensed he was proud to be speaking with the man of rank.

"Unfortunate business, Signore." The captain removed his hat. "But tonight, Signor Milanesi's cooking is what brings me to your fine neighborhood."

"You're in for a treat then." Vitelli sat back down with a huff.

I know I haven't prayed for much before, but I beg of you now, please tell me that my parents received the message from Francesca. Ezio begged Heaven, God, or whoever was listening. *Please don't let Faustina be inside the house.*

Yet his heart fell into his stomach when he opened the door and sitting at the top of the stairs was Faustina, looking down at them in surprise. Her suitcase was set beside her, and Ezio assumed she had been waiting anxiously for him to take her to the convent as he had promised.

"Sister." Captain Cacioppo looked up at the stunning woman, surprised to find a nun sitting on the stairs.

"Signore." Faustina swallowed and stood nervously with her hands pressed tightly against her skirt, and it was clear to Ezio that she assumed he had tricked her.

"My apologies, Signore." Ezio looked at his captain with feigned regret. "I had forgotten my obligation to Sister Faustina. I promised to return her to the convent after my shift. I, unfortunately, will not be able to join you for dinner."

"Nonsense." Captain Cacioppo scoffed and then spoke to Faustina in such a manner as if to pronounce that his word was final, "You will join us, of course."

"Signore, I—" Faustina began, but caught the swift shake of Ezio's head, warning her to not press the matter. "I would be delighted."

"Wonderful." Captain Cacioppo ascended the stairs toward her, where he took Faustina's hand in hers before offering a quick kiss on her gloved hand.

"Ezio?" Lorenzo also arrived at the top of the stairs with a washcloth thrown over his shoulder as he studied the captain curiously. "You should've advised us that we were to expect company."

"I requested Francesca to send you a message." Ezio gritted his teeth in annoyance.

"Message? What message?" Lorenzo asked in confusion, and Ezio assumed he was rather embarrassed for his state of undress.

"It doesn't matter now. This is Captain Cacioppo. Captain Cacioppo, this is Lorenzo Milanesi," Ezio introduced them.

"Your son advises me that you fought in the Great War." Captain Cacioppo looked at Lorenzo with admiration. "You have my greatest respect, Signore."

With a slight tear in his eye, Lorenzo morphed into an entirely new creation. The father retreated as the soldier emerged, and Lorenzo stood tall and proud as he saluted the captain, who returned the gesture.

"Papa?" Vittoria called from the balcony. "Is Mamma back yet?"

"We have company," Lorenzo called back, and at once, Vittoria abandoned her smoking corner as she rushed to see who the visitor could be.

"Santo cielo." The captain's arms fell to his sides when he spotted Vittoria. "You are beauty itself, my dear."

"Oh!" Vittoria blushed uncontrollably, and Ezio rolled his eyes in annoyance at how easily she was won over. "Now, now."

"You never mentioned how gorgeous your sister was!" The captain looked crossly at Ezio as Vittoria giggled.

Once you meet my mother, you'll understand, Ezio thought as he, too, ascended the stairs.

"I have something for you." The captain returned to a soft demeanor as he looked again at Vittoria.

"For me?" Vittoria pinched her lips together to try and hamper her excitement.

"Lieutenant." The captain waved emphatically for Ezio to bring him the painting, which he then presented to Vittoria.

"Bellissimo!" Vittoria threw a hand to her chest in astonishment.

"Do you like it?" the captain asked with a bright smile.

"I love it!" Vittoria grinned.

Glancing at Faustina, Ezio wished to convey his apologies, but she simply stood back, trying to be as inconspicuous as possible to repel any attention.

"Ezio, you didn't mention that your superior was so charming." Vittoria looked flirtatiously at the captain, and Ezio felt as though he may be sick.

I didn't mention him at all, you idiota! Ezio wished to say but kept his thoughts to himself as he instead addressed his father, "My apologies, Francesca was supposed to send a message home to you. Do you have anything that you can prepare for the captain?"

"I'm sure there is something I can put together. Sit, sit. I'll have supper ready shortly." Lorenzo waved for them to convalesce around the sofa and chairs.

"May I?" Captain Cacioppo held his arm out to Vittoria, who graciously accepted as she gave the painting back to Ezio who placed it carefully at the top of the stairs.

"Can he be trusted?" Faustina whispered to Ezio as the two remained near the top of the stairs while Vittoria and Captain Cacioppo walked to the living room.

"Not in the slightest," Ezio whispered back and shook his head swiftly.

"You promised you would take me!" Faustina clenched her jaw.

"I still intend to keep that promise," Ezio growled. "This is out of my control."

"Lieutenant?" Captain Cacioppo asked. "Is everything alright?"

"Perfectly, Signore. Just making arrangements for when I can take Sister Faustina to the convent. I'm sure her order is concerned for her whereabouts."

"Once she explains that she's with the one and only Captain Cacioppo, I'm sure they'll understand." The captain waved for them to join the group.

Reluctantly, the two joined them as Ezio sat on the couch with his sister and the captain, and Faustina sat on chairs facing the couch.

"Is this your first visit to Giulino?" Vittoria asked as she leaned forward and played with her hair.

Yet, oddly enough, the captain ignored her entirely, which Ezio found strange given his fascination with her a mere moment ago. Instead, he stared at Faustina in such a way that Ezio was certain the captain had already unraveled the truth.

"How does a nun come to be in the house of the Milanesi?" The captain asked as his cheer faded, and an intimidating frown crept onto his brow.

"She arrived yesterday with —" Vittoria began, but the captain held up his gloved hand to stop her.

"I'm asking the nun." Captain Cacioppo looked sternly at Vittoria, whose cheeks immediately grew crimson with embarrassment.

"Signor Lehner requested some prayer support. His wife passed not long ago, and he was feeling the burden of grief," Faustina replied as she stared at the floor.

"And they sent you?" the captain asked with incredulity. "Why not a priest? Why would they send a nun, alone, to console a lonely, grieving man? More specifically, why would they send you?"

"It's not my place to question orders, Signore." Faustina played with the cross around her neck nervously.

"Like a good soldier of Christ." Captain Cacioppo remained unconvinced. "How do you feel about Mussolini?"

"In what sense, Signore?" Faustina glanced quickly at him and then away, and Ezio felt his breathing laboring as he feared where this questioning would lead.

"I'm sure, as a good Christian, you're rather happy with his move to make Christianity the official religion of Italy, no?" Captain Cacioppo peered at her thoughtfully.

"My concern, Signore, is for the Kingdom of God only."

Seemingly impressed by the response, Captain Cacioppo leaned back in his chair as he placed a hand to his chin.

"Your accent..." Captain Cacioppo narrowed his gaze.

"I was born in Austria." Faustina offered a brisk smile to dispel the discomfort.

"Did you know of Signor Lehner's nature?" the captain asked as he again tested her.

"Nature?" Faustina feigned ignorance.

"He's a Jew." The captain narrowed his gaze.

"That nature is of no consequence to me." Faustina shook her head, but Ezio braced himself, wishing that she had lied instead.

"Then what is?"

"We have only one nature. The nature of sin." Faustina looked back at the captain with a sort of challenge.

"Are you aware of what happened to Signor Lehner?" the captain asked with a hint of sadism.

"He was arrested. I was at the property when the lieutenant took him into custody." Faustina glanced at Ezio. "He was kind enough to offer me passage to the convent today."

"Do you know where Signor Lehner is now?" The captain ran his tongue along the right corner of his lips as he seemed to relish the passing of this information.

"I would assume he's at the holding cells?" Faustina looked at the captain with concern.

"He's on his way to Trieste." The captain paused as he savored the moment. "From there, he will be sent to Poland."

As with Signor Lehner, the color left Faustina's face, and Ezio's heart broke for her to hear of this news in such a cruel fashion. How he wished to tell her that he had attempted to take him to Switzerland, but even there, her father's fate was no less barbaric.

"Does this bother you?" the captain asked, again enjoying the moment.

Yet Faustina couldn't reply as she struggled to compose herself, and Ezio watched helplessly as her eyes welled and her lips pursed.

"The kind lieutenant here was the one who sent him on his way." The captain turned his attention to Ezio, who refused to even look at Faustina.

"Those stupid kids!" Ludovica shouted from the foyer as she swung the door open, ignorant to the company in her house, and everyone's attention broke away from Faustina. All that is, except for the captain whose gaze remained fixated on her. "Their ball nearly made me drop these cakes."

"Ciao! We have company!" Lorenzo called out quickly before his wife had the opportunity to severely embarrass him.

"More company?" Ludovica asked grumpily.

Arriving at the top of the stairs, Ludovica, with a cigarette hanging out of the corner of her mouth and a pink box under her arm, looked at Captain Cacioppo in disbelief to see someone of his status gracing their humble home.

"Captain, this is my mother, Ludovica." Ezio stood as he introduced them. "Mamma, this is Captain Cacioppo."

"Come stai?" the captain asked as he also stood respectfully.

"Do you want cake?" Ludovica asked as her astonishment suddenly vanished, and she threw the pink box onto the coffee table in front of the couches.

"Where did you get cake?" Lorenzo asked from the kitchen.

"Signora Cianciulli," Ludovica replied, and Ezio's heart paused momentarily at the mention of the soap maker. It was likely that Leonarda had, as Vittoria predicted earlier, passed along some information about Ezio's conversation.

"She makes cakes now?" Lorenzo tilted his head in confusion.

"Said she had a recipe." Ludovica sat with a huff as she put her cigarette out in the ashtray before retrieving another one.

"Well, don't eat those. It'll ruin your appetite!" Lorenzo held up a finger in warning.

"What are you making?" Ludovica called over her shoulder.

"You'll see," Lorenzo replied.

"I hate when he does that," Ludovica grumbled. "Why the secrecy? Just tell me what you're making!"

"Actually, you might as well sit at the table. It'll be out in a moment." Lorenzo stirred sauce in a pot and began to sing cheerfully.

"Excellent." Captain Cacioppo stood and rubbed his hands together eagerly.

"Help your papa." Ludovica slapped Vittoria's thigh.

"Hey!" Vittoria's embarrassment soared as she glared at her mother.

"Go!" Ludovica threatened another slap.

"I'm going! I'm going!" Vittoria growled as she left to help Lorenzo, but not before offering a quick glance at the captain to measure his reaction.

"I've heard wonderful reports of your cooking." Captain Cacioppo shamelessly sat at the head of the table, and everyone, even Ezio, was surprised by this level of disrespect for their father.

Ezio, however, was careful to sit beside Faustina and prayed that he would have the opportunity to at least whisper to her when the captain's attention was diverted.

"Usually, this is made with fish or scampi." Lorenzo brought a large pot over to the table. "My mother's recipe, actually, but due to the rations, we will have to suffice without seafood."

Then, taking a ladle, Lorenzo half-slammed a tomato pasta mix onto the captain's plate, which splattered onto his uniform.

In alarm at the stain against his vanity, the captain nearly jumped out of his chair as he looked down at his uniform in disbelief before glaring at Lorenzo.

"Scusi! Scusi!" Lorenzo held his hands together apologetically. "Vittoria, grab the captain a cloth! Quickly!"

"Come with me, Signore." Vittoria led the captain to the kitchen.

"Your father is safe," Ezio whispered to Faustina while the captain was preoccupied in the kitchen and trying to clean himself up with a giggling Vittoria offering no real assistance.

"What do you mean?" Faustina whispered back as she waited eagerly for his reply.

"Switzerland." Ezio smiled slightly. He knew it was wrong to lie, but he was desperate to reassure her. Besides, it was still a possibility that Signor Lehner was not shot by the checkpoint guards, or so he convinced himself.

"And for you." Lorenzo dished out a serving for Ezio, being rather careful not to make another mess.

Glancing at the food, Ezio was startled to find that some of the pasta was undercooked while other portions were soggy and falling apart. The tomato mixture was runny, and the oil was poorly mixed.

"What are you doing?" Ezio whispered harshly after glancing at the captain to ensure he wouldn't be heard. "This food looks like you dug it out of the trash."

"Good." Lorenzo winked. "He'll never return."

With a slight grin of appreciation, Ezio watched his father in astonishment at his quick wit. It was then that he appreciated his parents' staunch hatred of Fascism and how beneficial it was for him this evening. Diving into his meal, Ezio savored each and every bite that hastened the end to this horrid evening.

"Lieutenant?" the captain asked with indignation as he returned to the table. "The nun should pray first."

With wide eyes of surprise, Faustina glanced at Ezio, who assumed she was terrified that the captain would expect a certain prayer.

"Let me grab my prayer book." Faustina moved to stand.

"Nonsense." Captain Cacioppo raised his hand to stop her as he chuckled. "Surely you know the prayers."

"May I let you in on a secret, Captain?" Faustina held her hands politely in front of her.

"Of course." The captain shrugged.

"No one in my order knows the prayers by memorization alone." Faustina continued to move toward her luggage that was still at the top of the stairs.

"Then pray from your heart." Captain Cacioppo held out his arm to stop her and looked at her with such a glare as to indicate he would not tolerate being tested further.

"From the heart?" Faustina again glanced at Ezio.

"Stop looking at him!" Captain Cacioppo barked. "Look at me when I'm speaking to you!"

Sharply, Faustina turned her attention to the captain, and Ezio sensed she was struggling to withhold her tongue.

"From the heart, you say?" Faustina clenched her jaw.

"From the heart." Captain Cacioppo placed his hands on the table as he nodded eagerly.

"If you wish." Faustina cleared her throat and closed her eyes as Ezio prepared for devastation.

"Deliver me, O Lord, from the evil man: preserve me from the violent man," Faustina began reciting Psalm 140, and Ezio couldn't help but offer a hidden grin, yet his cheer faded when he noticed that the captain was watching her closely. Faustina, however, couldn't withhold her defiance any longer and opened her eyes as she stared back at him with equal measure while continuing, "Which imagine mischiefs in their heart; continually are they gathered together for war. They have sharpened their tongues like a serpent; adders' poison is under their lips. Keep me, O Lord, from the hands of the wicked; preserve me from the violent man; who have purposed to overthrow my goings. The proud have hid a snare for me, and cords; they have spread a net by the wayside; they have set gins for me."

"Now from the New Testament," Captain Cacioppo challenged, and Ezio froze, understanding that he surely suspected her of being Jewish.

"Enough of this!" Ludovica's deep voice boomed as she stood and placed her fists on the table, and Ezio watched with silent amusement as the captain was taken back by his mother's ferocity.

Looking around the table, and still surprised by Ludovica's demeanor, the captain relented and gestured for Faustina to sit.

The table delved into an awkward silence as everyone ate the terrible meal with the eagerness to finish this evening as soon as possible.

Yet, as if appreciating the instability, when the captain had finished his meal, he sat back in his chair and examined Faustina carefully.

"I'm losing my eyesight," the captain began as he continued to study Faustina, and Ezio found it peculiar how adamant he was to share this information. "I may only have a few years left, but I could also lose my eyesight tomorrow. I'll never be able to witness my granddaughter growing. I'll never see what our glorious nation will become. Still, there's one thing I will always see. Do you know what that is?"

Faustina shook her head slowly.

"The heart of a person." The captain pointed at her chest. "That, to me, will always be laid bare. It's a gift, and a curse. What I know about you, Sister, is that you're not who you say you are. They may not be able to see it, but I do."

"Then what am I?" Faustina challenged, and Ezio bit his tongue from scolding her boldness.

"You're not religious." The captain ran his tongue along the inside of his cheek. "That much is certain."

"Certain?" Faustina took her turn to scoff.

"Without a doubt." He glanced at Ezio, who assumed the captain was now suspicious of him as well.

"Some wine, Signore?" Lorenzo asked cheerfully.

The captain didn't respond but instead looked at Lorenzo with slight disdain.

"Everywhere I look, I see corruption, falsehoods, and a world not as it should be." The captain kept his gaze fixated on Lorenzo. "Don't fool yourself into believing that I'm ignorant of your allegiances."

"We're loyal to Italy, Signore." Lorenzo threw his hands out in defense. "That is never in question."

"It is the only question!" Captain Cacioppo shouted, and the room grew quiet in surprise at his rage. "And it's the only reason I have come here this evening. You think I wanted to visit your shithole of a house and endure this communist sludge you call food? No wonder your son is crippled. Eating this food would malnourish anyone."

"How dare you speak about my Ezio in that manner!" Ludovica pointed wildly at Captain Cacioppo, and Ezio looked at her in bewilderment for her offense.

"You loathe your son." The captain retrieved his pipe and his tobacco as he glared threateningly at Ezio's mother. "Why should you care that I insult him?"

"Cause he's mine to hate." Ludovica patted her chest repeatedly. "Now, get out!"

With the slightest and most abnormal of smiles, Ezio, for the first time in years, felt the first real affection from his mother. Despite the harshness of her statement, Ludovica called Ezio her own, and in that small measure of care, Ezio knew that she still loved him, even if she didn't dare admit it.

"Lieutenant." The captain stood after lighting his pipe. "Take me back to the station."

"Signore." Ezio also stood, happy to see the light at the end of the tunnel on this evening.

"I would thank you for the meal, but I'm certain it is going to cost me dearly." The captain glared at Lorenzo. "Why is communist food so putrid? You really can tell the strength of an ideology by the culinary art it produces."

"You've spent too much time in the capital, Signore." Lorenzo looked back at the captain with a hint of menace. "You've forgotten what it's like up here in the north. There are many more of us than you realize."

"Lorenzo, please!" Vittoria tugged on her father's sleeve for him to not say another word that could potentially doom them.

"Fascism's day is drawing short." Lorenzo ignored his daughter's warning as he stared sheepishly at Captain Cacioppo. "Mark my words, the north will rise up, and you will see that the wickedness of your dogmatic view on life will never rear its ugly head again."

"Lieutenant!" Captain Cacioppo shouted as he turned and charged down the stairs before opening the door swiftly and exiting the house.

"I'll be right back to take you to the convent," Ezio spoke to Faustina as he hurried to follow the captain.

"At this hour?" Ludovica glanced at the clock. "You won't be back until the morning!"

"We don't have a choice." Ezio looked at Faustina with concern as he also exited the house to find the captain waiting by the vehicle while smoking his pipe.

Opening the back passenger door for the captain, Ezio brushed the smoke out of his face before throwing his cane onto the passenger seat and then entering the vehicle himself.

"Investigate her," the captain spoke coldly as he stared at Ezio's property.

"My mother?" Ezio asked, although he was fully aware of who the captain meant.

"I understand why you're blinded." The captain ignored Ezio as he stared at him through the rearview mirror.

"Oh?" Ezio tried to steady his nerves as he rolled down the window to let the smoke escape the vehicle.

"You're in love with her." The captain looked back at the house.

"Love?" Ezio was both baffled and caught off guard by the conclusion.

"I don't blame you. She's rather beautiful, but I think you're deceived by your own emotions." The captain rubbed his eyes. "I'm tired, Lieutenant, but the work never ceases. Take me back to the station. I have much to do. If you don't come to a satisfactory conclusion with the nun, I'll have Armando investigate both of you."

Satisfactory conclusion? Ezio grew cynical. *You've already decided what her fate is. Likely a quota he's required to fulfill, which means I'll have to be extra careful to protect her.*

"One other thing, Lieutenant." The captain raised his finger as a thought popped into his mind.

"Yes?" Ezio asked as he started the vehicle, wondering if the captain was going to demand investigations on his parents as well.

"There have been strange reports making their way to our superiors."

"What sort of reports?" Ezio glanced in the rearview mirror.

"Signora Setti," the captain sighed, and Ezio understood he had likely had some dealings with her. "The reports of her sister's disappearance seem genuine. I'm assigning you to investigate further."

"Do you believe this is an appropriate use of police resources?" Ezio frowned.

"I'm to be the judge of that!" Captain Cacioppo barked. "I make those decisions, and you follow orders."

"Si, Signore." Ezio cleared his throat.

"I suppose you're worried about what will happen with your parents?" The captain asked with a measure of compassion, and Ezio waited for him to continue.

"Their politics are wrong, but they're no threat. So long as you comply, that is." The captain looked menacingly at Ezio through the rearview mirror. "Don't fail me, boy. You did well with Signor Lehner, but Italy comes first, even above family. Your parents are communists in heart, but they don't officially belong to any of the illegal parties. If that changes, you'll have no choice but to arrest them."

Chapter Nine:
The Lake

"Above all the grace and the gifts that Christ gives to his beloved is that of overcoming self."

St. Francis of Assisi

"Where are we?" Faustina asked warily as they arrived at the pier near Signor Lehner's residence, and Ezio had made good on his word to return for her after he had delivered the captain to the station. "I thought we were driving to the convent?"

"That was the original plan, yes, but Captain Cacioppo's surprise dinner imposition altered the schedule. It will take too long to drive now." Ezio exited the vehicle after grabbing his cane. "We'll have to cross the lake instead."

"At this time of night?" Faustina's concern grew as she looked up at the overcast sky which hid the moon and stars. "Will it be too dark?"

"Captain Cacioppo has ordered that I investigate you, and he will only accept one outcome." Ezio looked at Faustina with understanding as he began to descend the ancient stone staircase that led to the boats. "This is our only chance."

"Do you have a boat?" Faustina walked swiftly behind Ezio and latched onto his arm, careful not to trip in the dark.

Ezio grinned at the slight affection, even though he understood it wasn't meant as a romantic gesture. He was starved for touch, and he held onto this moment dearly.

"It's a small rowboat, but it'll do the trick." Ezio pointed to the wooden rowboat tied at the end of the dock that Signora Soavi had gifted him only recently.

"That won't be too difficult for you?" Faustina asked with doubt in her voice.

"Fortunately, you don't need good legs to row." Ezio untied and removed the tarp.

"I meant the distance." Faustina slapped him gently on the arm. "I would never be so indelicate."

Clumsily, Ezio climbed into the boat after tossing his cane inside and nearly fell headfirst into the water before catching himself on the side.

"Are you sure this is wise?" Faustina watched Ezio trying to position himself gracelessly in the boat as she remained on the dock.

"Wise?" Ezio scoffed as he sat upright while trying to reclaim his dignity before securing the oars in place. "Of course not, but we have no choice. If we drive, I won't be home in time for my shift tomorrow which will only raise suspicions. I can make it across the lake and back in time for the captain to not notice my absence."

"I don't understand why you're helping me." Faustina looked at Ezio warily.

Ezio reflected for a moment as he looked up at her from the boat as it bobbed gently in the water, bouncing gingerly against the docks. He recalled the shot echoing throughout the hills and mountains after Signor Lehner had willingly gone into the hands of the checkpoint guards.

"I promised your father." Ezio drew a deep breath and closed his eyes as he knew he could never tell her the whole truth.

"He's safe?" Faustina's arms fell to her sides as she relaxed a little.

"He's in Lugano." Ezio continued the fabrication, convincing himself that it could be true.

"Why would the captain say otherwise?" Faustina held her conclusion in reserve.

"He believes I followed through with the orders." Ezio shrugged. "I don't suppose that will last long, though. Either way, I promised your father that I would watch over you."

Faustina stared at Ezio for a moment as she contemplated before turning away and stating, "I don't know what the truth is anymore. What proof do you have?"

"I..." Ezio huffed as he looked around aimlessly. "I have no proof. Unfortunately, all I have is a conscience that won't be quieted. Arresting your father was wrong, I knew it at the time, but I had my orders. I thought, at first, that he would be sent to a labor camp, but when I heard that the captain had other intentions, I had to act. I'm sorry I didn't proceed as you had advised earlier."

After watching Ezio for a few more moments, Faustina slowly and carefully climbed into the boat. Ezio offered his hand in assistance, but she swatted it away quickly.

"If anyone needs help, it's you." Faustina pointed to his leg, and Ezio turned away sharply at the sting.

"Sorry." Faustina swallowed. "I'm just nervous."

"I imagine you are." Ezio offered a brisk smile to dislodge his discomfort and grabbed the oars.

Yet before Ezio could place the oars into the water, he froze. The memory of his brothers dying in front of his eyes while he was helplessly pinned between the boat and the rock sprang back into his mind, and he was unable to move. All he could remember was their cold hands and lifeless eyes. Even after nearly ten years, this memory was still planted firmly in his heart. If he ever needed to recall their faces or small details that one usually forgets, all that was required was to remember that fateful day, and he was right beside them. Ezio knew that the moment he set the oars into the lake, he would have to face them. He had spent the years avoiding the terrible plague of memory, but now there was no choice but to stare this terror squarely in the face.

"What's wrong?" Faustina asked softly.

"I'm sorry I didn't tell you the whole truth about what happened to my leg." Ezio felt his palms becoming sweaty and his limbs weakening.

"You don't have to do this." Faustina looked at Ezio with sympathy. "My fate is my own."

"If only that were so." Ezio shook his head in bewilderment.

"What do you mean?" Faustina frowned.

"Do you believe in fate, Sister?" Ezio watched her carefully.

Faustina deliberated as she studied Ezio before quoting, "'The race is not to the swift, nor the battle to the strong, but time and chance happen to them all.'"

"Are you sure you're not a real nun?" Ezio grinned.

"I don't believe in fate, I don't believe in God, I don't believe in a higher power, and I certainly don't have faith in humanity." Faustina raised her eyebrows.

"Yet you're putting your faith in me," Ezio replied as the two bobbed gently in the boat.

"My father trusted you." Faustina nodded. "And that, I suppose, is good enough for me."

"I don't necessarily believe in fate, either." Ezio placed the oars into the water and felt a tightening in his shoulders as he began the arduous journey across the lake. "Still, these past few days have led me to believe that, perhaps, there is something unseen working in the background. I don't believe the Almighty is in control of everything that happens. I can't accept that He played a part in the death of my brothers, but maybe it's enough to know that someone is there. Maybe it's enough to know that they're with Him, and that these years I've spent in bitterness should instead have been rejoicing in the fact that death no longer has a sting, and the grave no longer has the victory."

"Maybe you're the nun?" Faustina jested, but Ezio frowned sharply and turned away.

"Sorry." Faustina realized her error.

"It's not easy for me to discuss this." Ezio focused his attention on rowing.

"What are their names?" Faustina asked.

"Grazie." Ezio paused from rowing as he stared at her in the darkness with the only illumination afforded them from the lights on the other side of the lake.

"For what?" she asked.

"For saying *are* instead of *were*."

"They're still with you." Faustina tilted her head.

"Luca and Alberto," Ezio trembled as he blurted their names.

Nearly ten years had gone by without him daring to utter their names aloud. Yet now, back on the lake where they had perished, he felt a closeness to them that would not have been possible without Faustina's prodding.

"Tell me about them."

"Absolute terrors." The lump in his throat swelled. "They drove me insane. They never left my side. How I begged them to give me a moment of peace, but now what I'd do to have them pestering me again with nonsensical questions. I didn't know it at the time, but they didn't really care about the answers, they just wanted to spend those moments with me. But, mio Dio, were they ever, what's the word, spirited. Not a day went by that wasn't an adventure. It's strange, looking back, it's almost as if they knew that time was short. Maybe not consciously, but inwardly they were so driven to accomplish everything they could."

"They sound lovely," Faustina replied, and in the darkness, Ezio caught the faint outline of a grin on her face.

As the two of them sat alone in the boat, Ezio couldn't help but examine Faustina carefully. Her smooth skin seemed more alluring in the dimness, her lips promised a pleasure he had not known, and her slender arms and hands made him desperate to embrace her.

"You're making me uncomfortable." Faustina scratched her forehead, and Ezio immediately diverted his gaze, feeling foolish.

"You were right about me." Ezio cleared his throat.

"What do you mean?" Faustina asked nervously.

"About the sort of man that I am. I couldn't carry out my orders with your father."

"I cannot tell you what that means to me," Faustina spoke tenderly.

"Or maybe I am that sort of man." Ezio grinned cheekily as he grabbed the oars and began rowing again. "Maybe this was my plan to get you alone all along."

"Or maybe it was my plan," Faustina retorted with a chuckle.

Then, suddenly, a splash came from what Ezio guessed was about a hundred yards back in the direction that they had come. At first, he assumed it was nothing more than a fish, but then it came again and sounded, to Ezio, to be intentional.

"What are you doing?" Faustina watched Ezio nervously when he stopped rowing.

"Shh!" Ezio held a finger to his lips as he looked behind her into the darkness.

"What is it?" Faustina's eyes grew wide with panic.

"We're not alone." Ezio retrieved his pistol and held it at the ready as he waited for the noise to come again.

"What do you mean?" Faustina whispered harshly, but Ezio shook his head for her to be quiet.

Ezio held his breath as he waited anxiously for the splash to come again, praying that it was, in fact, nothing more than a fish. After what seemed like an age of silence, Ezio slowly handed the pistol to Faustina.

"What are you doing?" Faustina shook her head in refusal.

The splash came again.

"Aim true!" Ezio shoved the pistol into her hand and swiftly placed the oars back into the water as he heaved and pulled with all his might to speed Faustina to the other side of the lake.

Confirming Ezio's fears, the splash intensified, and he was certain that someone was chasing them, but he couldn't imagine who. He wondered if the captain had

Armando follow them but doubted the second lieutenant would be on their tail.

"What's going on?!" Faustina panicked as she turned to look behind her and held the pistol down by her side.

"I don't…know, but…I'm not…about to find out." Ezio spoke between reps, utilizing all his strength as they sped across the river.

With adrenaline coursing through his veins, Ezio struck the water again and again with the oars as he hurried to deliver Faustina to safety.

A shot rang out.

Ezio startled as a bullet hissed by, mere inches above his head.

"What do I do?!" Faustina panicked.

"Shoot back!" Ezio shouted.

"I can't see anything!" Faustina barked.

"Shoot at anything, then!" Ezio yelled.

"That will give away our position!" Faustina replied. "They'll see the spark from my gun and know where we are."

Another shot fired, and the bullet cracked loudly into the hull of their little rowboat.

"I think they know where we are!" Ezio heaved with all his might.

Taking aim with the pistol, Faustina tried to gauge where the shot had come from. Finally working up the courage, Faustina squeezed the trigger, but nothing happened.

"The safety!" Ezio cried.

"Right!" Faustina drew the weapon back to her side as she inspected it in the dim light.

"Got it!" she shouted as she aimed again and squeezed the trigger, firing a shot into the unknown.

"Keep shooting!" Ezio demanded.

Obeying, Faustina fired off round after round into the dark until the pistol offered the horrific click, signifying it was out of ammunition.

"I'm out!" Faustina turned to Ezio.

"I don't have spare bullets." Ezio shook his head apologetically.

"What?! Why not?!" Faustina griped.

"That's the first time...the gun has been...fired in action," Ezio replied while running out of breath.

Turning her attention to the assailant hidden in the darkness, Faustina held the gun up and ready to fire, but Ezio assumed she meant to intimidate and appear as though she had simply reloaded.

"It's quiet," Faustina whispered.

Rowing with less enthusiasm, Ezio, too, took a moment to listen. There was no splashing, certainly no gunfire, and the only sound was the soft wind rustling through the trees on the shore or the occasional sound of a laugh or a cry from the residents on the other side of the lake.

"I think we're safe." Ezio drew a deep breath when suddenly the boat lurched to a stop, and he toppled backward as Faustina fell beside him.

"Are we?" Faustina griped sarcastically as she began checking her head for cuts.

"Sorry, I didn't realize we were so close to shore." Ezio pulled the oars inside before jumping out of the boat, and Faustina helped him drag it further onto the beachhead.

With shaky knees, and arms that had turned to mush, Ezio felt as though he may collapse from the burden on his body and the thrill of the chase. Bending over, Ezio breathed heavily and felt his heart racing.

"Are you alright?" Faustina asked as she handed the gun back to Ezio.

"That's the first time I've ever been shot at." Ezio stood upright as he looked back out over the lake, making sure that whoever had pursued them had now given up the hunt.

"They didn't fire back after I shot off a handful of rounds." Faustina also stared out at the lake. "Do you think…"

"What? That you killed them?" Ezio shook his head to alleviate her concerns. "Unlikely. They probably got scared."

"Who do you think it was?" Faustina asked as she stood close to Ezio, and he felt the warmth of her body radiating against his arm.

"I wish I knew, but whoever it was, they're gone now."

"They'll never be gone." Faustina threw her hands onto her hips as she looked at Ezio knowingly. "If it's not whoever was on the lake, it's the captain, or the Nazis, or others who hate that I was ever born."

"I don't pretend to understand what you're going through," Ezio began. "I imagine it feels as though the whole world hates you, but there are some who still care."

"You're very kind." Faustina turned toward him and gently patted his shoulder.

"Let's try and determine where we are." Ezio looked behind him at the properties near the shore but was unable to contain his smile from her affection. "Ah, perfect. The church is just up the road."

"I don't see a church." Faustina leaned forward for a better view.

"It's difficult to see in the dark." Ezio pointed in the direction.

"Where?" Faustina narrowed her gaze.

"See that tall white bell tower."

"I do," Faustina spoke, her voice absent of enthusiasm, and Ezio assumed she was feeling rather hopeless. "I suppose no one is awake at this time."

"The nuns rise early, which is partly why, I believe, they're so intolerably grumpy. We won't have to wait long." Ezio rubbed his tired eyes before sitting on a large log closer to the beach.

"You don't have to wait with me." Faustina sat beside Ezio, but by her tone, he understood she was merely being polite.

"I'll keep my word to your father and make sure you're safe. Although, I'm not sure who will save you from the nuns." Ezio grinned.

"I'm worried that you won't make it back across the lake in your condition."

"I'll wait until sunrise. By then, I will be fine." Ezio slumped down into the sand and rested his back against the log as he closed his eyes.

"You've been very kind to me." Faustina squeezed his shoulder gently, and he looked up at her in the darkness, wishing that this moment could stretch for eternity.

"I still wish I knew who was after us." Faustina cleared her throat as she looked back out at the lake.

"Something tells me they weren't after you." Ezio sat upright.

"Oh?" Faustina waited for him to continue.

"If they were after you because they knew you were Jewish, they wouldn't need to act in such a manner at night. Whoever it was didn't want to be seen, which means they were after me."

"What would they be after you for?" Faustina tilted her head.

"I have an idea, but I need to ponder first before I act rashly."

"So, you weren't rowing so hard to save my life, but rather, your own?" Faustina removed her veil and placed it on the ground as her hair fell to her shoulders, and Ezio's heart surged within his chest.

"At the time, I thought they were after you." Ezio picked up her veil and held it out to Faustina.

"One moment without it, please." Faustina looked at Ezio with large, pleading eyes.

"Someone is always watching." Ezio tilted his head in apology.

"It's late in the night." Faustina shrugged. "I can barely see you even though I'm a mere foot away."

"And if we're discovered, they'll either believe you're a fraud or you're not taking your vows seriously. Either way, it will be catastrophic." Ezio placed the veil in her lap, but his hand lingered slightly as he tried to feel her thigh without being entirely obvious.

"Fine." Faustina grabbed it from Ezio and returned the veil to her head. "Worst part about being a nun."

"Hopefully this war ends soon, and you won't have to worry about that much longer."

"Even when the last bullet in this war is fired, my people will still be hunted," Faustina spoke solemnly.

"Perhaps you're right," Ezio sighed.

"Did my father find a place in Lugano?" Faustina asked.

"Pardon?" Ezio cleared his throat.

"My father. Did he find somewhere to stay?" Faustina watched Ezio carefully.

"He's at a nice hotel, for the moment." Ezio looked back at her while thankful the darkness of the night concealed the truth behind his fabrication.

"Good." Faustina drew a deep breath before slumping down beside him as well.

Then, suddenly, Faustina leaned her head on Ezio's shoulder. Surprised by the affection, Ezio wasn't sure how to respond. Then, after a moment, Ezio leaned his head against hers, and the two sat on the beach as they listened to the quiet, still lake gently brushing up against the shore.

"You mentioned you didn't believe in God," Ezio spoke after a minute, although he wished he had remained silent as she sat upright to look at him.

"Does that matter?" Faustina asked.

"No." Ezio shook his head. "Curious is all."

"You believe in God?" Faustina looked at him with incredulity.

"I didn't for quite some time." Ezio frowned as he pondered. "But these last few days have made me question if there is more than what we can see."

"How so?" Faustina pressed.

"Meeting you, for one." Ezio paused as he studied her timidly.

"Meeting me?" Faustina scoffed. "I've been nothing but a terror on your existence. Because of me, you risked your life by taking my father to safety."

"It was the right thing to do." Ezio waved to brush away her admiration.

"If they weren't sending him to Poland, would you still have saved him?" Faustina watched him closely.

"I don't know." Ezio threw his lips upside down as he played the scenario over in his mind.

"I appreciate the honesty." Faustina returned to staring out at the lake.

"You seem to know the scriptures well," Ezio spoke quietly to her.

"My father, well, the man I grew up to believe was my actual father, I should say, was rather observant. He forced me to memorize the Psalms." Faustina rolled her eyes. "I never believed I would use them to save my life."

Ezio smiled as he studied her, taking full advantage in the dim light to examine her lips closely.

"There's no Signora Milanesi waiting for you somewhere?" Faustina asked quietly, and Ezio thought that she possibly felt a similar kindling.

"I have my mother to disappoint, I don't think I could handle letting another woman down." Ezio smirked cheekily.

"You should hear how she speaks of you when you're not there."

"Really?" Ezio shot his head back in disbelief. "What did she say?"

"Nothing memorable, but she's proud of you." Faustina smiled at him encouragingly.

"What do you mean, nothing memorable?" Ezio shrugged before demanding, "Specifics!"

"Well." Faustina stared up at the night sky as she searched her memory. "She was speaking with your father, and she said something along the lines of no other family in the neighborhood could boast of having an officer as their son."

"Heh." Ezio smiled brightly, feeling a warmth otherwise absent.

"She loves you." Faustina turned again to look at the lake as her shoulder rubbed against his, and Ezio felt a shockwave of anticipation nearly bursting through his chest.

"I wish she would say such things to me." Ezio swallowed as he wasn't entirely concerned with the topic of his mother any longer.

"Why haven't you married?" Faustina changed the subject.

"There aren't many women who fantasize about marrying a cripple." Ezio lifted his cane. "When they imagine themselves walking down an aisle, this is absent."

Faustina didn't reply but instead tilted her head as she peered into Ezio's eyes, and he struggled to control his urge to grab her by the neck and plant his lips on hers.

"Can I ask you an odd question?" Faustina began.

"Of course," Ezio replied quickly as his nervousness soared.

"Will you wait for me?" Faustina asked plainly, as though she were bartering goods at the market. "To marry me, I mean."

"I—" Ezio choked on his tongue, which was suddenly swollen with fear.

"There's something different about you." Faustina smiled before placing a hand to his cheek. "You bear hardship with grace. Many wouldn't be able to endure having their own mother behave so cruelly toward them."

Ezio didn't entirely know how to reply but felt a lump forming in his throat for the acknowledgment.

"I need you, more than you understand." Faustina paused as she collected her thoughts. "I need something to strive for; a reason to live. I want to be with you, but if we behave recklessly now, I think the desire would lessen. So, can you wait for me? When this war is over, we'll be together?"

"I..." Ezio felt the moisture in his mouth rapidly evaporating.

"I hope my Jewishness isn't a factor in your hesitancy?" Faustina looked somewhat hurt.

"No, not in the slightest." Ezio threw his eyebrows up as such a hateful thought was rather foreign to him. "I...I just don't know if I can believe you."

"How so?" Faustina frowned.

"Why would you have any interest in me?" Ezio shrugged. "You're the most beautiful woman I have ever laid eyes upon, and I'm merely a cripple."

"I'll answer that with a story." Faustina turned her attention back to the lake as she again leaned her head on his shoulder.

"A story?" Ezio chuckled.

"Shh! Listen!" Faustina slapped his chest playfully. "A long time ago, when the temple still stood in Jerusalem, three men attended to pray. While they were praying, an angel appeared to them. He advised that God would grant them anything they desired. Whatever they asked, it would be given. The only condition is that they could only make one requisition. They could wait and make their request later, but God would only listen to them once."

"Everyone knows that you would ask for a million wishes." Ezio grinned.

"Quiet!" Faustina barked before continuing, "The first man asked for all the money in the world. So, God granted it to him. The rest of the world was left destitute as all wealth had transferred to him. The problems he was trying to solve with endless money only multiplied with the sorrows of everyone else. He was attacked by a mob and killed for his greed.

"The second man asked for eternal youth, which he was granted. He lived as a young man for many years, watching the people he loved pass away. His wife, his children, his friends, and all acquaintances passed, but he remained. In the end, he took his own life to escape the loneliness.

"The third man was wise. He watched to see how the other two men's prayers were answered before submitting his own request. So, when he was old and weary, he came back to the temple and, before the angel, he made his request."

"What did he ask for?" Ezio grew intrigued.

"He asked for nothing."

"Nothing?" Ezio shot his head back in surprise. "I don't understand."

"The wise man realized that there was no good desire in his heart. If he wished for wealth, it would either harm others or multiply his troubles. If he asked for eternal life, he would only experience unending grief. If he asked for love, it wouldn't be genuine, but forced. Anything he wanted to ask for, he realized, was not what he needed. Our desires blind us to reality. We want perfect health, love, and happiness, but we forget the importance of suffering. Blessed are those who mourn, blessed are those who are poor in spirit."

"So, if I'm hearing you correctly, being with me is equivalent to suffering?" Ezio tilted his head as he tried to decipher her meaning.

"I want to be with someone who knows what it is to endure adversity." Faustina ran her hand along his chest, and Ezio could scarcely contain himself. "I don't want a rich man, or a youthful man, I want someone who knows what it is to suffer. Because life is suffering, and if you're with me, then maybe we can face the suffering together, with understanding. To quote from the New Testament, as I was so brazenly challenged earlier, 'suffering produces perseverance, and perseverance character, and character, hope.' Together, Ezio, we can endure and hope."

Without another word, Ezio and Faustina sat intimately beside each other on the shore of Lake Como, listening to the waves gently press and retreat on the beach.

Closing his eyes, Ezio felt a connection to another person he didn't believe possible. Without being too obvious, he inhaled the scent of her hair through the veil, pressed his cheek against her head, and wrapped his arm around her shoulder as he pulled her close, latching onto that hope that she promised.

Chapter Ten:
The Order

"You have power over your mind – not outside events. Realize this, and you will find strength."

Marcus Aurelius

A bell rang.

Ezio opened his eyes to find that the sun was rising and realized he had slept longer than he intended.

"Faustina." Ezio tapped her shoulder to wake her.

"What?" she asked grumpily.

"The nuns are ringing the morning bell."

"I'm so tired." Faustina rubbed her eyes.

"I know." Ezio stood and held out his hand to her. "Come on. We'll find you a place among the order. You'll be safe with them. I promise."

Reluctantly taking Ezio's hand, Faustina stood to her feet but held her gaze low as they walked.

"Look." Ezio put his arm around her and pointed at the church.

"Oh, it's beautiful." Faustina looked up at the church. "I wish I wasn't so exhausted and I could appreciate it better."

Agreeing with a nod, Ezio examined the church with a sense of wonder.

Painted white with a dark orange trim around the windows and columns, the church seemed rather exotic for such a small little town. It reminded him of paintings of Spanish or Mexican churches that appeared bright and inviting as opposed to the usual grey brick churches that he believed were built for intimidation alone.

Knocking on the small side door that was beside the large doors meant for the congregation, Ezio stood back and waited.

"Is anyone around?" Faustina asked with worry.

"Someone was ringing the bell." Ezio shrugged.

"It's so early. I doubt they have visitors at this time." Faustina rubbed her arms as a cool breeze suddenly enveloped them.

"Maybe there's another door I could try?" Ezio peeked around the corner.

But just as he left to inspect, the lock on the door clicked, and Ezio returned to standing beside Faustina as they waited for it to open. Another lock clicked, and then another, and Ezio glanced at Faustina in annoyance at the tardy pace.

Finally, the door opened slowly, but Ezio was surprised to find that, instead of a nun, they were greeted by an elderly monk who offered them a severe frown from bushy eyebrows as he glanced between them.

It was then that Ezio realized how peculiar they must've appeared. Glancing down at his uniform, Ezio noticed that it was disheveled and wet. Then, glancing quickly at Faustina, he noticed that her veil was slightly askew while her dress was dirty from the sand on the beach.

"Buongiorno," Ezio began warmly as he removed his cap but found himself in the awkward position of being unsure of what to say next. He had expected to address the nuns, and having a monk greet him was entirely unpredicted.

The monk nodded his greeting as he continued to eye them suspiciously.

"This is Sister Faustina." Ezio pointed toward Faustina, who offered a quick curtsey. "She's of the Franciscan order, and I—"

The monk scoffed.

"We're...looking for her order..." Ezio frowned, wondering what he had said to give the monk such a reaction. "I was under the impression that they inhabited this church."

With another scoff and shake of his head, the monk returned inside the safety of the church and closed the door. Ezio and Faustina listened with sinking hearts as lock after lock clicked into place.

"What the hell was that?" Faustina looked grumpily at Ezio.

"I have no idea!" Ezio defended with a shrug. "The nuns are always here!"

"He didn't believe a word you said!" Faustina delved further into her annoyance. "I'm not sure if I should believe you, either!"

Ezio knocked loudly again on the door in his irritation.

"Arrivederci!" The monk sang from further inside the church.

"That's absolutely unacceptable!" Ezio pounded on the door again.

"Save your strength," a voice called from behind them, and Ezio and Faustina turned to find a nun walking toward them with a basket of bread under her arm.

"See! A nun!" Ezio offered a quick elbow to Faustina, happy to be proven right.

"Brother Giovanni enjoys aggravating others," the nun continued as she stood before them.

"Not very Christian of him." Ezio looked back at the church crossly.

"He believes that suffering produces character." She offered an annoyed look.

"Don't fall in love with him," Ezio whispered in jest to Faustina before addressing the nun, "I'm Lieutenant Ezio Milanesi. This is Sister Faustina. Do you think you can help us?"

"You may have fooled the lieutenant." The nun looked at Faustina with a measure of sympathy. "But you're not a nun."

"How did you know?" Faustina swallowed. "I was instructed by other nuns on how to dress."

"You look the part, but a real nun would know which order she belongs to." The nun tilted her head. "Franciscans, my dear, wear brown. Or, at least, around here, they do. You're adorned in black, which is why Brother Giovanni behaved so rudely."

"Can you assist us?" Ezio pleaded.

"You're Jewish?" the nun asked Faustina.

Faustina nodded in her despair.

"It's not me you have to convince." The nun shuffled her jaw as she thought.

"Then who?" Ezio asked.

"Sister Rosa." The nun drew a deep breath. "She's the head of our order. Compassion is her trade, which sounds lovely, but if you can't provide some reason why you should stay, it's likely she will not accept you."

"What sort of reason?" Faustina pressed.

"What service can you provide to assist the order?" the nun asked.

"I don't have a skill, if that's what you mean." Faustina grew nervous and glanced at Ezio. "But I'm hard working. I will perform my duties with diligence. I'll remain unseen and unheard."

"There are plenty of hard-working nuns." The nun shook her head. "That isn't what our order requires. Besides, you're not a Christian. Why should the order accept you, given your religious views?"

"I may not be a Christian, but I find value and courage through the prayers."

"Which ones?" The nun narrowed her gaze as she tested Faustina.

"The rosary, for one." Faustina tapped the prayer beads attached to her hip. "The prayer of humble access as well is rather poignant."

"That prayer is reserved for communion." The nun frowned. "Why would you know that prayer? Only baptized Christians can receive the Eucharist."

"The prayer of St. Francis is beautiful," Faustina continued, ignoring the nun's concerns.

"No." The nun shook her head and looked at Faustina with sorrow.

"No?" Ezio asked in surprise before addressing her grumpily, "I thought Christian charity extended to helping those in need!"

"And what of the nuns that I care for?" she asked with indignation. "Should I not care for them? Anyone with even a basic understanding of our order would see right through this charade. I can't put all our lives at risk for her sake."

Ezio gripped his cane tightly as he imagined cracking it over her head. Though, he supposed he shouldn't be all that surprised. The nuns that taught him in school were just as stubborn.

"I will take you in for one night," the nun began, and both Ezio and Faustina looked at her with wide eyes. "But not as a nun. Tomorrow, we will find some accommodations for you. There are some eligible bachelors in town who are looking for a good wife."

"Eligible?" Ezio's heart sank.

"I use the term lightly. They're only eligible because no one else will endure them." The nun shrugged. "But a beautiful woman like you would be taken care of and sheltered."

"I..." Faustina was lost for words.

"I'm not forcing you to marry," the nun continued. "I'm merely advising of your options. You can stay with us for the day. Tomorrow, our order will assist you in whatever capacity we can, so long as it will not put the ladies under my charge in danger."

"Sister Rosa then, is it?" Ezio clicked his tongue.

"Perceptive," Sister Rosa replied sarcastically.

"I appreciate your help." Faustina looked back at Sister Rosa with sad, tired eyes, and Ezio felt for her.

"I'll write to you tomorrow," Ezio spoke kindly to Faustina.

"You'll do no such thing!" Sister Rosa spoke harshly. "She doesn't exist. For our safety, and yours, this woman no longer exists. You cannot write to her. You cannot attempt to reach her by any means. There is to be no mention of her at all. Do you understand me, Lieutenant?"

With a heavy heart, Ezio nodded, knowing this would likely be the last time he ever laid eyes upon Faustina. Despite their promises of devotion in the early morning hours, Ezio felt in his soul that this would be the last he ever saw her.

"I appreciate everything you've done for me," Faustina stood close to Ezio. "Wait for me!"

"Time is drawing short." Sister Rosa grabbed Faustina's arm and began to lead her away.

"Ciao!" Ezio raised his hand to wave, and it stuck in the air as he watched Faustina being swept away swiftly by Sister Rosa.

"This is the bread for the Eucharist. Let's have some fun with Brother Giovanni and tell him you ate some. He's as sharp as soggy pasta." Sister Rosa chuckled to herself, but Faustina paid her no attention as she looked over her shoulder at Ezio with tear-filled eyes.

"Arrivederci!" Brother Giovanni called from inside the church after Sister Rosa knocked on the door.

"It's me, you baboon!" Sister Rosa shouted. "Open up!"

Swiftly, the locks clicked as the door was opened, and Sister Rosa pulled Faustina, who was still staring at Ezio, into the church before closing the door behind them.

Standing alone in the little square before the church, Ezio felt an emptiness enveloping his soul. He was appreciative of Sister Rosa and knew that her callous approach would likely be life-saving for Faustina, but Ezio couldn't help but feel that his time with Faustina had been cut short, and wished he had expressed what was truly in his heart.

After a moment or two of staring at the door, hoping it would open again, Ezio glanced at his watch and realized that time was against him, and he would likely make it back to the office just before his shift started. He prayed that Captain Cacioppo would believe his false report, which, Ezio reminded himself, he still needed to fabricate.

With Faustina as safe as she could be for the moment, Ezio decided to brave the return journey. His strength was severely drained, but the pace back to the other side wouldn't be nearly as arduous, especially without bullets flying by his head.

Pushing the boat into the lake, Ezio threw his cane inside before climbing in and using the oars to row gently out to the calm waters. While Lake Como was generally known for its peaceful demeanor, Ezio grew acutely aware of its tranquility this morning.

The sun shone gently down on him as the wind softly brushed through his hair, and Ezio felt a calm that he thought to have long been forgotten. He felt as if the spirit world, if he even believed it existed, or God, was consoling him that Faustina would be alright, and that he had behaved justly.

But just as swiftly as the calm had descended upon him, it fled when Ezio spotted a rock protruding from the water, reminding him of the fateful event so many years ago.

The closer Ezio came to this rock, the more unusual he began to feel. Eventually, when he was close enough to reach out and touch the rock, he ceased rowing. A strange sensation set on his shoulders, and Ezio felt as though he was no longer alone. Again, he didn't necessarily believe in fate or the supernatural, but Ezio couldn't deny that something otherworldly was at work in his heart.

Looking around at the other fishing vessels or ships going about their business, Ezio felt foolish for what he was about to do.

Casting aside his pride, Ezio closed his eyes and spoke to his brothers inwardly, *I'm sorry.*

There was no response. Apart from the dinging of a bell on a ship not too far from him, or the call of a sailor on their vessel, it was entirely quiet.

I'm not sure what else to say. Ezio opened his eyes and stared at the rock, remembering what it was to see them lifeless. *The rock looks different than how I remember. I thought it was bigger or more menacing. Yet now that I'm beside it, it appears small and inconsequential. Mother still hates me, by the way.* Ezio grinned slightly, knowing that his brothers would take a morsel of pleasure from this.

"Meh, this is stupid." Ezio shook his head in frustration and grabbed the oars again when something stopped him.

He couldn't quite explain why, but he was frozen in place. His arms had turned to lead, and he merely stared at the rock in stupefied silence.

Suddenly, a breeze rushed around his boat, through his hair and clothes, across his face and hands, and then as quickly as it appeared, it vanished.

The hair stood on the back of Ezio's neck, not entirely sure what to believe about what he had just experienced. He knew that if he told another soul that they would only laugh at him. He would openly mock anyone who told him a similar story.

Wind rushed around you while you were in the middle of the lake? He imagined their jeering.

"I suppose that was just for us, then?" Ezio spoke aloud to his brothers.

No response.

"Please don't misunderstand my absence as ignoring you." Ezio swallowed to try and rid himself of the lump in his throat. "It's too hard of a burden to bear."

The moment the words left Ezio's mouth, his mind was flooded with happy memories of his brothers smiling and laughing. He recalled the time they hid their father's shaving cream. It was a harmless prank, really, but they couldn't stop laughing at Lorenzo's reaction and Ludovica's mockery. He recalled the time when they caught their first fish, and how proud they were of such a feat. Simple memories, yet so undeniably precious.

The more he thought about these pleasant memories, the more Ezio's heart began to shift. The bitterness of their death began to fade, and Ezio began to think of them as they were; happy, fearless, energetic, and playful. Instead of terror, his heart was filled with purity, simplicity, and joyfulness that he had such brothers to call his own.

With happy tears running down his cheeks, Ezio bowed his head in thanks, knowing that his brothers, or some otherworldly spirit, had shown mercy to him, before continuing his journey with haste across the lake.

Returning to the pier outside of Signor Lehner's residence, Ezio threw his cane onto the dock before climbing out of the boat. But as Ezio was tying the boat to the dock, something caught his eye.

Giuseppe's little vessel, which wasn't far from Ezio, had some noticeable damage and what appeared to be a bullet hole. Glancing around quickly to make sure he was alone, Ezio walked over to Giuseppe's boat and began inspecting it. Placing his fingers to the hole on the boat, Ezio was certain that it was from a bullet. He wondered why Giuseppe had shot at them last night, and if he knew that he was transporting Faustina.

Glancing again at his watch, Ezio realized that time was running short, and he somehow had to return to the station and report to Captain Cacioppo in such a disheveled state.

Taking the stone stairs beside the pier, Ezio returned to his vehicle and was about to open the door when he spotted Giuseppe leaning against his mother's shop while smoking. The soap maker's son was staring back at Ezio and looking smug. Even from a distance, Ezio could make out a malicious grin plastered across Giuseppe's face.

Deliberating his course of action, Ezio tapped the pistol down by his hip as he double-checked it was still with him, but remembered he was out of ammunition.

Then, closing the door to his vehicle, Ezio walked as swiftly as his cane would allow him toward Giuseppe, who, he noticed, was becoming increasingly nervous with his proximity.

"Late night on the lake?" Giuseppe asked as he took a puff and feigned a casual appearance.

"How did you know I was on the lake?" Ezio squinted.

"I saw you come up from the pier." Giuseppe pointed behind Ezio.

"Or maybe you followed me last night?" Ezio veiled his accusation.

"Why would I follow you?" Giuseppe took another puff.

"I noticed you had some damage to your boat." Ezio ran his tongue along his teeth as he examined Giuseppe with malice, though the poor sleep and the threat of violence were souring his mood.

"Damage?" Giuseppe reacted in such a way that Ezio almost believed he was truly ignorant.

"Looks like a bullet hole." Ezio remained staring at Giuseppe.

"I'll have to investigate." Giuseppe threw his lips upside down, and Ezio found it odd that he wasn't all that perturbed by the news. "Or, better yet, I'll put in a police report, and you'll have to investigate."

"Why did you tell my sister to come alone?" Ezio tilted his head back as he studied the boy closely for his response.

"What?" Giuseppe scoffed.

"My sister. Yesterday morning, you told her to come alone."

"I never saw your sister yesterday." Giuseppe shrugged.

"I don't know what you're up to with her, or with the other women that have come through here." Ezio clenched his jaw. "But it stops now!"

"I'm not up to anything," Giuseppe growled back. "What women are you talking about?"

"Stay away from my sister!" Ezio pointed his cane at Giuseppe's chest.

"Not a problem." Giuseppe looked back at Ezio with slight disgust.

"Is it not?" Ezio tilted his head, unconvinced.

"Have you seen the men in this town?" Giuseppe grew a wry grin. "Why would I sharpen my pencil at the same station where they have?"

"You little shit!" Ezio raised his cane.

But before Ezio could behave rashly, the door to the shop opened, and Leonarda charged out in defense of her son.

"Get away from him!" Leonarda shouted.

"Tell him to learn some manners!" Ezio pointed at Giuseppe, who was now hiding squarely behind his mother.

"Him? You're the officer! He's just a boy! What are you threatening him for? Smoking? He wasn't doing anything wrong!" Leonarda's face grew crimson with rage, but before Ezio had a chance to answer, she swiftly turned toward her son and snatched the cigarette out of his mouth. "You look ridiculous with these! Grow up!"

"He disrespected my sister!" Ezio defended his actions.

"She disrespects herself." Leonarda returned her attention to Ezio and threw her hands on her hips. "I asked you to assist my son, not threaten to beat him."

"Signora Cianciulli," Ezio began with a more measured tone, "I cannot help your son. He is of the legal age and may enlist as he chooses. Though, I would argue that if he needs his mother to protect him from a cripple, then facing bullets may not be the right path for him."

"I'll do anything to be out of her shadow." Giuseppe stormed into the shop and left Ezio and Leonarda on the street, which, Ezio noticed, was now filled with peering eyes for the disturbance.

Then, suddenly abandoning her outrage, Leonarda leaned in and asked, "Did you make the right choice?"

"What do you mean?" Ezio asked, caught off guard by the swift change in her demeanor.

"I told you, when you came to see me yesterday morning, that you would have to make a choice." Leonarda looked intensely into Ezio's eyes.

Pausing for a moment to collect himself, though still not entirely believing that Leonarda actually held powers of divination, Ezio replied, "I chose with my conscience."

"Good," Leonarda sighed. "Now do you believe me?"

"Yes," Ezio lied, wanting to be done with this conversation.

"Help my son, and I'll help you," Leonarda whispered. "Remember, I know about your Jewess."

"She's safe now," Ezio replied swiftly. "Far from anyone who would seek to harm her."

"You think she's safe?" Leonarda let out a cruel chuckle before nodding to the lake and stating, "Sister Rosa will hand her over at the first sign of trouble. She's safe from your captain, but not from me."

"How…" Ezio darted his eyes as he tried to comprehend how she would know about Sister Rosa, and began to believe she was, perhaps, genuine.

"Binoculars, Lieutenant," Leonarda explained with a slight roll of the eyes.

"But Sister —"

"I get my flour from Sister Rosa." Leonarda shrugged. "Did you try the cakes, by the way? I sent some home with your mother."

"Yes, very good," Ezio again lied briskly, feeling foolish for not being as discreet as he had hoped, and also wondering who else had tracked his path across the lake.

"I asked you to help my son, but instead, you become threatening and drive him further away from me." Leonarda frowned.

"He shot at me!" Ezio grew impatient, and Leonarda's eyes flew wide at the allegation. "He could've killed me last night."

"Stupido ragazzo!" Leonarda gritted her teeth as she turned toward the shop but then returned her attention to Ezio before asking, "What proof do you have?"

"That's classified." Ezio didn't dare advise her of the bullet hole in the boat, knowing that it would likely be miraculously repaired in short order.

"It was at night, you said?" Leonarda grew suspicious.

"Stay away from the nun, and I won't arrest your son," Ezio grew bold as he threatened.

"That's not the bargain." Leonarda threw her lips upside down as she shook her head, entirely unmoved by his tactic. "Help my son, and I'll stay away from her."

"The bargain has changed." Ezio remained defiant.

"One word, and she's sent away forever." Leonarda raised a threatening finger.

"I will talk to my captain today, I promise." Ezio drew a deep breath. "Perhaps he can persuade Giuseppe."

"Good," Leonarda sighed her relief. "I will help you with the nun. She's not safe across the lake. I told you yesterday morning that I would help her. I could've saved you the difficulty of the journey."

"If I'm going to talk to my captain, I need assurances. How can you help her? I want specifics." Ezio demanded, still not sure why he was entertaining this lunacy apart from his unquenchable curiosity.

"Bring her to me. I'll help her out of the country."

"I've tried that avenue." Ezio's mind flashed back to the gunshot that he believed had killed Signor Lehner. "It's not possible."

"Bring her to me, alone, and I'll get her to safety."

"Why alone?" Ezio frowned. "I told you I need specifics."

"Because then you won't be forced to lie if they question you, and if you're tortured, and your tongue slips, you won't be able to give them accurate information. I can't give you the details as it would endanger me, and if I'm not around, then no one will be able to protect Giuseppe."

"When?" Ezio shuffled his jaw as he thought.

"As soon as you bring her to me, she'll be taken to safety."

"I can try." Ezio recalled that Sister Rosa would only permit Faustina's stay for the day.

"I ask again, Ezio, when you were given the choice I predicted, did you make the right decision?"

"That's yet to be determined," Ezio replied, although warily, wondering if she truly knew what was going to happen.

"Is your conscience clear?" Leonarda pressed.

"Yes, actually." Ezio raised his eyebrows in surprise at the admission.

"Then you made the right choice." Leonarda patted his shoulder awkwardly as she attempted to make a connection with him, yet it was so forced and uncomfortable that Ezio was tempted to use the pistol on himself to end the moment.

"It's settled, then. Talk to your captain, who will convince my son to see the folly of his ways, then bring the woman you love to me. Remember, Ezio, remember the law of equivalent exchange." Leonarda turned and entered the shop, leaving a baffled Ezio alone in the street.

Equivalent exchange, Ezio thought, but was distracted by the curtain moving near Signor Lehner's property. Glancing quickly at the window, Ezio locked eyes briefly with the neighbor who was watching him closely.

Chapter Eleven:
Drops in the Ocean

"We become strong, I feel, when we have no friends upon whom to lean, or to look to for moral guidance."

Benito Mussolini

Arriving at the station, Ezio felt his stomach churning as he walked inside to find Armando leaning over the reception desk while still attempting to woo Francesca.

"Maybe you'll have to take me to dinner sometime and find out?" Armando flirted, and Ezio rolled his eyes.

"The only reason you and I would ever be dining together would be to discuss how I would never have to see you again," Francesca replied sarcastically.

"It's a date then!" Armando grew excited.

"Is the captain in?" Ezio asked as he came to stand beside Armando.

"You smell fresh." Armando leaned away as he scrunched up his nose in disgust.

"Is he in?" Ezio pointed toward the office grumpily.

"He never left," Francesca replied.

"Are you certain?" Ezio asked.

"Quite." Francesca also covered her nose, but in a more polite manner than Armando.

"Hmm." Ezio tapped his chin.

"Where's Wolfgang?" Francesca asked as she stood and leaned over the desk to see if the cat was by his feet. "He wasn't in the office when I arrived. You don't think the captain..."

"Heaven's no." Ezio shook his head quickly. "Wolfgang is at home. He's not feeling well."

"Your cat told you he was unwell?" Armando glanced quickly at Francesca for the odd statement.

"He was vomiting." Ezio griped before striking his cane against Armando's leg. "I'll be in the office."

With that, Ezio stomped away from reception and toward the office, still not entirely certain how he would lie to the captain.

Thankfully, Ezio was reminded of his low ammunition, and he decided to visit the armory first. Walking to the back of the station, Ezio unlocked the small cabinet containing the rifles and bullets.

Refilling the clip, Ezio placed the pistol back in its holster, yet his hand lingered as he stared down at it. He remembered the night before, when Faustina bravely warded off their attacker, and he wondered if it really was Giuseppe on the river with them.

Returning to his office, Ezio knocked loudly and swiftly on the door as he awaited a reply. When none came, he knocked again. Still without a reply, Ezio opened the door to find the captain sitting at the desk and reading the paper.

"Did you not hear me knocking?" Ezio asked without saluting the captain and trying to hide his grumpiness.

"There are only three possibilities as to who was at the door. You were either the annoying receptionist, the incompetent second lieutenant, or yourself. In the latter, this is your office, so there is no need for you to knock." The captain remained fixated on the paper. "You're late, by the way."

"I was investigating a lead." Ezio sat in the small chair facing the desk, wondering how he was expected to conduct his work if the captain remained in the office.

Yet from his vantage point, Ezio noticed a can of shaving cream half-opened and sitting on the floor beside the desk, intended to be unseen. Inspecting the captain, Ezio spotted a touch of the white cream on his lower neck and surmised that Francesca had deduced correctly that the captain had remained in the office the whole night.

"I hope it was a lead on the nun." The captain looked up briefly from the paper at Ezio.

"Giuseppe." Ezio bit his lip as he thought and felt the weight of his exhaustion descending on him. If he only closed his eyes, he knew that he would drift into a blissful void. "Giuseppe Cianciulli."

"The soap maker's son?" the captain asked as his interest aroused.

"He tried to lure my sister alone to his property." Ezio rubbed his chin.

"That's hardly evidence." The captain chuckled as he returned his attention to the paper. "Being alone with your sister isn't entirely unique in this town."

"I believe he's connected to Signora Setti's disappearance." Ezio glanced at the captain, who was again enraptured in his story.

"In what capacity?" The captain frowned. "Elaborate."

"I believe he finds unseemly work for women who are desperate." Ezio scratched the stubble on his chin.

"What sort of unseemly work?" The captain's concern grew.

"That is yet to be determined." Ezio threw his lips upside down. "The sort of work, I suppose, that makes these women cut themselves off from their families. Milan is a hub of degeneracy, and the clientele there are eager for anything new, no matter how old or how young."

"Go arrest Giuseppe, then." The captain nodded to the door.

"I will, but I'll have to let things cool down first."

"Cool down?"

"I spoke with him briefly this morning." Ezio clicked his teeth as he thought carefully about which information to leave out. "Let's just say it did not go smoothly. If I return now, I could jeopardize the investigation as being too personal. I'll send Armando later to bring him in for questioning."

"Who cares what these idiots believe." The captain shook his head in annoyance.

"I have…" Ezio cleared his throat. "I have a request."

Without reply, the captain looked down his nose at Ezio, indicating that whatever he asked better be worth his time.

"The boy, Giuseppe…" Ezio again cleared his throat. "I believe he could benefit from your guidance."

Sitting upright as he stared at Ezio with incredulity, the captain waited for him to continue.

"He's a lost soul, Signore, and — "

"Say no more." The captain waved for Ezio to be quiet. "Bring him in and I'll make sure to shepherd him."

"I have another lead I'd like to follow up first. Similar situation with Signora Setti." Ezio recalled Paola and her aunt, Signora Soavi.

"Another missing woman?" The captain leaned back in his chair.

"It would appear."

"That is interesting." The captain stared off into the distance.

"How long can we expect the pleasure of your company?" Ezio looked briefly around the room to find that a small mattress was rolled up in the corner and poorly hidden behind a table.

"Until the issue of these missing women is resolved." The captain glanced at Ezio, understanding that his presence was unwelcome.

A squeak came from the corner of the room.

"Where is your damn cat?!" The captain gritted his teeth. "Stupid rodent kept me awake all night."

"Do you need somewhere to stay?" Ezio asked with slight annoyance.

"Of course not! I was working." The captain leaned forward and flipped the page of the newspaper as he began reading angrily.

"Anything of importance?" Ezio pointed to the paper as he stood and made ready to leave.

"Just something of interest." The captain's countenance suddenly lightened as he flipped the page back. "The United States revealed, publicly, the extent of their losses at Pearl Harbor."

"Oh?" Ezio waited eagerly for the captain to continue.

"Twenty-four hundred souls were killed that day, and nineteen ships, including eight battleships, were damaged or destroyed." The captain tapped the article.

"And because of that, they're now bombing our cities." Ezio moved to the door.

"Explore your lead, Lieutenant." The captain rubbed his eyes in exhaustion. "Take the second lieutenant with you. I'd hate to believe that the taxes of these fine people are being used for nothing more than his romantic endeavors."

"Grazie, Signore." Ezio opened the door.

"But don't think I haven't forgotten about the nun. I need the report on her." The captain stared at Ezio earnestly. "I need the report by tomorrow at close of day."

With a quick nod of understanding, Ezio left the office, wondering how on earth he was going to bide time for Faustina and recalled Leonarda's request for her to come quickly.

"Armando!" Ezio barked as he hobbled toward the station doors.

"Lieutenant?" Armando looked at him with panic, wondering if something was amiss.

"Do you have your pen and notepad?" Ezio asked as he continued toward the exit.

"I do." Armando nodded.

"Good, come with me."

"Remember the mileage!" Francesca shouted after them.

"Where are we going?" Armando asked as they entered the vehicle.

"Does it matter?" Ezio asked grumpily as he started the vehicle.

"Have I done something wrong?" Armando asked gingerly.

"What do you think?" Ezio frowned sharply at him. He knew the second lieutenant didn't deserve this brashness, but exhaustion, hunger, and fear were embittering his mood.

"Because of Francesca?" Armando swallowed.

"I told you not to flirt while the captain was around. It reflects poorly on me." Ezio tapped his chest.

"Mi dispiace." Armando drew a deep breath, not appreciating the chastisement.

"Not to mention that Francesca is clearly bothered by your constant presence," Ezio continued to berate Armando.

"She's pretending." Armando shook his head in frustration. "Women have to feign dislike so they don't appear loose."

"Is that what you tell yourself?" Ezio glanced at the second lieutenant with incredulity. "Maybe she simply doesn't share the same feelings. Have you ever thought of that?"

Armando didn't reply but instead stared out the window as he pouted, and Ezio knew that he had possibly gone too far.

Eventually, they pulled up to a property that was, like Signor Lehner's, in a rather enviable location in town. The view of the calm lake and surrounding snow-capped mountains was picturesque.

"Where are we?" Armando asked as the two exited the vehicle.

"Signora Soavi's," Ezio replied with a hidden tone of remorse for his beratement of the second lieutenant.

"If she's missing, why are we here?" Armando asked with slight impatience, and Ezio gathered he was eager to return to Francesca's side.

"Maybe her niece lives here?" Ezio threw his lips upside down and knocked on the door.

"Did you really need me to tag along?" Armando continued in his impatience.

"The captain insisted." Ezio shrugged as he waited for someone to answer the door.

"He's insisting on a lot of things lately."

"What do you mean?" Ezio watched Armando curiously.

"Nothing." Armando waved to dismiss his concerns.

Ezio was about to press further when the door swung open, and Paola, Signora Soavi's niece, stood before them and seemed surprised by their presence.

"Oh, good, you're here." Ezio smiled politely. "I was hoping to find you. Paola, right?"

The niece didn't reply but instead looked back at Ezio and Armando with a measure of sorrow no one her age should understand.

"May we speak, Paola?" Ezio gestured to the door.

"I'm alone, Signore." Paola shook her head. "It wouldn't be appropriate."

"Quite right." Ezio removed his hat, feeling silly that he didn't consider the propriety of his request. "Are you free to speak here?"

Glancing around briskly, the girl checked to see if anyone was within earshot before looking again at Ezio with a nod.

"Good." Ezio withdrew a notebook and pen from his jacket pocket. "Can you kindly reiterate what you advised me the other day?"

"You don't recall?" Paola asked with a slight frown and looked at Armando to substantiate the sincerity of his request.

"A useful technique, Signorina. Sometimes people remember smaller details they might have overlooked." Ezio held his pen and pad at the ready.

"As I advised, I believe that my aunt is in trouble." Paola cleared her throat. "She was supposed to call me when she arrived in Milan, but I've yet to hear from her.

She received news that a gentleman was interested in her, and they were to meet in Milan."

"And you're still not aware of who this gentleman is?" Ezio asked.

Paola shook her head before continuing, "She hoped to find love, even in her old age, and I think she was blinded by her desire."

"Aren't we all?" Ezio shot Armando a knowing gaze, who offered a double take, surprised by the slight.

"And you think this man was merely interested in her wealth?" Ezio returned his attention to Paola as he glanced up at the large, spacious house.

"At first, yes."

"You've changed your mind?" Ezio squinted.

"No one has come to acquire the property, no withdrawals have been taken out of her account, no—"

"You have access to her account?" Ezio interrupted.

"She entrusted me with her financials." Paola shrugged.

"How old are you?" Ezio studied her with peculiarity.

"Fourteen."

"How are you able to access the accounts?" Ezio remained unconvinced.

"Not directly, Signore, no. The banker is a close relative. He keeps me informed."

"And you trust his word, this relative of yours?"

"He has no reason to lie."

"I'd say the temptation of wealth is reason enough." Ezio challenged.

"You're incorrect, Signore." Paola shook her head quickly. "He would not lie to me."

"Did your aunt mention anything about Signora Cianciulli?" Ezio asked, though he wondered if it was wise to broach the subject.

"No." Paola frowned. "What connection does the soap maker have to my aunt?"

"Just curious." Ezio closed his notebook.

"If you have information, please tell me." Paola pressed.

"Mi dispiace, I don't have anything." Ezio returned his cap to his head as he prepared to leave when he noticed that Armando was busy scribbling in his notepad.

"Per favore!" Paola drew closer to Ezio as she pleaded. "My aunt was everything to me. If you know anything, tell me, I beg of you!"

Examining her quickly, Ezio weighed his options before advising, "I saw your aunt enter Signora Cianciulli's shop with a suitcase."

"Giuseppe?" Paola clenched her jaw.

"What do you know of him?" Ezio re-opened his notebook.

"Not much other than he's strange."

"Strange? How so?" Ezio jotted down notes as he listened.

"I suppose it's not his fault."

"What do you mean?"

"His mother barely lets him out of her sight. We all understood, given her sorrowed past, but now that he's a young man, it's a little strange to not let him have some autonomy. I've heard rumors that she still bathes him." Paola scrunched up her nose in disgust. "I suppose those circumstances could create some devious behavior. I wouldn't be surprised if they're Jewish."

Ezio bit his tongue from lashing out. How he wished to chastise the young girl for her misguided bias, but kept silent for fear of reprisal. He needed to keep a low profile while he thought of a way to save Faustina, especially with the second lieutenant keeping a close watch.

"Sorrowed past, you said? Explain." Armando took a turn questioning.

"She lost ten of her fourteen children." Paola calmed a little. "I imagine that would make any mother become rather attached to her favorite child. I can't imagine what she's experienced."

A brief and terrible memory flashed through Ezio's mind as he recalled how his mother reacted when she heard the news of his brothers' deaths.

"I'm sorry, Lieutenant." Paola looked shamefully at Ezio. "I forgot about—"

"It's quite alright." Ezio held up a hand to stop her from elaborating. "You were very young at the time."

"Will you arrest him?" Paola asked eagerly.

"Who?" Armando asked absent-mindedly as he jotted down notes.

"Giuseppe, of course." Paola grew annoyed.

"I think I should question him first." Ezio recalled the morning's events. "I don't have enough information yet."

"Enough information?" Paola scoffed. "You saw my aunt enter his premises the night before she went missing! He obviously wanted her fortune so he could escape his own mother."

"He enlisted." Ezio closed his notepad and returned it to his jacket pocket. "He already has a plan to escape her clutches. Besides, seeing her enter the shop, while suspicious, is not enough to convict."

"Of course it is! If I—"

"I promise you I will look into your aunt's disappearance." Ezio interrupted as he grew annoyed. "I have a few more people to question. We'll get to the bottom of this, I promise you."

"Grazie," Paola replied swiftly yet unconvincingly.

Leaving the property, followed closely by Armando, Ezio returned to the vehicle to find that Paola was still watching them. She looked dejected, and his heart went out to her. She was rather intelligent for her age and not as naïve as one might expect, and Ezio recognized she knew as well as he that the odds of finding her aunt were next to none.

"You shouldn't have promised," Armando spoke softly as he, too, looked at Paola.

"I know." Ezio drew a deep breath. "Error in judgment."

"What if…" Armando began but paused as he waited for Ezio to show some interest.

"I'm listening." Ezio shrugged in his annoyance.

"What if these women joined the Resistance?" Armando cleared his throat.

"The Resistance?" Ezio threw his head back. "What resistance?"

"There's a movement." Armando avoided eye contact. "People are not pleased with the Fascist government, and they've begun to…collaborate."

"And you've heard of these collaborations?" Ezio eyed Armando warily.

"Rumors." Armando threw his lips upside down as he raised his shoulders.

"You believe Signora Setti and Signora Soavi to be partisan fighters then, do you?"

"Perhaps not fighters." Armando stared out the window. "Maybe they're cooks or cleaners? Perhaps that's why they're unable to write to their loved ones."

"What you're suggesting is the sparking of a civil war." Ezio raised his eyebrows in caution to Armando.

"I thought it prudent to explore all options." Armando threw his hands out in defense of his statement.

"Let's affix ourselves to plausible avenues, shall we?" Ezio shook his head in frustration.

"You have to sympathize a little with the anti-Fascist viewpoint." Armando cleared his throat.

"How so?" Ezio asked, wondering if this was some sort of orchestrated trap set by Captain Cacioppo.

"When's the last time you had a decent meal?" Armando looked briskly at Ezio.

"I'm not falling for this trap."

"Trap?" Armando frowned.

"The captain wants to flesh out my loyalties?" Ezio grew frustrated. "I'm as loyal to this country as any other man."

"I'm just stating that this movement exists. And it's not just Italy, either."

"Germany?" Ezio grew intrigued.

"There's a movement. They call themselves the White Rose. They're spreading anti-Nazi leaflets and pamphlets."

"I give them a few weeks." Ezio pondered. "They won't survive long."

"You said we had a few more people to question." Armando abandoned the subject and opened his notebook, prepared to write. "Who else is there?"

"Signora Setti." Ezio started the vehicle and grinned slightly as he watched Armando begin to shake while writing the mean lady's name on the page.

"You think there's a connection?" Armando asked as he attempted to appear indifferent and not in the least bit bothered.

"Both were advised of Milan as their destination." Ezio pondered as they drove. "It's smart, really. Milan is large, close by, and since it's much busier than here, one assumes a delay in letters, thus giving the killer, if it is that malicious, some extra time."

"Killer?" Armando chuckled. "The little weirdo probably has them tied up in his basement. I'm sure Paola will find a ransom note soon."

"Possibly." Ezio shrugged as they stopped in front of the house belonging to Signora Setti. "Problem is that the Setti family is impoverished. Not much wealth to be gained through ransom."

"Maybe Giuseppe nabbed the wrong old lady thinking she was Signora Soavi." Armando shrugged.

Turning off the vehicle, Ezio stared at Armando for a moment as he tried to gauge the seriousness of his suggestion.

"What?" Armando threw his hands out in annoyance.

"Why are you using your notepad?" Ezio asked.

"What do you mean?" Armando grew suspicious.

"You usually stand back and watch me. Why are you taking notes now?" Ezio squinted.

"I'm practicing." Armando remained wary of Ezio's interrogation.

"Good." Ezio patted Armando's arm. "I'll let you question Signora Setti alone then."

"Alone? What? Why?" Armando's eyes flew wide in panic.

"You don't need me." Ezio put his cap over his eyes and leaned his head against the headrest. "It's just a harmless old lady."

"Harmless?" Armando scoffed. "Hardly. She's intolerable."

"Then why are you taking notes?" Ezio peeked at Armando from under his cap.

"Like I said, I'm pract—"

"Armando." Ezio tilted his head.

"The captain wanted me to report on you." Armando relented.

"As I supposed." Ezio opened the door.

"Don't be cross!" Armando also left the vehicle. "I didn't have a choice."

"You had the choice to tell me." Ezio looked grumpily at Armando as he knocked on Signor Setti's door.

"You know the captain." Armando tried to garner some sympathy from his comrade. "You know I wasn't given the opportunity to tell you."

"I suppose." Ezio remained unconvinced as he again knocked on the door, his patience waning.

"I wasn't jotting down anything compromising," Armando pleaded his case.

"Everything is compromising." Ezio offered a warning glare at Armando. "But, yes, I understand your requirement. In the future, please be honest with me."

"Fair enough." Armando nervously retrieved his pen and notepad as the sound of heels could be heard approaching from the other side of the door.

Even Ezio wished he was back on the lake being shot at instead of having to deal with Signora Setti, and he knew that their interaction would be ill at best. Still, he needed to find some pertinent information on the disappearances of these ladies. Maybe his success could barter some time and appease the captain's blood lust for Faustina.

The door opened slowly, and a pair of sad, unthreatening eyes peeked out at the two men.

"Signora Setti?" Ezio asked, half wondering if they had the wrong address.

"What do you want?" Signora Setti asked grumpily, confirming her identity.

"May we speak?" Ezio gestured for them to come inside.

"About what?" Signora Setti remained in the doorway.

"About your sister, Signora," Armando interjected, although Ezio imagined he wished he had stayed silent as Signora Setti's eyes slowly moved over to look at him as though he were the very definition of an inconvenience.

"What about her?" Signora Setti returned her attention to Ezio.

"We want to ask you some more questions." Ezio removed his cap. "We would like to help you find her, if we can."

"If we can?" Signora Setti sneered as she turned and waved for the men to follow her inside.

"After you." Ezio held his hand out to Armando.

"I insist." Armando returned the gesture as neither wished to be among the front lines of this gruesome battle.

With a deep breath, Ezio entered the small property and walked down a narrow hallway into a small living room with a couple faded blue couches and chairs with intricate, wooden legs. The design was rather peculiar, and Ezio imagined they had been in the Setti family for quite some time, possibly since Napoleon.

"Sit." Signora Setti pointed to the couch as she sat on the chair facing them.

Again, Ezio noticed that the wrathfulness was slightly lessened as her soft, sad eyes stared at the floor hopelessly.

"I appreciate you allowing us into your home." Armando tried to gain some footing.

"Get on with it." Signora Setti rolled her hand regally for the questioning to proceed.

"Can you tell me, again, everything that transpired?" Ezio retrieved his pen and notepad before glancing at Armando, wondering what he would record about this interaction.

"You have the memory of a chicken," Signora Setti grumbled as she rolled her eyes before continuing, "My sister was set to move to Milan. She had found some sort of work. She sent a letter explaining everything, but I haven't heard from her since."

"Do you still have the letter?" Ezio asked.

"Yes, of course. Why would I throw it out?" She frowned severely.

"May I see the letter?" Ezio bit his tongue as he struggled to remain patient, but the lack of sleep was severely plaguing his reserve.

With a large sigh of frustration for the inconvenience, Signora Setti stood while paying special attention to the difficulty upon her aging body. Then, slowly and agonizingly, she took a few shuffled steps toward the coffee table in front of Ezio and Armando.

"It's in there." Signora Setti pointed to a small box on the table in front of the two men.

"We could've saved you the journey." Ezio pinched his lips together.

"Well, now you know." Signora Setti pointed again at the box before returning to her seat.

Drawing his hand into a fist, Ezio bit down on his cheek to stop him from lashing out at the poor yet decidedly deserving old lady.

"Grazie," Ezio spoke as politely as he was able and opened the box to find a few letters inside.

"The first one." Signora Setti gestured angrily.

"Got it." Ezio held the letter up and began reading carefully.

I have great news! I'm going to Milan tomorrow. I'm sorry I couldn't tell you in person. I will call as soon as I'm able, but it may take me some time to get things organized. I hope you understand.

"Odd, isn't it?" Signora Setti scratched her chin.

"I don't see anything odd." Armando frowned as he took the letter from Ezio.

"That's cause you're stupido." Signora Setti chuckled cruelly. "My sister was the mean one, you see. She would never write so pleasantly."

"But you confirmed that this is her handwriting?" Ezio pointed to the letter as he watched Signora Setti closely.

"It's undeniable, but I believe she wrote it under duress."

"Can you think of a reason why?" Armando asked, and Ezio admired his bravery.

"She didn't want to write it, you idiota, but someone made her."

"I meant, why would someone make her?" Armando closed his eyes as he, too, practiced restraint.

"That's your job, not mine." Signora Setti crossed her arms.

"Does she have any enemies?" Ezio tilted his head.

"Of course she does. Mean old grump hated everyone, and everyone hated her." Signora Setti paused as she looked at the carpet under her feet. "Except me."

"Do—" Armando began, but Ezio held up a hand to stop him.

"Thick as thieves we were," Signora Setti spoke softly. "We were never apart. I saw her every day as far back as I can remember. She would never leave without telling me, or at least trying to convince me to come. And Milan? She hated people, and crowds, and especially crowds of people. There's no way in hell she went to Milan."

Ezio and Armando remained quiet as they allowed this rare moment of vulnerability. The room grew deathly silent as neither man dared to utter a sound or even draw breath.

"Now, who can I talk to? No one understands my humor. They think I'm just crotchety and bitter. Meh, who cares what they believe. If they're too dull to understand, then why should I bother?" Signora Setti sighed as she raised her eyes and looked at Ezio with an unusual gentleness in her gaze.

"Do you mind if I take this letter back to the station?" Ezio asked after a moment.

"Whatever for?"

"Perhaps there is a clue?" Ezio threw his lips upside down. "Do you have anything else that she's written? I would like to compare."

"Of course." Signora Setti stood, again complaining bitterly with groans and moans, before taking a few steps to walk, again, to the table in front of the men and pointing at the box. "Here."

"I just realized something." Ezio looked at the old woman with a sense of admiration.

"What's that?"
"You're tremendously funny."

Chapter Twelve:
Cake and Soap

"You ask what is our aim? I can answer in one word: Victory.
Victory at all costs. Victory in spite of all terror. Victory
however long and hard the road may be. For without victory
there is no survival."

Winston Churchill

"This is wonderful, isn't it?" Vittoria asked cheerfully as the family met Ezio in the small square for the twelve days of Christmas countdown celebrations.

Lorenzo, although tired, appeared as a glimmer of his former self in his smart, navy blue suit and matching hat. His beard and mustache were trimmed, his ear and nose hair cut to acceptable lengths, and he had even dabbed some cologne on his neck.

Ludovica, however, was not as concerned as her husband with respect to vanity, but she at least had a head scarf on and wore the dress reserved for special occasions. Still, with a cigarette hanging out the side of her mouth, and a scowl that would stop even Il Duce in his tracks, she looked rather mismatched to her spritely and happy husband.

Vittoria, of course, wore the latest fashion and had her hair neatly curled and short. While Ezio found her dress way too revealing, he knew better than to comment, instead keeping a watchful eye out for any lingering gazes.

"Where is everyone?" Lorenzo looked around suspiciously at the mostly vacant square.

While the vendors were busy organizing their produce and trinkets, only a handful of shoppers and customers were wandering slowly through the market.

Suddenly, the church bells began to ring, and Lorenzo clutched his chest in panic.

"Easy, Signor Milanesi." Ezio chuckled as he placed a soft hand on his father's back. "We're not under attack."

"Ah, right, it's Sunday." Lorenzo looked at his son with slight embarrassment.

Shortly after the joyful, although terrifying, ringing of the bells, the church doors burst open, and the market was soon flooded with parishioners.

"Help me find a new hat before all the good ones are taken!" Lorenzo grabbed Vittoria's wrist as he tried to lead her away.

"I was going to meet up with my friends!" Vittoria withdrew her hand.

"After you help me!" Lorenzo panicked as he looked back at the hat merchant's stall, now surrounded by little old ladies. "The vultures are going to pick over the nice hats before I get a chance."

"Why me? Take Ezio!"

"You have a good eye for fashion, and I won't be outdone this year." Lorenzo again grabbed Vittoria's wrist and began to lead her away as she groaned in her annoyance.

Ezio and Ludovica chuckled slightly at Vittoria's irritation as they stood together on the edge of the market, neither all that interested in shopping or engaging with the incessant vendors.

"What did he mean by being outdone this year?" Ezio asked his mother.

"Vitelli, our neighbor, shows off his new hat each Christmas," Ludovica explained as she took a puff. "Somehow, it's always larger or fancier than your father's. I can't tell the difference. A hat is a hat to me, but your father insists that a hat is the mark of a man."

"I'd say it covers his mark." Ezio smiled cheekily and looked at his mother, who didn't seem at all amused.

"I hate Christmas." Ludovica stamped out her cigarette as she retrieved another from her purse and lit it quickly.

Ezio glanced briefly at his mother as he understood why she abhorred the supposedly jubilant time of year. Taking a deep breath, he braced himself for her beratement and why he was the reason she was so embittered.

"What would you like this year?" Ludovica asked, and Ezio shot her a surprised glance.

"I..." Ezio was lost for words.

"I haven't bought you a present in quite some time." Ludovica bit her lip as she stared at the pavement by her feet, and Ezio's astonishment delved to new depths at this unexpected display of vulnerability.

"I...don't...um...I don't need much." Ezio cleared his throat as he returned his attention to the market, where he spotted Francesca and Armando walking in his direction.

"There's nothing that interests you?" Ludovica pointed quickly to the vendors.

"I suppose I could use a new cane." Ezio held it up and inspected it briskly. "The handle is worn out, and I think it may just buckle one of these days."

"I'll see what I can find." Ludovica took her leave, and Ezio, in stunned silence, watched his mother begin Christmas shopping for him.

He wondered if the captain's visit the other night had changed her perspective a measure, but Ezio wasn't sure how to respond to her sudden kindness. He didn't need presents and certainly didn't expect them, especially not at his age, but Ezio began to believe that this year, perhaps, would be a more tender Christmas.

A smile crept onto Ezio's face as he thought of how significant Faustina had been in changing his life, despite the fact that he had only known her for so short a time. If he had not met Faustina, and she had not come to his house where the captain had inadvertently reminded Ludovica of her love for her son, then maybe this Christmas would remain a bleak affair.

How he wished that Faustina was beside him now, holding his hand as the two of them strolled through this pop-up market, free of the cares of the world. He imagined her fingers intertwined with his as she offered subtle hints of what she'd like for Christmas. Ezio, of course, would already have something planned out, ready to surprise her. He imagined her shocked expression as he wrapped the necklace around her neck, the warm embrace she would deliver as she squeezed him tightly.

"Ezio!" Francesca broke his trance as she greeted him warmly with a generous embrace and a kiss on his cheek.

"Come stai?" Ezio asked while still dumbfounded by his mother.

"Bene!" Francesca glanced at Armando with a large grin as he came to stand beside her with a stupid smile of his own.

Not sure if I can stand any more surprises today, Ezio thought as he sensed the two of them were now romantically involved.

"Are you not shopping?" Armando asked as he wrapped his arms around Francesca, and Ezio felt like gagging at their chumminess. Although, he also supposed that jealousy might be playing a part in his veiled reaction.

"My family doesn't celebrate Christmas." Ezio scratched his chin as he caught sight of his mother looking thoughtfully at a cane. "Or, at least, we didn't."

"I forgot about that." Francesca looked at Ezio with a sort of sadness, although her wide eyes almost made her sympathy seem sarcastic, which was rather comical.

"What are your plans for the holiday?" Ezio asked Francesca.

"My brother is currently in Africa, Tunisia to be exact, so my mother is beside herself with worry." Francesca twisted her lips. "I imagine it will be a bleak affair."

"You do have me this Christmas, darling." Armando looked hurt by the neglect.

"My statement stands then." Francesca jested as she poked her finger into Armando's side.

"That's not fair!" Armando poked her back as the two delved into a flirtatious skirmish and nearly knocked Ezio over as he stood awkwardly beside them.

"Sorry, Ezio!" Armando laughed as he helped steady his superior.

"It's quite alright." Ezio straightened out his jacket.

"Come shop with us for a minute," Francesca pressed. "You're not allowed to refuse."

"If I don't have any other choice," Ezio agreed reluctantly as the company walked through the little market, admiring the trinkets, knitted hats and mitts, and various perishables.

"Signora Cianciulli." Ezio removed his hat when they arrived at her stall, which was bustling with cakes and soaps.

"For your mother." Leonarda packaged up some soap and cakes, which she then handed to Ezio.

"We're fine, grazie." Ezio waved to dismiss her. "We're still eating the rest of the cakes you provided."

"Please, it's on me," Leonarda insisted.

With a reluctant nod, Ezio took the package from the soap maker and held it under his arm.

"I spoke with the captain." Ezio looked at Leonarda with a bright smile. "He agreed to speak to Giuseppe."

Leonarda didn't reply as she remained staring at Ezio before glancing quickly at his compatriots.

"I thought you would be pleased." Ezio narrowed his gaze slightly.

"I'll be happy when I hear from my son's own mouth that he will not leave me." Leonarda peered at Armando pensively.

"When is your son expected to enter training?" Ezio asked.

"Next month."

"He'll need a reason, likely medical, as to why he can no longer fulfill his obligations."

"I love your soaps," Francesca interjected politely, and both Leonarda and Ezio looked at her curiously for her inability to accurately read the situation.

"All I care about is the outcome." Leonarda returned her attention to Ezio. "Whatever reason is concocted by your captain is suitable to me, so long as my Giuseppe stays out of the war."

"Ezio?" Armando asked curiously, and Ezio noticed that he seemed suspicious. "What is she talking about?"

"My apologies for not introducing you sooner." Ezio looked contritely at Leonarda. "This is Second Lieutenant Arm—"

"I know who he is!" Leonarda barked. "The question is, Ezio, do you?"

"I'm not following." Ezio shook his head.

"There's more to him than you perceive." Leonarda leaned forward as she inspected Armando closely, who Ezio noticed was growing nervous.

"I doubt it." Ezio grew a wry grin as Armando glanced at him in annoyance for the jest.

"Careful with this one." Leonarda ran her tongue along her teeth as she seemed to stare off into oblivion.

"Wolfgang!" Francesca shouted excitedly.

Ezio's smile vanished as his heart fell into his stomach when he spun around to find Captain Cacioppo approaching them swiftly, and, to Ezio's horror, he was holding Wolfgang in his arms.

Swallowing to hide his discomfort, Ezio turned away as his mind raced to find some sort of plausible deniability. Glancing quickly at Leonarda, Ezio caught her worried expression, hoping that if she did have some actual witchcraft, she would employ it now.

"Lieutenant." Captain Cacioppo stood beside Ezio, and Wolfgang looked indifferently around the square.

Ezio's heart raced in his chest, and he knew beyond a shadow of a doubt that the captain had discovered his attempt to free Signor Lehner. He would never see Faustina again, nor his parents or his sister, and simply hoped that his end would be swift instead of drawn out.

"With your leave." Francesca offered a polite, swift curtsey, recognizing the gravity of the captain's demeanor as she and Armando abandoned Ezio in his hour of need. He didn't blame them, really, as they had no inkling as to what the discovery of Wolfgang meant.

"I thought you would be grateful?" Captain Cacioppo asked slowly as he pet Wolfgang.

"I knew it was a matter of time." Ezio moved to take Wolfgang into his arms, but the captain held firmly onto the cat as he stared at the lieutenant with a morsel of menace.

"You don't want to know where I found him?" The captain narrowed his gaze.

"He wanders from time to time." Ezio took Wolfgang from the captain, who finally released him. "I'm sure it wasn't far."

"Thirty kilometers!" The captain shuffled his jaw. "I found him exactly thirty kilometers away. Odd, don't you think? How could a cat flee so far away from a loving home?"

"He's rather resilient." Ezio began to pet Wolfgang anxiously.

"He must've learned how to hunt." The captain continued to watch Ezio warily.

"Hopefully, he can apply the skills in the office and rid ourselves of that rat." Ezio offered a brisk smile to ease the tension.

The captain remained unamused as he stared at Ezio, who was wondering how he could possibly escape this situation.

"Lieutenant, I want us to make a promise to each other," the captain began as he threw his hands behind his back. "A solemn, unbreakable vow."

"What sort of vow?"

"I believe a working relationship is based on mutual understanding and trust, don't you?" The captain asked as he politely turned down a passing vendor anxious to sell a scarf.

"Of course," Ezio replied quickly, his heart still pounding in his chest, and glanced over his shoulder to see if Leonarda was, by chance, listening.

"That makes me happy." The captain smiled genuinely as he looked out at the rest of the market. "Do you find it odd that we haven't received our promised promotions yet?"

"These things take time, I'm sure." Ezio shrugged as he tried to appear casual. "Besides, we are at war. I imagine it is not a priority."

"Which is, and I apologize for using this word so frequently, odd." The captain placed a finger to his lips as he appeared to be calculating, yet Ezio feared the destination of this conversation. "My superior was adamant and genuine that he would promote me. So, after some time without word, I humbled myself and telephoned Rome. It turns out that Signor Lehner never made it to Poland."

"Did you reach out to Trieste?" Ezio asked, his pulse raging in his neck.

"I did, actually." The captain rubbed his eyes. "He never arrived there, either."

"That is strange." Ezio threw his lips upside down.

"Lieutenant, will you be honest with me?" The captain leaned in, and Ezio could scarcely stand the stench of his cigar breath.

"I know of no other way," Ezio lied boldly.

"I checked the speedometer." The captain sighed as though he were a headmaster who had discovered that one of his pupils was cheating.

Francesca! Ezio bit his tongue as the receptionist's persistence for this information had likely sealed his doom.

"The distance to the station in Como is thirty kilometers, which is the distance that you drove. And yet..." the captain paused as he peered at Ezio. "You never arrived. There are no records of you attending the station, and no one I spoke to recalls an officer from our humble station attending. So, I pulled out the map and looked at the surrounding area, wondering where else you could've driven for thirty kilometers. And do you know what I found?"

"I had some other errands to attend to." Ezio waved at his father and sister, hoping to gain their attention to pull him away from this horrible encounter.

"Yes, I thought that may be the case." The captain tapped his chin as he pondered. "But then, by accident, really, I discovered that the speedometer matched the exact distance between the station and the border crossing near Switzerland. I thought to myself that you wouldn't possibly have tried to take that route, but curiosity won out, and that's where I found your cat."

"How unusual." Ezio chuckled nervously.

"I don't want to make accusations, Lieutenant." The captain waved politely to a passerby. "Because, as you promised me only a moment ago, we are going to be honest with each other."

Ezio didn't reply as he sensed that the captain was enjoying the mental torture he was forcing him to endure.

"I have a gift for you," the captain spoke softly, and it was in that moment that Ezio noticed the captain couldn't quite focus on Ezio's eyes. He wondered if the captain's disease had started to spread already, and how poor the captain's sight now was.

"A gift?" Ezio asked as he looked intently into the captain's eyes, studying them for any weakness.

"Come." The captain nodded in the direction of Ezio's vehicle. "You'll need to drive me."

"Signore, my family." Ezio pointed to his parents and sister, but by the look he received from the captain, he understood that there was no debating the matter.

"Bring the cat." The captain began walking slowly toward the vehicle as Ezio scooped up Wolfgang in his arm.

Trailing the captain, Ezio's mind raced as to how he could escape. He was thankful that he had refilled the bullets in his pistol, but doubted he would have the chance to use his weapon, especially not while in public.

With sweaty palms, Ezio opened the back door for the captain to enter, wondering if this was the last time he would ever see his parents or sister. He watched his father impatiently trying on hats while Vittoria grew annoyed at how long it was taking, he spotted his mother still looking through canes and testing out their durability, and then his eyes fell on Armando, who, surprisingly, was watching them closely. Ezio wondered how much the second lieutenant knew, and perhaps Leonarda was right with her assumption that there was more to him than he perceived.

Still, something within Ezio stirred him to believe that fate was at work, and he should trust that whatever was about to happen was for good and not for ill.

"Where to?" Ezio asked as he looked in the rearview mirror.

"Drive straight." The captain pointed before holding out his hand and demanding, "Your pistol, Lieutenant."

"My pistol?" Ezio feigned ignorance. "What would you need my —"

Ezio paused when he spotted that the captain had drawn his own weapon and was pointing it at the back of Ezio's seat.

"Signore, you don't need to do this." Ezio swallowed.

Without replying, the captain again waved for Ezio to hand over the gun.

Unholstering his pistol, Ezio paused momentarily as he contemplated using it on the captain. The captain's sight was diminishing, and Ezio believed he could use that to his advantage. He could squeeze off a few rounds, drive to the pier, take a boat across the lake to Faustina, and run into hiding with her.

"I'd prefer not to kill you, Lieutenant," the captain spoke softly, and Ezio obliged by reluctantly handing over his pistol.

"Grazie." The captain breathed his relief. "Straight, and then your first left."

"Switzerland?" Ezio asked, guessing the captain's intended destination.

The captain nodded.

"The quicker this is over, the easier it will be for everyone." The captain patted Ezio's shoulder gently, and he found the affection unusual.

Slowly, Ezio began the drive on the same route that he had taken Signor Lehner not so long ago. The two remained silent in the vehicle, and Ezio glanced in the rearview mirror to find the captain leisurely staring out the window as if they were on a simple country tour.

Ezio's arms began to shake as they drove, and his mind wandered to Faustina. He remembered how sore his arms were from rowing her across the lake after being shot at by Giuseppe. How he wished to return to that beach with her resting her veiled head against his shoulder.

That moment seemed so important, almost predestined. The way she spoke to him felt so real, and he firmly believed in his heart that he was her hope, as she had put it. A lump formed in his throat as he regretted not kissing her when he had the opportunity. Love from his mother, and from most women, had been withheld from him for nearly ten years, yet now, when he finally found someone so intolerably perfect, he would be cut off from her forever.

"It's time. For me, that is," the captain spoke after a moment. "I still have good visibility out of my left eye, but my right eye seems to have all but gone. I can only see shapes out of that eye. Without depth perception, it's difficult to tell if a shape in front of me is a tree or a mountain."

Ezio didn't reply as he watched the captain in the rearview mirror, hoping that his poor eye would give him the advantage if he was forced to fight for his life.

Rounding the corner to where he had taken Signor Lehner, Ezio's heart nearly collapsed when he spotted the border guards on their knees with their hands bound behind their backs and their mouths gagged. Other Carabinieri officers were standing over them with their rifles trained at their chests.

"Merry Christmas," the captain leaned forward and whispered, and Ezio knew that this was the end for him.

He understood that he would be bound and gagged like these border guards and shot just like Signor Lehner had been. He was tempted to press on the gas pedal and run through all of them, taking out as many Fascists as possible. At least then his life would be worth something, he believed.

"Pull over here," the captain demanded, and Ezio obeyed.

"I know what you're feeling," the captain began after Ezio turned the vehicle off. "You're feeling that slight twinge of hope that maybe, just maybe, this won't end as bad as you believe. Humans are unusual creatures, my boy. We cling to the slightest bit of hope, even when there is no advantage in doing so. I'm going to kill you, and even with that knowledge, you'll obey my orders until the last minute."

Wolfgang meowed as he warmed himself on Ezio's lap, who looked down at his companion with a heavy heart. He began to reflect on the last few days and realized that if he had simply arrested Signor Lehner weeks ago when it was required of him, he could've avoided all this sorrow. Then again, he would've never met Faustina, and his heart would never have been ignited. If only for a short time, the last few days actually meant something to Ezio, and that was more than he could say for the last ten years.

"Get out," the captain spoke plainly.

"Stay here," Ezio's voice broke as he spoke to Wolfgang, recognizing that it was the last time he would ever speak to his companion.

"Come here." The captain waved with the pistol, and Ezio walked slowly, leaning heavily on his cane as his arms shook.

Gesturing for Ezio to kneel, the captain signaled for one of the guards to proceed. The guard crudely latched onto Ezio's arms and threw them behind his back before tying them together with coarse rope. The harsh cord dug into his arms, and Ezio winced as they wrapped tightly around him.

"Not too rough!" The captain barked when he noticed Ezio's discomfort. "He's not an animal. And don't gag him just yet."

Glancing quickly at the two border guards tied up with him, Ezio noticed that they had accepted their fates. Their gazes were fixated on the earth by their knees and seemed to be lost to their own misery.

"Do you recognize them?" the captain knelt in front of Ezio.

Ezio nodded.

"I appreciate your honesty." The captain ran his hand along his chin in thought. "Is this where you brought Signor Lehner?"

Ezio again nodded, realizing that lying was of little use.

"What's your name?" the captain pointed to one of the border guards.

The border guard looked at the captain and attempted to speak through the gag, but it was too tight.

"Take that off him!" The captain looked at his guards with incredulity. "Have a little awareness of the situation!"

Swiftly, the guards removed the gag, and the border guard advised, "I'm Mario."

"Mario." The captain nodded his greeting. "Do you recognize this man?"

Mario nodded.

"He brought someone to you a few days ago, correct? A Jew?"

Mario nodded again.

"Where is this Jew?"

"I don't know." Mario cleared his throat, and Ezio offered him a surprised glance, wondering if Signor Lehner was, by chance, still alive.

"You don't know?" the captain tilted his head, and Ezio understood that he had already interrogated them, and that this was merely a show for Ezio.

"We were drunk." Mario shrugged. "He ran away. We tried to shoot him, but we missed."

"Gag him again." The captain nodded to one of his guards.

"Please! I didn't kno—" Mario appealed to the captain's mercy, but it was in vain as the gag was reapplied.

"Why did you bring Signor Lehner here?" the captain asked Ezio as he played with the pistol in his hand.

"I hoped to see him safely to Switzerland." Ezio swallowed.

"I see." The captain nodded. "Then why did you arrest him in the first place?"

"They were my orders."

"And you also had orders to deliver him to Trieste."

"Those orders were morally reprehensible." Ezio looked boldly at the captain.

"Sending him to a labor camp was alright, though?" the captain asked as he threw his lips upside down in feigned sympathy. "I think you fell in love with the nun who somehow is related to Signor Lehner. Would I be correct, Lieutenant?"

"Related by law, not by blood." Ezio shook his head as he lied.

"Don't you ever lie to me!" the captain screamed as he brought his face close to Ezio's. "You promised to tell me the truth!"

Ezio didn't reply as he, too, stared at the earth by his knees. He knew his life was forfeit, but he didn't dare offer any information on Faustina. If today his soul would be accounted for, then he would go to his grave with a clear conscience.

"It's noble to try and save her, it really is." The captain calmed a little. "But it's not just the nun who is in danger. I'll torture your parents and sister in the holding cells for months. Even after they've given me all the information they know, I'll continue destroying them little by little. Can you do that to your family, Ezio?"

Still, Ezio didn't reply as he clung to his silence, waiting for the moment when the bullet would rip through his flesh, ending him forever.

Yet in this moment of terror came a moment of peace. Ezio remembered Faustina's head leaning against his shoulder, promising a life of hope together. Closing his eyes, Ezio again inhaled her scent, felt the warmth of her body against his, and felt the longing in his heart to be with her body and soul.

"Remember when I told you that Italy comes first? Even above family?" the captain asked as he spoke softly to Ezio. "My wife is Jewish."

Ezio shot the captain a surprised glance for this admission.

"*Was* Jewish, I should say." The captain offered a sad grin. "She was sent to Poland, you see. I know what it is to make sacrifices, Ezio, and I know how difficult this is for you. Italy comes first. I was sent here to here to deal with the Jewish problem. You may be asking yourself why. Why all this trouble to rid the town of one, two, or possibly three people? Storks, my boy, kill their own young. When they have a nest of two or three chicks, they choose one to kill so that the others may survive. Sending my wife to Poland was a mercy to others. Because of her sacrifice, Italy will prevail. I only wish my son could understand this. He's adopted, you see, so he has no Jewish blood. Thankfully she never bore me a child. I don't know if I could bear such a burden."

"I believed the ideology of the Nazis and Fascists to be perverse." Ezio shuffled his jaw as rage overtook him. "Now I see that it didn't create these atrocities but merely exploited what was already in the hearts of lesser men like you. How could you possibly believe that killing your own wife is a mercy?!"

"No tree can touch Heaven without first reaching its roots down to Hell," the captain replied swiftly.

"You may have fooled the others, but I know better. You weren't sent here to deal with the Jewish problem. You were sent here as a punishment."

"How so?" the captain scoffed.

"They would've supplied you with lodgings, yet you sleep in the office. You've been the rank of captain for nearly twenty years. There's a reason you haven't climbed the chain of command. Now you're here, pretending to still carry some importance, yet I know what you really are."

"And what's that?" The captain squinted as he grew impatient.

"You're scared," Ezio challenged. "And you're alone. Because of what you did to your wife, you must prove to yourself that it was justified. Shame on you!"

"Where did you take the nun?!" the captain screamed as he placed the gun to Ezio's temple.

"She's the only light I have in my life." A tear escaped Ezio's eye and ran down his cheek as he stared into the captain's eyes. "Why would I ever tell you?"

"Even for the sake of your parents?" the captain tested.

"You want to torture my parents?" Ezio laughed. "Good luck! They've been tortured already for nearly ten years because of what I've done to them. You think my passing will crush them? You saw how my mother treated me! You'll be doing her a favor by ending my life."

"You're compassionate." The captain sighed in his disappointment as he stood. "Which is unfortunate for you. Stand him up."

"Where are we going?" Ezio asked as the guards grabbed him by the arms and stood him to his feet.

"You're going to choose which one I execute first." The captain pointed to the two border guards, and Mario looked up at them with wide, panicked eyes.

"This isn't legal!" Ezio shouted. "You're all committing murder. If they've done wrong, then they deserve a trial."

"They're not committing murder. You are." The captain grabbed Ezio by the back of the neck as he screamed, "Which one dies first?!"

"I won't do it!" Ezio shook his head adamantly.

"Take the vehicle. Go grab his sister." The captain nodded to one of the guards.

"His sister?" the guard asked warily.

"Now!" The captain shouted.

Abandoning any hope for himself, Ezio threw his body against the captain, making a desperate attempt to overpower him, but within mere seconds the guards pinned him down to the ground as they began beating him with their guns and boots.

"Stop! Stop!" the captain shouted. "We need him alive. I'm getting the Nazis a Jew! He knows where she is! I'll finally receive that promotion and —"

"And what?" Ezio asked as he spat blood onto the gravel. "You destroyed your life for a meager promotion? You know the Nazis have no power over your status. Even if they appreciated your contribution to their malevolence, you'll still be a lowly captain, groveling in the dirt for but a morsel of the glory you hope to achieve. And for how long? My father is right, you know. The north hates the Fascists. It won't be long before they rise up."

"Get his sister." The captain nodded again to the guard.

A shot rang out, echoing throughout the hills, and a bullet landed beside the captain's foot in the gravel.

At once, the guards raised their rifles as they aimed in every direction at the surrounding hills, eager to catch a glimpse of their attacker's location.

Dragging himself to his knees, Ezio began shuffling over to the vehicle for cover when another shot rang out, narrowly missing his leg.

"Who the hell is shooting at us?!" one of the guards cried out.

"Shoot back!" the captain screamed as he also took cover behind the vehicle.

"Untie me!" Ezio demanded of the captain. "I can help you."

"Ah!" a shout erupted, and Ezio peeked out of cover to find that Mario had knocked one of the guards to the ground, and the other border guard had also taken to assaulting his captor.

"You're outnumbered!" Ezio bartered with the captain. "Untie me. I'm an excellent shot. You can barely see as it is."

"Who are they?!" the captain demanded.

"How should I know?!" Ezio screamed back. "Untie me!"

"My men will handle them!" the captain began as another shot rang out.

With a thud, one of the captain's guards fell to the ground, clasping his neck as blood poured out and he struggled to take a breath. It was heart wrenching to watch him suffer, and Ezio knew the only thing that could help him would be another bullet.

Another shot shattered the back windshield of the vehicle, and Ezio winced as glass fell onto his shoulders.

Spooked, the captain stood swiftly and ran toward the cover of some nearby trees when a bullet sunk into his back, and he fell to the ground about ten yards from Ezio.

Wheezing in pain, the captain rolled onto his back as he looked at Ezio with wide eyes, desperate for survival. With the blood already soaking through his uniform, Ezio knew that the captain had met his end.

"Isabella!" the captain shouted toward Heaven as he began to weep. "My wife, my beautiful wife! I'm sorry! Isabella, forgive me!"

Another bullet landed in the captain's chest, forever silencing him.

"Help!" Mario shouted, now free of his gag, and Ezio turned to find him on his back with the guard trying to drive his bayonet through him. The other border guard was still bound and gagged and writhing on the ground in a frantic bid to free himself.

With his heart pounding, Ezio knew he had to act. Laying prone, Ezio rolled over to the captain and, with his hands still tied behind his back, retrieved the captain's knife. Rolling back to behind the vehicle as quickly as he could, Ezio sat upright as he began cutting at the rope.

"He's going to kill me!" Mario shouted to Ezio.

"I'm trying!" Ezio shouted back as he struggled to cut through the rope with such an awkward angle.

"Come on!" Mario screamed.

"Dammit!" Ezio stood and, as best as he was able without his cane, and still trying to free himself from the rope, hobbled over to the guard and threw his body against the guard in an attempt to break Mario free.

Swiftly standing with their hands still tied behind their backs, Ezio and Mario returned behind the vehicle for cover as another shot landed near them. Yet, by the sound of the gun, Ezio discerned that their attacker was closing in on them.

Carefully, Ezio peeked through the window of the vehicle as he caught a glimpse of a man about twenty yards away with his rifle trained on the guard who now had his hands in the air in surrender.

"Who is it?" Mario whispered to Ezio.

"I couldn't see his face," Ezio whispered back.

"You're safe now!" The man with the rifle called out, but Ezio wasn't entirely sure who he was addressing.

Armando? Ezio thought he recognized the voice.

"Lieutenant!" Armando called again, confirming his identity. "He surrendered. You're safe."

Chapter Thirteen:
The Stained Rose

"If everyone is thinking alike, someone isn't thinking."

General George Patton

"What the hell are you doing?!" Ezio berated Armando, more from shock than actual anger as he abandoned the cover of the vehicle.

"Saving your life." Armando moved closer to the surrendered guard as he gestured for him to turn around.

Yet Ezio noticed that the guard still clung to his rifle, staring back at Armando with such a look as if to indicate he meant to die in battle.

"Don't make me kill you!" Armando aimed at the guard's head.

"You're going to have to kill me no matter what." The guard glanced between Ezio, Armando, Mario, and the other tied-up border guard.

"He's right," Mario interjected. "Shoot him now. It'll be quicker for everyone."

"I'm not going to shoot him!" Armando griped before asking the guard, "What's your name?"

"Matteo," the guard replied quickly.

"How do you feel about the Fascists, Matteo?" Armando asked, and Ezio offered him a surprised glance.

"Are you a revolutionary?" Matteo smirked in mockery. "A partisan?"

"We're part of a resistance movement." Armando lowered his weapon slightly but remained at the ready.

"We?" Matteo scanned the surrounding hills, checking for others.

"I'm alone." Armando also glanced at the surrounding hills, and Ezio wondered if he was double-checking. "I didn't have time to gather anyone. I needed to act swiftly. But we are many. More are rallying to our cause every day. We're tired of the yoke of oppression set upon our shoulders by Mussolini and his thugs. We're tired of being Hitler's puppets."

"Italy has never been stronger." Matteo shook his head in disagreement. "We're on the path to rebuilding —"

"The Roman Empire?" Armando mocked. "We can't even feed our own people. When was the last time you had a decent meal? When was the last time you saw more than one vehicle on the road? For goodness' sake, our American relatives are sending postcards to us made out of copper because of the sanctions. We're losing our footing in Africa, Greece, and everywhere else that we've sent our men to die."

Ezio studied Armando in slight awe of his passion. He would've never guessed as to the second lieutenant's loyalties, and the disparities Armando was alluding to had, for the most part, become the new normal for Ezio.

"These are temporary setbacks." Matteo persisted in his delusion. "We all need to make sacrifices."

"You've been lied to." Armando looked at Matteo with a measure of sympathy. "Hitler is using Italy as a buffer to keep the south of Germany safe. As soon as we're not a benefit to him, we'll be overrun. The Americans are already bombing us in the south. Soon we'll be defending Italy on two fronts, most of our soldiers still in Africa or Greece. We need to put an end to this."

"You can't let him join." Mario shook his head.

"You're part of this resistance too?" Ezio frowned at Mario.

"If you'll have me?" Mario looked over at Armando.

"One recruit at a time." Armando grew flustered.

"Why can't we let him join?" Ezio asked Mario.

"You're joining?" Armando asked Ezio with hope in his voice.

"I don't really have a choice, I suppose." Ezio shrugged and looked over at the captain's lifeless body.

"Regardless." Armando held out his hand to refocus. "Matteo, can we count on you?"

"He'll turn us in the minute he can," Mario continued in his disapproval.

"Like you did to me?" Ezio grew cross with Mario.

"We never said a word." Mario shook his head and nodded to the other border guard, who was still gagged and also shook his head in agreement. "The old man escaped. If we said anything, we'd have to explain how we let him go."

"Hmm." Ezio remained wary of Mario.

"He's right." Matteo swallowed. "You can't trust me."

"You're really not helping your case." Armando huffed.

"You'll have to shoot me." Matteo began to raise his weapon slowly.

"Stop!" Armando aimed at Matteo's head. "I don't want to kill you."

"Why?!" Matteo demanded.

"I hate the death of any Italian!" Armando shouted back as he nervously gripped the rifle. "Killing you would tear at my soul. The other two that I killed here today will never leave me, and that is something I will have to contend with for the rest of my life. I'd rather not add your face to my nightmares if that's alright with you."

Matteo watched Armando closely as he still gripped his rifle, and Ezio knew he was pondering his options. Ezio also recognized that if Matteo was successful in subduing Armando, he would quickly turn his weapon on Ezio and Mario. Everything now hung in the balance as Matteo drew slow, deep breaths to try and steady his nerves.

"We don't have to live under their yoke any longer," Armando spoke with fervor, appealing to Matteo's better senses. "The Fascist's are weakening. There are rumors of discontent in Mussolini's party. I know you've heard them. It's only a matter of time."

Still, Matteo remained in the balance between life and death. One flinch of his rifle and Armando would surely kill him, yet Ezio recognized that joining the Resistance would result in Matteo turning his back on his oaths and all that he had fought for over the years.

"I'm no threat." Armando lowered his rifle slowly and raised his hand to indicate he meant no harm.

"What are you doing?!" Mario asked harshly.

Fortunately, this little stunt seemed to have paid off, and Matteo, moved by Armando's vulnerability, also lowered his rifle as Ezio breathed a sigh of relief.

"What if you're wrong?" Matteo shrugged.

"Then you'll die fighting for a righteous cause instead of being slaughtered, here, for the sake of a dead man." Armando lowered his rifle. "Per favore, amico mio."

"For sparing my life, I will keep silent." Matteo drew a deep breath. "I will tell them the truth, but I will not offer names. Anti-Fascist resistance fighters ambushed us. I fired back, scaring off the cowards who fled back to Switzerland."

"I don't like it." Mario again shook his head.

"You don't get the privilege of an opinion." Armando frowned at Mario. "You're just as trustworthy as Matteo. Maybe it's you we should shoot."

"Me? I didn't commit treason by killing the captain!" Mario shrugged as he defended himself.

"How are we going to account for that?" Ezio asked Armando reluctantly.

"Signora Setti and Signora Soavi are both unaccounted for." Armando tilted his head as he thought. "Maybe there is a killer after all."

"Earlier, you mentioned that they could've joined the Resistance…" Ezio narrowed his gaze.

"I was merely gauging your reaction." Armando scratched the back of his neck. "I was trying to recruit you."

"That's also why you asked what my opinion was about the Jews?"

"Not very subtle, I know."

"What do we call ourselves then? Or are we part of the White Rose movement that you mentioned earlier?" Ezio turned to Armando.

"They're nonviolent." Armando shook his head. "Fortunately for you, our movement no longer adheres to pacifism."

"No longer?" Ezio frowned.

"Well, we were." Armando again pointed to the captain's body. "I had to act."

"So, what do we call ourselves then?" Mario asked.

"The Resistance." Armando glanced at Ezio. "Original, I know."

"Gets the point across, I suppose." Mario threw his lips upside down.

"Let's deal with the bodies." Ezio scratched his chin. "Then we can discuss further."

"Agreed." Armando slung the rifle across his shoulder.

"You'll need to untie me first." Mario turned his back to them and gestured to his ropes.

"And what of your comrade?" Ezio pointed to the other border guard, who was still gagged, as he began cutting Mario's bonds.

"Flavio." Mario nodded to the other guard. "Will you join us?"

Glancing between the company, Flavio tried to speak through his gag but struggled significantly.

"Untie him," Ezio ordered Matteo, who reluctantly obeyed.

With his gag undone, Flavio looked at Ezio and Armando with a cruel gaze before spitting at their feet.

"Believe! Obey! Fight!" Flavio screamed the Fascist slogan as his face beamed red with rage and hate. "You cowards! You will all hang for this!"

Without hesitation, Matteo raised his rifle and pointed it at Flavio.

"Wait! Don't!" Ezio rushed over to Matteo, but it was too late.

Flavio lay swiftly dying at their feet as blood oozed from a bullet wound in his chest.

"I told you to wait!" Ezio grabbed Matteo's arm roughly.

"Ezio, it had to be done." Armando came to stand between them.

"Not like that!" Ezio barked.

"Why does it matter?" Matteo asked coldly. "He would've turned us in."

"It matters because we're not like them! We're not the cruel, unsympathetic Fascists." Ezio's eyes bulged with indignation. "We can't be! Otherwise, this movement is already damned!"

"I made a decision that you were incapable of making." Matteo looked at Flavio's lifeless body.

"Take him into custody!" Ezio demanded Armando and Mario.

"That's not your call to make." Armando shook his head. "Come, let's deal with the bodies."

"Armando!" Ezio looked at him with sincerity. "Think about what you're doing! You can't replace terror with more terror."

"Let's deal with the bodies," Armando spoke through gritted teeth as he walked over to the captain and began searching him.

Running his hand through his hair, Ezio felt at a loss for how to behave. Even though none of these men fell at his hands, his conscience was plagued for having any involvement. Seeing them in their cold, lifeless forms reminded Ezio of his brothers' passing, and he could scarcely stand the wretched memory.

Standing over the captain, Ezio looked down at the horrific man in wonder as Armando continued to search through his pockets. Ezio found it peculiar how innocent the captain now appeared, almost as if he was asleep, and wondered if he was now giving account of his actions to a higher power, or if this really was the end.

"What's this?" Armando asked curiously as he pulled out a photograph from the captain's breast pocket, and Ezio watched the second lieutenant curiously for his indifference.

"A picture of his granddaughter." Ezio looked at it with a measure of respect before folding it up and placing it in his pocket. He recalled that the grandchild was named Isabella, and the chilling call of Captain Cacioppo begging for his wife's forgiveness reverberated through Ezio's mind.

"Why are you keeping it?" Armando frowned.

"I don't know." Ezio swallowed. "Feels wrong to dispose of it."

"It'll be suspicious if you're searched, and you have that photograph on you." Armando held out his hand for the picture.

With a sigh, Ezio handed the photograph back to Armando, who placed it back in the captain's breast pocket.

"We should hurry before anyone comes by this way." Armando grabbed the captain's arms and nodded for Ezio to take his legs.

"Where are we taking him?" Ezio asked as he looked around.

"Just over that hill." Armando nodded behind him. "There's a spot out of the way where no one will find him."

"I can't carry him with my leg." Ezio shook his head.

"I'll carry him. You dig." Armando let the captain's arms flop to the ground before opening the back of the vehicle, where he retrieved a shovel that he threw at Ezio, who caught it with his free hand.

"He's too heavy to carry all that way." Ezio looked at the shovel in his hand, feeling the burden of its duty.

"I'll drag him." Armando shrugged.

"And leave a trail in the snow that leads right to the body?" Ezio studied Armando in disbelief.

"What's your idea, then?" Armando grew annoyed.

"Take the body with one of them." Ezio pointed at Mario and Matteo. "Then come back and grab the other body.

"We don't have enough time." Armando looked down the road. "Someone could come at any minute."

"Pile them on top of each other," Mario suggested.

"Alright, here's what we'll do. The three of us will carry them, Ezio will bring the shovel and begin digging." Armando scratched his forehead as he pondered, and Ezio felt sick for how callous it felt to discuss their predicament like they were trying to figure out how to get furniture inside a house.

Agreeing, the company piled the three bodies on top of each other, and, using rope to keep them bound together, struggled greatly to move them through the rugged terrain. Traversing a little hill, they came to a ravine that was guarded heavily by trees where the branches and vines on the ground caused everyone to lament their task.

"Here...is...good..." Armando panted when they came close to the stream. "The water...will help...disguise their...scent."

"Get digging." Matteo nodded to Ezio before bending over to try and catch his breath.

"I'm of rank here." Ezio grew indignant. "I give the orders."

"In the Resistance, I outrank you." Armando brushed away the sweat on his brow.

"The Resistance isn't recognized by Italy." Ezio grew annoyed. "I'll dig because you assisted with the carrying, but remember, I'm in charge here."

"Signore." Matteo offered a sarcastic salute.

With a shake of the head, Ezio drove the shovel into the dirt, but noticed that the ground was hard and this would take some time.

"Signore," Mario spoke quietly as he walked over to Ezio. "What are you doing?"

"I'm digging," Ezio replied, confused.

"I meant about Matteo." Mario glanced over his shoulder at the guard before continuing in a soft voice, "He disrespected you."

"He's tired." Ezio waved to dismiss the topic. "We all are."

"We need him on our side." Mario ran his hand through his hair as he tried to be diplomatic. "If you don't command his respect, he will turn on you."

"What do you want me to do?" Ezio's face grew crimson with rage. "Shoot him?"

"There are other methods of discipline." Mario tilted his head.

"We're not the Mafia, and we're not the Fascists." Ezio shook his head as he continued to shovel. "We can't be like them."

"I've said my peace." Mario raised his hands to signify he was now innocent in whatever befell Ezio.

Continuing as swiftly as he was able, Ezio finally had the first grave dug. Climbing out of the hole, he signaled for the first body to be brought in, and the men unsympathetically threw Flavio's body into the earth as it landed with a thud.

"I'll take a turn." Armando held his hand out for the shovel.

"Are you sure?" Ezio asked, but instead of replying, Armando snatched the shovel out of his hand and began on the next grave.

"How did you hurt your leg?" Mario asked Ezio as the company watched Armando.

"Long story." Ezio laid his cane across his lap as he sat on the ground near Armando.

He recalled Faustina and her persistence in unraveling the truth behind his condition. He wondered if it would've been better had he been honest from the very onset, but even with her prodding, he couldn't bear to tell her the truth. Still, after the whole story had been revealed, Faustina had not judged him poorly. He recalled how she asked about his brothers the night before while they were on the lake. How he wished to be back at the moment, playing the role of the hero once again as he rowed her to safety. Although, the more he contemplated, the more Ezio realized that, in reality, she was the hero for shooting back at their assailant.

Giuseppe seemed genuinely surprised at my accusation when I saw him this morning, Ezio recalled the moment. *I wonder if there is some truth behind his reaction. But if it wasn't Giuseppe, then who?*

What does it matter? Ezio grew dejected as he watched Armando shoveling. *If I thought my life was forfeit by helping Signor Lehner, there really is no escape for me now. A resistance fighter? Crippled old me? What a laugh! And all of this because I acted upon my conscience. If I had stayed quiet, obeyed my orders, then I would likely be living in peace.*

Peace? Ezio argued with himself. *I wasn't at peace! I hated my life. My mother despised me, I had no romantic prospects, and other than Wolfgang, I was virtually without companionship, and I was wasting away in that cramped office.*

I hate that these men were killed, but I half wonder if they deserved it. Captain Cacioppo sent his own wife to a death camp! What a wicked, horrid man.

After all the graves were dug, and the bodies placed in the earth, Armand covered them with dirt before Ezio placed branches, leaves, and snow over them to try and cover their tracks.

"Where are you going?" Ezio asked as the men began to leave.

"We're done." Armando shrugged.

"Shouldn't we say a few words?" Ezio asked.

"Why do you care? They were evil Fascists." Armando scoffed. "I didn't consider you to be religious."

"I'm not necessarily, but I still believe in the sanctity of life." Ezio cleared his throat, feeling awkward with the looks the men were offering him. "They're still human. They still knew love, fear, anger, and everything else we feel. They're still owed dignity."

"They wouldn't offer us any." Matteo shook his head.

"That's why we have to." Ezio drew a deep breath. "Again, we cannot become like them. We value life, no matter who it belonged to."

"If it's so important to you, say a few words and meet us by the vehicle." Armando turned to leave, and the others followed him.

Feeling foolish, Ezio stood in front of the graves as he stared at the snow-covered earth at a loss for what to say. He listened to the wind gently rustling through the trees, he looked up at the overcast sky littered with thick grey clouds, and only now felt the sting of the cold on his fingers. The shock and adrenaline had caused him to almost forget the cold entirely, but the skin on his knuckles and hands were ghostly white, and his hand seemed frozen to his cane.

Ezio drew a deep breath before beginning, "I commit these bodies to the ground. Earth to earth, ash to ash, dust to dust."

Unable to continue the half-baked funeral rights, Ezio gripped tightly to his cane before a rage overtook him and he erupted, "You deserved this! It's not my fault either, so I'm not sure why the hell I feel guilty. You were a terrible man. You were hateful, cowardly, and sent your own wife to die for your misplaced sense of loyalty. And I shouldn't say this, but for Faustina's sake, I'm thankful you're gone. Without you, she can finally be safe. She's a perfect woman, but all you could see was the lie that she's less than human."

With that, Ezio began his slow trek back to the vehicle, where he found the company waiting for him. While they pretended to be uncaring about the deaths of the captain and Flavio, their silence seemed to suggest otherwise.

What annoyed Ezio the most, however, was Wolfgang's attachment to Mario. The cat was perched lovingly in the guard's arms and twitching its tail as it looked around in happy wonder.

"How are we to explain this?" Mario pointed to the shattered window when Ezio arrived.

"We were attacked." Armando shrugged. "We were heavily outnumbered and fled with our lives. We returned later to inspect, but the bodies of our fallen brethren were removed."

"Why did we bury them, then?" Mario squinted, and Ezio's annoyance soured further when he heard Wolfgang purring. "If we were ambushed by the Resistance, why didn't we just leave the bodies?"

"Don't think about it too hard." Matteo groaned.

"What were we doing out here?" Mario continued.

No one replied.

"They're going to ask questions." Mario threw his hand out in frustration and Wolfgang meowed in his annoyance at the sudden movement. "We need to have a unified account."

"Tell them exactly what happened," Ezio leaned against the vehicle. "The captain was following the lead of a Jew who escaped to Switzerland. While we were discussing with the guards, which is you, Mario, we were ambushed. We fired back. After the captain, Flavio, and..."

"Alberto," Mario advised.

"Alberto," Ezio spoke as his brother's name nearly stuck in his throat. "After the three men fell, we retreated to safety. When we returned, the bodies were gone. The partisans likely took them to be mutilated."

"What happens now?" Matteo cleared his throat.

"Mario will radio his superior." Armando pointed and Mario and then at Matteo. "You will do likewise."

"What is our part in this Resistance of yours?" Mario asked.

"It's not *my* Resistance." Armando frowned at him. "You will be called upon shortly. Continue in your position as normal."

"You trust us that much?" Matteo scoffed in his disbelief.

"I wasn't lying when I mentioned there are more of us than you realize. If I hear anything, I will finish what I started." Armando glared at the two men.

With an uneasy alliance that was based on shaky trust, the men offered nods of agreement before leaving to return to their perspective posts, but not before Mario handed Wolfgang back to Ezio with a glance of sorrow.

"I parked my vehicle just before the bend." Armando pointed in the direction.

"Your vehicle?" Ezio frowned as the two men entered the car. "I've never seen you drive before."

"It's not my vehicle," Armando loosely explained.

"The Resistance?" Ezio asked.

"Francesca's." Armando cleared his throat.

"I see."

"I'll meet you back at the station?" Armando asked as Ezio started the ignition.

"I'm going home." Ezio shook his head as his tiredness began to envelop him.

"You should write your report first." Armando cleared his throat, and Ezio offered him a crooked glance for his attempt at outranking him.

"What happens now?" Ezio looked down at Wolfgang, feeling slightly hurt by his companion's adoration of Mario.

"Tomorrow, I'll consult with the Resistance." Armando began to stare out the window. "After we get the rear window fixed, of course."

"What do you need to consult with them about?"

"They'll know how to proceed with what happened here. There are some in places of power that could divert attention. You're welcome, by the way."

"You want my gratitude?" Ezio frowned sharply at Armando.

"I saved your life!" Armando grew animated. "I risked my neck to save yours."

"You didn't save me!" Ezio barked back. "You delayed the inevitable. Do you really think they'll buy our story? Even if they do, an ambush of a police captain in such a strong communist sector is the sparking of a civil war. This area will be swarming with men searching for any clues about the Resistance. When they find the bodies, and they will, the evidence will lead to us."

"How will it lead to us?" Armando defended. "The bodies are near a ravine."

"How many bullets did you fire?" Ezio asked.

"Six, maybe seven." Armando shrugged. "Why does that matter?"

"Some ambush." Ezio raised his eyebrows. "If I was investigating, I'd be looking for the bullet spray of chaotic and panicked men, marks in the terrain where they were laying in hiding, and anything else that shows some sort of coordination or planning."

"As I said, there are men in the Resistance who have considerable power. They will be able to steer attention away from us." Armando looked grumpily at Ezio before continuing, "Look, I know you probably have reason to doubt my capabilities, but—"

"Be quiet." Ezio rubbed his eyes as they arrived at Armando's parked vehicle. "I need sleep. We'll talk tomorrow."

Chapter Fourteen:
Ti Amo

"Life is a shipwreck, but we must not forget to sing in the lifeboats."

Voltaire

"I thought you were going home?" Armando asked when Ezio walked into the station with Wolfgang.

Armando was sitting behind the reception desk, filling out some sort of report. Ezio was glad to find that Francesca was not at the station. He didn't suppose he could handle her demand for the mileage again, especially knowing that the captain had used it against them.

"I told you I need to do the report first." Ezio pinched his lips together; he hated admitting Armando was correct. "Also, did you tell Francesca where you were going?"

"I don't believe she would've been thrilled." Armando shook his head before elaborating, "Although, if she knew I was behaving so rashly for your sake, I'm certain she would understand. I'm sure she's wondering where I am, actually. Maybe I should locate her and explain, without too much detail, of course."

"Grazie, by the way." Ezio cleared his throat as he looked at Armando with a measure of humility.

"For what?" Armando asked with a slight grin.

"Are you going to make me spell it out?" Ezio groaned as he walked toward the office.

"Absolutely," Armando spoke proudly as he trailed Ezio.

"Why are you following me?" Ezio glanced over his shoulder as Wolfgang jumped out of his arm, excited to be back in a familiar place.

"Waiting for the apology," Armando replied briskly as Ezio opened the door to the office. "And to see what we can find out about the captain."

An eerie sense fell over Ezio as he stood in the office while surrounded by the captain's personal effects. Armando, too, must have experienced something akin to Ezio as he also remained quiet.

If spirits did exist, then Ezio felt the captain in this room. It was as if a presence was watching him, unable to interfere but watching with menace, nonetheless. Ezio wanted nothing to do with anything belonging to such an evil man, and wondered if he should hire movers to empty out the office.

"Don't disturb his stuff too much," Ezio warned as Armando began rummaging through the drawers.

"Why?" Armando frowned.

"Why?!" Ezio barked back. "Because I'm your commanding officer, that's why! Also, it will look suspicious, or at least look unkind, if we examine all his effects."

"Maybe I'll have Francesca do it then." Armando stood and threw his hands onto his hips. "She has a gentler touch than I do. Besides, my hands are still shaking."

Watching Armando for a minute, Ezio realized that maybe the second lieutenant had been more troubled by the killings than he initially believed. He had assumed that the second lieutenant was a man absent of ambition, yet now Ezio understood Armando as someone rather clever who only acted when absolutely necessary.

There's more to him than you perceive, Ezio recalled Leonarda's warning, and wondered if she, too, was part of this Resistance. It would, possibly, explain some information she knew. Maybe she had intercepted the captain's orders and knew beforehand that he would ask Ezio to dispatch Signor Lehner to Poland.

"Are you alright?" Ezio asked, feeling uncomfortable with his display of vulnerability.

"I'll be fine." Armando nodded as both men avoided eye contact.

The rat squeaked from the corner of the office, and both Ezio and Armando looked in the direction and then back at Wolfgang, wondering if he would now become decisive.

"I almost missed the rodent." Ezio smiled bleakly before petting Wolfgang's head and mentioning, "It's alright. You don't have to kill if you don't want to."

"But you should kill when necessary," Armando interjected, and Ezio understood that he was not merely addressing the cat, but rather, his own guilt.

"So, Francesca?" Ezio asked, swiftly changing the subject.

"She's one of us." Armando scratched his chin, and Ezio noticed that his hand was, indeed, shaking. "Her affection for me is a clever deception."

"Those times you were flirting with her at the desk?" Ezio squinted.

"All a ploy." Armando exhaled quickly through his nose, but Ezio sensed a degree of disappointment. "Initially, I did approach her with the intention of pursuing a serious relationship, but she thought it better to enact a romance as a distraction from our actual activities. I hate to admit it, but it worked like a repellent against you and the captain. Whenever we flirted, the two of you fled as quickly as a mouse from a cat. Or, some mice from some cats. I can't think of a good metaphor at the moment."

"This disappoints you?" Ezio asked, leaning on his perception.

Armando paused as he sat in the chair beside the desk before replying, "She is the most amazing woman I have ever met. You should see how dedicated she is to the cause. She discovered this method for invisible ink."

"Invisible ink?" Ezio frowned as he grew intrigued.

"Ingenious, really." Armando crossed his arms. "You take some sort of bodily fluid; blood, urine, or even semen. You use that as your ink, and it's invisible unless heated. Where she discovered this, I have no idea, but it works. She's written dozens of correspondences on police reports or other documentation from the station. No one is the wiser."

"If you ever write to me in such a method, please use urine." Ezio scrunched up his nose in disgust.

"Or was it lemon juice?" Armando studied the ceiling as he tried to recall. "She may have been toying with me, but I can't remember what she actually uses. Regardless, she's selfless, caring, and wittier than you know. If I could marry her today, I would."

"She'll come around. I'm sure of it." Ezio nodded encouragingly. "You're not so bad yourself."

Armando shot Ezio a peculiar glance.

"Don't worry, I'm not about to propose to you." Ezio smiled, but as soon as the words left his mouth, a dangerous thought dropped into his mind. "I should leave. You'll be alright here?"

Armando nodded quickly before closing his eyes and leaning his head back. Ezio felt for the second lieutenant, and his conscience stirred him to remain, but there was a pressing matter set upon his heart that wouldn't depart from him.

Rushing out of the station, Ezio threw his cane into the vehicle as excitement mixed with terror built within him. He was being impulsive, irrational, and potentially dangerous, but his experience on the road with the captain had ignited a sense of impending doom, and Ezio would not miss out on this chance.

Starting the vehicle, Ezio drove as quickly as he was able back to his house, making sure to avoid the children playing in the streets or the old ladies slowly walking arm in arm without paying much attention to their surroundings, until he finally arrived at the property.

Hobbling quickly to the door, Ezio offered a happy wave to Vitelli, who stared back at him with a concerned gaze for the lieutenant's cheer.

"Ciao!" Ezio called loudly and happily when he entered the house and made his way up the stairs to find his father and mother listening to the radio.

"What has you so excited?" Ludovica asked with annoyance, and Ezio spotted a half-empty bottle in her hand while the usual cigarette hung out the corner of her mouth.

"I'm going to ask her to marry me." Ezio's eyes welled as he looked at his parents expectantly.

"Who?" Lorenzo slowly looked up at his son with a worried gaze.

"Faustina." Ezio continued in his excitement, but both Ludovica and Lorenzo glanced at each other in confusion.

"The nun! The one who was here only yesterday!" Ezio explained.

"Ragazzo mio," Lorenzo began sympathetically, "I don't think you can marry nuns."

"I'm aware!" Ezio squeezed his eyes shut briskly in frustration. "She's not a real nun."

"She's not?" Lorenzo remained in his confusion before adding, "I'm pretty certain she is."

"She's pretending to be a nun to escape persecution," Ezio explained. He wasn't entirely convinced that advising his parents of this deception was wise, but he thought it best to offer all the information now before the questions came later, and potentially in front of others.

"Pretending?" Ludovica again looked at her husband with peculiarity, wondering if Ezio had become mad.

"I doubt that." Lorenzo shook his head adamantly. "Only someone with God's help could beat me in chess that easily."

"She's a Jew!" Ezio blurted, but still, his parents remained doubtful. "For goodness' sake, I'm going to ask her to marry me!"

"Just..." Lorenzo scratched the back of his neck as he struggled for the right words. "Just don't be too heartbroken when she declines. Nuns don't break their vows easily."

Slapping his hand onto his forehead in exasperation, Ezio decided to abandon his pursuit in convincing them and asked, "I would like to take a ring to propose to her, and I was hoping that, perhaps, I—"

"A ring?!" Ludovica cackled. "You were born into the wrong family, you idiota! Who is going to marry you, anyway? You don't have a chance with her, or any woman I can think of. You'll die alone which is a just reward for your sins. Kill your brothers, and you believe you can still find happiness? Heh!"

Ezio's heart sank as he listened to his mother. A part of him hoped that with the morning's activities in the market, Ludovica had softened her heart toward him, but her harsh words sunk into his spirit like a hot knife.

"Did your sister mention which friends she was with?" Lorenzo asked, ignoring his wife's cruelty to their son.

"No." Ezio swallowed to try and remove the lump in his throat. "Why?"

"She should be back by now." Lorenzo glanced at his watch.

"I'm sure she lost track of time." Ezio turned and was about to leave when his mother snapped her fingers.

"I got you something." Ludovica pointed at the kitchen table, and Ezio spotted a cane leaning against a chair.

"For me?" Ezio asked, unsure what to expect from his mother's behavior.

She had spoken to him so cruelly, yet now she wanted to make sure he saw her present? He couldn't wrap his mind around her behavior toward him and struggled to determine if she actually loved him or not.

"Who else?" Ludovica ridiculed. "Do you like it or what?"

"It's very nice." Ezio swallowed as he examined it carefully.

The handle was a solid white that mimicked marble patterns, the body was sturdy and a polished light brown, and there was even a rubber grip at the bottom for extra traction. This, Ezio understood, was not a cheap item, and he looked at his mother inquisitively, still unsure of her duality. Did she buy him the gift out of guilt, or had she truly wanted to purchase something meaningful for her son?

"Don't wreck it like you did the last one." Ludovica took a generous sip. "It set me back."

"Set you back? Set me back, you mean!" Lorenzo studied his wife with slight offense. "I'd love to hear how you financially contribute to this family, and how this could possibly—"

"I'd enjoy setting you back!" Ludovica raised a hand, ready to slap him, and at once Lorenzo cowered in submission.

"You really didn't have to." Ezio felt embarrassed by his parents' difficulties and hated that he contributed to their financial woes.

"You can't walk around with the one you have." Ludovica shrugged before waving. "Take it and leave us."

Without another word, Ezio took the new cane and, quickly testing its durability, descended the stairs and walked out the door.

Arriving at the pier, Ezio hurried down to the boats, where he climbed into the one that was, again, gifted to him by Signora Soavi. Glancing over at Giuseppe's vessel, Ezio was surprised to find that it was already repaired, and wondered if he should've kept quiet before he had the chance to take it in as evidence.

Regardless, Ezio's priorities at this moment were rather selfish, and he quite honestly could care less about what happened in the world. With his near brush with death still fresh in his mind, anything that didn't involve Faustina was trivial and not worth the attention.

Huffing and puffing while rowing quickly, Ezio rushed as quickly as he could to the other side of the lake. He didn't dare spend another minute without the one person that he cared about more than anything in the world.

Passing by the rock where his brothers perished, Ezio offered a quick nod of acknowledgment, wondering if they had any part in watching over him earlier that day.

Eventually making it across the lake without incident, Ezio pulled the boat into shore as best as he was able with only one good leg. Then, he sped toward the church, where he knocked generously on the door.

When there was no reply, a horrible thought entered Ezio's mind that Faustina was already gone. Or, worse yet, as Sister Rosa had so kindly offered, she was already married to someone else.

Knocking again, more from panic than anything else, Ezio grew impatient with each passing second that went without answer.

Lifting his arm to pound on the door again, Ezio was about to lose all patience when a shout from deep inside the church called out angrily, "It's open!"

Didn't think of that, he felt silly for not even considering trying the door first.

Opening it slowly, Ezio peeked his head inside to find a peculiar sight.

Sitting near the altar, Faustina and Brother Giovanni were embattled in a fierce chess match with six or so nuns, including Sister Rosa, standing around them and watching intently while whispering their own strategies to one another.

Quietly, and with a grin of anticipation, Ezio walked slowly down the outside aisle before sitting in a pew near the front, but far enough away to not be noticed.

"If you're here for confession, the priest is away," Brother Giovanni spoke grumpily, and Ezio understood that he was not pleased with the added distraction.

Not wanting to give away his voice to Faustina, Ezio waved in dismissal, and Brother Giovanni grunted in his acknowledgment before returning his attention to the chessboard.

"Check," Faustina moved her queen, but Ezio was too far from the board to get an accurate reading.

"Heh," Brother Giovanni huffed as he ran his hand along his chin. "I should've seen that one coming."

The door where Ezio had entered opened again, and glancing over his shoulder, he spotted another nun who walked briskly to her compatriots where she whispered to Sister Rosa, "What's the tally?"

"Sister Faustina is undefeated. I think this is their fourth game," Sister Rosa replied.

"She looks bored." The nun giggled.

"I'm trying to concentrate!" Brother Giovanni barked and waved for the nuns to be silent.

After a few minutes, and with Ezio's anticipation swelling with each and every second, Brother Giovanni finally made his move. Unfortunately for him, Faustina seemed to have anticipated this move and swiftly captured a piece. Brother Giovanni clasped his hands onto his cheeks as he appeared dismayed at his poor decision that had been so calculated.

As he waited impatiently, Ezio took a moment to inspect Faustina while she was unaware of his presence. In the dim church light, Faustina appeared irresistible to Ezio. Her soft lips, smooth skin, and gentle features made him burst with desire, and he knew that if he didn't kiss her today, then everything he survived would account for nothing.

"Alright! What do want?!" Brother Giovanni berated Ezio. "Are you here to pray or watch? Either way, you're distracting me!"

"I'm here because she's wrong." Ezio stood, and at once, Faustina's eyes lit up when she recognized his voice and turned to look at him.

"Ezio?" Faustina asked as she tilted her head in happy surprise, but also confusion his statement.

"I'm not finished!" Brother Giovanni tugged on Faustina's sleeve.

"There is no move you can make which will spare you," Faustina spoke to Brother Giovanni as she looked at Ezio with a growing smile. "Because rook to h1 is checkmate."

"What? That can't be!" Brother Giovanni stared at the board intently.

"Look." Faustina lost patience as she took control of the pieces. "Your best move is rook to e2, but it doesn't matter because as soon as I move to e1, your king has nowhere to escape to."

"What about f3?" Brother Giovanni moved his king to the position.

"Have you already forgotten how the knight moves?" Faustina pointed to her piece guarding f3.

"Again!" Brother Giovanni began resetting the board.

"Perhaps later." Faustina returned her attention to Ezio as he walked closer to her. "What are you doing here? What do you mean I was wrong?"

"You were wrong about waiting." Ezio smiled tenderly at her. "I can't wait a moment longer."

"Ezio." Faustina glanced bashfully down at her hands as she nervously played with her fingers. "I don't know if you've thought this through entirely. What do you expect to happen next?"

"I'll marry you," Ezio spoke confidently as he moved closer to Faustina. "We'll live in moderate happiness."

"Moderate?" Faustina raised an unimpressed eyebrow.

"I'll never overpromise," Ezio explained quickly as he continued to approach her. "You know as well as I do that life will never be easy. Still, we'll have four children to fill our hearts."

"Four?!" Faustina's eyes flew wide in surprise.

"Fine, six then." Ezio stood about a foot away from Faustina, who glanced out the corner of her eye at Brother Giovanni and the other nuns, but their opinion didn't concern Ezio.

"But the captain!" Faustina frowned as her uncertainty grew.

"He's not a concern anymore." Ezio shook his head.

"He's not?" Faustina held her conclusion in reserve.

"You are the light of my life, Faustina." Ezio placed his hand gently on her cheek.

"This is a house of God!" Brother Giovanni scolded Ezio for his shameless attitude.

"God created love, Signore," Ezio replied swiftly.

"He also created propriety!" Brother Giovanni protested.

"Oh, shush!" Sister Rosa slapped Brother Giovanni on his shoulder. "Let them have their moment."

"I don't usually fall prey to impulsiveness," Ezio began, but Brother Giovanni scoffed. "We've only known each other a short time, but in this brief spell you've been in my life, existence finally has a meaning. I never knew what living was before I met you."

"For goodness' sake." Brother Giovanni rolled his eyes but received another swift swat from Sister Rosa.

"I didn't believe that I would ever find someone like you who loved me in return." Ezio paused as he tried to discern what he would say next. "I can't promise you happiness. I can't guarantee that with me, you'll always be safe. We're both susceptible to the realities of this world. But I swear that I will endure with you. Together, we'll endure the injustice levied against us, we'll endure the sleepless nights spent in hiding, we'll endure the sorrow of never having the life that comes so easily to others, and, finally, together we'll suffer. Together we'll build endurance, together we'll build character, and together, we'll hope."

Brother Giovanni sniffled as he wiped his nose, and Sister Rosa took her turn rolling her eyes at the monk's antics.

"Answer him!" one of the nuns demanded of Faustina.

"What else can I say but…" Faustina paused as she stared into his eyes. "Yes!"

With that, Ezio dropped his cane and wrapped his arms around her tightly as his body and soul were raptured in a euphoria otherwise foreign to him. This moment was perfect to Ezio. All the hatred, grief, and loneliness he endured over the last ten years were suffocated in a crescendo of pure, unadulterated love. Ezio's heart was finally whole.

He felt the spirits of his brothers surrounding him. He felt the years of his mother's tormenting melting away in the purity of passion. He felt the pain mixing with joy as his heart tore and healed in the same fluid motion.

"When?" Faustina wiped her eyes as she broke the embrace.

"When what?" Ezio asked.

"When are we to be wed, silly?!" Faustina chuckled.

"Today if we can!" Ezio looked at the nuns and Brother Giovanni. "We have witnesses."

"The priest is out of town." Brother Giovanni held his hands up to wash away any responsibility in this matter.

"Per favore!" Faustina pleaded with him, and she was soon joined in by the nuns demanding that he marry the couple.

"I'm not some parrot you can order around! Marriage is sacred!" Brother Giovanni began cleaning the chessboard in irritation.

"You should unify them in holy matrimony before they consecrate their union without your blessing," Sister Rosa persisted, and the nuns giggled.

"I'm old enough to know the danger of marrying someone without their parents being present." Brother Giovanni snapped and stood as he grabbed the chessboard. "I should amend that statement, actually. Rather, I'm old enough to know the danger of marrying someone without their mother present."

"My mother is dead, Signore." Faustina pressed, and Brother Giovanni looked at her with a measure of sympathy as his mood softened.

"What about yours?" Brother Giovanni asked Ezio.

"She..." Ezio wondered how to phrase his response. "She won't be a problem."

"No, no, no." Brother Giovanni wagged a finger. "That's what I was told last time, and I'm still receiving an annual letter from an embittered mother-in-law. That was twenty years ago. I don't believe I could handle another onslaught."

"I'll give you a chess lesson!" Faustina threw her hand in the air as the idea struck her.

Pausing to reflect, Brother Giovanni squinted at Faustina as he tried to gauge her sincerity.

"An hour lesson." Brother Giovanni bartered.

"Thirty minutes." Faustina negotiated.

"No wedding." Brother Giovanni began to leave.

"Fine! An hour!" Faustina relented.

"An hour?" Brother Giovanni waited for her confirmation.

"An hour." She nodded adamantly.

"You must really love this man." Brother Giovanni narrowed his gaze.

"Or I don't think I could truly teach you anything in less than an hour," Faustina quipped, and Brother Giovanni smiled ever so slightly.

"So be it." Brother Giovanni set the board down on the pew, and the nuns clapped giddily in their excitement.

"Do you have rings?" Sister Rosa asked.

"No, actually." Ezio swallowed as he grew nervous. He half-expected Faustina to say no, let alone proceeding with the actual wedding now.

"That's fine. We have witnesses, the rings can come later." Sister Rosa waved to dismiss his concerns before gesturing for the nuns to take their places in the pews.

"I should've remained a simple monk and never have been ordained," Brother Giovanni grumbled as he grabbed a stole, kissed it, and placed it over his shoulders before grabbing a Bible.

Taking Faustina's hand, Ezio led her to just in front of the altar where Brother Giovanni was now impatiently waiting. Staring lovingly into her eyes, Ezio couldn't contain his smile, and felt as though this moment, like the one they shared on the beach, was somehow predestined. He felt loved, desired, respected, and that he had found not only a suitable companion but a woman more beautiful than he could've ever imagined.

"Will you be partaking in Communion?" Brother Giovanni asked as he inspected the altar to see if there was any consecrated bread or wine available.

"I'm Jewish," Faustina blurted with a measure of enjoyment as Brother Giovanni half froze in place.

"I know your nature is Jewish, but certainly you adhere to Christianity?" Brother Giovanni grew concerned.

"I don't adhere to any religion." Faustina shook her head quickly, and Ezio wondered if the monk was about to collapse.

"But you're marrying a Catholic?" Brother Giovanni asked in such a way as if to determine if she was aware before turning his attention to Ezio and inquiring, "Please tell me you're at least of the faith?"

"I am." Ezio nodded.

"When was the last time you attended Mass?" Brother Giovanni remained unconvinced.

"Ten years ago." Ezio grew reflective.

"A literal nightmare," Brother Giovanni ran his hand across his face in dismay before addressing Faustina. "I cannot marry you without partaking in Communion, and without being a baptized Christian, you cannot partake. Unless, of course, you'd like to convert?"

"If I may, according to the order of celebrating matrimony, there are alternatives to officiating without communion," Faustina challenged, and Ezio appreciated her close studying of the prayer book.

"If a word of this escapes these walls..." Brother Giovanni held up a stern finger to everyone in the church. "I could lose these privileges. Actually...maybe...yeah, maybe spread word of this. They'll discipline me with never being able to perform another wedding which, would save us all some grief. Let's proceed then."

The ceremony progressed as Brother Giovanni read from scripture, offered a few words on the importance of marriage, and again encouraged Faustina to convert before requesting that they sign the marriage certificate.

"I should change my name," Faustina paused as she contemplated before signing.

"Smart." Ezio nodded. "What would you like?"

"Perhaps my middle name?" Faustina thought for a moment.

"Put Moses for all I care," Brother Giovanni griped. "Just get it over with."

Ignoring the priest-monk, Faustina thought for another minute before printing and signing the name, Nora Milanesi.

"Nora." Ezio grinned. "That's beautiful."

"You may take your bride." Brother Giovanni fanned the certificate to dry it off.

With giddy clapping and happy tears, the nuns watched with hidden jealousy as Ezio placed his hands gently on Faustina's jaw before pulling her in close for a kiss. As their lips pressed together, Ezio's heart erupted with emotions that transgressed into the physical realm and his heart ached with desire. His fingers tingled, his breathing began to labor, and it felt to Ezio that every part of his being had been anxiously waiting for this moment.

"Alright, that's done with." Brother Giovanni removed his stole as he folded it gently before grabbing the chess board. "Lesson time."

"Leave it!" Sister Rosa barked. "Let the husband take his bride!"

"She promised!" Brother Giovanni snapped.

"I will come back soon." Faustina chuckled at the aged old monk.

"So be it." Brother Giovanni waved for them to leave, but Ezio caught a smirk of happiness.

"I appreciate your kindness." Faustina touched him gently on the shoulder.

"Yes, yes." Brother Giovanni again waved.

"So, where are we going now?" Faustina asked Ezio.

"Our honeymoon." Ezio smiled.

"Honeymoon?" Faustina frowned.

"I'll show you." Ezio nodded to the doors.

Chapter Fifteen:
Vittoria

"The best revenge is not to be like your enemy."

Marcus Aurelius

"Well, what do you think?" Ezio asked Faustina after he had rowed them out to the middle of the lake.

"About what?" Faustina asked while confused.

"About our honeymoon." Ezio gestured to the lake around them.

"This is the honeymoon?" Faustina grew unimpressed.

"My wife, you've forgotten that you're in the most beautiful place on earth." Ezio pulled the oars in as they drifted on the middle of the gentle lake.

"I haven't forgotten." Faustina looked at the mountains surrounding them, and then back at Ezio with a squint.

"They've become common to you." Ezio leaned forward and held her hand.

"Not quite." Faustina shook her head. "I simply haven't been afforded the time to appreciate them."

"Then this is my wedding gift to you." Ezio held his hand out to the scenery.

"A little cheap," Faustina muttered under her breath with a grin.

"Cheap is all I can provide." Ezio chuckled. "I do hope you weren't marrying me just for my wealth?"

"Any man is rich if they have what they already want." Faustina grinned.

Ezio smiled as he watched his bride for a moment as they sat in silence, appreciating the calmness of the lake, the gentle breeze coming down from the mountains, and the bright sun blessing them with warmth.

"Four kids?" Faustina asked after a moment.

"I like the sound of six better."

"You just want the tax break, don't you?" Faustina narrowed her gaze.

"What can I say? Mussolini wants to swell Italy with Italians. The tax breaks for large families are enticing. Maybe then we could afford an actual honeymoon." Ezio gazed at the snow-topped mountains.

"There are better reasons to have children." Faustina lowered her gaze in disappointment.

"Such as?"

"Such as blaming them when our marriage falls apart."

"You make it sound inevitable."

"If this is my wedding gift, then you know who to blame." Faustina smirked.

"I thought I was blaming the children?" Ezio squinted.

"Have you thought of names for them?"

"Names? Goodness, no." Ezio chuckled. "I would never be so bold as to name Vittoria, Alberto, Luca, and Ezio Jr."

"Three boys and a girl?" Faustina raised an eyebrow.

"Four boys. Unfortunately, Vittoria will be teased often in school."

Faustina laughed but then grew solemn as she mentioned, "Speaking of names...you'll have to remember to call me Nora when you're addressing me publicly."

"You'll always be Faustina to me." Ezio placed the oars back into the water as they began rowing slowly.

"Ezio," Faustina sighed.

"I know." Ezio nodded reluctantly. "Don't worry, Nora, there are a few people less cautious than me."

"Listen, uh..." Nora began slowly. "I don't mean to inquire where I maybe shouldn't, but the captain..."

"He's not a threat anymore." Ezio offered her a knowing look. "Anyone who knew about your existence is, well, not a problem."

"I hope you didn't...you know...for my sake?" Nora asked hesitantly.

"The thought did cross my mind, but, thankfully, the circumstances arose outside my control and...well, maybe I should leave it at that."

"What about his replacement?" Nora asked.

"We've only filed our reports. We'll wait to see what Rome replies with. I've been running this station well enough on my own, and I doubt they'll give us a second thought." Ezio contemplated. "Besides, as it happens, I may have some allies in positions of prominence that I wasn't aware of."

"I don't understand." Nora drew a deep breath as she looked intently into Ezio's eyes. "But maybe that's for the best."

"There was a moment…" Ezio paused as he recalled the captain's pistol at his temple. "I didn't believe that I was going to see you again."

Nora remained silent as she leaned forward and touched his knee lovingly, and Ezio's soul relished the affection.

"You don't have to explain further." Nora squeezed his knee gently.

"What was your plan? If I didn't return, that is?" Ezio asked.

"I didn't have one." Nora shook her head in wonder. "I was convinced I would be found out. I was tempted to run, but I have no money, no papers, no food, and nowhere to go."

"I'm glad I returned then." Ezio spotted the rock in the lake as he rowed past and offered an inward nod to his brothers.

"I don't mean to sound ungrateful…" Nora paused as she looked at Ezio with a measure of discomfort. "But please tell me that we're not staying with your parents."

"Of course we are!" Ezio teased, but he couldn't contain his grin.

"You must have a plan for where we'll live!" Nora grew worried.

"We'll stay a couple nights in a hotel." Ezio closed his eyes as he savored the very thought of privacy and comfort. "Then we'll find a place to call our own."

"Where?" Nora shrugged.

"Anywhere you'd like." Ezio threw his lips upside down.

"I can't leave Italy without proper documentation." Nora tilted her head in annoyance.

"We will remedy that." Ezio nodded confidently.

"Really?" Nora looked at him hopefully but with a measure of cynicism.

"We'll find a way. I promise you."

"Well, then." Nora grew pensive. "Where would you like to live?"

"How about America?" Ezio shrugged. "They hate Fascists and Communists equally."

"So far away!" Nora grimaced.

"Where were you thinking?"

"I would love to see my father."

"Switzerland." Ezio grew intrigued. "We could move to Lugano. I could see if there is any work there for me."

"Really?!" Nora's excitement soared. "But how?! I don't have the paperwork. They won't let me in!"

"I might know a way." Ezio thought about Mario and wondered if his new relationship with the border guard could prove beneficial.

"This sounds too good to be true." Nora looked at him reluctantly.

"I'll make an inquiry." Ezio drew a deep breath, hoping that he hadn't overpromised. "But first things first, let's enjoy our honeymoon. Perhaps we could honeymoon in Switzerland? I would have to provide proper notice to my superiors, but I doubt it would take me long."

"Sounds so strange." Nora laughed. "Honeymoon. I didn't imagine I would ever hear those words, especially not so soon!"

"I'll have to grab some items from my house first, then we'll head to Lugano," Ezio spoke quickly as they arrived at the pier, and the two disembarked before entering the police vehicle.

"How will your parents react?" Nora asked nervously as they drove through the town.

"I tried to tell them that you weren't a real nun, but they refused to believe me." Ezio recalled the painful exchange.

"You did?" Nora frowned. "That was dangerous."

"Possibly." Ezio shrugged. "But you saw how they were with the captain. They hate the Fascists with a passion."

Yet whatever cheer Ezio was feeling suddenly vanished when they drove past a poster with the Fascist slogan: Believe! Obey! Fight! For the briefest of moments, the man in the poster took on the countenance of Flavio, the guard who had spit at their feet in defiance while repeating the very slogan.

"Are you alright?" Nora placed a gentle hand to his arm.

"Yeah, why?" Ezio snapped back to reality.

"You're swerving."

"Sorry," Ezio offered a chuckle to ease the tension. "I'm tired, is all."

Arriving back at the house, Ezio parked the vehicle and exited to find Vitelli sitting in his usual spot on his balcony, sipping some wine and smoking a cigarette.

"Signore!" Ezio tipped his hat excitedly at the old man, who seemed a little caught off guard by the lieutenant's euphoria.

"You've returned?" Vitelli asked Nora.

"Signor Milanesi's cooking is too good, Signore," Nora called back.

Opening the door to his property, Ezio walked inside to find it suspiciously quiet. The radio was playing softly, but there was no singing of an aria from Lorenzo, and no disgruntled barking from Ludovica.

"Anybody here?" Ezio called out but was met with no response.

Walking up the stairs, Ezio was almost startled to find Armando sitting on a chair in front of Ezio's parents, who were on the couch and looking distraught.

"What's wrong?" Ezio panicked when he caught the worried expression from Armando, wondering if some news had escaped of his sudden involvement in the Resistance.

"Vittoria," Lorenzo explained despairingly but offered Nora a double take when he noticed her ascending the stairs behind Ezio. "She hasn't been seen or heard from since this afternoon."

"She's likely with her friends." Ezio shook his head in confusion. "It's not even that late in the day. Why the agitation?"

"We also assumed she was with her friends until we received *that*." Ludovica pointed to the table where a letter was folded. "We used the neighbor's phone to call the station the moment we read it, but you weren't there. Fortunately for us, Armando was available to come to our aid. Some son. He's in the police force but is absent when we need him."

"What does the letter say?" Ezio asked, impatient to read it himself as he snatched it off the table.

"It states that she went to Milan." Armando looked at Ezio with regret for delivering the news as he understood the significance.

"No, that's not right." Ezio clung to denial as he skimmed the letter. "Why would she go to Milan?"

"The letter states she found some work," Lorenzo explained as he stood and came to stand beside his son as he also glanced at the letter again.

"This could be legitimate." Ezio grasped the letter tightly as he looked at Armando with a bold gaze of defiance. "She could have actually gone to Milan."

"Ezio, it's—" Armando began softly.

"Don't you dare!" Ezio pointed at Armando as he screamed. "Don't you dare finish that sentence!"

"I think it would be best if we were realistic." Armando swallowed.

"Did you tell them?" Ezio asked Armando as he pointed to his parents.

"About the other letters?" Armando asked rhetorically as he nodded.

"That's not their business to know!" Ezio grabbed Armando's shoulder tightly in a rage. "We don't know for sure what those other letters meant."

"Ezio—" Armando looked solemnly at Ezio.

"Not another word!" Ezio struggled to maintain his emotions as he rushed to his room, trailed swiftly by Nora.

Grabbing a suitcase from under his bed, Ezio began throwing clothes in hurriedly, as well as some toiletries.

"What's going on?!" Nora grabbed his arm to stop him as she began to panic.

"I can't take you to Switzerland." Ezio closed his eyes as he breathed deeply to calm himself. "I'll see if Armando can take you in my place."

"I don't understand?" Nora pulled Ezio closer as she pressed him for clarification. "What is so significant about Milan?"

"My sister is in danger." Ezio clenched his jaw as he felt a fury building within him.

"Then I'm coming with you!" Nora demanded.

"Faust—Nora," Ezio corrected himself. "We need to get you out of Italy. This may be your only chance. I would take you myself, but I can't see another sibling taken from me."

"Your fate is mine." Nora placed a gentle hand to his chest.

"That's brave of you to say, but I don't know if I can be split between you and my sister. I need to focus all my attention on her. You're safe, for now, and getting you to your father will guarantee that." Ezio held her hand lovingly.

"There is no guarantee." Nora shook her head. "For all we know, the Nazis could invade them at any time. I'd rather be with you. Besides, I can help."

"It's a husband's duty to protect his wife." Ezio looked at her repentantly. "I can't bring you with me."

"I'm not leaving your side." Nora grew defiant. "The only way I'm leaving is if you force me."

Studying her for a moment, Ezio judged if she was sincere and wondered if it would be wise to go without her.

"I'm good with a gun." Nora threw her hands onto her hips, further selling her merit for the venture.

"Let's hope it doesn't come to that."

"So, what is it about Milan that has you so concerned?" Nora asked.

"I'll explain on the way," Ezio spoke swiftly as he returned to throwing shirts and trousers into the suitcase.

"On the way?" Nora asked.

"We're going to Milan," Ezio explained as he rushed back out of the room and toward the kitchen.

"Where are you going?" Ludovica asked when she spotted Ezio's hurry.

"To find my sister!" Ezio barked as he rummaged through the pantry for some perishables.

"Do you believe that's prudent?" Armando asked softly.

"I have to do something!" Ezio shouted over his shoulder.

"Ezio," Armando continued in his soft demeanor as he approached the lieutenant and began in a hushed voice, "After what happened yesterday…"

"You can speak freely." Ezio nodded to Nora to signify she was trustworthy.

"Leaving now would look suspicious." Armando placed a hand on Ezio's arm to try and stop him. "It would look like you're running."

"I'm not leaving Vittoria alone!" Ezio gritted his teeth. "I don't know if this is some twisted killer, or if she's engaged in some untoward activity, but I'm not about to abandon her!"

"Where are you going to even start in such a big city?" Armando attempted to make Ezio see reason.

"I'll start on one street, and then go to the next, and the next, and the next, until I find her." Ezio grabbed a can of food.

"This could be misdirection." Armando pointed to the letter. "If this is some scheme, they could be trying to throw us off the scent."

"Go arrest Giuseppe," Ezio ordered as he ignored the second lieutenant's words of caution.

"Giuseppe?" Armando squinted.

"He's involved in all of this. Some way or another." Ezio moved toward the door. "Interrogate him, keep him for a week, torture him, bribe him, I don't care, just get the truth out of him."

"Ezio, you can't—"

"I'm not losing another sibling!" Ezio screamed and the room drew deathly silent.

Ezio watched as Ludovica and Lorenzo held hands while they sat on the couch, both clearly disheartened by the news, and Ezio's heart shattered for his parents. He should've listened to them when they first mentioned that Vittoria was missing, yet Ezio assumed innocently.

"I can't arrest him without a charge." Armando looked at Ezio with remorse.

"Why not?" Ezio stared back at Armando with a challenge. "They would do the same to us."

"You have to give me something," Armando pleaded.

Pausing as he tried to decide whether or not he should offer the information, Ezio advised, quietly, "He shot at us on the lake."

"Giuseppe?" Armando narrowed his gaze. "When?"

"Last night." Ezio glanced at Nora, who confirmed with a nod.

"Last night?" Armando remained unconvinced. "It was overcast last night. How did you know it was him?"

"I saw the bullet hole in his boat from when we fired back. I also saw him with a pistol earlier. He had been trying to lure Vittoria alone as well."

"Is this true?" Ludovica stood as she glared at her son. "You knew about this young man, and you did nothing? Don't tell me another one of my beautiful children's lives is at stake because of you."

"This isn't the time." Lorenzo shook his head as he defended Ezio.

"When will it be time?" Ludovica asked her husband as she glared at Ezio. "You're a curse upon this house. I wish I had never given you life."

Ezio's heart broke at his mother's condemnation. Vittoria's disappearance was disturbing enough, especially given the letter, but having his own mother offer such a cruel wish was unbearable for Ezio.

"I'll take this with me." Ezio grabbed a photograph of Vittoria and handed it to Nora to carry. "By the way, everyone, this is my wife, Nora Milanesi."

No one responded, but they all looked at Nora curiously as she was still dressed in her habit, but Armando seemed to be more confused than anyone.

"We bring you breaking news," an announcer's voice cut off the music on the radio, and Ezio's ears perked up, wondering if, by any chance, this would somehow involve Vittoria. "The Americans have landed in Sicily."

"Did he say the Americans?" Lorenzo asked.

"Most of the fortifications have fallen without so much as a single shot being fired," the announcer continued, but even behind his professional voice, Ezio discerned hints of embarrassment. "Il Duce has requisitioned reinforcements to be dispatched by the Nazis, but Hitler has yet to respond to our demands."

"The war is lost then." Armando drew a deep breath. "Maybe this will be the final blow to Mussolini."

"The war was always lost." Ezio grabbed his suitcase and began descending the stairs. "I will call the station to advise you of where we're staying. You can reach me by phone there if you hear of anything. I want a report of Giuseppe's arrest and how the interrogations are proceeding. Use every means at your disposal."

"Ezio, wait!" Armando chased him into the street and grabbed his arm to stop him.

"What?!" Ezio asked angrily.

"There's something else." Armando glanced at Nora. "We need to speak alone."

"She can hear whatever it is you have to say!" Ezio berated his subordinate.

"It's alright. I'll be in the vehicle." Nora grabbed the suitcase from Ezio and walked away.

"What is it?" Ezio demanded.

"Orders came in…" Armando didn't know how to finish the sentence.

"Spit it out!" Ezio grew annoyed.

"Orders to arrest her." Armando nodded to Nora, and Ezio's heart sank. "If I'm correct in my assumptions, that is the nun, Faustina, that the captain was so obsessed with?"

"I…how?" Ezio stared at the pavement.

"Captain Cacioppo must've sent the requisition in himself before…you know." Armando shrugged.

Looking at the vehicle with Nora sitting patiently inside, Ezio understood that they would once again have to part. If there were orders to arrest her, and Ezio ignored them, it wouldn't be long before Captain Cacioppo's replacement arrived.

"You need to take her to Switzerland." Ezio turned back to Armando.

"Me?!" Armando frowned. "I don't have the capacity."

"I'm your superior officer!" Ezio grew indignant. "And I deman—"

"There are bigger things at stake than your romantic interests!" Armando shouted at Ezio, and then continued in a harsh whisper as he drew close to the lieutenant, "I'm sorry about your sister, and I'm sorry about your new bride, I really, truly am, but we finally have a chance to bring Italy out of the Fascist shadow. Think of thousands of sisters you could be saving by adjusting your focus."

Pausing for a moment to gather his thoughts, Ezio replied, "You ask the impossible. I'm not a revolutionary. I'm not a soldier. I'm a simple man who, for the last ten years, was convinced my life was nothing more than simply surviving each day as it came." Ezio glanced back at the vehicle to see that Nora was watching them inquisitively for their hushed debate. "Yet now, I've found someone who has given me purpose. I cannot throw that away."

"You're being selfish." Armando removed his hat as he grew flustered and ran his hand through his hair.

"Maybe I am." Ezio leaned on his cane.

"I'll send a message to the station in Milan if I hear anything about your sister." Armando left Ezio and went back inside the property.

Turning to leave and rejoin Nora, Ezio was startled to find Leonarda approaching with a basket of cakes and soaps. Yet what was most surprising about the diviner was her countenance. She seemed, to Ezio, to have expected him, and was approaching him with purpose.

"You can rest easy now," Ezio spoke to Leonarda with a measure of cruelty. "Your son won't be enlisting."

"No?" Leonarda grew surprised, which Ezio counted as overwhelming evidence against her acclaimed powers.

"I'm sending Armando to arrest him." Ezio watched her carefully for her reaction.

"Arrest him?" Leonarda frowned. "For what?"

"If he's hurt my sister in any capacity, I swear to God, you'll need more than your magic to protect him." Ezio moved within inches of Leonarda's face, but was surprised when she offered no reaction.

"What have you done?" Leonarda looked at him inquisitively, and Ezio felt as though she was peering into his very soul before looking over her shoulder to inspect Nora in the vehicle.

"Stay away from her!" Ezio grabbed Leonarda's arm as he forcefully drew her attention away from Nora. "Your threats are idle now."

"Again, I ask, what have you done?" Leonarda looked intently into Ezio's eyes.

"I've done what was necessary," Ezio defended, and by the way she spoke, he assumed she already knew that the captain was dead. How she was aware was beyond him, but Leonarda, if she wasn't genuine, was, at the least, convincing.

"I fear that you've awakened a greater evil." Leonarda stared off into the distance. "You've merely cut off one head. Seven more will grow in its place. She might be safe for the time being, but an evil you cannot even begin to fathom will descend upon us."

"Ludicrous generalizations." Ezio shook his head in mockery. "Did you come here to tell my parents that you can find my sister? How much are you going to charge them for this reading?"

"Do you really believe my Giuseppe has anything to do with your sister?" Leonarda frowned.

"I think you might have some part to play as well." Ezio narrowed his gaze at her.

"Lieutenant." Leonarda chuckled. "It's been a while since you've had a decent sleep, hasn't it? Your mind is playing tricks on you. Besides, if you really thought I had some part in whatever it is you're imagining, why not arrest me?"

"You're tied to your son," Ezio spoke with a measure of menace. "You won't be far from his side which, shortly, will be the holding cells at the station."

"Harm him and there's nowhere you can run from the curse I will unleash upon you!" Leonarda pointed a finger in Ezio's face.

"If he hurt my sister, there's no curse or spell you can cast that will save him." Ezio pointed a finger back in her face. "And don't fill my parents' minds with rubbish. Tell them honestly if you don't know."

"Cake for the road?" Leonarda offered an insincere gesture as she held the small cakes up to Ezio's nose, who then smacked them onto the ground.

Without another word, Ezio brushed rudely past Leonarda and entered the vehicle to find a confused and concerned Nora.

"What was all that about?" Nora asked.

"They…" Ezio pondered if he should tell his wife about the orders to arrest her. "You're not as safe as we hoped."

Drawing a deep breath, Nora ran her hands along her thighs as she tried to calm herself.

"I meant it." Nora looked at him with worry. "When I said that our fate is tied to each other, I meant it. Where you go, I will go."

"After we find my sister, I'll take you to Switzerland." Ezio started the vehicle but felt in his heart that such a promise was made in vain.

All he wanted was to live decently with his new wife. His greatest ambition now was nothing more than raising a family. Still, he knew that such simple dreams would likely never be his to obtain. He just prayed that he could find his sister. That was his priority. Nothing else mattered until he knew that she was safe and back with his parents.

Chapter Sixteen:
Milan

"Retire me to my Milan, where every third thought shall be my grave."

William Shakespeare

Ezio gripped the steering wheel tightly as he waited for Nora outside of Signor Lehner's. Nora had urged him to allow her to change her clothing so she wouldn't draw too much attention. He argued that her nun disguise allowed her to blend in, but Nora believed otherwise, and, although an infant in marriage, Ezio was already assuming his husbandly role of reluctant agreement.

Glaring at Leonarda's shop, Ezio decided to leave the vehicle and inspect. He imagined Nora would take a moment to find some appropriate clothes that had belonged to Signor Lehner's late wife, and figured he had a minute to investigate.

Trying the door handle, Ezio was annoyed to find it locked. Looking in the window of the shop, Ezio noticed that it was deathly quiet. The lights were off, and he was certain that Giuseppe was not around. He wondered if the young man had a part to play in his sister's disappearance, or if she truly had run away to Milan and the letter was merely a ghastly coincidence.

Without breaking a window, there was no option for Ezio to inspect inside the shop, so he decided to withdraw. Returning to the vehicle, Ezio noticed that Giuseppe's boat was missing from the pier and surmised that the young man was likely on the lake.

Armando better follow through with my orders and arrest him, Ezio thought as he inspected his new cane. It was a thoughtful gesture from his mother, despite the harsh words that accompanied her gift. He wondered if his mother truly blamed him for his sister's disappearance and knew that she would only heap on insult if the worst should come to pass.

Don't think like that! Ezio shook his head as he was at once by his brothers' gravesides, watching them lowered into the earth. *She's going to be rescued. I have to believe that! I have to! She will not meet the same fate as my brothers.*

"I'm ready," Nora spoke while slightly out of breath as she returned to the vehicle. She was dressed modestly in a long navy-blue dress and a plain, white headscarf.

Yet even this modesty was a marked improvement from the puritanical nun outfit, and, despite the dire circumstances, Ezio found it difficult to think of anything besides being intimate with his new wife. While the dress was long, it still revealed a measure of skin on her leg previously hidden, causing Ezio's imagination to nosedive into thoughts of passion.

"What?" Nora frowned sharply at him.

"You..." Ezio cleared his throat. "You look nice."

"In this?" Nora scrunched up her nose in disbelief.

"Especially." Ezio returned his attention to the task at hand as he started the vehicle, but paused before he mentioned, "This is your last chance. I can take you to Switzerland. Just say the word, and I'll drive you to safety. You don't have to be involved in tracking down my sister. I'd understand, seeing as she's not your family."

"She's my family." Nora nodded adamantly. "And if you ever ask me that question again, I'll divorce you."

With a slight smirk, Ezio started the vehicle, and they drove swiftly toward the highway. While most of the roads in such remote parts of Italy were either gravel or dirt, Ezio was relieved to be driving on pavement as they headed toward Milan.

"Why is Milan so significant?" Nora asked after a moment of silence. "In the letter, I mean. You turned white when the second lieutenant mentioned the city."

"We received two other letters quite like it." Ezio glanced at her. "The others were for two women who are reportedly missing. They haven't been heard from in some time, and both sent letters to family members mentioning their move to Milan."

"Hmm." Nora pondered. "You don't believe the letters are legitimate?"

"It was Vittoria's handwriting." Ezio shrugged. "The others confirmed likewise with their own relatives."

"They haven't received any other contact since?" Nora grew intrigued.

"Nothing." Ezio shook his head. "They send a letter and then disappear."

"Why Milan, I wonder?"

"It's a large city. It would take some time to search for someone, but by then they've either been kil—" Ezio chocked, unable to finish the sentence.

"Your sister is going to be fine." Nora put a soft hand to his shoulder. "We'll find her. I'm certain she's with a stupid boy who convinced her to move to the big city with him."

"I want to believe that." Ezio looked tenderly at Nora. "But my heart says otherwise. Thankfully, we have a wider net. I'm not looking for one woman, but three."

"Find one of them, and you'll likely be able to find the others." Nora agreed.

"I need to find her…" Ezio paused as he glanced at his wife. "My parents lost their two sons, and they haven't been the same since. My mother never touched alcohol before, or even smoked for that matter. She used to be pleasant, but nearly a decade of pain has turned her bitter and spiteful."

"What about you?" Nora tilted her head as she looked deep into his eyes. "You've mentioned your parents' pain, but what about your sorrow? This can't be easy for you, either."

"It's my fault they're gone." Ezio felt a lump growing in his throat. "My father told me not to take the boat out on the lake. The waves were too choppy, but I didn't listen. How do you imagine I feel?"

"What about your father?" Nora continued. "Your mother has her vices, but what about Lorenzo?"

"He's the silent sufferer." Ezio looked out the window. "His errors are less noticeable. He doesn't condemn me, but he never defends me, either. When my mother enters her monologue of hate, he listens to the radio on the couch or sings his arias from the kitchen while he cooks. He pretends that all is well and nothing is out of the ordinary. Enough about me, what is there to know about Nora Milanesi?" Ezio looked at her with a slight smile.

"Not much to tell." Nora turned away as she shrugged her shoulders.

"That sounds intriguing." Ezio took a moment to inspect her closely with her gaze turned, again feeling a drive to experience her in every possible aspect.

"It's really not." Nora turned back to look at him, but Ezio darted his gaze away, still feeling prohibited from such licentious thoughts.

"Please." Ezio looked at her with soft eyes. "There's another two hours on the drive. I could use the distraction. I'm going insane thinking about my sister."

"We'll need some food then." Nora looked through the cans that Ezio had taken from his home.

"I don't think either of those will interest you." Ezio watched her warily.

"Fruit salad and pickled hot dogs." Nora's nose scrunched up in disgust.

"The pickled hot dogs taste about as good as they sound." Ezio twisted his lips in apology. "I just grabbed something quick."

"Did you grab anything for me?"

"The fruit salad." Ezio pointed to the can.

"No cutlery?" Nora looked quickly around the car.

"Just open the can and...you know..."

"Pour it into my mouth?" Nora studied him with incredulity. "Are you an animal?"

"I do it all the time." Ezio shrugged.

"Because you're not a woman and expected to look your best at every available occasion." Nora crossed her arms. "That spills on me, and it's never coming off."

"You're being dramatic." Ezio offered a teasing roll of his eyes.

"Dramatic?" Nora's eyes flew wide in disbelief at his boldness.

"We'll grab you some food after I stop at the police station in Milan." Ezio chuckled.

"I don't ask for much out of this marriage." Nora looked passionately at Ezio. "But you damn well better feed me more than canned fruit salad and pickled hot dogs."

"So, what's your story then?" Ezio asked before whispering, "Tell me about...Faustina."

"Nora," she corrected him.

"No one else is in the car." Ezio chuckled. "We can speak freely here."

"Someone is always watching. At least that's the line you fed to me whenever I removed that horrid veil."

"Fine, then, Nora, what is your story?"

"Not worth telling." Nora stared out the window.

"Still, I'm intrigued." Ezio watched her carefully.

"I like the way you look at me." Nora turned back to gaze at him. "If I tell you the truth, that will change."

"I doubt that." Ezio snorted.

"I wish that were so." Nora offered a little pinch on his cheek.

"Maybe get some sleep then." Ezio's smile faded as he remembered the harrowing task awaiting him in Milan.

"Are you sure?" Nora asked hopefully.

"It's another two hours or so until we're at the station." Ezio took her hand in his. "I need to strategize how I'm going to find her, and, more painfully, how I'm going to convince the detachment in Milan to assist me."

"We're here." Ezio tapped Nora gently to wake her when they arrived on the outskirts of Milan.

While he could have enjoyed the view of her sleeping forever, Ezio assumed that she would appreciate the sights of the beautiful city.

"Here?" Nora asked groggily.

"Milan."

"Oh, right!" Nora quickly sat upright and began to rub her eyes to clear them of any tiredness. "I'm sure you're used to this. You must come here often, being so close and all."

"This is my second time, actually." Ezio grew tense as they moved through the city, which was growing narrow with vehicles and people.

"Really?" Nora shot him a surprised glance. "Why?"

"This is why." Ezio pointed to a few men who walked across the street without looking over their shoulder to make sure the path was clear, a car behind Ezio honked at him for having the audacity to slow down for the jaywalkers, and a rather disgruntled old man offered him an unkind gesture for driving too close to the sidewalk.

"This bothers you?" Nora scoffed.

"Not just me!" Ezio defended. "It bothers everyone! These people are miserable. They've been crammed in together with rations that are much tighter than ours, dealing with the hustle and bustle of a big city life, having to make ends meet while they're locked in a war none of them chose."

"Well, I love it!" Nora smiled tentatively.

"You love it?" Ezio studied her with peculiarity.

"I love the pacing, the overcrowding, the city atmosphere, and the grand architecture." Nora rolled down her window and leaned her head out as she took in the sights.

"You think you know a person," Ezio teased.

"It is odd, thinking about our impulsive decision." Nora glanced at him. "I truly know next to nothing about you."

"And yet you still said yes." Ezio smiled. "I'm just that handsome."

"It can be difficult to accurately assess ourselves." Nora offered a cheeky grin. "While I married you for your character, I'm fortunate that I find you a touch handsome as well."

"Just a touch?"

"How close are we to the cathedral?" Nora shifted the subject as they drove by a large church.

"I don't believe we'll have the chance to see it, unfortunately." Ezio looked regretfully at Nora. "It's not far from the station, but I can't promise that our path will take us there."

"I would love to view it in person someday." Nora mused, and Ezio hoped that she understood his reasoning.

"If not today, then sometime soon I'll bring you back. Maybe when we have our proper honeymoon." Ezio patted her hand, yet Nora clasped onto him and wouldn't let go as she offered a faintly seductive bite of her lip.

"Focus!" Ezio shook his head and Nora chuckled.

Driving through the city, Ezio remained in his annoyance with the crowds and the hazardous drivers. Watching Nora immerse herself into the atmosphere, however, did allow Ezio a measure of adjustment to his perspective. He wished that he could see this world through her eyes and witness Milan only for its good and not for its inconveniences.

Another aspect that Ezio despised about the city was how long it took to get anywhere. In his little town, he could drive home in less than five minutes. Yet here, in Milan, he had driven for ten minutes already, and they were nowhere near the station.

"That's quite the pothole!" Nora offered Ezio a curious glance as they maneuvered around a large gouge in the pavement.

"That's not a pothole." Ezio looked at Nora with sad eyes. "Rather, it's evidence of past bombings."

"I see." Nora swallowed and glanced up at the sky.

"Don't worry, the air sirens will warn us if there is any imminent danger."

"They don't always give sufficient warning, though." Nora bit her cheek, and Ezio understood that the subject was a difficult one for her.

He wondered if she had experienced a bombing raid before but felt that he shouldn't broach the subject quite yet. Still, there was much about Nora that Ezio didn't know. He was aware that she was born in Austria, and that her home had been raided by the Nazis, but how she came to Italy was not entirely clear to him. If she didn't have documentation to leave Italy, Ezio wondered how she had entered the country in the first place.

Yet Ezio was distracted from these concerns as the further they drove through the city, the more damage became noticeable. Some buildings had entire sections missing, while others left only their frames standing. Builders were hard at work repairing the destruction or removing rubble, but surprisingly, some areas were entirely free of damage. Buildings that were erected centuries prior stood without a scratch beside other buildings that were flattened or wrecked — an embodiment of chance.

"Finally!" Ezio groaned when he parked the vehicle.

"This is the station?" Nora asked as she inspected a seven-story building.

With respect to the rest of the buildings in Milan, the station was particularly unadorned, and its plainness caused it to appear rather intimidating and imposing. An old poster of Mussolini was hanging nostalgically in a window, his face was surrounded by the word *sì* as a reminder to the public, or rather, a threat, as to who they were to vote for.

"The station isn't quite as grand as mine, I know." Ezio grabbed his cane as they stepped out of the vehicle.

"It's massive." Nora tilted her head back as she stared up at the building.

"Stay close to me." Ezio held his arm out for Nora, who accepted the gesture happily.

"You're kind to me." Nora looked at him with a measure of suspicion. "I hope you remain so."

"As long as you are by my side, I will be by yours." Ezio winked as a car sped by and honked its horn at the content couple for being too close to the road.

"I should report him!" Ezio shook his cane at the driver, who paid them no more attention.

"Leave it." Nora chuckled at her husband. "It doesn't matter."

"These people need to learn!" Ezio frowned sharply.

"You should practice stoicism, my love." Nora looked both ways down the street before they sped quickly across the road to the station. "Your emotions govern you too much."

"Me?" Ezio raised his eyebrows at her. "I've witnessed you becoming rather reactive."

"I didn't say I should practice stoicism."

"Just me?"

"Correct," Nora clarified with a grin. "What I mean is, that man honking his horn at you really didn't affect you at all, did it? The only thing that bothered you was your own reaction. Stop allowing the outside world to dictate how you will feel inwardly."

"So, I shouldn't let what happens to my sister bother me?" Ezio studied her warily.

"I meant within reason. If you weren't bothered by your sister's disappearance, then you wouldn't have reacted. My point is, in some circumstances, maybe letting things go would be suitable." Nora shrugged.

"Feels like you're rather attached to this subject." Ezio offered a cheeky wink.

"Clever." Nora remained emotionless as she opened the door for Ezio. "After you, my love."

"Another lesson in stoicism?" Ezio asked as he looked at the open door.

"Humility, actually." Nora offered a cheeky grin. "In chess, the pawns go first."

"I'm a pawn to you then, am I?" Ezio tilted his head.

"Don't worry," Nora leaned in and whispered. "If I get you to the other side of the board, I promise to make you my queen."

"Move!" a shout came from inside as a handful of officers stormed out of the station in a hurry.

Yet as the officers ran by, one of them glanced at Ezio, who, in the briefest of moments, was almost certain it was Captain Cacioppo. His heart froze as he locked eyes with the man he had witnessed passing from this life, begging for forgiveness from his wife.

Watching the officers run out of the station, the man Ezio thought was the captain glanced over his shoulder in curiosity for Ezio's gaze. Satisfied that this was merely a trick on his mind, Ezio returned his attention to Nora.

"What was that about?" Nora asked, slightly offended at the officers' rude demeanor.

"I'm not certain I want to find out." Ezio straightened out his uniform as the reality of what they were attending the station for returned swiftly to him.

Entering the station, Ezio was at once struck by the polluting noise of phones, typewriters, telegrams, and frantic shouts from officers and personnel running throughout the office in alarm. Ezio had almost forgotten how chaotic this environment was, and in an instant, he decided that his small, dark office was, in fact, a morsel of paradise.

Walking over to a large reception desk, where five receptionists were talking loudly on phones that seemed to be ringing endlessly, Ezio and Nora waited patiently to be noticed.

Yet Ezio's patience began to wane with every second that they were not addressed. In his line of work, Ezio knew how critical it was to find someone who went missing as soon as possible. Dark thoughts began to plague his mind, influenced by his memory of his brothers.

"I doubt Francesca could handle the stress of this station," Ezio spoke to Nora, trying to distract himself from his worries.

"Who?" Nora asked, half paying attention.

"The receptionist at my station. Sorry, I forgot you had yet to be introduced. She's a panicked person, to say the least, and even with our small station, she can become overwhelmed."

"Is she pretty?" Nora asked.

"I didn't imagine you were the jealous type." Ezio squinted at her.

"I'm not." Nora threw her lips upside down. "I just want you all to myself."

Ezio chuckled quickly before returning his attention to the receptionists who were still busy on the phones. Glancing at his watch, Ezio wondered how much longer they should wait.

"Allow me." Nora walked swiftly over to one of the receptionists, and, grabbing the phone, placed it back on the receiver.

"You're fortunate that wasn't an emergency!" the receptionist barked as her eyes bulged at Nora, and an officer on guard began walking toward them to inspect the disturbance.

"The lieutenant here needs your assistance." Nora pointed to Ezio. "His sister is missing. We believe she came to Milan."

"Finding anyone in Milan is difficult as it is," the receptionist spoke harshly as she remained in her offense. "Especially today of all days."

"What do you mean?" Ezio asked as he came to stand beside his wife.

"You haven't heard?!" The receptionist darted her eyes between Ezio and Nora as her phone began to ring again.

"Heard what?" Nora pressed.

"The Americans have overrun Sicily. Mussolini's government is about to collapse. They're rioting all over the south of the city. How did you not know this?" The receptionist moved to pick up the ringing phone, but Nora put her hand out to stop her.

"What do you mean Mussolini's government is collapsing?"

"I need to answer this!" the receptionist swatted Nora's hand away.

"What seems to be the problem?" the officer on guard who had been observing them interjected.

"Salve, I'm looking for my sister." Ezio scratched his neck, now feeling that his problems paled in comparison to the fate of Italy.

"Where are you from?" the officer asked as he retrieved a notepad.

"Giulino," Ezio replied, not at all convinced that this officer would follow through.

"Giulino?!" The officer shot Ezio a surprised glance. "You're familiar with Signora Setti?"

"That's one way of phrasing it." Ezio raised his eyebrows.

"My condolences to you, then." The officer looked at Ezio with a measure of disbelief. "I'm familiar with Second Lieutenant Armando, but you're clearly not him."

"Lieutenant Ezio." Ezio struck out his hand in greeting.

"Milanesi?" The officer narrowed his gaze as he took Ezio's hand.

"That's me." Ezio watched him warily, wondering if he had any news on his sister.

"We have something for you." The officer held his finger up to gesture that he would be back momentarily.

Opening the small gate beside the reception desk, the officer he began sifting through some papers.

"What did he mean by 'we'?" Ezio whispered to Nora.

"Armando mentioned you would likely be by," the officer explained loudly as he retrieved a folded-up piece of paper that he then handed to Ezio carefully.

"Is this to do with my sister then?" Ezio asked before unfolding the paper.

"Indirectly." The officer made a so-so gesture with his hand.

"Indirectly?" Ezio remained confused when he opened the paper to reveal an address. "Is this where she is?"

"Listen," the officer spoke quietly as he glanced over his shoulder before leading Ezio and Nora to the center of the room where no one was within earshot. "I heard what happened."

"Oh?" Ezio looked at the officer with a touch of distrust.

"You're a hero to us." The officer looked back at Ezio with tearful eyes.

"Us?" Ezio shook his head in confusion. *Hero?*

"Armando sent his report. There are more of us than you think." The officer tilted his head, and Ezio understood he was referring to the Resistance. "Things are now in motion to finally be rid of the plague of Fascism."

Glancing over his shoulder, Ezio checked to see if anyone was listening. Such a bold statement offered so freely and publicly was the mark of lunacy.

"Go to the address. They will help you find your sister." The officer tapped the letter before saluting proudly and walking away briskly.

In stunned silence, both Ezio and Nora offered each other a clueless glance before again inspecting the paper that the officer had handed them.

"I don't understand." Nora shook her head.

"Me neither." Ezio also shook his head. "But it looks like we'll be seeing the Cathedral after all."

"What do you mean?" Nora asked.

"This is the address."

Chapter Seventeen:
Cathedral of Deception

"Of all man's works of art, a cathedral is greatest. A vast and majestic tree is greater than that."

Henry Ward Beecher

"Does it say who you're supposed to meet?" Nora asked as they arrived at the cathedral, although Ezio noticed she could scarcely pay attention as she inspected the majestic structure.

Regrettably for Nora, however, the damage to the cathedral from previous bombing raids was rather prominent. Thankfully, the damage was minor, but still, Ezio wished she could witness its full splendor.

"Unfortunately, no." Ezio again looked at the paper. "It merely states the address."

"Let me see." Nora took the paper from him and inspected it.

"I don't even know where to begin." Ezio looked around the square in front of the cathedral that was beginning to swell with those discontented with the current state of affairs.

A small group of young men were gathering in the plaza, and some seemed rather pleased with the reports of Mussolini's weakening hold on Italy while his supporters were enthusiastically defending him.

Soldiers were amassing near the far end of the square, ready to suppress any anti-Fascist outbreaks, and Ezio spotted a squad of German Nazi soldiers among them. They wore their characteristic swastika armbands around their bleak, grey uniforms, and Ezio assumed that they had been dispatched to Italy to prepare Milan for Allied invasion. Either that or they were sent as a mere display of good faith from Hitler that he intended to support Italy.

In either case, it bothered Ezio tremendously to see them standing shoulder to shoulder with his Italian brothers in arms. He also understood the implication of what would happen should they discover that his wife was Jewish, and he found himself wishing to return home as soon as possible.

When Ezio spotted a Communist flag being held high in opposition to the other Fascist flags, Ezio knew that a violent outbreak was imminent, and that they needed to make haste before they became caught up in the raging storm.

"Shame." Nora tapped her chin as she continued to look over the paper. "It would be nice if...wait a minute...what's this?"

"What's what?" Ezio grew intrigued as he looked over her shoulder.

"There's something else written. I couldn't see it until the sunlight hit it just right." Nora tilted the paper as she tried to recreate the scenario.

"Bastardo!" Ezio cursed Armando as he looked around frantically.

"What is it?" Nora grew concerned.

"I need a match," Ezio explained.

"You're going to burn the paper?" Nora frowned. "Why? What does it say?"

"Signore?!" Ezio hailed a passing gentleman who grew concerned with the lieutenant's vibrancy.

"I'm not with them!" the man shouted as he pointed toward the group of men and began to walk briskly away.

"That's not—" Ezio stopped himself as the man was too far away.

"A match, Signore?" Ezio called to another passerby before realizing that the man was a Nazi supporter. With a quick nod, the man tossed him a small box of matches to Nora with a wink before proceeding to join the fray.

It was an odd interaction, Ezio thought. The man, who likely held similar anti-Semitic beliefs to his Nazi compatriots, had not only assisted a Jew, but even winked at her—a telling display of how illogical the Nazi hatred of the Jews really was.

Ezio quickly lit a match and, grabbing the paper from Nora, held the light close to the letters.

"What are you doing?!" Nora grabbed his arm to stop him.

"Give it a minute."

In a few seconds, the invisible became visible as words formed on the page, and Nora gasped in her surprise.

"Father Alexander," Ezio read the newly formed words aloud.

"How is that possible?" Nora asked.

"You don't want to know." Ezio cleared his throat, feeling slightly disgusted to be holding this paper with what he hoped was lemon juice.

"Do you know this priest?" Nora asked as a few men ran by them toward the plaza where battle lines were being drawn.

"I don't." Ezio shook his head as he grabbed Nora's hand. "Let's be quick about it. I don't want to be caught up in this storm when it boils over."

Moving swiftly through the swelling crowds of men who were growing bolder with defending their political leanings, Ezio and Nora drew closer to Milan Cathedral.

Glancing up at the striking columns, Ezio felt small and insignificant in the face of such imposing craftsmanship. A sense of wonder fell over Ezio as he looked up at the carved figures guarding the five large doors into the cathedral. There was such a wealth of history, culture, and knowledge embedded into the very rocks and stones which comprised this magnificent structure, and Ezio wished he had the time to explore the richness in greater detail.

At once, Ezio's breath was stolen from him when they entered the cathedral as he looked upon the splendor of the church. Large, thick columns with carved saints looking gracefully down upon the long rows of pews that faced a resplendent altar with a large crucifix extended far above. The marble floors with their intricate designs of varying flowers and shapes made Ezio feel as though he was unworthy to tread on this holy ground.

Adding to the imagery was the enchanting tune from a beautiful choir practicing a Gregorian chant, and Ezio felt as though he had stepped into paradise. The light from the stained-glass windows spilled into the cathedral, filling it with a heavenly glow as the music elevated his spirit to another dimension.

Without a word, Nora put her arm through Ezio's and leaned her head gently against his shoulder as the two stood in awe. Ezio never knew that his heart could feel this full after enduring such hardship, but in this cathedral, Ezio felt as if his brothers were also standing right beside him. All the sorrows of this world felt so trivial as he listened to the angelic music among the imposing yet inviting architecture.

"Blessed are those who mourn," a voice spoke from behind them, and Ezio turned to see a priest with a thick, red beard and curly red hair watching them closely.

He seemed, to Ezio, to be rather kind and have a soft expression. He was a little shorter than average yet carried himself with confidence in his poise with his hands held firmly behind his back and his chest puffed a small measure.

"For they shall be comforted," Nora finished the quote, and Ezio again wondered if she still clung to her feigned religious convictions.

"Lieutenant Ezio, I presume?" The priest struck out his hand in greeting.

"Father Alexander?" Ezio asked, and the priest nodded.

"I've been expecting you. Come with me, we have much to discuss." The priest nodded for them to follow him.

"We do?" Ezio asked as he remained in place, still not entirely sure what business this priest had with respect to his sister.

"Armando didn't fill you in, I see." The priest stopped when he realized they weren't following him.

"I'm in Milan on behalf of my sister." Ezio retrieved a photograph of her and held it out to the priest.

"She doesn't look familiar." Father Alexander took the photo and inspected it quickly.

"Armando didn't mention her?" Ezio asked, still confused about the priest's involvement.

"What's her name?" Father Alexander handed the photo back to Ezio.

"Vittoria. Vittoria Milanesi."

"Milanesi?" the priest asked with a twinge of excitement.

"You've heard of her?" Ezio grew hopeful.

"No, sorry, but the name is interesting. Your family is from Milan, then?"

"A few generations ago, our family emigrated." Ezio placed the photo back in his breast pocket. "I don't mean to be rude, but if you haven't heard of her, then I must beg your leave. I need to find her."

"She's missing?" the priest asked with a slight frown.

"Yes, and there's a chance she's somewhere in the city. I went to the station, and that's when I was provided with your address and your name," Ezio explained, although he wondered if he was wasting his breath. "I was hoping that meant you could help me."

"Indirectly." Father Alexander glanced between the two of them.

"Indirectly?" Ezio shook his head as he grew annoyed. "I've heard that before. What do mean by it?"

"Come with me." The priest again nodded for them to follow.

With a reluctant glance at Nora, the two began to follow the priest, who remained a few steps ahead of them.

As they walked through the church, Ezio spotted a couple construction workers climbing a scaffold under an arch between two pillars.

"Would you believe that we're still under construction?" Father Alexander asked over his shoulder.

"They're not repairing damages?" Ezio asked as he inspected the work.

"They're balancing their duties between repairing and building anew." Father Alexander also glanced up at the men. "Construction of the cathedral began in 1386, and, who knows, maybe I'll live long enough to finally see it completed. Napoleon was crowned King of Italy here, you know?"

"Is that right?" Ezio's interest was piqued.

"Maybe someday we'll have the chance to discuss the rich history of this cathedral." Father Alexander looked throughout the church with a gaze of admiration.

"I would love that," Ezio replied, still unsure if he should trust this priest. For all Ezio knew, Father Alexander was in the pocket of the Fascists, and he was being led, willingly, into a trap.

"Just through here." The priest dug out a large, medieval-looking key from his pocket and placed it to the keyhole of a dark brown door with iron plates across it for extra support.

Opening the door to a dark and windowless hallway, Father Alexander held his hand out to Ezio and Nora, who both glanced at each other in uncertainty. Ezio believed that his wife shared the same suspicions of Father Alexander that he did, and looking down the dark hallway, Ezio imagined secret police officers waiting to grab him.

"After you," Ezio insisted.

"As you wish." Father Alexander nodded and passed through the door, where he waited with his hand on the door handle.

Armando did give us his name, Ezio convinced himself that it was acceptable to trust Father Alexander, and, with a quick nod to Nora, walked into the hallway.

"I just have to lock the door," Father Alexander explained as he closed it behind them, and Ezio nearly startled when the sound of the lock echoed throughout the hallway.

But then, as Ezio's eyes adjusted to the dark, he noticed a faint light coming from a room near the end of the hallway.

"Almost there," Father Alexander placed a gentle hand to Ezio's shoulder as he walked by them and toward the light that Ezio had spotted.

Following the priest, Ezio and Nora came to a small, windowless room that was dimly lit with candles on a little chandelier over a round table.

Sitting at this round table were three men who all seemed, to Ezio, to be quite dejected and depressed. In the middle of the table was a map of northern Italy spread about it, and the men seemed to be studying it like treasure seekers searching for some sort of clue.

While Ezio would've found this sight curious enough on its own merit, he was distracted by two women standing over a small table in the corner of the room littered with rifles, pistols, grenades, mines, knives, and an array of melee and missile weapons.

One of the women was showing the other how to clean and reload a rifle, and Ezio found it curious that she wore a uniform as well. She seemed, to him, to be military, and he wondered what on earth she was doing in a dark room in the back of the cathedral showing a laywoman how to use this weaponry. Then again, he feared that he already knew the answer.

More damning of this little company's allegiances was a picture of Mussolini hanging on the wall that had tears and scratches near bullseyes that were drawn around his eyes and in the middle of his forehead.

It was a peculiar impression indeed, and Ezio knew that he was in an extremely dangerous room. They were likely involved with the Resistance, and Ezio knew it would be best if he simply turned around and left. Still, his curiosity drew him in, and he would endure any threat to his life if it meant he had the chance to locate Vittoria.

"What's this?!" one of the men asked angrily as he stood quickly when he finally noticed Ezio and Nora behind Father Alexander.

The military woman immediately stopped her demonstration and withdrew her pistol, pointing it at Ezio.

"They are here on my request." Father Alexander raised his hands to calm everyone down.

"And who the hell are they?" another man demanded.

"They are our hope." Father Alexander smiled brightly as he turned toward Ezio and Nora, who both looked at each other in confusion, wondering if they had faulty information.

"I don't understand?" Ezio looked about the room.

"This is Walter." The priest pointed to a middle-aged man with a thin mustache. He was plainly dressed and seemed rather uninteresting to Ezio. "He's part of the Communist Party and is actively establishing guerilla groups."

"Next, we have Alessandro." The priest pointed to another man who was smoking a pipe and seemed wary. "For his activism against Fascism, he spent eight years in prison."

"Finally, we have —"

"With all due respect, Padre," Ezio interrupted. "What does any of this have to do with my sister?"

"This is Palmiro," Father Alexander continued as he pointed to the man who had taken issue with their presence when they first arrived. He was an older man with large glasses and a somewhat soft expression. "He was in exile since 1920 and has an extensive underground network. If anyone, he can help find your sister."

"I see." Ezio cleared his throat.

"We don't have time to find anyone right now." Palmiro frowned at the priest. "And you still haven't explained what the hell they're here for!"

"These men," the priest turned to Ezio as he explained while ignoring Palmiro, "are all partisans who seek to rid the country of Fascism in all its forms."

"Listen," Ezio rubbed his eyes. He didn't know how much more of this he could stand. "I—"

"Take a seat, and we'll discuss your sister." The priest dragged two chairs over to the table and gestured for Ezio and Nora to sit.

"Maybe she wants to help us?" the military woman asked. "Also, I note that you introduced the men and forgot to introduce us."

"This is Carla." Father Alexander held his hand out to excuse Nora if she so preferred, but Ezio took note that he didn't bother to list Carla's achievements or her involvement with the partisans.

"I'm good with a gun," Nora spoke proudly to the women as she swiftly left Ezio.

"The men can sit and talk. Action is for women." Carla offered a sharp look to the priest, who, Ezio noticed, seemed rather familiar with her antics.

"Would someone explain what the hell this is all about?!" Alessandro barked as he lit another match for his pipe that had burned out.

"We have more important matters than babysitting this lieutenant's sister," Walter leaned forward in his chair as he spoke softly, not wishing to be too rude to the newcomers.

"Lieutenant Ezio, where are you from?" The priest smiled proudly, relishing in the point he was about to make.

"Giulino." Ezio scratched the back of his neck, still unsure as to the intention of his presence, and his mind dwelled on his sister.

"That's on Lake Como." Alessandro frowned as he studied the map.

"That's in the north." Father Alexander drove home the purpose of Ezio's involvement.

"You can help us navigate?" Palmiro studied Ezio cautiously.

"He's also, currently, the highest-ranking officer in his district. He can silence or divert any attention from headquarters," Father Alexander spoke to the other men as if Ezio wasn't even in the room. "He's an invaluable asset. We all know the great work that Armando has achieved. Imagine if we have another officer just as dedicated to the cause."

"I don't know what you're scheming." Ezio stood as this traitorous rendezvous filled him with dread. "I won't say a word of what I've seen today, but I won't have any part of it."

"Why have you brought him here?!" Walter looked angrily at Father Alexander. "You've placed all our lives in jeopardy by exposing our plots to him."

"Ezio, you have more reason than any of us here to hate the Fascists." Father Alexander pressed.

"Has he spent the last twenty years in exile as well?" Palmiro scoffed.

"His wife is of the tribe." Father Alexander looked at Nora, and the men around the table understood his meaning and offered Ezio a sympathetic gaze. "The

Fascists in our own land are brutal enough to Jews, but they pale in comparison to the barbarity of the Nazis."

"Even so." Ezio shook his head. "I'm not seeking revolution. I simply want to find my sister, then settle down and have a family."

"It's a noble ambition." Palmiro threw his lips upside down. "But without revolution, you will forever live in fear."

"We're not asking you to do anything…yet," Father Alexander spoke softly.

"Yet?" Ezio held his conclusion in reserve.

"We believe that if Italy surrenders, the Nazis will swiftly invade," Father Alexander continued. "Milan is Mussolini's headquarters. The battle to end Fascism starts here, but the north is key to keeping the Nazis at bay."

"Why the hell are we even bothering with this man!" Alessandro barked as he pointed at Ezio. "He clearly has reservations. Not that I blame him, but we need someone who won't buckle under the pressure."

"Are you not with us?" Walter asked Ezio warily.

"You're all part of Armando's resistance then?" Ezio asked.

The room erupted into laughter, but none greater than the women as they looked at Ezio with a touch of disdain.

"Did he tell you this was his movement?" Palmiro chuckled. "Stupido."

"To answer your question, I'm guilty by association." Ezio recalled Armando's heroics that saved his life. "But I don't care. I need to find Vittoria. If you can help me locate my sister, then I will play a part in your Resistance, but not a moment sooner."

"What about the thousands of sisters, daughters, and mothers who are about to be endangered?!" Palmiro griped. "The threat from the north is real. Our intelligence suggests that the Nazis plan to invade if Italy surrenders."

"They're our allies." Ezio frowned. "There's a squad of Nazi soldiers in the plaza before the cathedral as we speak."

"But only until Italy remains in the war. We all know Hitler has no affinity for Mussolini apart from how he can use his favorite puppet," Father Alexander explained. "The Americans and their allies are taking the south swiftly, and Hitler will not accept that his southern flank is exposed. We need to be prepared and do our part to ensure that if, God willing, Fascism collapses in Italy, Nazism does not gain a foothold. We'd only be bringing upon ourselves a greater evil."

Leonarda feared the same, Ezio recalled the soap maker's prophecy about cutting off one head and seven more will grow in its place. Still, he doubted that his actions with the captain had any part to play in global politics.

"The Nazis have been amassing soldiers near the border." Walter pointed to the location on the map as he added to Father Alexander's point. "Mussolini's government is weakening by the day. They're ready to conquer, and we must be ready to defend."

"Mussolini requested reinforcements to combat the Americans." Ezio shrugged. "There's nothing out of the ordinary for that."

"Yet why haven't they come?" Alessandro took a puff of his pipe.

"They're preparing their strategy." Ezio scratched his chin. "It takes time to—"

"They have their strategy! It's called blitzkrieg!" Walter pounded his fist on the table. "We saw it in France, Poland, and everywhere else that has been subjected to German tyranny. Waiting is not part of their strategy."

"You know we're right," Father Alexander spoke tenderly.

Ezio's shoulders slumped in disbelief when he realized the impending danger. The Fascists in his own country were cruel enough, but the Nazis were another level of depravity. At least, from the stories he'd heard.

"And we need to be ready," Nora interjected, and Ezio glanced over at her with marvel as she appeared all too comfortable with a rifle slung over her shoulder.

In that moment, Ezio understood there was nothing he could say or do that would persuade her otherwise. Besides, she of all people had experienced Nazi brutality firsthand. Nora looked fierce, determined, angry, and Ezio wondered how far she would be willing to take her revenge.

"I'm not a fighter." Ezio shook his head before turning his attention to the priest. "I'm surprised you, of all people, would be advocating for violence."

"Another reason why you're here." Father Alexander smiled softly. "I need someone to caution against violence. My reasoning for pacifism is rather biased, but with you, they'll listen to your calculated approach. Besides, none of these men here are fighters. Palmiro and Alessandro are all part of the Communist Party seeking to gain more members. Their war lies not with flesh and blood but with party members and due process. Walter runs an illegal radio that attempts to persuade others to join against Fascism. Carla here is the only one, actually, who is actively arming citizens—I've made clear my reservations on the matter."

"With all due respect, Father, Communism isn't without its own sins." Ezio looked briefly at the men, hoping to not offend. "I'm surprised to find you in their camp."

"You misunderstand me." Father Alexander folded his hands. "'My kingdom is not of this world,' as Christ spoke to Pilate. I'm not concerned with the temporary political landscape, but rather, men's eternal souls. These men here seek elected representation. I may disagree with their politics, but I support their right to free assembly."

Glancing around the table at the three men, the priest, and then the women with Nora, Ezio felt an entirely unexpected burden placed upon his shoulders. He was a simple man whose greatest ambition was raising a family with Nora, yet now he was being asked to counsel in matters of rebellion.

"Why me?" Ezio scoffed.

"That's what I'd like to know." Alessandro leaned forward as he watched the priest intently for his answer.

"Because you're a good man, Ezio." Father Alexander folded his hands. "And in these trying times, good men are a disappearing commodity."

"That's his qualification?" Walter threw his hand out in disbelief.

"You don't even know me." Ezio laughed, agreeing with Walter and feeling that this whole venture was traveling down a ridiculous path.

"Do you remember a man named Flavio?" The priest tilted his head, and at once, Ezio was at the roadside where the guard had been gunned down in cold blood by Matteo.

"I do." Ezio swallowed.

"You tried to save him. He spit at your feet, but still you, didn't want to 'become like them'." Father Alexander looked knowingly at Ezio. "Armando provided me with a full report, but I want to hear from your own lips why you tried to save a man who would not show you the same clemency."

The room grew silent as everyone watched the lieutenant closely, wondering how he would respond. The women held their guns at the ready, the men smoked as they glared at Ezio, and the priest leaned in as he struggled to contain himself.

"We have to be better." Ezio stared at the table. "I've known this tyranny for most of my life. I've grown up under the shadow of Mussolini. I've witnessed neighbors turning neighbors into the secret police over petty grievances. I've seen the phony cheering at Fascist rallies for fear of being taken away by the secret police. They operate on hate. They believe their opponents are sub-human and use pseudoscience to support their ridiculous claims. Everything that is beautiful about Italy is no longer permitted. We cannot allow ourselves to fall to the Fascist level of depravity, degeneracy, and cruelty. Otherwise, we'll only replace tyranny with more tyranny. We need to build our house on a solid foundation, and I believe that reconciliation is possible."

"Then you should realize, young man..." Alessandro puffed his pipe, "that there is no longer impartial ground. The fate of Italy lies in our hands. If you are not with us, then you are against us."

"My sister comes first," Ezio replied swiftly, and Walter threw his hand in the air in annoyance.

"We'll assign a team to locate your sister." Palmiro crossed his arms. "How many men do you want?"

"Thirty." Ezio nodded.

"Thirty men?!" Walter choked on the spit caught in his throat.

"We can't spare thirty." Palmiro shook his head.

"Twenty, then." Ezio bargained.

"Ten."

Ezio sighed as he felt his shoulders tightening.

"Surely ten is better than one." Palmiro shrugged. "It's either you're looking through the city by yourself, or we can send ten men for you."

"What do you need from me?" Ezio rubbed his forehead in frustration.

"Subterfuge, sabotage, espionage, and diversion." Walter folded his hands as he leaned forward. "We can oversee Milan, but the north is unfamiliar to us."

"Be ready at any given moment." Alessandro pointed the butt end of his pipe at Ezio. "When we call upon you, you must act."

"The ambiguity of that command is concerning." Ezio crossed his arms.

"No one will force you to do anything you're uncomfortable with." Father Alexander placed his hand gently on the table. "In fact —"

"Nonsense!" Palmiro barked. "He's either in or out. No half measures!"

"What's that noise?!" Nora asked loudly as she held up a hand to silence everyone.

"I don't hear anything?" Father Alexander turned his ear.

Ezio, too, strained his ear before looking at Nora, wondering if she had merely imagined it.

"As I was saying..." Father Alexander began again. "The —"

A small thud.

Glancing around the table, Ezio and the others inspected to see if anything had fallen onto the floor.

Another thud, followed quickly by yet another.

Glancing around the table, Ezio grew confused as to the cause of the sound. The other men and women, too, looked at each other with curious glances.

Then, starting slow, but building with intensity, the air raid sirens began to squeal their warning, piercing Ezio's very soul.

"Follow me to the shelter!" Father Alexander stood and rushed over to the door, swinging it open and waving for everyone to follow.

At once, Ezio jumped up from the table and grabbed Nora's hand as they began trailing the company through the church. Yet Ezio's leg caused them to fall behind, and Nora wrapped her arm through his in an attempt to help speed him along.

The thuds grew louder and more prominent as dust shook from the rafters and pillars. The once beautiful choir was now an unharmonized frenzy of chaos as they scattered to the nearest exits. Everyone was aware of what it meant to be trapped inside this cathedral should one of the bombs dislodge its structural integrity.

Thud! Boom! Crack! The bombs grew louder and closer, and Ezio could now hear the buzzing of the bomber's engines and knew that at any moment, a bomb would come crashing through the church ceiling. The sound became deafening as Ezio and Nora followed loosely behind Father Alexander and the Resistance members.

"I'm holding you back!" Ezio shouted over the noise.

"What?!" Nora shouted back.

"I'm slowing you down! Go! I'll catch up!"

"Our fates are tied together! Whatever happens to you, happens to me!" Nora looked at him sternly, signaling that she would not accept another word on the subject.

Bursting out the doors of the cathedral, Ezio's spirit was filled with dread when he looked up at the sky to see it littered with planes. The bombs released indiscriminately from the sea of aircraft grew larger as they fell to the earth, and the ear-piercing whistle they released was horrific.

What Ezio hated most was the injustice. These planes weren't bombing military sites or training barracks. They were targeting civilians, cultural areas, and historical sites that had no part to play in the war. There was nothing that these mothers, daughters, fathers, sons, brothers, sisters, aunts, uncles, nieces, and nephews could do to fight back. They were helpless and entirely at the mercy of chance.

"Let's go!" Nora grabbed Ezio's hand, and they continued to chase after Father Alexander, hoping that the shelter was close by.

Boom!

A bomb exploded about ten yards behind Ezio, right where he had been standing only moments ago.

Crack!

Another bomb struck a statue of Caesar, obliterating it into thousands of pieces, replacing it with a shroud of earth and shrapnel.

Bang!

A bomb landed squarely on top of a mother with her two children, wiping away any trace of their existence, and Ezio froze in place, disturbed by what he had just witnessed.

"We have to keep moving!" Nora screamed as she grabbed Ezio's arm, and they continued onward without another consideration for the poor family.

"Help!" a man shouted as Ezio hobbled by, and he glanced at the man to see that the lower half of his leg had been torn to shreds.

"Ah!" A woman screamed as she tried in vain to remove the shrapnel from her eye while running aimlessly to rid herself of the pain.

Crash!

An entire house crumbled in on itself as the screams from those trapped inside tore at Ezio's heart.

"Go to hell!" a police officer screamed as he aimed his rifle at the sky, firing off round after hopeless round in wrath. Ezio knew as well as the officer that the bullets from his rifle were inadequate to impede the planes, but the tears from the policeman's eyes signified to Ezio that he had lost someone dear to him.

"Over here!" Father Alexander called loudly to anyone who could hear and began waving his arms wildly.

Ezio noticed that the priest was standing beside a small stone stairwell that led to an underground tunnel below a road. Swiftly rushing by the priest, Ezio and Nora began descending the stairs that were now packed tightly with those in a panic to find safety.

"Move!" Ezio shouted to those in front before glancing above him. If a bomb landed on the stairs, dozens would be dead within seconds.

"We're stuck! The door won't open!" a shout returned from near the front.

Suddenly, more people began packing in behind Ezio, and they, in turn, were pushed from those behind them, crushing him and Nora in the middle of the crowd.

The eerie whistles of death above continued, the thunderous crashing with the earth sent shockwaves through the ground, and the crushing of bodies pressing against Ezio convinced him that this was how he was to meet his end.

"Vittoria!" Ezio shouted to Heaven.

Even in such desperation, his mind dwelled on the safety of his sister. He thought of his mother and wondered if she would weep when she read of his death. If he could've found Vittoria, then maybe, perhaps, Ludovica would love him again as a mother should love her son.

Yet, oddly enough, Ezio's mind also dwelled on the captain. He remembered the horrid man's screams for forgiveness from his wife before Armando's bullet silenced him.

"We're through!" the saving call came from the front of the line, and within seconds, the crowd was able to surge forward into the shelter.

Rushing inside, Ezio immediately regretted his decision. The shelter, if he would dare to call it that, was a cemented room that was maybe six hundred square feet. In the center of the room were four wooden posts that supported the ceiling, and Ezio knew that they would do nothing against the mass of a bomb.

Still, even if Ezio wanted to retreat, there was no option as the crowd was packed too tightly and the entrance was entirely blocked by their continuous pouring into the shelter.

"Over here." Nora grabbed Ezio's hand and led him to a corner of the shelter where they both sat.

Trying to catch his breath, Ezio glanced over at Nora and shook his head, lost for words. Nora, too, shocked into speechlessness, grabbed onto Ezio's hand, and the two sat under the cover of the shelter as the bombers showed no clemency and continued their strike. The civilians continued to pack inside the small shelter, hoping to escape a terrible death and mourning the loss of their loved ones who died so needlessly in a war that they held no part in.

Shaking in fear and unable to rid himself of the terrible sights he had witnessed only moments ago, Ezio leaned his head on Nora's shoulder and closed his eyes, wishing with all his heart that Vittoria would escape this tragedy.

Chapter Eighteen:
Surrender

"And those who were dancing were thought to be insane by those who could not hear the music."

Friedrich Nietzsche

"Sounds like the bombing has stopped." Ezio sat upright as he strained to listen in the dark.

It was now in the evening, although Ezio was unaware of the exact time, but there was some issue with the power, and Father Alexander was unable to get the lights working. The only illumination afforded to them was from a slit under the metal doors.

The bomb shelter was packed, and likely overcapacity, with people who were tired, hungry, and grieving. They mourned for their loved ones, for their city, for their nation, and mourned with the wretched understanding that nothing they could do would right the wrongs.

"The bombing never stops," Nora replied as she leaned forward and rested her elbows on her knees. "The next group of bombers will begin at night. If they can't kill everyone, they can at least keep us awake. They'll weaken us through a war of exhaustion."

"This isn't your first experience with a raid, is it?" Ezio asked as he watched her closely.

"Vienna." Nora scratched the back of her neck, and Ezio knew that she was uncomfortable. "The Soviets showed no restraint."

"I understand." Ezio nodded, realizing she didn't want to discuss it further. "If you don't—"

"I need you to understand something." Nora turned toward him sharply, and Ezio was surprised by her insistence.

"Go on." Ezio waited anxiously.

"You can't ask me about my past." Nora looked at the cement floor. "That woman is gone. I'm Nora Milanesi now. My past is dead and buried, and I can't allow you to resurrect it. Please, for your safety, don't ask me again."

Watching her for a moment, Ezio judged if he should, indeed, keep her request. It was odd, at the least, and he wished that she trusted him enough to explain. Then again, if the position was reversed and her safety would be at risk, he would request the same of her.

With a nod, Ezio accepted her conditions.

"I do have to say…" Nora paused as she offered a slight grin. "As far as honeymoons go, I did expect a little better."

"Women these days with their unreasonable expectations." Ezio smiled back at her, and in the dim light, his eyes were once again drawn to her lips, her soft jawline, and her gentle neck.

"You can't look at me like that." Nora tilted her head toward him as she studied his lips.

Ezio was about to lean in for a kiss when he noticed black robes walking in their direction and knew that Father Alexander wished to discuss something with them. How Ezio wished to have this shelter alone with his new wife, and begged God in Heaven to at least allow him one moment with Nora before his life was cut short.

"Are you two alright?" Father Alexander knelt in front of Ezio and Nora, and Ezio noticed that the priest's hand was wrapped in a bloodied rag.

"It's nothing," Father Alexander explained as he pointed to his hand. "I'm much more fortunate than many others were."

"Is that you, Father?" asked an old man, leaning against one of the wooden beams supporting the roof. He was trembling and looked to be taking shallow breaths, but in the darkness, it was hard to discern if he was wounded or merely in shock.

"Si." Father Alexander turned to the old man.

"I think I'm dying. Can you hear my confession?" the old man asked with a shaky voice.

"You're not dying, Signore," the priest replied softly. "You've experienced something dreadful, and your soul is having difficulty comprehending it."

"Why would they do this to us, Father?" another man asked, and Ezio noticed that he was quite young, possibly younger than himself, but again, in the dark, it was difficult to determine. "Why would God allow it?"

Father Alexander paused for a moment as he stared at the concrete floor before replying loudly so that all within earshot could hear him, "I've struggled with 'why' for many years. As some of you know, I had a family once. I moved to Italy from Scotland when I was but a wee lad, as they would say back home. I found a beautiful Italian woman, and we settled and raised a family. Two boys and a girl. I was working out in the field, helping a neighbor with the harvest, when an earthquake struck. My family was in the home when it collapsed, and they all perished instantly."

A couple of gasps and a few clicking of tongues could be heard throughout the shelter as they listened to the priest.

"For decades after that tragic event, I asked 'why'." Father Alexander stood and looked about the shelter as best as he was able. "One answer is that creation, and us as humans, have fallen from grace. We require redemption, that much is true, but it doesn't answer why God would allow it. But the more I pondered the question of 'why', I realized something."

"What's that, Father?" the old man asked.

"I think 'why' is the wrong question. Why doesn't change what happened, why doesn't make it any easier when I think about what my boys and my girl could've become, and 'why' won't bring my wife back to me. What does matter, however, is how we respond." Father Alexander paused as he choked. "I'm ashamed to say I responded rather poorly at the time. I allowed the tragedy to cleave my soul in two. I hated everyone, especially those who were happy, and I rendered a sword between my parents and myself in a way that will likely never heal."

The room grew quiet as they waited for the priest to continue. They needed to hear his words of hope and courage, and even Ezio listened intently.

"But one day, I heard a man on a street corner reciting Dante's *Inferno* from memory, and listening to these beautiful passages, I realized something rather tragic."

"What's that?" The old man asked.

"I was already in Hell. Namely, a hell of my own making. The man was reciting the canto pertaining to the fifth circle of Hell. Does anyone remember what punishment awaited sinners in this circle?" Father Alexander looked about the room.

"Wrathfulness," Nora replied, and the priest nodded as Ezio again found her knowledge of religious instruction to be without depth.

"In this fifth circle, Dante sees men fighting with one another in front of a muddy river and gnashing their teeth in hatred." Father Alexander stared at the ceiling as he recalled. "But then something happens in the canto that forever changed my life. Virgil asks Dante about the other souls in this circle. Confused, Dante looks around, but only sees these men. Virgil explains that there is another group, but that they're trapped in the river, forever doomed to suffocate in the muddy waters.

"I saw myself in this canto, suffocating in a muddy river of my own sullenness. I saw my own anger, tearing at anyone who dared come near me. I could've chosen to be thankful for having such beautiful children and such an admirable woman in my life, I could've accepted the love shown to me by my parents, and I could've sought out God's peace that surpasses all understanding long ago. So, please, learn from me. Choose love, and don't condemn yourself to a hell of your own making. Blessed are those who mourn, for they will be comforted."

"Cazzo!" a man cursed at Father Alexander through gritted teeth. "I lost my wife too. I'll kill everyone one of those Americans."

"They were British," someone corrected.

"I don't care!" the grieving man screamed. "I'll kill them all! If I'm going to Hell, then I'll drag them all down with me."

"My son, you're already there," Father Alexander spoke softly. "I can't pull you out of this mirey pit, only God can do that, but I can guide you if you only but extend your hand."

"Vaffanculo!" the man swore again and spit at the priest's feet.

"Your wife is with God and his angels. Bear this tribulation with honor, and you will be rejoined to her," Father Alexander spoke with a measure of tact that Ezio knew he himself would never be able to summon before leaving the man alone.

"We're having a meeting." Father Alexander again knelt in front of Ezio and Nora.

"Now?" Ezio frowned as he looked behind the priest at the grieving man who was now weeping.

"You have something better to do?" Father Alexander also looked back at the man, and Ezio noticed the priest's gaze was full of empathy.

"This is our honeymoon." Nora shrugged as she offered a response.

Darting a surprised look between the two of them, the priest seemed to be judging if they were sincere.

"We were married earlier today, if you can believe it." Ezio looked at Nora with an ironic chuckle before explaining, "We found out my sister was missing after the ceremony and came straight to Milan."

"You have your priorities straight," Father Alexander spoke to Ezio as he looked at Nora with understanding that few men would be able to divert their attention from her. "Come with me. The others are waiting, and they'll likely be unhappy I took the time to offer a small sermon."

Following the priest in the dark, and careful not to dig his cane into anyone's feet, Ezio noticed that the three men and the woman from the room in the cathedral were huddled around a flimsily, circular table. The table was likely one that was taken from a bar or a pub, and Ezio noticed that there was barely enough room for two people, let alone the seven that now crowded it.

As Ezio grew closer to the table, he realized that it was piled high with thin navy-blue blankets, rigid white pillows, and a handful of canned food.

"You should've stocked the shelter with more supplies," Walter griped to Father Alexander.

"We used almost all the provisions from the last raid," Father Alexander explained. "Besides, this bombing run will be over by the morning, God willing."

"There's nowhere to properly use the facilities." Alessandro took his turn complaining.

"There's a spot in that corner." Carla pointed, and Ezio looked to see a couple wooden crates sectioning off a small hole.

"As I said, there's no proper place to —"

"We should focus," Palmiro interjected before the discussion took a direction that no one would appreciate.

"Agreed." Father Alexander nodded.

"I still don't know why we're trusting them." Alessandro narrowed his gaze at Ezio and Nora.

"You can trust them to hand out pillows." Father Alexander groaned at the mistrust as he began piling up the blankets and pillows before handing them to Ezio.

"This is the meeting?" Ezio frowned.

"Part of the pacifist approach." Walter looked at Ezio with a touch of admiration.

A small thud.

The shelter slowly drew quiet as everyone waited for another one to land, wondering if, or when, a bomb would smash through the ceiling.

"Our approach is simple, but it will take coordination and it will test all our resolve," Father Alexander continued, ignoring the imminent threat of a nightly bombing raid.

Another thud, followed quickly by another, and a gasp or two escaped from those still in shock from the earlier bombing run.

"We shouldn't speak so freely," Alessandro whispered. "And what business is it of yours to be preaching such bleakness as Dante's inferno? You should be telling them that everything is going to be fine. Peace and understanding and all that nonsense."

"I happen to believe that we are meant to suffer," Father Alexander replied curtly, and Ezio was a little surprised by the priest's demeanor, and, not to mention, his rhetoric. "I'm sorry to say it, and I know this isn't what everyone would like to hear at the moment, but it's the truth. You think that an easy life without tribulation is our right? On what grounds? Unless a seed falls into the earth and dies, it remains nothing more than a seed. But because of the death and suffering the seed bears, it produces many more seeds. I promise you this: the suffering we're enduring now is bitter indeed, but it will produce a better Italy, and a better world."

Ezio watched the priest, mesmerized. He hadn't witnessed this Scotsman's fervor before and was happy to learn how committed he was to this cause which, in turn, made Ezio wonder if he should reexamine his own priorities.

"Faith without works is dead," Walter spoke after a moment. "And words without action are meaningless."

"How right you are." Father Alexander drew a deep breath. "Then if not words, we can at least take action.

Ezio and Nora, will you assist me in handing out the blankets? Carla, can you see if anyone has brought food with them? Alessandro and Walter, you two look into the radio and see if you can find a signal. Palmiro, see if you can fix the broken light. Everyone clear?"

With some grunts and nods, the company took to their assignments, and Ezio, still not sure how he fit into this Resistance, began handing out blankets.

"Grazie, Signore!" an older woman clutched onto her blanket and pillow with a strong grip.

"Is this it?" another man complained when he felt how thin the blankets were.

"Do you think you two can share?" Ezio asked a pair of small children huddled together against their father, and they nodded in their agreement.

Then, Ezio came across a soldier who was sitting alone with his back against the post in the middle of the room. Ezio was about to hand him the blanket when he suddenly stopped. On the man's arm was the band of a Swastika, and Ezio understood that he was likely a Nazi soldier who had become separated from his troop during the raid.

The man looked up at Ezio with a vacant expression before holding out his hand to receive a blanket. Yet Ezio was almost frozen in place. He wanted to see the human behind the uniform, but Ezio loathed the Nazis, especially with their cruelty toward people like Nora.

"Do you speak Italian?" Ezio asked.

The man lowered his gaze, not understanding Ezio.

"Or do you speak German?" Ezio asked in broken German. His understanding of the language was poor, at best, but living in northern Italy did provide the benefit of learning a few phrases here and there.

The man shot Ezio a peculiar gaze before replying in German, "Yes."

"What is your name?" Ezio continued in German, almost depleting his entire comprehension of the language.

"Hans."

"Where are…" Ezio struggled to find the word. "The rest?"

Hans frowned with a lack of understanding.

"The rest." Ezio pointed to the man's armband.

Hans shook his head in such a way as to signify that he didn't know.

Either way, Ezio decided to heed Father Alexander's instructions and handed a blanket and pillow to the soldier.

Ezio continued to hand out blankets and pillows then returned to their little 'headquarters' to grab more before proceeding to hand out the remaining supply, which, unfortunately, fell bitterly short of reaching everyone in the shelter. Finally, when there were no more left, Ezio returned to the corner of the room where he and Nora had first arrived and sat on the floor as he waited for her.

"That's all of them," Nora spoke quietly as she returned to Ezio with a pillow and blanket, but then asked in surprise, "You didn't keep a set for yourself?"

"I didn't think of it." Ezio rubbed his tired eyes.

"That's alright. You can share mine." Nora lay on the floor and patted the spot beside her.

Glancing around, Ezio felt a little awkward for the thought of being so familiar with his wife publicly, but realized that, as it grew darker and darker in the night, it was nearly impossible to see anyone more than a foot away.

Clearing his throat, Ezio lay beside Nora, who rested her head against his chest, and he was unable to contain a smile. Running his fingers through her hair, Ezio felt a peace emanating through his body that was interrupted briefly by stirrings of romance.

"Are you comfortable?" Nora asked as she looked up at him, her chin digging into his breast.

"Are you?" Ezio asked in return.

Thud, thud, thud.

The bombs grew louder as Ezio and Nora both looked at the ceiling, wondering how close the bombs were to their shelter.

"We'll be fine." Nora ran her hand along Ezio's cheek.

"I'm not worried." Ezio shook his head as he lied.

Suddenly, a high-pitched squeal came from the other side of the shelter, and Ezio shot upright in a start.

The squeal quickly lessened as music began playing from a little radio, and Ezio understood that the two men were able to complete their task of making it operational.

The happy toon of *Occhi Blu* began, with some static interference, from the little radio, and Ezio listened as others in the shelter joined in the joyful tune that was sung with such passion and sorrow.

"You're not worried?" Nora grinned at him as he still clutched his chest.

"I'm on edge." Ezio rubbed his eyes in exhaustion, understanding that there was no hope of sleeping in this shelter on a concrete floor with a hard pillow and a thin blanket.

"Come here." Nora forced Ezio to lie back down with her.

"I hope she survives this." Ezio thought of his sister.

"She'll be fine, I'm sure of it." Nora touched her fingers gently to his lips before she shuffled up on the floor so that her head was parallel to his. "Besides, what can you do while we're trapped in this questionable shelter? I'm not asking rhetorically. I want to know what you, Ezio Milanesi, can do to help out Vittoria while sitting here, in the dark?"

Ezio pondered for a moment but couldn't think of a single, reasonable response.

"My point exactly," Nora continued. "Breathe, my dear husband, for the next breath might not be guaranteed. You can spend these moments driving yourself insane with worry, or you can spend them now, with me."

Then, slowly, Nora leaned in and kissed his lips.

"What are you doing?!" Ezio whispered harshly as he looked around, wondering if anyone else had seen.

"It's pitch black," Nora whispered as she climbed on top of Ezio.

"They can still hear!"

"Then," Nora brought her mouth close to his ear and whispered seductively as Ezio's soul melted in the heat of her desire, "we'll just have to be quiet.

"Thank God you're not an actual nun." Ezio kissed her passionately.

Rolling onto her back, Nora pulled Ezio in close and his heart surged as he pressed his body against hers. Kissing her cheek, then kissing her neck, Ezio struggled awkwardly to unbutton her dress as Nora chuckled slightly at his troubles.

Ezio felt her warm breath against his cheek as she struggled to keep quiet. In the darkness, with the music blaring over the radio while others joined in the song, and bombs continuing to fall about the city, Ezio and Nora consecrated their marriage on the hard cement surface, giving themselves over to each other in body and soul.

While Ezio would've preferred privacy, he abandoned such concerns as he delved into a love that he was, unfortunately, unversed in. Someone who loved him as equally as he loved them was entirely foreign to Ezio, and in this act of passion he was reborn. The old Ezio was buried in this baptism of devotion, and he rose anew as a man who no longer needed to fear a life spent alone.

There was nothing else in the world that mattered in that moment. He was entirely enraptured in her body as he pressed his lips against hers, ran his hand through her hair, and felt every part of her body without reservation.

It was scandalous, fringing upon iniquitous, but without a doubt gratifying. This was the epitome of the romantic experience, despite the fact that they were surrounded in a dark shelter by other people. To Ezio, nothing outside of him and Nora existed. His concerns and worries were pushed aside, the hurtful words of his mother subsided, and the destruction he experienced only moments ago now seemed like a distant memory. All that mattered, all that existed, was Nora.

"Next...time..." Ezio whispered as he panted. "We'll have to...do that...when we can be louder."

Nora giggled as she flicked his nose playfully.

"We bring you breaking news," the announcer cut into the music, and both Ezio and Nora sat upright as they listened intently. "Italy has dropped out of the war."

"What does that mean?" an older man asked.

"Dropped out?" Another repeated.

"Mussolini has been arrested," the announcer continued, and a gasp went about the room.

It wasn't merely a gasp of surprise, but rather, one of relief. A sudden air of liberation seemed to enter the shelter as everyone began to chatter excitedly with one another.

"Quiet!" someone shouted so that they could hear the next announcement, and the room returned to stillness as they hung upon the words of the announcer.

"An anti-Fascist government, under the approval of the king, has been established."

A cheer erupted throughout the shelter, and Ezio felt his eyes welling with tears. Glancing at Nora, he noticed that she was smiling brightly with her eyes closed as if she was relishing in a cool, refreshing breeze by the ocean.

"Ezio!" Father Alexander called out.

"Stay here." Ezio squeezed Nora's arm. "I'll find out what the priest wants."

Walking back through the crowded and ecstatic shelter, Ezio came across the Nazi soldier but noticed that his armband had been removed. With a look of fear, the soldier glanced up at Ezio who realized that he now held this young man's fate in his hands. With a quick nod, Ezio signaled that he would keep his silence, and the young man frowned in surprise before staring off into the distance in contemplation.

"Ah, Ezio." Father Alexander latched onto Ezio's arm. "We have to act quickly. Go home. We'll find your sister, I promise you, but we need you in the north. Report on everything that happens."

"Sì, Padre!" Ezio grew excited.

The very idea of a free Italy was not something Ezio ever imagined experiencing in his lifetime. An Italy where he and Nora didn't have to hide, where he could settle down, and where he could live peacefully, seeking nothing more than a happy home.

"This is it, ragazzo mio!" Father Alexander squeezed Ezio's shoulder. "This is the start of a new chapter for our people!"

Chapter Nineteen:
Ludovica

"While you do not know about life, how can you know about death?"

Confucius

"I need to stop at the station quickly, then we can go to my parents' place for something to eat," Ezio explained to Nora as they arrived back in Giulino, fortunate that his vehicle was not destroyed during the bombing raid and only suffered some minor scrapes from shrapnel.

"Alright," Nora replied briskly, and he understood that she was likely just as tired as he was.

Neither of them had slept the night before in the shelter, nor had they eaten, and Ezio, although happy to have her company, was feeling the itch of irritation at even the trivial matters. Nothing worthy of divorce, of course, and Ezio was aware that his lack of sleep and nourishment played a factor in his sour mood, but still, he wished for a moment of solitude to regain some energy.

Apart from the fact that he still lived with his parents, Ezio had virtually lived alone his whole life in the sense that his decisions were his own. With Nora, that changed, and it changed drastically. He no longer had to concern himself with what he would eat but also how he would provide for her. He was comfortable at his parents' place, but he understood Nora's need to have a home of their own.

He appreciated the opportunity to provide and to have a wife as beautiful and as elegant as Nora, but Ezio wasn't foolish enough to dismiss that change, in most senses, is usually uncomfortable and this one was plaguing his ability to remain patient.

"You're welcome to come in, if you'd like?" Ezio asked Nora, half hoping she would decline.

"Will you be long?" Nora looked at Ezio with tired eyes.

"That's impossible to tell," Ezio replied with slight annoyance. He intended to be brief and knew he should've simply mentioned as much to Nora, but he grew annoyed at her unassuming question.

"I'll wait." Nora leaned her head against the window and closed her eyes.

"We'll get some sleep and food soon." Ezio patted her hand lovingly as he exited the vehicle and walked toward the station.

Entering inside, Ezio was surprised to find Armando at the reception desk instead of Francesca, and he was busily scribbling on some papers as the phone rang incessantly.

Wolfgang was sitting on the edge of the desk twitching his tail as he meowed indifferently when he saw Ezio.

"Armando?" Ezio asked as he leaned against the desk and petted Wolfgang.

"Thank goodness you're alright!" Armando shot Ezio a look of relief. "I heard about Milan. I was worried."

"I appreciate that." Ezio nodded. "What's happening here?"

"It's begun." Armando swallowed, and he seemed nervous as he glanced at the ringing phone.

"What's begun?" Ezio frowned.

"The Nazis. They've already overrun most of the rural north. There are reports that a small detachment is on its way to Como, and they'll be making their rounds through our town." Armando bounced his knee, and Ezio wondered what he had left unsaid.

"Do you think some soldiers will stay in Giulino?" Ezio asked as he thought of Nora and wondered if he had time to take her to Switzerland.

"Some of them might." Armando glanced quickly at Ezio before looking away.

"Armando, what have you done?" Ezio asked slowly as the second lieutenant grew increasingly nervous.

"I'm not permitted to be part of it." Armando shook his head. "They said it would appear dubious if an officer was involved. They need me to remain above suspicion."

"Part of what?" Ezio grew impatient as he planted his hands on the reception desk, and Wolfgang jumped down as he began inspecting around the station.

"Promise me that you'll steer clear." Armando looked at Ezio in such a way as if he understood his request was already forfeit.

"Armando!" Ezio shouted as he leaned over and grabbed the second lieutenant's collar. "I'm ordering you to tell me what is going on!"

"The Nazi detachment is passing through the main road," Armando broke free from Ezio as he explained. "The Resistance has set up an ambush."

"The main road is close to my parents' place!" Ezio barked. "How could you have put my family in such danger?!"

"It wasn't my decision!" Armando barked back. "In either case, you'll have to stay here until it's over. We need to remain above suspicion."

"Like hell I'm staying here!" Ezio stormed toward the exit.

"We found your sister!" Armando stood as he shouted to stop him, and Ezio turned while he looked at Armando expectantly.

"Where?" Ezio shrugged in annoyance, waiting for Armando to elaborate.

"Francesca recruited her into the Resistance," Armando began slowly. "I didn't know until just recently. Your sister is safe."

"Where is she?!" Ezio shouted.

"She's in Milan," Armando sighed. "Francesca heard from her this morning, so she's also, thankfully, unharmed."

"How could you possibly bring her into this?!" Ezio walked toward Armando and pointed his cane at his subordinate's chest. "She's much too young and far too naïve."

"She made up her own mind." Armando raised his hands to free himself of any guilt.

"She doesn't even know her own mind!" Ezio screamed. "She thinks of nothing else but stupid boys."

"She's committed to the cause," Armando continued quietly as he threw his hands onto his hips.

"Did you arrest Giuseppe like I ordered?" Ezio began walking toward the holding cells.

"I did, but once I heard from Francesca, I let him go, seeing as he had no part to play in her disappearance."

"That was not your call to make!" Ezio frowned sharply at Armando. "I give the orders here! I decide who leaves the holding cells and when!"

"What did you need him for?" Armando threw his hands out in defense of his actions. "He wasn't involved with your sister."

"He's still up to something!" Ezio berated Armando. "There are still two more missing women."

"We have no proof that he's involved." Armando crossed his arms.

"Regardless, I don't have time for this. I'm going to get my parents out of there." Ezio moved toward the door.

"I can't let you do that," Armando spoke commandingly, and Ezio thought he heard the sound of a gun cocking.

Looking slowly back at Armando, Ezio confirmed his suspicions when he saw the second lieutenant pointing his pistol at him.

"You're not going to kill me." Ezio shook his head as he tested Armando.

"I can't let you walk out that door!" Armando shouted as he moved closer to Ezio. "We need to remain above —"

"Say it again! Tell me again that my parents' lives are valued less than how much the Nazis *might* trust us!" Ezio screamed. "Who are you?! What have you become?! You're going to kill me so that I don't look suspicious?

Armando! Wake up! You've become the very thing you set out to destroy."

Armando trembled as he continued to train his weapon at Ezio, who noticed that the second lieutenant was beginning to sweat. His heart softened for the young man as he understood how troubled he likely was from killing the captain and the other guard.

"Achieving your goal won't justify your actions," Ezio spoke softly. "I appreciate that you saved my life, truly I do, but what happened on the road to Switzerland was unjust, and I believe you know that as well. You're doubling down, throwing all your chips into the pot, but a free Italy won't come by friends pointing pistols at each other."

Finally, and slowly, Armando lowered his weapon and turned away as he walked toward the office.

Swiftly exiting the station before Armando changed his mind, Ezio rushed toward the vehicle.

"Is everything alright?" Nora asked with concern.

"We found my sister," Ezio explained as he started the vehicle after handing his cane to her.

"That's great news!" Nora sat upright as she remained confused by Ezio's elevated state. "Isn't it?"

"She's with the Resistance." Ezio offered Nora a cross glance.

"I see." Nora nodded, understanding her husband's hesitancy.

"Also, the Nazis are invading. I'm taking you to Switzerland, and if—"

"As I said, our fat—"

"Enough!" Ezio yelled as he slammed his fist against the steering wheel and the car grew deathly quiet. "I won't hear another word on the matter. I'm taking you to Switzerland. You're my wife, and I'm taking you to safety. First, however, I need to stop by my parents and warn them to leave the area. If only they weren't so cheap and paid for a damn phone, I could warn them already."

Driving swiftly through the town, Ezio ignored the kind wave from Luigi and his family, who were now a marked improvement from when he had last seen them, honked his horn liberally to speed the little old ladies along who offered him irritated glances, disregarded Nora's demands that he slow down, and finally arrived back at his property to see that the street was still, fortunately, empty.

Exiting the vehicle, and with a touch of relief that he still had time, Ezio looked up and waved at Vitelli, who, oddly enough, seemed rather distracted. Vitelli was looking away from Ezio, down the street, and Ezio wondered if the old man knew that the Nazis were coming.

"There's no one here!" Nora griped when she stepped out of the vehicle. "Did we really need to drive at such ridiculous speeds?"

Yet as soon as the words left Nora's mouth, the purring of an engine rumbled through the street. Ezio paused as he listened to try and determine what direction they would be coming from when he soon heard the heart-shattering stomping of boots.

Within a few seconds, about three hundred yards from where Ezio stood, an armored transport vehicle, along with twenty Nazi soldiers, rounded the corner and began marching in their direction.

But Ezio's heart sank even further when he spotted the grey uniformed soldiers hoisting an SS flag. This was no ordinary Nazi troop, these men were unquestionably brutal, as was required by the SS. They would search every home, question anyone they thought suspicious in order to route out traitors, Jews, and anyone else they arbitrarily deemed as 'undesirable.'

Glancing back at Vitelli, Ezio frowned when the old man gave him a quick shake of the head as if he was pleading with him to not draw attention. It was then that Ezio noticed Vitelli was not alone, and standing behind him, in the shadows of the house, was Mario with a rifle trained on the SS column.

Glancing up at the other balconies, Ezio spotted two more rifles trained on the approaching SS troops, and further down on another roof was Matteo, also preparing for the ambush.

Ezio's heart began to pound as he realized this neighborhood was about to become a warzone, and he spotted another man getting into position on top of a roof.

With the sound of the engine, the street was soon filled with families, including children, awaiting the parade and entirely ignorant of the planned ambush. If they dared to be absent, the SS would surely take them for questioning, and no one was willing to risk such a horrific event.

"Do we tell them?" Nora asked as she, too, recognized what was about to happen.

"It will draw too much attention to us. We'll either be killed by the SS or our own partisans. We need to get you, of all people, away from here. Let's get my parents and go to Switzerland. Together. All of us." Ezio took Nora's hand in his and was about to walk toward his parents' house when their door suddenly opened and both Ludovica and Lorenzo walked out to be ready for the approaching parade.

They were both dressed as best as they were able, but Ezio noticed how worried they appeared. Lorenzo looked downcast, and Ludovica fidgeted with her hands as she was absent of a cigarette.

"You're back in time," Ludovica called nervously to Ezio as she looked down the street at the Nazis approaching.

"Come here!" Ezio waved at his parents.

"What? Why?" Lorenzo asked with a frown, scarcely paying attention as he, too, was affixed to the approaching Nazis.

"We need to leave!" Ezio lost his patience, and both Lorenzo and Ludovica offered odd looks to each other.

"We can't leave now." Lorenzo gestured to the SS.

"Please, come. I'll explain everything!"

But it was too late.

Glass shattered from a window down the street, followed quickly by a shot from a rifle and an explosion from a hand grenade that landed near the armored transport.

Immediately, the Germans responded by opening fire chaotically, not knowing, or caring, who was an innocent bystander or an active insurgent.

"Get down!" Ezio latched onto Nora and the two hid behind his vehicle for cover as it was peppered with bullets.

Glass fell onto their shoulders, bullets whizzed above their heads, the tires wheezed out air from the bullets now embedded in them, and a body fell with a thud beside Nora, who let out a chilling scream. It was Mario, and his lifeless eyes stared at Ezio as if in warning that he would be next.

Glancing up at Vitelli, Ezio's eyes welled with sorrow and hatred when he noticed Vitelli hunched over the table with blood running like a stream down his arm and onto the balcony.

Harsh orders from the Germans, shouts of freedom from the partisans, screams of terror from the innocent caught in the crossfire, the cracking of guns, the roar of automatic weapons, the shattering of glass, and the whimpering of the wounded caused a panic in Ezio akin to the Milan bombing raid.

Yet there was one sound above all others that caught Ezio's attention. It was the cry of his mother.

Glancing over, Ezio saw that she had fallen against the door of their house, and she was covering her chest where she had been shot by a stray bullet.

"Mamma!" Ezio shouted, glancing out from behind the vehicle to see if there was an opening for him to reach her.

"There's no chance, Ezio!" Nora grabbed onto his arm, understanding his intention.

"I don't have a choice." Ezio wrung himself free before running, as best as he was able with a cane, to his mother's side.

"Ezio..." Ludovica spoke with a gurgle as blood spilled out of her mouth before looking down at the wound on her chest.

"Let's get her inside!" Ezio commanded his father as a bullet shattered glass just above them and the shards fell just shy of his mother.

"You shouldn't have left me!" Nora scolded Ezio after she had also braved crossing the street.

"You should have stayed there!" Ezio berated her as a grenade exploded near Vitelli's house with a deafening crack. "You could've easily been shot!"

"I'll help you with her." Nora nodded to his mother.

As quickly as they were able, the three of them pulled Ludovica into the small foyer before the stairs as they closed the door behind them. Ezio wasn't sure what protection a wooden door would provide, but it felt more secure, at least.

"Ezio," Ludovica spoke with a weak and scared voice as the gunfire and explosions shook the house.

"Try not to talk." Ezio took his mother's hand in his as he inspected her wound.

He knew that her injury was fatal, but still, something within Ezio didn't want to believe that his mother was dying in front of his eyes. He tried to deliberate how he could assist her, but as the seconds stretched on, Ezio lost himself to a horror he struggled to consider was real.

"Ezio." Ludovica reached up her hand and placed it gently to her son's cheek as she looked at him lovingly.

With teary eyes, Ezio looked down at his mother. She was pale, her gaze was glassy, and Ezio knew there was no chance of getting her medical assistance in time.

"You'll be alright," Ezio lied.

"Ezio." Ludovica's lips trembled. "Mio dolce ragazzo."

"We found Vittoria," Ezio continued, happy that he could at least share the good news with her. "She's in Milan. She's fine."

"You've made me proud." Ludovica smiled at Ezio. "You always have."

Then, suddenly, her breathing changed. Ludovica stared off into the distance as she began taking shallow breaths until, finally, she inhaled as if to take a large breath, but never exhaled again.

"Mamma?!" Ezio asked as he watched the life leave her eyes.

"Amore mio?!" Lorenzo shook his wife's shoulders.

"Mamma?!" Ezio shouted. He knew it was useless. He knew she was dead, but there was a small hope within him that she was merely sleeping. He thought, perhaps, if he could shake her awake, as he had done so often as a child after crawling into bed with his parents in the early morning hours or when she protected him after a nightmare.

"She's gone." Lorenzo covered his mouth as he fell backward.

"Mamma?!" Ezio screamed as he buried his face into her chest.

Weeping as he sat beside his mother, Ezio didn't know how to respond. He didn't know if he should shout or charge into the street with his pistol, killing as many of the SS as he could before being gunned down.

He was angry, beyond angry. He recalled feeling this rage at his brothers' deaths, yet now it was maximized as if expounding upon his suppressed emotions. All the hatred and fear that he had tried to suffocate over the years now surged forward, breaking free from their chains and enjoying free reign over Ezio's spirit.

Eventually, the gunfire quieted while Ezio, Nora, and Lorenzo sat motionless in the foyer with Ludovica's body. The stench of gunpowder wafted under the doorway, mixing with the stench of Ludovica's blood that was now covering Ezio's hands and clothes.

A shout in German came from nearby, and Ezio understood that the SS would be going door to door to secure the area.

Withdrawing his pistol, Ezio aimed it at the door, ready to fire upon any German who dared to enter.

"Put that away!" Lorenzo barked.

"What do you care?!" Ezio remained fixated on the door as tears continued to stream down his face.

A knock came to the door as a command in German came from the other side.

"Ragazzo mio," Lorenzo spoke softly as he reached his hand out slowly and placed it to the pistol.

Again, the shout came in German, angrier and with a measure of fear.

"Ezio, amore mio," Nora also spoke softly, and glancing at her tender gaze, his heart melted a measure.

With a nod, Ezio stood and limped over to the door, where he spoke quietly in broken German that he was going to open it.

Slowly, Ezio opened the door, and the SS looked at him curiously for the blood.

"My mother." Ezio swallowed as he pointed behind him, and the SS soldier nodded before proceeding to the next house.

"Why did they leave us alone?" Nora asked.

"My uniform." Ezio sniffled before closing the door again. "He knows I'm just a police officer."

Glancing at his mother, Ezio couldn't believe what he was seeing. He knew it was real, but a part of him wouldn't accept it. He didn't know who to hate more, the Nazis that killed her with a stray bullet, or the partisans for being so reckless around civilians.

Further embittering Ezio's heart was the fact that Switzerland was now entirely out of the question. With his car destroyed, and the Nazis now overrunning this part of Italy, there was no option of escape. They would have to endure and hope beyond hope that the Allies would come to their aid. If not, Ezio knew that he would likely also lose Nora, and he didn't know if he could bear any more.

Ezio ran his tongue along his cheek before uttering through gritted teeth as his rage resurged, "They'll pay for this! I'll kill them all! Every last one!"

Chapter Twenty:
Major Meyer

*"The quick pain of truth can pass away, but the slow eating
agony of a lie is never lost."*

John Steinbeck

"We, therefore, commit this body to the ground," Brother Giovanni began the burial rites for Ludovica, having been called over from across the lake to assist in laying Ezio's mother to rest along with ten other souls who had perished in the partisan ambush, including the bodies of Mario, Vitelli, and Matteo. "Earth to earth, ashes to ashes, dust to dust; in sure and certain hope of the Resurrection to eternal life."

"Amen," those who had gathered replied weakly as they stood close to the perspective graves of their loved ones, and Ezio noticed that no one was present for either Mario or Matteo.

Ezio stared angrily at his mother's casket as the men began shoveling dirt to cover her, sealing her to the earth beside her two sons. While Ezio did appreciate the measure of reconciliation he shared with Ludovica at her passing, he would rather have her alive and hating him than dead.

What Ezio despised the most was how beautiful the weather was. The birds chirped happily, the sun shone brightly from a cloudless sky, and the breeze from the lake was warming. It made Ezio feel as though the world was somehow indifferent to the death of someone so precious to him.

Lorenzo sniffled beside Ezio, but he was unable to console his father. He had no energy left to spare, and even Nora felt the brunt of Ezio's detachment as she reached out to take his hand, but he made no effort to reciprocate the affection.

Glancing around at those gathered, Ezio spotted Leonarda nearby, and she seemed to be looking at him with a sort of purpose as if she had something important to relay. He assumed she likely wanted to swindle some money out of him by pretending she could still communicate with his mother, and Ezio determined to avoid Leonarda altogether.

As the men continued to shovel dirt into the graves, Brother Giovanni, as well as the other priests in attendance, made their consolation rounds to the grieving. Ezio thought it was an absolute joke that Brother Giovanni would take part in these activities as he, more than anyone Ezio knew, was ill-qualified to address someone's feelings.

Standing in front of Ezio, Nora, and Lorenzo, Brother Giovanni drew a deep breath as he held his Bible in front of him and unable to offer any words of comfort. Instead, Brother Giovanni simply offered a forced smile to Ezio before staring at his feet uncomfortably.

"I lost my mother." Brother Giovanni cleared his throat and glanced briefly at Ezio before looking away. "I know the pain you're enduring."

Ezio didn't reply, understanding that Brother Giovanni was simply carrying out his duty and would rather not discuss such sensitive things. Not that Ezio blamed him, either. The priest-monk only knew Ezio briefly, and such serious topics, when it was so raw, were often better seen as dismissed.

"Ezio!" Nora inhaled quickly with a start as she tugged on his sleeve before pointing toward the town.

Looking in the direction, Ezio spotted ten Nazi soldiers marching toward them swiftly, an officer bringing up the rear. They seemed intentional in their advance, and Ezio's shoulders tightened as he feared their objective.

A murmur began to spread throughout the crowd as they, too, took notice of this approach and were just as worried as Ezio. Glancing around at those gathered, Ezio noticed that Armando was not among them, and realized that he alone was the only one with a weapon. The mourners had no chance of defending themselves.

Shortly, the SS soldiers reached the bereaved, and, with indiscriminate precision, the ten soldiers spread out and surrounded the group, causing them to huddle and squish together as they feared the intention. Then, more terrifying still, the Nazis trained their weapons on the crowd, who let out terrified gasps, still in shock from the previous day's slaughter.

"It's going to be alright." Ezio gripped Nora's hand tightly, wondering if he even believed it himself.

He had heard stories of Nazi brutality, killing thousands of civilians after forcing them to dig their own graves. They showed no clemency, no discrimination for age or sex, and looking at the dead eyes of these SS soldiers, Ezio knew the stories to be true.

Nora didn't reply but squeezed Ezio's hand in return as she pressed herself close to him.

With the soldiers surrounding the group, and their weapons trained on the defenseless innocents, the officer stepped forward to address them.

He was a younger man but carried an air of arrogance with his soft chin held high and his arms held firmly behind his back. He wore shiny black boots, an impeccably clean uniform, and even donned a little riding whip that Ezio feared was not used for horses.

With a menacing smile plastered across the young officer's face, he began in Italian with a thick German accent, "This is an illegal assembly."

"Illegal?" Brother Giovanni asked with a measure of defiance that made Ezio nervous. "We are burying the men and women you killed!"

"We killed them?" the officer threw a hand to his chest in surprise at the accusation, taking no pains to hide his sarcasm. "You're mistaken."

"If you won't hold yourself to account, then you know these killings were unjust!" Brother Giovanni grew crimson with righteous anger, and Ezio feared for the priest-monk's life.

"Come here." The officer waved at Brother Giovanni, who, with a reluctant glance at Ezio and Nora, left the safety of the group.

"Irrespective of how they died, it is right that we bury the bodies," Brother Giovanni explained with a touch more tact.

"I am Major Meyer," the officer extended his hand in greeting to Brother Giovanni.

Staring down at the open hand, and then glancing over his shoulder at Nora for guidance, Brother Giovanni looked back at Major Meyer without shaking his hand.

"Aren't you instructed to love your neighbor? Bless those who persecute you? Pray for those who would do you ill?" Major Meyer tested the priest-monk.

"Those instructions relayed to our fellow humans," Brother Giovanni replied sharply, and Ezio's shoulders slumped, knowing that the cleric's defiance was dooming them all.

"I'm not human?" Major Meyer tilted his head, and Ezio believed the officer seemed to be enjoying the interaction. "Am I not made in the image of God? Do I not deserve mercy and grace?"

Brother Giovanni didn't reply, but instead stared defiantly back at the officer.

"You are all fortunate," Major Meyer continued as he looked at the crowd. "You may not feel fortunate, but you are. Not a single one of my men fell in the ambush, which, I might add, speaks volumes as to the Italian fighting spirit. If even one, only one, of my men had been killed, reinforcements would have been dispatched and we would've purged every living soul from this town as an example to the rest of Italy."

A rage grew inside Ezio as he stared at this major, wondering if Leonarda's words were true and that they had merely cut off the head of one serpent. Glancing again over his shoulder at the soap maker, he spotted her gazing at him intently with a sort of knowing.

"Still, an example is necessary for the actions and for supporting the partisans. I was sitting in my office trying to determine a fitting punishment when I was alerted to this illegal gathering. No requisition has been made to our office for the burial, which provided me with quite the opportunity, I must say." Major Meyer began to pace, leaving Brother Giovanni to stand awkwardly outside of the group.

"It's a funeral!" Brother Giovanni griped.

"Or, it could be a gathering of partisans? Maybe you're all gathering to determine how you will exact your revenge." Major Meyer inspected the crowd with a narrow gaze until his eyes locked onto Ezio's.

"You." The major pointed at Ezio, and his heart sank into his stomach. "Come here."

"Me?" Ezio pointed to his chest, feigning ignorance.

"Yes, come." The major again waved with waning patience.

Glancing at Nora, and then at his father, Ezio wasn't sure how to proceed. The major's demeanor didn't seem to indicate anything threatening, but Ezio recalled the stories of civilians being gunned down by coldhearted SS.

"Don't!" Nora latched onto Ezio as he began to walk toward the major.

"It'll be alright." Ezio planted a kiss on her forehead before forcefully withdrawing his hand.

"Your rank?" The major held his chin high as he inspected Ezio's uniform, taking special notice of his cane.

"Lieutenant," Ezio replied quietly as he cleared his throat, holding himself at attention with his cane resting against his leg.

With his hand down by his side, Ezio wondered how quickly he could withdraw his pistol. He would take out the major and as many of the soldiers as possible before being gunned down. It was foolish, selfish, and would likely cause the death of everyone in the crowd. Still, Ezio was partially convinced that mass murder was the Nazi plan anyway.

Yet, as if in contention with his violent idea, a soft breeze blew in from the lake, wrapped itself around Ezio, and then departed as swiftly as it had arrived. It was the same experience from when he addressed his brothers near the rock, and Ezio felt as though they were nearby, consoling him.

"You're part of the local police force?" The major walked closer to Ezio, who, curiously, noticed that the officer's pupils were dilated.

Ezio had heard reports of the Nazis using drugs to instill their soldiers with the ability to work without cessation and eradicate empathy. He remembered reading in the papers how the Nazi blitzkrieg into France was so successful because the soldiers, under the influence of drugs, didn't require sleep.

And now, looking into Major Meyer's eyes, Ezio knew that it was true. He was aware that without empathy, there was little that he could use to implore the soldier to show clemency.

"That's correct." Ezio nodded.

"And you weren't aware of a plot to ambush our detachment in your own town?" the major eyed Ezio suspiciously.

"I was in Milan, Signore," Ezio answered swiftly in the manner that a soldier would.

"You can verify this?" The major remained unconvinced.

"I can." Ezio nodded.

"You're either terrible at your job, or you're part of this Resistance, as they call themselves." The major retrieved a cigarette.

"This is a small town, Signore." Ezio remained disciplined as he stared beyond the major. "I didn't expect such a horrible tragedy to occur here."

With a deep inhale of his cigarette, the major nodded his understanding before casually stating, "Take your uniform off."

"Signore?" Ezio frowned, wondering if he had heard the order correctly.

"Take your uniform off," the major again spoke casually as if he were alone with Ezio. "You're not worthy to wear it."

"Off?" Ezio still didn't quite understand.

"Now!" The major withdrew his pistol and pointed it at Ezio's head as the crowd gasped in terror.

"Do as he asks!" Lorenzo called out to his son.

With a glance back at Nora and his father, Ezio again contemplated using his weapon but knew that he likely stood no chance in even taking down the major.

With a quick breath out to steady his nerves, Ezio began undressing. Removing his uniform and his trousers, Ezio stood, embarrassed, in nothing but his undershirt and underpants.

"And the rest." The captain waved with his gun for Ezio to continue.

"Signore, I—"

Aiming his pistol instead at Brother Giovanni, the major stared at Ezio, who understood the threat.

"We're an odd species, don't you agree?" the major asked with a cruel smile. "For this man's sake, you will humiliate yourself?"

Again glancing at Nora and his father, Ezio began to remove his undershirt and underpants as he stood entirely naked in front of the graves of his mother and brothers. Holding his hands in front of him to provide himself a least a measure dignity, Ezio continued to stand at attention, refusing to offer the major the satisfaction of embarrassing him.

"I should arrest you for public indecency," the major spoke in German as he laughed, and the guards with him also chuckled. "Give me your pistol."

Obliging, grudgingly, Ezio handed the officer his weapon. Adding to his unprovoked hatred, the major kicked his cane a fair distance away, but Ezio didn't bother to look, remaining in his decision to not allow the major this victory.

Despite his resolution, Ezio's face burned crimson in an unholy mixture of rage and embarrassment. He loathed this man, entirely. It was one thing to be cruel, but to take pleasure from needlessly humiliating another person was beyond disgusting. This was a crime not only against Ezio but against the whole of Giulino, and with a glare at the major, Ezio promised himself that he would exact his revenge.

"May we continue the funeral?" Brother Giovanni asked as he came to stand near Ezio, shielding his nakedness from the rest of the crowd.

"As I stated, this is an illegal gathering." The officer shook his head before he addressed the crowd, "Form a line behind the lieutenant here."

"What's the meaning of this?" Brother Giovanni asked.

Without hesitation, the major smacked Brother Giovanni on the side of the head with his pistol, and he fell to the ground as blood poured from the wound. A hush rushed through the crowd at not only the unexpected brutality but that it would be met upon a holy man.

Still, Ezio noticed that the measure worked, and a line soon formed behind him.

"We are looking for partisans, Jews, and anyone else who may be of interest," the major explained. "I'll review your documentation as you come forward."

Nora! Ezio began to panic as he recalled that she had no papers on her.

"Is this necessary?" Brother Giovanni stood as he gingerly touched where he had been struck. "Do you have no respect for the dead?"

"Why should I? They're dead." The major waved for the person behind Ezio to step forward. "Name?"

"Luigi," the man replied, and Ezio noticed Luigi and his wife turned slightly away from the lieutenant as to offer him a measure of dignity that he appreciated.

The major reviewed their documentation carefully, and Ezio assumed he was looking for any flaws or reasons to believe they were forged.

Satisfied that the documents were legitimate, the major pointed in the direction where he wanted Luigi and Isabella to move to before waving for the next person to come forward. As the line progressed slowly, Ezio understood that his humiliation would last for a while and that he would only be met with further punishment if he dared to request reprieve.

"Papers?" the major asked the next person in line.

"They were destroyed in a fire," the reply came timidly, and Ezio squeezed his eyes shut, knowing that it was Nora.

"Fire?" the major asked in such a tone that Ezio knew he didn't believe her.

"Will my marriage certificate suffice?" Nora reached into her purse before retrieving it for the major.

Grabbing it roughly from Nora, the major sighed as he looked over it before frowning.

"You were just married?" the major pointed to the date.

"That's correct." Nora swallowed.

"Brother Giovanni married you." The officer continued to look through the certificate.

"I'm Brother Giovanni." The priest-monk remained brave, despite the wound on his head. "I can vouch for the authenticity."

"Is that so?" the major asked while remaining suspicious before turning his attention to Nora again "You know, I was reviewing the documents at the station—I like the desk, by the way." He offered a cheeky wink to Ezio. "And I came across an arrest order for a woman by the name of Faustina."

Ezio's heart sank into his stomach, and he struggled to contain his reactions, fearing that he would inadvertently give Nora away. *Why didn't Armando dispose of the order?!*

"Oh?" Nora asked, and Ezio was glad that she, at least, could keep her composure.

"The last name was omitted, but the order came with a description: an attractive woman with brown eyes and brown hair." The major shredded the marriage certificate and scattered the pieces to the wind. "Unfortunately for you, this document will not suffice. I need your proper papers."

"I..." Nora cleared her throat. "I don't have any."

"The order also mentioned that, despite her Italian name, this Faustina isn't Italian." The major drew closer to Nora while placing his hand gently on her shoulder, and Ezio's rage nearly overpowered him. "She's Austrian."

Nora didn't reply, and Ezio assumed that the major had already detected her accent.

"What I found most shocking about the report is that it mentions she's wanted for murder," the major continued, and Ezio frowned at the condemnation before glancing at Nora to realize that it was true.

Again, Nora didn't reply, and in her silence, she offered the major the truth.

Recalling Nora's refusal to discuss her past, Ezio wondered if she truly was a murderer. Perhaps he was blinded by love, but Ezio assumed that her reasoning was just.

"She killed a Nazi border guard." The major brought himself within inches of Nora as he placed his hand on her other shoulder and looked down at her lustfully.

That's how she entered Italy! Ezio studied his wife while wishing she would've divulged this information to him so that he could try and protect her from it. Still, there was nothing Ezio could do while standing naked and the major holding his weapon.

"Take her." The officer nodded for a couple of guards to separate Nora from the rest of the group. "We'll hold you at the station until we can procure the truth."

Everything within Ezio wanted to fight. His heart shattered for Nora as she was taken away, her eyes staring at the earth before her feet. He knew that they would torture her in the cells, and Ezio almost collapsed at the very idea. How he wished that he still had his pistol. He would gun down this wicked major. He would die in the process but considered it to be worthwhile if he could spare Nora from what they would likely unleash upon her.

Still, Ezio remained in place as he stood, naked, before the line of people as, one by one, they provided their documentation to the captain. Anyone who couldn't prove their identity was set aside with Nora, ready to be taken to the station.

The minutes felt like hours as Ezio's embarrassment remained without diminishing as each new person, men and women that Ezio had known all his life, such as Luigi and his wife Isabella, provided proof of identity.

"Don't touch her!" a man in Nora's group shouted, distracting the major.

With the major's gaze diverted, Ezio felt a poke in his side. Turning slightly, Ezio spotted Leonarda, who was still offering him a determined look.

"I can help her," Leonarda whispered. "Bring her to me. I'll get her out of the country."

"Ah!" the man who had shouted from Nora's group collapsed as he received the butt end of a rifle to his stomach.

"I appreciate your cooperation," the major addressed the crowd when the last person's documentation had been reviewed, turning to his guards before stating, "Take them to the station. You two, destroy these graves."

"What?!" a cry erupted from the crowd.

"You didn't have permission to congregate." The major shook his head as if his decision was entirely rational and he couldn't comprehend the reason for their outrage. "These graves are illegal."

"Signore, per favore!" Brother Giovanni left Ezio's side and pleaded with the captain, his hands collapsed together. "Don't commit this sacrilege."

"They're dead." The major scoffed. "They no longer care if their body rots below the ground or above it."

"Do you have no faith?" Brother Giovanni scowled.

"We have the swastika." The major pointed to his armband. "We don't need the cross anymore."

"What about your humanity?" Brother Giovanni continued in his indignation.

"Proceed." The major raised his arm, and the group that was assigned to the station was taken under armed escort.

Nora's eyes locked with Ezio's as she was led by him. How he wished to tell her it was going to be alright, but by the look in her eyes, Ezio knew that she had accepted her fate. With a slight, loving smile, Nora turned her gaze away, and Ezio watched with a broken heart, knowing the pain she was about to endure.

Without hesitation, and despite the wailing and pleading from loved ones, the two guards assigned to the horrific task began destroying the graves by smashing the gravestones.

"Cease your desecration!" Brother Giovanni stood in front of the two guards as he held his cross out to them, stopping them from attacking Ludovica's grave, which had not yet been filled entirely with dirt.

"Get out of the way!" one of the guards spoke unkindly as he shoved Brother Giovanni backward, and the priest-monk fell into the grave on top of Ludovica's casket.

"I have an idea." One of the guards looked maliciously down at Brother Giovanni, who was scrambling to climb out of the earth. "Get me a shovel."

"No!" Ezio shouted, unable to contain himself any longer. "Do your evil, then leave. Don't multiply sorrow if it's unnecessary."

"You wanted a shovel?!" an older man asked angrily as he held a shovel high above his head, ready to strike the guard.

Yet the guard, without even flinching, aimed his rifle at the man's leg and squeezed the trigger.

The man screamed and fell as he clasped his hands to leg, and the guards laughed liberally at his pain. They had no empathy, no humanity, and Ezio wondered if it was merely the drugs, or if the drugs were magnifying the indecency that was already within them.

"Let's finish and get back," the other guard said, and Ezio noticed that he had a bit more compassion. "I'm tired."

"I could do this all day," the first guard replied as he stepped into Ludovica's grave and, with the shovel, began cracking open the casket.

"Stop this at once!" Lorenzo shouted, but the guard turned and pointed his rifle.

"No!" Ezio jumped in front of his father, and the guard lowered his weapon before continuing to smash open the grave.

"I can't allow it!" Lorenzo tried to get in front of Ezio, but he refused to let his father pass.

"Listen to me!" Ezio grabbed his father's shirt. "I lost my brothers, my mother, and now my wife. I can't lose a father too!"

"They can't do that to her!" Lorenzo screamed, but Ezio pushed him away.

Grabbing his clothes, Ezio dressed himself quickly while glancing out the corner of his eye to see who was watching, thankful to see the level of respect shown to him.

Looking back at the guards, Ezio noticed that they had now opened the casket, and he stared down at his mother's lifeless, pale body. She looked at peace, despite the fact that her grave was being defiled, and the jewelry around her neck was taken by the greedy guard.

"Ludovica!" Lorenzo wailed in his horror at the sight, and Ezio put his arm around his father as he forcibly dragged him away from the scene.

But depravity begets depravity, and when the guards were finished with Ludovica, they moved on to the next grave, opening that casket as well and stealing the jewelry, untroubled by the wailing and pleading from loved ones. The graves that were already long established were spray painted with crude black swastikas, and then, adding to the disgrace, the two guards took a moment to rest from their labors as they began smoking.

The wailing for the humiliated and disrespected deceased continued in its heartbreaking discord, and Ezio stared at the open casket of his mother, wondering if her spirit was nearby or if she was at rest with God and his angels. He hoped, that if the spiritual world did exist, and he was growing more convinced of it each day, that she was with her sons at last and her heart was finally at peace.

"Come." Ezio placed his arm around his father's shoulder. "That's not my mother. That's just her body. Her spirit is at rest with my brothers. We will take revenge on these men. I promise you. We will have our justice."

Chapter Twenty-One:
Partisan

"To know your Enemy, you must become your Enemy."

Sun Tzu

Ezio and Lorenzo sat around the kitchen table in the late evening, neither knowing what to say nor how to process what they had just experienced. Even if Ezio had some words of encouragement to give his father, he wouldn't be able to deliver them effectively as his mind was ravaged with worry for his wife.

Standing slowly, Lorenzo shuffled his feet as he walked over to the kitchen. Grabbing a few glasses and Ludovica's booze, Lorenzo returned to the table before filling each glass.

"I hated this stuff." Lorenzo shot his drink back as he grimaced at the burn before intentionally spilling the third glass onto the floor.

Ezio stared at his glass, unable to lift the cup to his lips.

"Drink," Lorenzo demanded.

Taking the glass, Ezio also shot his drink back as he tried to hide the burning in his throat.

The two returned to silence as Ezio played with his empty cup before a rage overtook him and, screaming, he threw the glass against the wall where it shattered.

Without reacting, Lorenzo poured another glass for himself before shooting it back as well.

"You hungry?" Lorenzo asked as he stared half-heartedly at the table.

Ezio shook his head.

"You have to eat," Lorenzo pressed.

"I wouldn't be able to force it down," Ezio spoke dejectedly.

"You need to keep your energy up." Lorenzo sniffled.

"What about you?" Ezio asked as he looked at his father.

"Bah." Lorenzo waved to dismiss Ezio's concern.

Again, the room returned to silence as Ezio felt the weight of his mother's absence. What he would do to have her chastising him at this moment. At least then he would feel something instead of this unquenchable emptiness.

"I...I'm not sure what to say." Ezio rubbed the back of his neck.

"Nothing to say." Lorenzo shrugged before pouring another glass.

"Per favore, Papa." Ezio reached out and grabbed the bottle. "I can't have you becoming like her."

"You think it was the booze that turned her bitter?!" Lorenzo offered a cruel chuckle as he glared at his son, and Ezio's heart began to ache as he understood his father's reference.

"You nev —"

"I told you not to take the boat out on the lake!" Lorenzo stood as he screamed, and his chair fell backward with a crash.

Ezio remained silent as he played nervously with his hands, understanding that his father's rage was not to be trifled with.

"Ten years we've suffered because of your disobedience! You became a cripple in body, and we were broken in spirit." Lorenzo's eyes bulged with indignation.

"I thought you remained silent out of pity, but now I understand that you agreed with your wife." Ezio looked up at his father.

"Of course I agreed with her!" Lorenzo aggressively grabbed the bottle off the table and retreated to his bedroom before slamming the door loudly.

Alone in the uncomfortable silence, Ezio sat at the table, unable to form a complete thought or decide what he should feel. His spirit was being torn between sorrow, rage, hatred, loneliness, anxiety, and every other ungodly and loathed emotion under the sun.

Feeling aimless, Ezio moved over to the balcony and sat in Vittoria's spot, wishing that he could contact her and wondering how to break the news of their mother's passing. He doubted that she would take it well, despite the fact that she also experienced Ludovica's callousness, albeit not as fiercely as Ezio.

Then, Ezio's gaze caught something peculiar. Vittoria's cigarettes were sitting on the table beside the chair, and Ezio wondered why she would've left them. Surely she had returned home to pack before she left for Milan. If she did, she would've never left her smokes behind. Or, Ezio figured, she could've been nervous and in a hurry.

What are you up to in Milan? Ezio thought as he retrieved the picture of Vittoria from his breast pocket. *How on earth did Francesca convince you to join the Resistance? Never in all my days would I have imagined you as a partisan.*

Ezio's mind delved further down into the pit of worry as his thoughts wandered to Nora. He knew that there was no hope for her. If the Nazis didn't kill her at the station, or do unspeakable things to her, then she would be sent to Poland. And there was nothing Ezio could do to help her. She was entirely at the mercy of Major Meyer, and that was a bleak statement in and of itself. Ezio had no weapon, no ability to get into the station, no keys, no vehicle, and no one to assist him.

He pondered the direction his life had taken if this was how it was to conclude. Meeting Nora felt predestined, and his spirit seemed to confirm that his life over the past ten years had led to such moments. Yet now, as he sat alone on the balcony without Nora, Vittoria, or any friends, Ezio was tempted to jump.

"May I join?" Lorenzo asked, startling Ezio, who didn't realize that his father had snuck up on him.

"Si." Ezio gestured to the open chair. "Of course."

With a grunt, Lorenzo sat on the chair while still clutching the bottle that Ezio noticed was nearing empty.

Without a word, the two men sat beside each other, staring out at their neighbor's houses. Glancing out of his peripheral, Ezio judged whether he should broach the subject of how his father was coping. The bottle of booze seemed to be an answer anyway, and Ezio kept silent. Besides, men didn't speak of such things, and Ezio wasn't about to disrespect his father by forcing him to become any more distressed than he already was.

"Have you heard from your sister?" Lorenzo asked, and Ezio sensed in his voice that he was feeling somewhat sorry for what he had yelled at his son.

"No." Ezio drew a deep breath. "I should ask Francesca to send her a message."

"She should know." Lorenzo took a generous sip. "About her mother."

Ezio nodded in his agreement as he stared out into the starry night sky.

"Do you like your new cane?" Lorenzo pointed to Ezio's cane.

"I do," Ezio replied quickly. He knew his father was trying to ease the tension, but he had no interest in discussing such matters when his wife was being held at the station.

"You know, your mother..." Lorenzo cleared his throat as he became uncomfortable.

"You don't have to say anything." Ezio reached over and patted his father's shoulder to relieve him of the burden.

"I was just going to mention that—"

"Per favore, Papa," Ezio interrupted. "I don't think I have the capacity to hear it right now."

"What's your plan, then?" Lorenzo drew a deep breath.

"Plan? For what?" Ezio asked.

"You're going to leave your wife in the hands of the SS?" Lorenzo frowned at Ezio. "What's your plan to free her?"

"There's no plan!" Ezio grew animated. "What can I do? I have nothing and no one to assist me."

"Don't you have connections?" Lorenzo narrowed his gaze. "You know, with headquarters in Rome."

"None." Ezio shook his head.

"Milan?"

"There's no one, Papa." Ezio looked regretfully at his father. "We can't fight this. Even if I did have connections, the Nazis are overrunning Italy."

Lorenzo paused as he examined his son for a moment before saying, "Your mother despised you for what you did, but I—" he tapped his chest—"I despise you for what you don't do."

Ezio shot his father a surprised glance at the curt statement.

"You're brimming with potential!" Lorenzo sat forward as he grew vibrant, and Ezio wondered if this was the booze speaking or his father. "You're smart, witty, perceptive, but you squandered these gifts at some small-town police station because you're afraid."

"Afraid?" Ezio grew annoyed at this condemnation.

"You're afraid that if you do anything out of line again, it will bring further ruin. You don't take risks, you accept what life gives you without complaint, and, Mio Dio, you should've told your mother long ago to go to hell for the way she spoke to you." Lorenzo's eyes bulged as he berated his son. "You're more than a lieutenant wasting away behind a desk in a tiny station. You're more than a man who's given up because life is cruel. Your wife sees it, I see it, but you, dammit, are blinded to it."

"Moving words," Ezio spoke sarcastically. "But they count for nothing in the face of this Nazi cruelty. Most of the men I did know in the Resistance died not far from where Mother fell. So, pardon my potential, because it is nothing more than an illusion. I appreciate you listing my qualities, but they count for nothing when it matters.

Without weapons, or soldiers, there is nothing we can do but hope that the Allies arrive sooner than later."

"You want soldiers? Take me!" Lorenzo stood and pounded his chest as his drink spilled.

"You?" Ezio scoffed and shook his head in annoyance.

"I know how to fight, ragazzo." Lorenzo gritted his teeth. "I fought for four horrendous years in the trenches and the mountains. Put a rifle in my hand, give me a target, and it will be done."

"Do you see any rifles?" Ezio gestured around the balcony.

"I'll kill them all!" Lorenzo shouted.

"Quiet!" Ezio glanced at the neighboring houses as a couple of lights flicked on. "They'll come for us next, and then we really won't be able to help Nora."

"Let them hear!" Lorenzo spread his arms out in a boldness encouraged by his consumption. "I'll kill every last Nazi for what they did to my wife and the graves of my sons. I'll bury them all alive if I can. A fitting end for wretched lives."

Yet this sudden boldness morphed into a surge of tears, and Lorenzo fell to his knees as he covered his eyes while he wept openly.

"Amore mio!" Lorenzo's hands trembled as he covered his shame. "Ludovica! Amore mio!"

Placing a hand to his father's back, Ezio didn't know what else to do, and he certainly didn't know what to say. Lorenzo continued to weep, not caring that anyone should witness his shameful state of vulnerability.

A knock came to the door.

Ezio and Lorenzo froze as they glanced at each other, both hoping that the other had been expecting someone.

The knock came again.

"What do we do?" Lorenzo whispered.

"Grab a knife." Ezio stood and rushed over to the kitchen, where he retrieved a large knife that he handed to his father and then grabbed one for himself as well.

"Won't be much use against guns." Lorenzo held his knife reluctantly down by his side.

Another knock, louder and more aggressive.

"I'm not dying without a fight!" Ezio summoned his courage as he descended the stairs while hiding his weapon behind his back.

With the unbridled rage of a man without hope, Ezio swung the door open with a puffed chest, furrowed brow, and gritted teeth, only to be shocked to find Armando and Carla standing with large coats that were pulled tightly across their bodies with the buttons nearly bursting.

"Quick!" Armando didn't offer an explanation as he and Carla brushed past Ezio and entered the house.

"Close the door!" Carla whispered harshly, and Ezio didn't wait for clarification as he obeyed swiftly.

"What the hell is happening?" Ezio asked in a hushed tone as he followed Armando and Carla up the stairs.

"We're taking back Giulino." Armando undid his coat to reveal three short rifles, a few pistols, and a handful of grenades that fell onto the kitchen table with a loud racket.

"What are you doing?" Lorenzo asked angrily, growing annoyed at the intrusion.

"Scusi, Signore," Armando spoke with respect. "We didn't have anywhere else to go. The station is now the headquarters for the SS."

"You little shit!" Lorenzo grabbed Armando by the collar and spun him around. "You brought this on us!"

"Me?" Armando looked back at Lorenzo with confusion.

"The SS would've simply carried on through this town without stopping had you not attempted a foolish ambush!" Lorenzo continued to hold Armando roughly.

"Because of your 'heroics'," he added sarcastically, "my wife is now dead, and the SS have set up headquarters here. Stupido! Idiota! How could you be so thoughtless?"

"I'm sorry for your loss, Signore. I truly am." Armando broke free from Lorenzo as he straightened out his uniform. "But I had nothing to do with the plans for the ambush."

"You didn't do anything to stop it, either!" Lorenzo flared his nostril.

"It doesn't matter. The Nazis are here now, and that's the situation we're forced to deal with. Let's take our revenge." Armando handed a rifle to Lorenzo, who looked at it with hesitancy.

"What can I do?" Lorenzo asked as he suddenly grew timid, and Ezio remembered how only moments ago, he bragged about his previous wartime experience.

"Kill Nazis," Carla interjected without reservation as she organized her weaponry, and Ezio watched her closely, questioning her motives.

"Let's take the station, Ezio." Armando handed him a pistol. "Your wife is still in there. Let's free her, and Italy, from this scourge."

"How do you know she's still there?" Ezio narrowed his gaze.

"What have I always told you, amico mio?" Armando asked with a slight smile.

"There's more of us than you know," Ezio replied with a nod.

"There are men and a handful of women who have been reporting to me on Nazi movement in Giulino and around the station," Carla advised as she checked over her rifle. "Thankfully, the Nazis decided to interrupt the burials earlier today, sending those who otherwise would've remained neutral right into our cause."

"Still, there's four of us." Ezio looked around the room.

"And there's only three at the station." Armando drew a deep breath. "The rest are patrolling the town. Major Meyer is concerned about the backlash from the deaths of our comrades and the scene at the cemetery. If we can make it to the station undetected, we can establish a headquarters for ourselves with which to drive them out."

"Strike the shepherd and the sheep will scatter, is that it?" Lorenzo began to inspect his weapon with uncertainty, and Ezio wondered if his father was reliving wartime memories.

"If we fail, the backlash could be catastrophic." Ezio remained wary. "They could kill everyone in the holding cells, including Nora, and then purge the town, as the major threatened earlier."

"You'd rather stay here?" Carla moved closer to Ezio, challenging his doubt.

While she wouldn't be what Ezio described as a dainty woman, she was still quite feminine. Not at all like his mother with broad shoulders and patches of hair on her chin. Still, Carla's demeanor was aggressive, to say the least, and Ezio admired, but also feared, her fighting spirit.

"I can't lose anyone else." Ezio looked back at Carla as she sized him up.

"Staying here and waiting for a savior to arrive is exactly how you'll lose her." Carla grabbed Ezio's hand, turned it upward, and placed a pistol in it roughly. "Take back your town, save your wife, be the man that is needed for the hour."

"We have a mutual objective," Armando pressed. "We'll assist you with freeing your wife. In turn, help us clear out the rest of the town."

"Even if we free the town, Germany will only send reinforcements." Ezio shrugged. "Then what? We're not equipped to fight off hundreds of men."

"What makes you think we're alone?" Carla tilted her head. "Dozens of towns across the north are fighting back."

"Really?" Ezio felt a lump forming in his throat.

"You continually underestimate how large the Resistance is." Armando smirked proudly. "We need you. Every soul counts."

"I need to get my wife to safety." Ezio examined the pistol in his hand. "Once I know she's safe, I'll assist you. You have my word."

Sighing in his frustration, Armando threw his hands onto his hips before stating, "I know there's no arguing you out of this. I'll accept whatever help you can provide."

"I appreciate your understanding." Ezio nodded.

"There's one more thing," Carla began.

"Oh?" Ezio waited for her to elaborate.

"Mussolini was rescued from his imprisonment. His government has been propped up by Hitler. We can expect him and his Fascist cohort to litter the north soon. If we can fight off the Nazis in time, then we can deal with Mussolini, but we can't fight on two fronts. We need to hit the Germans hard and fast."

Glancing at his father, Ezio felt a hopelessness descending on his shoulders. It seemed, to him, that there was no end to oppression. If it wasn't the Italian Fascists, it was the Nazis, and he worried that once they drove the Nazis out, or rather, if they could achieve such a feat, then the vacuum would only be filled by even greater tyranny.

"I'll get my wife to safety, then I'll return to help you. You have my word." Ezio nodded adamantly.

"Let's get to it, then." Lorenzo took one last large gulp from the bottle as he abandoned whatever reserve he was feeling. "I want to see my revenge dealt swiftly."

"He should stay back," Carla spoke to Armando as she nodded to Lorenzo.

"Like hell I'm staying back!" Lorenzo shouted.

"You're drunk and you'll be a liability!" Carla pointed angrily at him. "You're too unhinged, and you threaten the success of this whole operation!"

"I fought for four years when you were but the runt of the litter." Lorenzo carried himself with a greater sense of self-control. "I know what war is. I relive it every night. I'm not going to jeopardize this opportunity to pay retribution."

"I don't approve." Carla shook her head.

"We'll split up." Armando scratched his chin as he addressed Carla. "Signor Milanesi and I will approach the station from the west. You and Ezio will take the east."

"Why the hell would we split up? And why not my father and I on a team?" Ezio frowned.

"Because this way we double our chance of making it to the station. We need one of us to be on a team who is familiar with the layout," Armando explained. "The patrols are everywhere. Going unnoticed with four of us and, not to be insensitive, your leg, is too difficult."

"The station is likely locked." Ezio shook his head as he understood this plan was a Hail Mary, at best.

"That's why I stole the keys." Armando dug into his pocket and tossed one of the two sets to Ezio.

"If they know the keys are missing, they'll become suspicious." Ezio shook his head. "They'll bar the door with something."

"They underestimate us." Armando shrugged in his disagreement. "I don't blame them, either, considering our failed attempt at an ambush."

Ezio exhaled as he contemplated what he considered to be a foolhardy plan.

"You can't just sit here." Lorenzo looked at his son with empathy. "You've been waiting around for the last ten years as life has dragged on by. You squandered your time. No more. Take action, ragazzo mio. Kill the bastards who took your mother's life. Kill the bastards who desecrated the graves of your brothers. Kill the bastards who now have your wife locked up in a cell."

With a glance around the room at Lorenzo, Carla, and Armando, Ezio snatched the bottle away from his father before taking a swig and stating, "Viva l'Italia."

Chapter Twenty-Two:
Terror

"The supreme art of war is to subdue the enemy without fighting."

Sun Tzu

Placing a pistol, a knife, two hand grenades, a canteen of water, a can of pickled hot dogs, and a can of fruit salad into a little knapsack, Ezio wished his father and Armando the best of luck, demanding that if he fell in battle, they would do anything within their power to ensure Nora's safety. They, of course, agreed, but he assumed Armando would say anything at that moment to convince Ezio to proceed.

Heading out the door with Carla, who was now wearing Ludovica's dress (which Ezio found rather uncomfortable) and pretending to be Ezio's wife, the two walked carefully along the street, staying as close to the shadows as possible. Thankfully, Giulino wasn't what one would call a 'modern' town, and the few streetlights they did possess were rather dim.

"Your mother had quite the shoulders." Carla ran her hands along the dress. "And don't worry, I mean that as a compliment. I admire a tough woman."

Tough is right! Ezio thought.

Feigning a contented married couple, Ezio and Carla walked arm in arm through the dimly lit roads, thankful that it was now overcast and there was no moonlight to aid their enemy.

Turning down a street, Ezio swiftly pulled Carla back when he spotted a patrol of two men walking in their direction. He couldn't tell if they were part of the SS or simply citizens, but he didn't want to be discovered with the contents of his knapsack should it be a SS patrol.

Thankfully, it appeared that these two men had not spotted Ezio and Carla as they turned down a perpendicular alley.

Continuing throughout the town, Ezio was starting to grow suspicious of how easy it had been to avoid any patrols. They were now within a few blocks of the station, and Ezio allowed himself the dangerous thought that their plan might bring fruition.

But then, as they turned down another street, and two men with flashlights came into view at the end of the sidewalk, Ezio was certain that they were, in fact, SS patrolmen. Confirming Ezio's suspicions, he noticed the automatic rifles slung over their shoulders as they walked up to a house before knocking liberally.

With a nudge, Carla pulled Ezio to the other side of the street, where they both walked as quietly as they were able, hoping to avoid detection altogether while the SS had their attention to whatever task they had with this household. There was no other avenue or street with which they could get to the station, and Ezio prayed they could pass by the SS without discovery.

"Open up!" one of the men shouted, and Ezio recognized his voice. It was the same man who had desecrated his mother's grave.

Ezio squeezed his eyes shut as he reminded himself of Nora's plight, but his spirit yearned for vengeance on this deserving and pitiless creature. Ezio and Carla were close enough now that they could attack the SS from the rear without detection, but Nora came first, and Ezio knew that he would simply need to continue walking and the urge would subside.

The door to the house opened slowly, and Ezio's heart sank when he spotted Paola, Signora Soavi's niece, and recognized that this must be where she lived.

Ezio tried to discern his course of action. He wondered what business these men had with her, and contemplated if he should become involved.

Nora! Ezio reminded himself of his charge. He couldn't afford to be distracted, regardless of how noble the pursuit was. Besides, if they lingered, Armando and Lorenzo might assume the worst and make a rash mistake if they got to the station first.

"Is your father or mother home?" the man asked in terrible Italian.

Paola didn't reply, and Ezio assumed as much as these SS that her silence indicated she was alone.

"I'm guessing no?" the man spoke to his compatriot in German and offered a wicked chuckle.

"May we come inside? We have something we need to discuss," the other man spoke to Paola in better Italian.

Waiting anxiously to hear how this would turn out, Ezio slowed his pace a little.

"We have to keep moving," Carla pressed Ezio onward.

"I know her," Ezio replied with a harsh whisper.

"I'm sorry, then," Carla whispered back. "It's either her or your wife, you can't save both."

"That would be inappropriate," Paola replied bravely.

"Keep an eye out," the first man spoke over his shoulder to the other patrolman before he barged into the house as Paola offered a stifled scream that was soon silenced by the closing of the door.

"We need to help her," Ezio demanded of Carla.

"She's one girl." Carla shook her head. "If we take the station and set up headquarters, we'll save countless others."

"You go on then." Ezio freed himself from her arm. "I'll meet you there."

"Ezio!" Carla grew irate in a hushed voice, but the lieutenant was already silently crossing to the other side of the street and toward the SS.

The other patrolman, thankfully for Ezio, had taken a rather complacent attitude to 'keeping an eye out', and was busy rolling a cigarette as he sat on the front steps of Paola's house.

Walking as quietly as he was able, and trying to control his breathing as his heart pounded in his chest, Ezio tried to decide how to best approach the situation. Ezio knew he couldn't shoot him as it would draw too much attention, and it would be nearly impossible to get close enough with a knife. Still, he knew he had to try. He couldn't permit Paola to endure this evil without attempting to save her.

Kneeling beside a neighboring tree when he was about twenty yards away from the patrolman, Ezio set his knapsack and cane down on the ground and searched for his knife. His hands shook as he looked through the bag, wondering how he could possibly take another man's life. His position was precarious, and even in the dark, Ezio knew that if the patrolman simply turned to his left he would be spotted.

"Excuse me," Carla asked loudly as she approached the patrolman, and Ezio's heart nearly leaped out of his throat at her boldness.

"Signorina?" the patrolman asked quickly, also a little startled, but when he realized who was approaching, he relaxed substantially.

"I seem to have become lost; would you be so kind as to help me?" Carla asked as she pretended to be looking through her purse for something pertinent.

"Why are you out so late?" the patrolman stood and walked close to Carla. "You know there is a curfew, right?"

"Silly me." Carla giggled and walked just to the patrolman's left as he turned slightly, exposing his back to Ezio.

Perfect! Ezio thought as he found his knife and resumed his quiet sneak towards the SS, whose attention was now entirely on Carla.

"Would you like to keep me company tonight?" the SS man asked with such a tone as if to indicate his question was rhetoric.

"I don't think my husband would approve." Carla again giggled. "I'm not from around here. We're visiting my sister, and our car broke down."

"Where?" the patrolman looked over his shoulder, wondering if the car was nearby when he spotted Ezio.

Turning sharply, the SS man shone his light on the lieutenant while raising his weapon. He was about to shout at Ezio when he suddenly took a gasp inward, and, dropping his flashlight and rifle, he fell to the pavement. Standing behind him as she breathed heavily, Carla stood over his body before pulling her knife out of his back.

The patrolman struggled for breath, and it was evident that Carla had punctured his lungs. It was wretched business to watch him writhing as he slowly suffocated. In a mercy that he likely didn't deserve, Carla grabbed him by the hair and forced his chin up before taking her knife and quickening his death by cutting his throat. Blood sprayed onto her dress, and the man gurgled blood from his mouth as death hastened to collect his soul.

"Who are you talking to?" the first SS man asked as he opened the door, his belt undone, and Ezio saw into the house as Paola was strewn out on a couch with tears running down her face and her dress raised up to her waist.

Taking a moment to realize what he was seeing, the first SS man leaped into action as he reached for his rifle that was leaning against the doorpost.

Fortunately for Ezio, Carla was quicker, and with two quick squeezes of the trigger, she put two bullets in his chest. The man fell face-first onto the stairs, dead in an instant. Blood trickled down like a stream, and Paola let out a shriek as she came over to the door to find the men dead.

"Is anyone home with you?" Ezio rushed up the stairs as he asked Paola.

But in her shock and terror, Paola couldn't reply. She continued to scream and held her hands on her cheeks.

"Paola!" Ezio shouted as he took hold of her shoulders and she looked into his eyes. "Is anyone home?"

She shook her head.

"Go to my house! You'll be safe! You understand?" Ezio asked.

She nodded.

"You remember where I live?" Ezio asked.

"By Signor Vitelli's," Paola spoke through sniffles.

A shout in German came from down the street, and Ezio knew that other SS were coming to inspect the gunshots.

"Ezio!" Carla shouted, also hearing the guards.

"Go! Now!" Ezio pushed Paola in the opposite direction of the approaching SS, and she ran into the black of night.

Grabbing his knapsack and cane, Ezio followed Carla through the street, sticking to the shadows as the heated shouts from the SS grew louder and louder, until eventually, their flashlights could be seen bouncing a good distance behind them.

Ducking down an alley, Ezio and Carla stuck to unconventional routes on their way to their objective. After scaling short stone walls, sifting through bushes and trees, and nearly being spotted on a couple occasions, the two arrived near the parking lot of the station.

"There's a lot more than three guards!" Ezio griped as they took cover in a thicket by a stone wall overlooking their target.

Two SS were standing guard outside the door with another four in the parking lot inspecting the armored vehicle.

"What are we going to do?" Carla asked rhetorically, and Ezio understood she was not looking to him for advice on military matters.

"You don't want my opinion, I take it?" Ezio asked grumpily.

"Your opinion nearly got us both killed!" Carla whispered harshly. "You're fortunate that neither of them believed I was armed."

"I did what I thought was right." Ezio scowled at her under the cover of darkness.

"Next time, warn me, and I'll leave you to die." Carla scowled back as she continued to scout the terrain.

Ezio watched her for a moment and noticed that she appeared quite collected. Her hands weren't shaking, she didn't seem to have any crises of conscience after killing the two SS guards, and even now, she seemed calm, collected, and analytical.

"You seem oddly comfortable with this." Ezio studied her.

"I have to be." Carla swallowed as she continued to watch the SS, and Ezio assumed she was looking for a weak point or some way they could sneak inside the station.

"How does a woman like you become so violent anyway?" Ezio asked but regretted it from the look Carla offered him.

"I'm not violent," Carla replied swiftly. "Not by nature, at least. I was studying law when the war broke out. Military aspirations were as laughable to me then as they likely are to you now. I employed principle to fight against our own Fascists, but these Nazis only know one language. Do..." she paused as she glanced at him, showing a measure of vulnerability. "Do you remember your first kill?"

"I've yet to take a life." Ezio cleared his throat. "I've witnessed death plenty, but never by my hand. Not directly, that is." He thought of his brothers.

"That will likely have to change tonight." Carla returned her attention to the SS. "I remember mine."

Ezio watched Carla as he waited for her to continue.

"He was a Nazi official. I was tasked with assassinating him after he had acquired the defense plans for Rome, Milan, and some other cities. I waited for him outside of his hotel. I remember every single detail of that moment. It was raining, not hard, just drizzling. I was standing on the corner of the street, pretending to be enthralled by a novel, but thankfully, no one even thought to ask me what I was reading. Because I was so nervous, I don't think I could read a single word properly. I remember the minute I saw my target exit the hotel. He was wearing plain clothes, I think to hide his identity, but I knew what he carried in his briefcase. I walked up behind him with my pistol and put it to his head. I felt like I should've called to him, told him to turn around so that death didn't find him so cheaply. I knew he was armed, that's the only thing that stopped me from calling out to him, and I pulled the trigger, stole his briefcase, and ran away with tears streaming down my face."

One of the SS inspecting the armored vehicle began shouting angrily in German and kicking the vehicle in anger, and Ezio wondered if the partisans had damaged it during the ambush.

Another shout in German came, but this time closer to Ezio and Carla, and Ezio's heart began to race as he realized that a handful of soldiers were marching in their direction and toward the station. They would walk right by Ezio and Carla, and both of them held their pistols at the ready as they expected to be discovered.

But either by divine providence, or pure chance, none of the SS that walked by Ezio and Carla noticed them hiding a mere few yards away.

"Hey!" one of the guards that walked past them shouted to his compatriots in the parking lot.

"What?" the reply came grumpily.

"Is no one on the radio?"

"What for?"

"If someone was on the radio, you'd know that! Karl and Klaus were killed by partisans. We're tracking them down."

Hearing the names of these men somehow enraged Ezio. They were less than human to him when they were simply SS guards who spawned into existence. Hearing their names reminded Ezio of the mothers who birthed and raised them and named them personally. Still, Ezio didn't regret what happened to them. He felt their deaths were just for their actions at the cemetery and with Paola.

"You four, spread out and find them. And if you can't find them, make some arrests. We'll draw these delinquents out, and, if not, we'll get revenge for our fallen."

The parking lot soon emptied as four more were added to the patrol, leaving only the two guarding the door.

"Maybe listening to my conscience paid off," Ezio spoke with a little smirk.

"You were lucky!" Carla berated him. "Fortune, in war, rarely picks sides, and I'd rather not be near you when the tide turns."

"What's the plan then?" Ezio asked as he studied the area, wondering if there was a way to call one of them away from the door.

"We need to be quiet." Carla also studied the area. "If we are too loud, the men inside will be alerted."

"Obviously!" Ezio grew annoyed. "I'm well aware of what is at stake."

"What's your idea then?" Carla scowled at him.

"Damsel in distress?" Ezio shrugged.

"That…" Carla wanted to berate Ezio for his suggestion, but he could see from her reaction that she had the same idea. "Dammit, that might work!"

"I'll be close by in case this goes sideways." Ezio checked over his pistol.

"You've never killed a man?" Carla asked again as she watched Ezio earnestly.

Ezio shook his head. It was odd that he felt almost a sense of shame, like he hadn't accomplished this feat yet. Especially compared to a civilian like Carla, who, to a degree, seemed more 'manly' than he was.

"Whatever you do, don't hesitate." Carla patted Ezio quickly. "If you do, we're both dead."

"I won't." Ezio offered a tough look back at Carla, who rolled her eyes.

"Officer! Help!" Carla practiced her lines quietly as she began sniffling and threw her lips upside down as she procured forced tears. With a quick breath to steady her nerves, Carla stepped out of cover.

Yet, as Ezio watched the station, he noticed something moving near the guards. Reaching out swiftly, Ezio latched onto Carla to stop her, but this was a fatal move. The guards, now seeing this woman in distress, also spotted Ezio holding onto her. At once, they began shouting harshly in German and raised their weapons.

"What the hell was that?!" Carla raised her hands as she glared at Ezio, who also was now out of cover and surrendering.

"On the ground!" the guard shouted, and Ezio obeyed quickly before noticing that Carla stood her ground.

"Trust me!" Ezio barked, but still, Carla remained in place. "They'll shoot you."

Suddenly, a dark figure rushed the guards from behind, tackling them both to the ground. Without hesitation, Carla withdrew her knife and ran to assist. Ezio, however, was not as swift to action as Carla, and hobbled as best as he was able to help.

The dark figure that Ezio now recognized as Armando was embattled in a bitter attempt to wrestle the rifle free from one guard while Carla had already sunk her knife deep into the neck of the other one, who, clearly, did not expect violence from her.

Another dark figure emerged from the shadows, and, coming into the light of the parking lot, the now illuminated Lorenzo rushed to the guard Armando was wrestling with, and sunk his bayonet deep inside his back. With a gasp, and wide, terrified eyes, the guard arched his back as he tried to free himself of the pain. Rolling on the ground, the guard reached for his pistol, but Lorenzo was too quick and stepped on the guard's hand before driving the bayonet into his chest.

The guard gurgled blood as he looked up at Lorenzo with dread, and Ezio's stomach churned at the sight. Especially as this guard was just a boy, no older than eighteen, maybe nineteen, and his life had already been cut short.

Watching his father, Ezio saw a different man than the one who had raised him. The man who heartily sang arias from the kitchen as he made delicious food had retreated, and the killing beast within emerged. Even when Ezio looked into Lorenzo's eyes, the man he had known his whole life was no longer present. Or perhaps, Ezio thought, this was who Lorenzo always was, and the man who had raised him was merely an imposter.

Ezio stood over the dying guard as he looked down at him with pity while the life swiftly left his eyes. He wondered if the young man had been excited to join and serve his country. He wondered if the guard had felt patriotic, or if he felt that he was making his father proud or impressing his peers. He knew there was no excuse for the guard's actions, but still, in his death, Ezio saw that, when everything is stripped away, there was little difference between them. This guard was still human, despite his hatefulness.

"Hide the bodies!" Carla whispered harshly as she ordered the men. "We can't let them be seen if the patrols come back."

Swiftly, the men hid the bodies behind the armored vehicle, which would buy them a few minutes should the patrols return.

"Andiamo!" Armando grabbed the rifles from the dead guards and handed one to Carla.

"I need my cane." Ezio looked back at the cover where he had left it.

"We don't have time!" Carla waved for them to follow her as she approached the doors.

Limping, Ezio, naturally, took the rear. Carla and Armando, with rifles at the ready, aimed at the door while Ezio and Lorenzo stood on either side of the door, ready to open them. Now the station doors in question, regrettably, opened outwards instead of inwards, meaning that if anyone was waiting on the other side, they would have the upper hand.

"On three," Carla spoke quietly, and Ezio sensed she was nervous. "One, two, three."

With a nod to his father, and with pistol drawn, Ezio pulled his door open as Lorenzo did likewise.

Immediately, shots fired from inside the station.

Armando fell, clutching his stomach while Carla fired off a few rounds before taking cover beside Lorenzo, who, twisting his body around the door, fired in a few rounds of his own.

"Help!" Armando called to Ezio, who noticed the second lieutenant was struggling to breathe.

Peeking around the corner quickly to see if he had the opportunity to help Armando, a bullet landed in the concrete right beside Ezio's head, and the dust flew into his eyes, momentarily blinding him.

"Get him!" Lorenzo shouted to Ezio. "I'll cover you!"

Turning to fire in another few rounds, Lorenzo shot wildly to provide Ezio a moment.

Still partially blind in one eye, Ezio crawled on the pavement, latched onto Armando, and dragged him back to his side of cover. He didn't know how he managed the strength to drag a full-grown man with one arm and while he was on his knees, but he assumed adrenaline was playing a part.

Standing again with his back pressed against the open door, Ezio heard a sharp ping and watched as Carla tossed a grenade into the station.

"Grenade!" a Nazi from inside shouted in warning, but it was of little use.

The explosion rocked the building, shooting debris that was mixed with blood out the door and onto the pavement. A horrendous, high-pitched scream of agony came from inside the station, and Ezio took the opportunity to prove his mettle by being the first to storm the building.

Stepping over some upturned tile and rubble, Ezio spotted a few SS, including Major Meyer, retreating down the hallway to the holding cells, leaving behind their compatriot, who was now without a knee and holding his leg in pain as he writhed on the floor.

With his pistol trained in the direction of the hallway, Ezio watched carefully for any SS who might pop out of cover and try to catch him unawares.

"Help!" the injured SS shouted in German. "Please! Help! God! Mamma! Help me!"

And with what seemed to be an almost automatic reaction, Carla aimed her rifle at the man's head and squeezed the trigger, ending his suffering.

"We could've asked him for information!" Ezio shouted at Carla. "We don't know how many more are inside."

A shot echoed from down the hallway, and Ezio thought it was near the holding cells.

Fearing that the major was killing off the prisoners, Ezio limped quickly to the wall perpendicular to the hallway and peeked around the corner to see that his fears were justified.

With pleading and begging as they squirmed inside the holding cells, the prisoners were shown no mercy as the major murdered them indiscriminately.

"You son of a bitch!" Ezio screamed as he aimed his pistol, and, without hesitation, fired off a few rounds, killing one of the guards beside the major as the other fled further into the station.

"Do it!" the major shouted as he grabbed Nora through the open bars of the holding cell and roughly pulled her against the bars as he held his pistol to her head.

"Let her go!" Ezio shouted back.

"She's a fucking Jew!" Major Meyer screamed back, and Ezio saw only emptiness in his eyes.

"She's my wife!" Ezio pondered if he should shoot the major before he had the chance to kill her, but with Nora so close, he didn't want to miss and hit her.

"Are you going to make me undress?" Major Meyer asked with a demented cackle.

"That would make us equals." Ezio shook his head swiftly as he continued to slowly approach the holding cell without deviating from his aim. "Leave her alone, and I'll let you live."

Without hesitation, Major Meyer spit vehemently in Ezio's direction. Whether it was drugs, or mental incapacity, or ideological indoctrination that was eradicating Major Meyer's empathy, Ezio wasn't sure, but all he knew, or cared about, was Nora.

A moment passed as Ezio trained his pistol on Major Meyer, a moment of an infinitesimal passing of time, yet for Ezio, the world stood still. He looked at his wife and saw the terror in her eyes, the tears streaming down her cheeks, and the trembling lips begging for this to be over. He looked at Major Meyer with his vile eyes bulging with hateful rage, spit slopping down his chin from his open mouth with gritted teeth, and his finger on the trigger.

As swiftly as the moment arrived, it vanished, and Ezio squeezed the trigger. The bullet landed just above Major Meyer's right eye, and he died in an instant. His body fell limp against the bars, his fingers still clinging to the sleeve of Nora's shoulder.

"Get me out!" Nora screamed as Ezio rushed over to pry Major Meyer's hand away from her.

Glancing in the cell as he searched Major Meyer for the keys, Ezio's heart shattered. Two men and an elderly woman, all of whom Ezio had known since a young age, lay dead, huddled against the back of the cell for cover.

"Hurry!" another person inside the cell shouted, desperate to escape their cage, and Ezio noticed that it was Francesca.

Finally finding the keys, Ezio unlocked the cell as those who were forced inside, including Francesca, rushed out and bolted for the door, anxious to get back to their families.

"Nora!" Ezio squeezed her tightly as the two wept in each other's arms.

She seemed limp, weak, and Ezio used all his strength to hold her upright as she shook in his arms. He loathed what the SS had put her through, what she had endured since this Fascist scourge had wrecked Europe, and didn't, for a moment, want to let her go.

He felt her soft arms wrapped around his neck, her tears staining his shoulder, and her warm breath filling his nostrils. He squeezed her tighter, pressing her as close to him as possible. He thought his wife was gone, but now he had hope again and didn't want to let go.

"Ezio!" Lorenzo called from back near the entrance. "We need to prepare! The patrols will be back soon!"

Ezio ignored his father as he continued to embrace his wife. "You're my home. You're my hope."

Chapter Twenty-Three:
Fate

"Those who choose the lesser evil forget very quickly that they chose evil."

Hannah Arendt

"Armando!" Francesca cried when she spotted him leaning against the door, holding his bleeding side with Carla inspecting him.

"Ow! Careful!" Armando winced when Francesca jostled him too much.

"Stop complaining!" Carla barked. "You're going to be fine."

"We need to prepare before the patrols return." Lorenzo glanced out the door nervously as he kept his rifle at the ready.

"Francesca." Ezio waved for her to come over to him.

"Si?" Francesca asked as she wiped the tears away, and Ezio noticed that her usually large eyes seemed narrow and downcast.

"Are you going to be alright?" Ezio inspected her quickly, making sure she wasn't injured.

"I'm not hurt." She sniffled. "I was at the station when they first arrived. They threw me in the cell without even asking me a question. They thought I might be some woman named Faustina."

"I'm sorry to do this now, but I need you to get a message to my sister." Ezio glanced at his father, who understood what was about to be relayed. "She needs to know about her mother."

"Sure." Francesca wiped her nose with her sleeve, and her hands shook as she looked through the partially destroyed reception desk for a pen and paper. "Where am I sending it?"

"What do you mean?" Ezio shook his head.

"Where am I sending the message?" Francesca looked at him with confusion.

"I thought you would know." Ezio frowned.

"Why would I know?" Francesca continued in her confusion.

"Armando said that you had —" Ezio stopped himself short, realizing the deception.

Shooting Armando an incredulous look, Ezio knew, by the second lieutenant's expression, that he had exposed the fabrication.

"You lied?!" Ezio shouted as he walked over to Armando.

"Listen, I can explain!" Armando held his hand out to stop him.

"What is he saying?" Lorenzo grew worried. "Ezio, where is Vittoria?"

"That's what I want to know!" Ezio grabbed Armando by the collar as he forced him to his feet, and the second lieutenant winced in pain.

"Listen, I know this looks bad, but—" Armando held his hand up to profess his innocence.

"Where is she?!" Ezio screamed as he pushed Armando up against the door, his face crimson with rage. "Where is Vittoria?!"

"I…" Armando swallowed.

"You don't know, do you?" Ezio looked intently into Armando's eyes.

"We thought it best," Carla spoke softly.

"Best for what?!" Ezio turned to her as he continued to hold on tightly to Armando.

"If you believed she was alright, you'd focus on what was important," Armando explained.

"Important?" Ezio nearly laughed at the absurdity. "You mean the Resistance?"

"We need every available hand," Armando spoke gently.

"You told us she was in Milan!" Lorenzo joined in Ezio's outrage.

"Where is Vittoria?!" Ezio again screamed at Armando. "Did they even send men to look for her in Milan?"

"No," Carla replied quickly.

"Come!" Ezio grabbed Nora's hand, and they began to walk out of the station with Lorenzo not far behind.

"Where are you going?" Carla asked as she caught up to them.

"I'm going to find her!" Ezio barked.

"The Nazis still control this town!" Carla pulled on his shoulder to stop him. "We achieved our goal of securing the station, now we need your help clearing the town."

"I need to find her." Ezio shook his head and began limping away again.

"And who will help the rest of your defenseless countrymen? Who will help the other women and children when you're off trying to find your sister?" Carla threw her hands out in anger.

"Look!" Ezio spun around. "I'm sorry if this is selfish, or if I have my priorities in the wrong order, but I've experienced too much loss to not protect what I still have. Besides, what are we fighting for? We'll drive out Fascism and then replace it with what, Communism? Do you really believe that those living under Stalin have any more liberty than those under Hitler or Mussolini? It doesn't matter what I do; the world will always be oppressive and cruel. There is no system of government that will not, in some shape or form, harm its own people. I admire your ideals, I really do, but they're not realistic. The only thing I know, in my heart, that carries no dispute, is that finding my sister is the right thing to do."

Carla watched Ezio angrily as she clenched her jaw, and he feared her backlash.

"I'll stay in his place," Lorenzo spoke quickly in an attempt to ease the tension.

Frowning, Ezio looked back at his father curiously.

"Go find your sister." Lorenzo's lips trembled. "I'll make sure Giulino is safe for her to come back to."

With that, Lorenzo slung his rifle over his shoulder and swiftly retreated to the station with Carla. Ezio watched his father walk away and wondered if he would ever see him again. He wanted to tell Lorenzo what an excellent man he was, and that any boy would be fortunate to call him his father. He wanted to tell him that he was sorry that he had ignored his warning ten years ago about not taking the boat out on the lake. He wanted to tell him how heartbroken he was for the passing of his wife. Still, Ezio kept quiet and hoped that, in his heart, Lorenzo knew these things as well.

"Leonarda's shop isn't far from here." Ezio nodded in the direction. "It's the soap maker's place near your father's house. I'll get you to safety first, then go look for my sister. Something tells me that I'll find both answers at Leonarda's."

"We should stay with them." Nora hesitated as she looked at the station.

"What? Why?" Ezio frowned.

Nora paused as she contemplated before answering, "This is my father's town. His house is my ancestral right. I want to defend that. I don't want to run away. If we flee, they'll come after us. We can't rely on others to save us because, honestly, who knows if they'll even come. What if the Americans, or the British, fail in driving out the Nazis in the south? Hitler's gaze is set upon the whole world. If we don't stand here, then there's nowhere we can run that will be safe."

Ezio watched Nora for a moment. She looked tired, her eyes seemed sad and hopeless, and Ezio pondered as to the correct course of action.

"If we can get to Switzerland, then we can at least try to go further west." Ezio stared at the pavement as he mapped it out in his mind, although he felt as though his argument was useless given her adamancy for fighting.

"I'm a good shot. I can help," Nora pressed.

"I've lost too many." Ezio's eyes welled. "I can't lose you as well."

"That risk will always exist." Nora reached out and took his hand in hers. "You can't save me from life or suffering. You have to realize that you're not in control. I can't run any longer. I need to make a stand. *We* need to make a stand. We need to fight this evil and drive it from our home."

"You're right." Ezio pinched between his eyes as he felt lost in direction. "But I need to find my sister."

"As I've always stated, my husband." Nora looked into his eyes as she ran her hand along his cheek. "Our fates are tied together. Whatever happens to you, will happen to me. If we find your sister, will you help us fight?"

Ezio drew a deep breath before replying, "Major Meyer, and his guard, were the first two people I have ever killed. I don't know if I can kill again."

"Then maybe you're the exact person we need fighting." Nora smiled slightly out of the corner of her mouth. "Someone with a conscience."

The beams from flashlights came into view a few blocks away, and Ezio knew that they were running short on time. Grabbing Nora's hand, Ezio returned to the cover where he had left his cane, grabbed it along with the knapsack, and the two walked back through the town, careful not to be spotted.

Returning to the pier outside of Signor Lehner's old residence, Ezio and Nora arrived at Leonarda's shop to find that it was closed. While Ezio expected the store not to be open during these hours, he was hoping to find Leonarda nearby.

"What do we do now?" Nora asked.

"Looks like there's a light on in the backroom." Ezio hammered on the door.

When there was no response, Ezio took his cane and smashed the window on the door as Nora held her hand over her mouth to stifle a surprised scream. Reaching inside, Ezio unlocked the door and opened it carefully.

Gunshots erupted in the distance, and Ezio wondered if a counterattack was being launched on the station, hoping that his father would survive the onslaught.

"Who's there?!" a shout came from the backroom of the shop, and Ezio recognized Leonarda's voice. "I'm armed!"

"It's me, Ezio," he called back, and at once the door to the backroom opened.

Walking closer to them, Leonarda seemed to view Ezio and Nora with a sort of marvel, almost as if she had been expecting them but that they had arrived too early.

"What do you want?" Leonarda asked slowly, and Ezio found it peculiar that the broken glass didn't seem to bother her.

"You said you could get her to safety." Ezio nodded to Nora.

Examining her closely, Leonarda seemed to be inspecting Nora for some sort of flaw or blemish. He wondered if she was looking for anything mistrustful as Leonarda ran her hand down Nora's arms, back, and briskly through her hair.

"Come with me." She returned to the backroom after she was satisfied with the inspection.

"I told you I didn't want to leave." Nora hesitated as she placed a gentle hand to Ezio's chest.

"I think she knows where my sister is." Ezio drew a deep breath. "I'll ask about Vittoria when she's caught off guard."

"Something seems off with her." Nora glanced at the backroom.

"She's unconventional, but she's kind," Ezio pressed.

"I trust your judgment," Nora relented reluctantly.

Entering the backroom, Ezio watched with peculiarity as Leonarda filled two glasses with wine and set them on the table. It was the same table where she had prophesied about the task Captain Cacioppo would give Ezio, and he was beginning to believe that fate might be playing a part in his life.

"Drink this." Leonarda pointed to the cups.

"We don't need any, grazie," Ezio politely declined.

"I need you to be calm," Leonarda pressed. "Your eyes are dilated, your breathing is quick, and you have the look of trauma about you."

"Still, we don't need wine. We just need to be—"

"If you don't drink, I can't help you." Leonarda scowled, and Ezio found it curious how adamant she was. "You need clear minds and restful hearts."

"Still, I—"

"Oh, if it'll appease her!" Nora griped as she drank her whole glass quickly.

"Good." Leonarda nodded and then pointed at Ezio before she replaced the bottle in a cupboard near the back of the room. "You, too."

With Leonarda's back turned, Ezio took a small sip before dumping the rest of his glass into a bucket beside the table.

"Alright, what is the plan?" Ezio sighed.

"Sit." Leonarda pointed.

Both Ezio and Nora sat in the chairs in front of the desk when Ezio began to feel strange. His hands turned numb, and he noticed that he was losing feeling in his lips. Ezio's heart began to race as numbness spread throughout his body, and glancing at Nora, he noticed that she was she was feeling similar.

"Some...some...something's...off," Nora looked at her hands before her head fell backward and her arms dropped limp beside her.

"Nora!" Ezio tried to reach for her, but his arm wouldn't respond, and he felt as though his lips were beginning to droop.

With her head resting against the back of the chair, Nora stared up at the ceiling with expressionless eyes and limp arms and legs. Ezio would've believed her to be dead if not for the groaning that sounded like she was attempting to scream.

Much quicker than Ezio appreciated, he began to lose control of his neck, and, reaching for the desk, he tumbled and fell onto the floor. Staring up at the ceiling, Ezio was only able to slightly move his eyes, otherwise he didn't have control over any part of his body. He was completely numb.

The wine! Ezio thought. *She's poisoned us! But why?*

A slight shuffle of shoes on the cement floor approached Ezio until, finally, Leonarda was standing over him with a cold expression. She seemed to be studying him, much like she had inspected Nora only a few minutes prior, and Ezio's heart felt as though it would burst out of his chest in terror.

"It'll be over soon." Leonarda knelt beside Ezio and ran her hand through his hair like she was consoling her child.

What will be over? He wanted to scream, but his voice was trapped inside and all that escaped was a groan, much like Nora's.

"My son was born the same year that Il Duce seized power." Leonarda stood and walked to the back of the shop and out of Ezio's view. "He's studying literature, my Giuseppe. At least he was until the war started and then everything became about the 'glory of Rome'. Son of Mars, he called himself. Stupid boy worships Mussolini."

Ezio detected the sound of metal clanging against metal, and he thought she was looking for tools in a chest of sorts. Whatever the case, it unnerved him terribly, and, again, he tried to scream but all that escaped was a trickle of air. It reminded him of nightmares as a child where he would try to shout for help but was unable to.

"I didn't know that he had enlisted until Signor Lehner, actually, offered me best wishes for Giuseppe. When I found out the truth, I collapsed, right where you are Ezio, and begged God to give my son a change of heart.

"I don't know why he enlisted. It doesn't make sense to me. I gave that boy everything. He was my miracle child. I buried ten of his brothers and sisters, and he repays me by signing his own death warrant?"

Some more metal clanking together, and Ezio heard what he thought was an 'ah ha' from Leonarda, who had found what she had been looking for.

"My mother, as I told you before, hated me. Yet through her curses, I found a blessing. Without her love of witchcraft, I would've never discovered a spiritual world; a world that for so many is out of reach or hidden. I've used my magic to counter many diseases, but my mother's curse is potent. A powerful curse requires a powerful spell, and now my magic will save my Giuseppe."

Ezio could hear some more shuffling of feet, and this time Leonarda went over to inspect Nora. Ezio tried to look in her direction, but his eyes could now barely move, or even blink, and they began to dry out while remaining exposed to the air.

"She's very pretty," Leonarda spoke casually, and Ezio could hear a groan from Nora.

"Oh, dear, my apologies, Ezio. You can't see her." Leonarda walked briskly over to the lieutenant, whose heart only raced further when he spotted a crude axe in her hand.

With a huff, Leonarda grabbed Ezio's arm and spun him slightly so that Nora would be in his sight.

"That better?" Leonarda asked in such a way as if she expected a reply.

"Good," she said as she returned to inspecting Nora with her axe in hand.

"Don't worry, Ezio, I'm going to explain everything. You're a good boy, and you deserve some answers." Leonarda tried to catch her breath, and Ezio thought that she seemed nervous or, possibly, excited. He wasn't sure which was more terrifying.

"Do you remember when I told you about the law of equivalent exchange?" Leonarda asked rhetorically. "In order to save a life, namely that of my son, I need to take a life."

Ezio screamed internally. He tried every possible attempt at moving a muscle, desperate not to watch whatever obscene plans Leonarda had with her axe and Nora.

"I must admit that when I first read about this law, the very thought disturbed me. I'm not a violent person, and taking a life doesn't give me pleasure, but I will not bury another child. You've lost loved ones, Ezio, and I know how painful that is, but I promise you that it pales in comparison to losing a son or daughter. Nothing compares to that agony, and I cannot experience it again."

Setting the axe down on the table, Leonarda grabbed a little bucket of water with a sponge inside and began washing Nora's face.

"Signora Setti was my first...well...victim I suppose you would call her. Lonely old bag. Terribly rude. She had a sad existence and felt as though her sister was suffocating her. She had wanted to marry on a few occasions, but her sister would always interject and drive the men away. She was resentful toward her sister and regretted the years not telling her the truth. She needed her own life she told me, which, at seventy-six, was rather peculiar to me. Still, in her sacrifice, I gave her some meaning and ended her suffering.

"I had her come here early in the morning. She wrote a letter to her sister explaining that she was moving to Milan. Then I gave her the same concoction that you and your Jewess drank."

Taking the bucket of water and sponge, Leonarda knelt beside Ezio and began washing his face as well. The sponge was old and well-used, and Ezio spotted traces of fat and other bits that he hoped was merely dust.

"I do feel bad for her, though." Leonarda paused as she looked into Ezio's eyes. "I was so nervous. I spoke the spell, and, with shaking arms, I tried to kill her on the first strike with my axe. Unfortunately, I was so anxious that I missed her head entirely, and instead, the axe embedded right in her shoulder." Leonarda pressed on Ezio's shoulder. "She could feel everything, despite not being able to scream. It took me a while, but I was finally able to pull the axe out of her bone. Breaks my heart to recall the tears running down her face.

"Still, I had to try again. I closed my eyes," Leonarda pressed her eyes shut as she mimicked the moment. "I thought of Giuseppe being happy and free because of this sacrifice. I imagined what it would be like to hold the grandchildren he would give me, and finally be released from my mother's curse.

"With those images in mind, I brought the axe down again and it struck her right in the middle of the head. But a human skull is no malleable object, and she was still alive. I dug out the axe again and struck her over and over, mutilating her head beyond recognition!" Leonarda simulated the movements as the fat jiggled on her arms, her face grew red as the blood flushed, and her hair became unkempt as Ezio was powerless to do anything but watch.

"Blood was everywhere." Leonarda looked around the room, and Ezio thought she appeared to be relishing the memory. "Parts of her skull were in my hair, under my fingernails. It took me forever to clean up. Still, that wasn't nearly as gruesome as dismembering her body, and I'm glad that I had some skill in butchering animals.

"I hung her body parts on hooks, right in this very room. No one noticed." Leonarda chuckled. "My customers were so used to seeing animal parts hanging from my walls they didn't even think twice.

"Do you want to know what I did with the fat?" Leonarda leaned over and whispered in Ezio's ear. "Did you like the soap and the cakes?"

Go to Hell! Ezio wanted to scream, but still, his voice was stifled inside his paralyzed body.

"Fortunately for you, I've become rather skillful and I know how to kill swiftly. You won't endure much pain. I've had the opportunity to practice twice before. That's right, Signora Soavi, the other woman I heard you were searching for. She was so desperate for love. At her age?" Leonarda again chuckled casually as if she was discussing a charming story. "I did her a favor. She no longer longs for love or suffers the endless lonely nights. I took that pain from her.

'Thankfully, with the old spinster, I was able to strike true. I hit her on the side of the head." Leonarda touched Ezio's skull to indicate the part. "She died instantly. Another batch of soap and cakes."

Then Leonarda did something which Ezio found peculiar. She looked down at her hands and began to tremble slightly.

"But your sister…" Leonarda glanced at Ezio.

No! No! No! Ezio begged inwardly. *Please don't tell me she met this horrible fate! Not my sweet Vittoria!*

"That one was…difficult for me," Leonarda's voice cracked. "She was sweet and innocent, which unfortunately, made her the perfect sacrifice."

You bitch! I'm going to kill you! I'm going to cut you into a thousand pieces!

"I do hope you enjoyed the cake and soaps of her," Leonarda spoke with a measure of remorse, yet Ezio knew she wasn't repentant. "That was my way of bringing her back to you."

You demented old hag! I'll kill you! Please, God, give me the chance! Don't let us die like this! I can't leave my papa all alone! He has to know what happened. At least that much, please! Let him know what happened!

"She was brave, you know." Leonarda nodded as she reflected. "She wanted to move to Milan to make some money to help her family. Her motives were pure. The other two women were selfish, and their own desires caused them to suffer. Not your sister.

"I'll make you into some tea cakes as well. Don't worry, your life won't go to waste. You're a good boy." Leonarda grabbed the axe from the table and walked over to Nora. "It's probably best that I sacrifice her first. It would be the gentlemanly thing to do, I suppose. For you, I mean. If you had a choice, I'm sure you wouldn't want her to watch what I do to you. I'm going to help you, Ezio. I'm going to take away your pain. You won't have to suffer this life any longer."

Leonarda stood over Nora, and, with the blade of the axe, gently brushed the hair out of Nora's face. Running her hand along Nora's cheek, Leonarda seemed to show a measure of sorrow as if she was being forced to kill Nora.

Then, standing back, Leonarda closed her eyes, took a few measured breaths in, and began chanting in Latin.

Please! Ezio begged, using every part of his being to try and move or bring any control back to his body.

A sudden breeze rushed through the room, wrapped itself around Ezio, and then left.

Leonarda opened her eyes suddenly, and she seemed to be startled by the strange occurrence.

"My mother is here," Leonarda whispered as she looked around the room carefully, and Ezio assumed she was watching for another sign.

Ezio didn't know what the breeze meant. He didn't understand it on the lake, or at his mother's graveside, and he certainly didn't understand it now. All he could decipher was that breeze was meant for him. Somehow, someway, this gave him hope.

"After my mother passed, and she uttered a curse upon my life, I went to see a fortune teller." Leonarda stepped away from Nora as she continued looking through the room, taking soft steps and holding her axe high in anticipation. "I asked what my mother's curse meant. I thought I would die young, but the fortune teller told me I would live a long life, and I would bury all my children. My magic countered some of my mother's curse, but still, ten of my precious babies were taken from me. Every night I would dream of small, white coffins that were swallowed one after another by the black earth."

An explosion echoed from outside, further within the town, followed by gunfire, and Ezio knew the battle for Giulino had begun.

This caused Leonarda to grow even more worried, and she returned to Nora with a sort of urgency to complete her task.

Another explosion, and Leonarda looked at the door to the backroom. Grabbing the chair that Ezio had fallen out of, Leonarda dragged it over to the door, where she propped it against the handle to block it.

Ezio's finger twitched.

He tried again, and his finger moved. He had only taken a sip of the wine, and thought, perhaps, the effects were already beginning to wear off. Now all he needed to do was hope for time.

"I'm sorry about this, my dear." Leonarda returned to Nora and began lining the blade of her axe up with Nora's forehead.

Please! I need time! Just give me a few more minutes! Ezio begged Heaven, God, his mother, his brothers, his sister, and anyone who would listen as he could now move his toes.

Raising her axe, Leonarda made ready to bring it down.

Please! Ezio cried inwardly, and suddenly, there were flashes in his mind of memories both horrid and pleasant. He remembered his brothers lying dead against the rock. His leg twitched. He recalled the order from Captain Cacioppo to send Signor Lehner to Poland. Another twitch. He evoked the feeling of seeing Nora for the first time, her alluring brown eyes staring at him defiantly. He could now move a few more fingers. He recalled the experience on the lake as he rowed hastily away from their attacker. His hand was now entirely under his control. He thought of his wedding day and then returning to his home to hear of Vittoria's disappearance. He remembered the bomb shelter where he made love to Nora, the graveside where he was humiliated by Major Meyer, the SS who desecrated the graves, and how he had ended the major's life.

He could now breathe voluntarily, and a rage arose within him unparalleled to anything he had ever experienced before. This was the clinging to life, the desperation to save Nora, the hatred of Leonarda, and the hope that life could be beautiful.

"No!" a scream escaped Ezio's mouth. It was a terrible scream, a loud and deep scream. The sort of scream that is brought on by the weight of a decade of self-loathing. The scream that is released from a man whose own mother heaped insult upon insult on his shoulders. The scream that would save his wife and avenge his sister.

Startled, Leonarda dropped the axe and fell backward as she looked at Ezio with wide eyes.

His arm was now under his control, and Ezio reached into his holster, unbuckled the strap, and withdrew his pistol.

"How?!" Leonarda scurried to her feet as she scrambled to grab the axe.

"Drop it!" Ezio aimed at Leonarda, who paused, and Ezio realized that she was contemplating her course of action.

"I can't!" Leonarda grew desperate as she turned her attention to Nora. "I need to protect my son!"

Aiming at her leg, Ezio squeezed the trigger, and Leonarda fell, grasping her wound as she screamed in pain.

"Why?!" Leonarda shouted. "Why would you do that?!"

Ezio didn't reply as he struggled to sit upright, still not able to move his legs very well.

More explosions and gunfire came from outside, this time drawing closer to the shop, and Ezio imagined the fighting was happening just down the street, closer to Signor Lehner's house.

"You understand?" Leonarda sat her with back against the wall as she held her leg. "Don't you, Ezio? You understand why I need to do this? You have to let me finish. I need to stop my mother's curse. You know what it's like to have a cruel mother. You, of all people, understand. I saw it when you came to my shop the first time with your sister."

"I understand more than most, yes." Ezio kept his pistol trained on Leonarda.

"Then you know why I have to end this suffering." Leonarda leaned forward and grabbed the axe.

"You will never end suffering." Ezio shook his head. "Suffering exists without your mother's curse. Suffering is the base point of all life. Our suffering brings salvation or damnation, depending on how we respond to it. You could have forgiven your mother, but you choose the path of resentment, creating your own hell by becoming vengeful and hurting yourself, and then hurting others."

"She beat me! Everyday!" Leonarda shouted. "I was two, three years old, and terrified of the one person a child should cling to. How can you forgive that? How can you forgive the one person who is supposed to love you unconditionally?!"

"I did it." Ezio's lips trembled. "I chose compassion. I knew why she was angry. I chose the path of grace, because suffering, if you allow it, produces perseverance, and perseverance produces character, and character produces hope. Instead, you damned yourself to a life of misery until your resentment boiled into what you believed to be justified murder."

Leonarda didn't reply as she remained staring at Ezio with angry eyes. He had stripped away her façade, revealing that the murders were unjust, and Leonarda, or rather the menacing creature that had taken over her, was enraged.

With a hateful scream of vengeance against her mother, Leonarda stood and raised her axe far above her head as she charged at Nora.

Ezio squeezed off another shot, this time hitting her in the arm, and Leonarda fell beside Nora as she screamed in pain.

"It's over." Ezio kept his pistol trained on Leonarda as he crawled over to Nora and embraced her, and he wept for his sister. "It's over. It's over. It's over."

Chapter Twenty-Four:
Il Duce

"I never worry about action, but only about inaction."

Winston Churchill

Walking into the empty police station that was still partially destroyed, Ezio looked around with a sense of hopelessness. The reception desk was nearly cleaved in two from the grenade that Carla had thrown in, and blood and bits of bone were still scattered throughout the station.

A few days had passed since that fateful night when they stormed the station and rescued Nora. The Nazis had made the disastrous error of splitting into patrols which allowed the Resistance to reduce their numbers with ease while Ezio and Nora were dealing with Leonarda. If the Nazis had stayed at the station, there would have been no hope, and Ezio was thankful that the enemy had underestimated them.

Thankfully, Armando had agreed to transport Leonarda to Milan to await trial, as Ezio would've been tempted to enact his own justice if that responsibility had fallen to him.

Gently kicking aside some rubble, Ezio didn't know where to begin cleaning. Sticking his hand into his pocket, Ezio simply stood in silence as he replayed the events of the evening. He pondered how he had been so blind to Leonarda's depravity. He knew that she wasn't entirely reasonable, but he would've never guessed that she, of all people, had butchered not one but three women in such a horrific manner.

"What a mess!" Francesca spoke behind Ezio, startling him.

"What are you doing here?" Ezio clutched his chest in fright.

"I saw you walking into the station. I thought I would join." Francesca looked back at him with her exceptionally wide eyes. "I'm sure there's lots to do."

"We'll hire someone to clean this all up." Ezio returned to inspect the mess.

"Then why are you here?" Francesca asked.

"I can't find Wolfgang." Ezio threw his hand back into his pocket. "I hope he's in the office."

Ezio and Francesca stood beside each other quietly as they looked around at the empty station. Ezio wanted to tell her that he was sorry she had been caught up in the nightmare when the Nazis took over. She could've easily been killed by Major Meyer when he was murdering others in the holding cell, and he was certain that must've disturbed her.

"I enjoyed my time as a receptionist," Francesca broke the silence.

"You're leaving?" Ezio narrowed his gaze.

"Milan." Francesca nodded slowly. "Armando and I found a place there. I don't think I could work here any longer after what happened. It's difficult enough as it is just to stand here."

"I..." Ezio shook his head as he was at a loss for any consoling words. "I'll miss you."

"You're a kind soul. I'm sure your wife is a very happy woman." Francesca put her arm through Ezio's as she offered him platonic affection.

"When are you leaving?" Ezio asked.

"In a few minutes."

"You're not staying for the meeting?" Ezio glanced at his watch.

Francesca looked down at her hands nervously before replying, "We thought it best to cut off our involvement with the Resistance."

"But this is the pinnacle of the movement!" Ezio looked at her with incredulity. "This is what you and Armando worked so hard to achieve. Why leave now?"

"Armando thinks—"

"Where is he, by the way?" Ezio interrupted. "If he's leaving, I'd like to say goodbye."

"He was worried that you were still upset with him." Francesca looked sheepishly back at Ezio.

"Still, I'd like to bid him farewell. Leaving without acknowledging him would seem—"

"Would you just come in already?!" Francesca called over her shoulder to the door.

Slowly, peeking his head around the corner, Armando peered into the station and offered a little wave to Ezio as if he had not been waiting for the signal.

"You're leaving?" Ezio asked as he watched the second lieutenant walking gingerly toward him, holding his side where he had been shot.

"Si," Armando replied quietly as stood beside Francesca.

"Why did you quit the Resistance?" Ezio studied Armando curiously, wondering if the gunshot he received had changed his mind.

"You were right." Armando scratched his forehead, and Ezio knew it was difficult for him to admit it. "I became the sort of person I was trying to eradicate from Italy. I put the Resistance above all else. I mean, for God's sake, I lied about your sister to focus your efforts. I knew it was wrong at the time, but I convinced myself it was for the cause."

"You shouldn't have lied." Ezio shook his head as he looked at Armando with a measure of sympathy.

"I imagine that you're still cross with me." Armando swallowed.

Ezio stared back at Armando for a minute, inspecting the second lieutenant closely before replying, "I certainly have the right to be. Still, I've seen what bitterness can do to the soul. Anger is an unlimited resource. There is no end to it, and it consumes everything else in its path. I won't let it consume our friendship. Besides, you weren't the one who killed her."

"That's..." Armando cleared his throat. "I don't deserve your pardon."

"What are you going to do now?" Ezio asked as he changed the subject.

"We're getting married," Francesca interjected happily as she slung her arm through Armando's.

"Congratulations." Ezio smiled.

"Brother Giovanni is marrying us!" Francesca squealed.

"Little bit of advice." Ezio tapped his chin as he thought. "Don't take to heart anything unkind he might say."

"We've already met him." Francesca smirked.

"He was far from withdrawn with respect to his condemnation of my conduct, especially with respect to you," Armando explained, again sheepishly. "Ezio, amico mio, I'm forever sorry."

"Unburden yourself." Ezio extended his hand. "Be whole. If not for your sake, then for Francesca's. She deserves a good husband."

"Grazie." Armando shook Ezio's hand strongly. "Grazie mille."

"One last assignment together?" Ezio asked as he clung to Armando's hand.

"Anything," Armando replied quickly, though Ezio sensed he was nervous.

"Help me look for Wolfgang?" Ezio glanced in the direction of the office.

"That I can do." Armando nodded, and the two men walked toward the office carefully.

"I hope he's still alive," Ezio mentioned with a sense of hopelessness when they arrived at the office door to find that it was barred.

"Something must've fallen against the door from inside the office." Armando attempted to open the door, but something held it in place.

Slamming his shoulder into the door, Ezio felt it budge. Again and again, Ezio crashed into the door until it finally gave in and flew open to reveal a pitch-black office. The window had been covered with what Ezio assumed was a cloth or a blanket, but Ezio couldn't tell if it was intentional or accidental.

Peering into the dark, Ezio's heart slumped as he expected to find his companion lying on the floor, dead from starvation. He felt terrible that he had neglected his cat, but they were busy clearing the town from the Nazis, and he didn't have much time to think about Wolfgang.

"Is he in there?" Francesca called nervously from behind them.

"Wolfgang?" Ezio asked, hoping that he would receive a response.

Suddenly, green, reflective eyes opened and stared at Ezio from the corner of the desk, followed by an indifferent meow.

"Santo cielo!" Ezio threw a hand to his chest in relief and embraced Armando in joy.

"What does he have in his mouth?" Armando asked as he walked toward Wolfgang.

But before Armando could inspect, Wolfgang jumped down from the desk and casually walked out of the office and by Ezio, who laughed when he noticed that his cat was carrying a rat in its mouth.

"I would've locked you in here earlier if I knew that would solve the problem." Ezio chuckled at his friend as Wolfgang walked toward Francesca as if nothing was out of the ordinary.

"Ciao, Wolfgang!" Francesca knelt in front of the cat, who sat at her feet to be petted. "Oh, you poor little guy. All locked up and alone."

"That's a relief," Armando spoke cheerfully as he stood beside Ezio while the two watched Francesca smothering Wolfgang with kisses.

"We should be on our way." Francesca glanced at the clock.

"We'll miss you at the meeting." Ezio nodded to Armando.

"When are they arriving, by the way?" Armando asked, and Ezio sensed he was tempted to join.

"They should be here within the hour." Ezio glanced at his watch.

"Well, if you need me to—"

"Armando." Francesca glared lovingly at him.

"Right." Armando drew a deep breath.

"Take him with you." Ezio nodded to Wolfgang as he drew closer to Francesca.

"What? Wolfgang?" Francesca stood as she held the cat lovingly in her arms. "I couldn't possibly."

"Take him," Ezio pressed.

"What do you think?" Francesca looked at Armando.

"He never liked me all that much." Armando moved to pet Wolfgang who meowed angrily at him. "See?"

"He's perfect, then!" Francesca squeezed Wolfgang tightly. "Are you sure?"

"Perfectly." Ezio tapped his cane on the ground to signify his word was final.

"Why is it perfect that he doesn't like me?" Armando asked Francesca with a slight scowl.

"Because now I have two sensitive men in my life." Francesca smiled at Ezio before heading toward the door.

"Sensitive?!" Armando asked with annoyance as he chased after his fiancé.

"Arrivederci." Ezio waved as Francesca and Armando left the station, and he knew that would be the last time he would ever see them.

"I found him!" Ezio called out as he returned home but was met with no response. "He was in my office, believe it or not."

Arriving at the top of the stairs, Ezio was surprised to find that Nora and Brother Giovanni were huddled over a chessboard at the kitchen table.

"So, you see, if I move my queen here," Nora instructed Brother Giovanni. "Then you are in check. But, if you move your knight here, there is now nowhere for the queen to move. You've trapped her."

"Brilliant." Brother Giovanni leaned forward, happy to receive his promised chess lesson.

"I heard that you were officiating a wedding." Ezio sat at the table with them.

"I have some time before the ceremony." Brother Giovanni glanced at the clock. "Thought I would cash in on the promise from the last wedding I was forced to oversee."

"But that's not the end." Nora ignored Ezio as her excitement overtook her. "It's a gambit. I've let you focus on my queen, because if you take her, my bishop slides over here, and checkmate."

"Mio Dio!" Brother Giovanni rubbed his forehead in astonishment. "Again."

"Alright. Let's reset. See if you can't find the correct move to escape the trap." Nora began to organize the board, and Ezio watched her with a touch of sadness.

It had been a few days since they narrowly escaped Leonarda's clutches, and Nora's behavior showed clear signs of trauma. She ignored Ezio, delved into chess or anything that might amuse or distract her, and at times, she even seemed happy. Still, Ezio knew these were masks, and he feared the repercussions if she didn't properly deal with the trauma.

A bottle rolled from the balcony, and Ezio glanced over to see his father resting on a chair with his arms limp by his side.

"You should speak with him." Brother Giovanni nodded to Ezio.

"I don't think he wants anything to do with me." Ezio shook his head. "He was rather close with Vittoria. He loved his wife, too, and now he's left with nothing but the cripple."

"You're not omniscient." Brother Giovanni scowled at Ezio. "You don't know what he's thinking. Go and find out."

"Doesn't that fall within your purview?" Ezio crossed his arms. "I'm no priest. I don't have the skill set to console him."

"You're his son." Brother Giovanni looked at Ezio with a measure of sympathy. "You have what a priest-monk like myself will never have."

"Nora?" Ezio asked his wife for her opinion.

"Whatever you choose," Nora replied quickly as she focused on the chessboard.

"They'll be here soon, by the way." Ezio glanced again at his watch.

"I know," Nora replied quickly, still offering Ezio a cold shoulder as she remained fixated on the board.

He sensed that she was upset with him, but he wasn't entirely certain why. He didn't know that Leonarda was so demented, or that she would have tricked them so effortlessly. He couldn't comprehend why Nora was punishing him for the soap maker's cruelty.

With a heavy sigh, Ezio left the table and walked over to the balcony and sat on the chair beside Lorenzo.

The two sat in silence as Ezio listened to Nora offering another lesson to Brother Giovanni and his admiration of her knowledge.

"Come stai?" Ezio cleared his throat and glanced at his father, who didn't reply. "If you need to talk about—"

"The whore fed me my own daughter," Lorenzo began, absent of any emotion as he stared out at the sky with solemnity. "Thank God your mother died before she knew. If only the Nazis had killed me too before I found out."

Ezio remained silent as he watched his father.

"She sat on our couch, in our own damn living room, feeding us our own daughter. If I—" Lorenzo turned away as he choked. "Why did you let her live?"

"She needs to stand trial," Ezio replied quickly. "Vittoria wasn't her only victim. The other families deserve justice, too."

"Always by the book," Lorenzo scoffed. "Just for once, if—"

"Do you want to know why I disobeyed you when I took the boat out?" Ezio looked sternly at his father. "You told me the lake was too choppy, but I took my brothers out anyway. Do you want to know why?"

Lorenzo watched Ezio for a moment as he ran his tongue along his teeth before offering a faint nod.

"Because Luca and Alberto were manipulative little schemers." Ezio looked out at the clear blue sky as he huffed. "They knew how to make me do almost anything they wanted. Even when I was aware of their scheming, they were too clever to offer me a way out. If they hadn't twisted my arm, they would've taken the boat out themselves. You know how they were. Once an idea was in their head, it never left. I thought that if, at least, I was there with them, I could keep them safe."

Lorenzo remained staring at Ezio as he allowed his son a moment to express himself.

"You spent the last ten years grieving over what could've been, or what should've been," Ezio continued as his emotions began to overpower him. "All the while, you ignored what you still had. I know I don't have the right to feel angry, since it was my fault they're gone, but you shut me out."

Lorenzo looked away from Ezio, and he knew that he had upset his father.

"I'm still here," Ezio continued. "You still have a son. You can spend the rest of your days mourning what once was, or you can spend them in the present, with me, and, who knows, with grandchildren. Taking pleasure in life is not dismissing the pain of losing those who were closest to you. It's how we honor them."

"Ezio!" Nora called from the table, and he turned to see her walking toward the stairs. "They're here."

"I could use your guidance with this meeting." Ezio looked hopefully at his father.

"Are you certain about the plan?" Lorenzo glanced back at Ezio.

"I am." Ezio nodded.

"Then you don't need me. I'll take part in the execution, but I'll leave the planning to you."

Understanding his father's position, Ezio left him on the balcony and entered back into the property.

Filing into his little house, Carla, Palmiro, Father Alexander, Walter, and Alessandro walked up the stairs and organized themselves around the kitchen table.

"We'll continue this later." Brother Giovanni began putting away the chessboard.

"You've been kind to me." Nora looked at the priest-monk with an affection Ezio felt she was withholding from him.

"Will we get another chance?" Brother Giovanni tapped his chessboard, but by the tone of his voice, Ezio recognized that the priest-monk knew this was goodbye.

"Lieutenant." Walter removed his hat as he waved for Ezio to join them at the table. "Time is of the essence."

"With your leave." Brother Giovanni waved goodbye to everyone before offering Nora a steady gaze as he descended the stairs and out the door.

"Come stai?" Father Alexander asked Ezio sincerely as he sat at the table beside the priest.

"He's fine," Walter interjected. "This is war, Father. If you ask everyone how they're doing every time you meet, we'll never get to the topics at hand."

"Kindness will never be out of fashion," Father Alexander spoke softly to Walter, who shook his head in annoyance.

"There's no time to spare," Carla began. "The Nazis have all but been driven out of Italy. Partisan groups in Milan have launched successful coordinated measures and have mostly secured the city. We've received reports that Mussolini is fleeing Milan and intends to seek refuge in a neutral country."

"Switzerland?" Nora interjected.

"That's what we assume." Father Alexander confirmed.

"And here we come to the crescendo of your involvement with the Resistance." Palmiro leaned forward as he folded his hands and looked excitedly at Ezio.

"I told you that you were our hope." Father Alexander added.

"If Il Duce is, in fact, fleeing to Switzerland," Alessandro dug out a map from his pocket and spread it over the table. "What route would he be taking?"

Ezio looked around the table as he studied the faces of those gathered. He looked at Father Alexander, who appeared genuinely innocent, Carla, whose bloodlust was palpable, Walter, who seemed politically driven, Alessandro smoking his pipe, Palmiro examining the map, and, finally, at Nora, who appeared downcast yet determined.

"What's your intention with Mussolini?" Ezio asked.

"We'll ambush his convoy." Walter shrugged.

"I won't be involved in his murder." Ezio crossed his arms.

"Murder?!" Palmiro chuckled. "What would give you that impression?"

"We want to capture him; alive. Bring him to justice." Father Alexander placed his hand softly on the table.

"My dear priest." Ezio looked at him sympathetically. "They've convinced you of what you want to hear. They have no intention of ending this without violence."

"Mussolini needs to answer to the Italians and in an Italian court." Carla pounded her fist on the table.

"We have an hour to get ahead of him. Now, which route would he take," Palmiro pressed, pushing the map closer to Ezio.

Looking at the map, and then at Nora, then at his father, and again at those around the table, Ezio stood, grabbed the map, and began heading toward the door.

"Where the hell are you going?" Palmiro barked.

"I'll show you where he'll be." Ezio waved for them to follow him.

"Why not tell us?" Alessandro asked as he followed Ezio down the stairs.

"Because I need to be there."

"For what purpose?" Carla asked.

"To make sure that you don't kill him." Ezio opened the door and exited the property, where he nearly fell back in surprise to find about fifty men and women standing outside, armed to the teeth with rifles, automatic weapons, grenades, explosives, and melee weapons.

"What did Armando always tell you? There are more of us than you know." Father Alexander placed a strong hand to Ezio's shoulder.

"That there are." Ezio swallowed as he studied the faces of these partisans.

They were not soldiers but ordinary people. Modest mothers with headscarves and cigarettes hanging out the corner of their mouths while holding semi-automatic weapons watched Ezio eagerly. Sons who had grown weary of witnessing their fathers and brothers die for Mussolini's vainglorious ideal of a Roman Empire now looked to Ezio for direction. Paola was among them, Luigi and his wife also, as well as many others whom Ezio had known since he was but a boy.

"He needs to answer to them," Walter spoke quietly to Ezio as the partisans waited eagerly for direction.

"Do we have enough vehicles?" Ezio asked Father Alexander.

"They didn't all walk here." Father Alexander offered a veiled answer.

"Well..." Ezio cleared his throat. "Follow me, then."

"Are you sure this is the right place?" Walter asked as he hid with Ezio behind a hill near the checkpoint where he had taken Signor Lehner.

Ezio didn't reply as he stared in the direction of the ravine where they had buried Captain Cacioppo and Flavio. He wondered if he should give their families the satisfaction of knowing where the bodies were.

"This is where you took my father?" Nora asked Ezio as she, too, inspected the area.

Ezio nodded as he remembered the event, and how he had given Wolfgang to Mario while abandoning Signor Lehner.

"Do you think we have enough partisans?" Father Alexander grew concerned.

Ezio glanced at the surrounding hills as he spotted the fifty-some hiding behind bushes, trees, rocks, hills, and anywhere that would conceal them.

"Let us hope." Ezio drew a deep breath. He didn't want to be involved in another firefight like they had at the station. He was tired of violence, of the intimate dance with death, and longed for peace and quiet.

"Do you think I should say something?" Walter scratched his chin.

"What do you mean?" Father Alexander asked.

"Something inspirational." Walter shrugged.

"Do we have time?" Father Alexander asked Ezio.

"As long as you stay hidden." Ezio threw his lips upside down.

Standing, but making sure to remain hidden behind the hill, Walter stood and cleared his throat before beginning, "How often have you been called the Sons and Daughters of Mars by our Fascist overlords? No longer do we hold you to that pagan accounting. You are sons and daughters of Italy — of humanity!"

The partisans murmured quietly in their agreement.

"Listen," Ezio whispered to Nora as Walter continued to address those gathered. "I don't mean to pry, but are you alright?"

"I'm fine," Nora replied swiftly as she kept her gaze fixated on the road, waiting for any sign of the convoy.

"If I upset you, or if I — "

"It's not you!" Nora growled at Ezio.

"Then why are you shutting me out?" Ezio pressed.

"It's not…" Nora squeezed her eyes shut as she bit her tongue. "Let's talk about it later."

"We might not have later." Ezio glanced at the road.

With a heavy sigh, Nora began, "I…I…I don't know how to articulate it."

"You're angry?" Ezio asked as he studied her reaction.

"Very." Nora swallowed and glanced at Ezio with a soft expression, and he understood that she was growing resentful toward him.

"With me?" Ezio continued, and Nora nodded.

"If you had listened to me, we could've stayed to fight instead of nearly dying by that maniac's hand." Nora closed her eyes quickly, and Ezio knew that the experience had significantly traumatized her. "I couldn't do anything. I couldn't move, cry, or scream. Nothing."

"You were powerless." Ezio nodded in his understanding.

"I can't sleep." Nora's voice shook. "When I close my eyes, I see her standing over me, running her crude axe through my hair like a brush."

"She's gone now." Ezio squeezed Nora's hand.

"No." Nora shook her head. "No, she's not."

"I know it won't be easy." Ezio continued to hold her hand. "But stay with me, and I'll help you through this."

Nora looked back at Ezio with a sort of hopelessness that shattered his spirit.

"If you're angry," Ezio continued, "then tell me. If you hate me, tell me. If you want to smash my head in with your rifle, tell me. Please don't keep me in the dark."

"I want to smash your head in with my rifle," Nora replied with a slight smile, and Ezio felt her squeezing back on his hand.

"Promise you won't keep me in the dark."

"I promise." Nora drew a deep breath.

"Today, we take back our country!" Walter encouraged those in hiding. "Today, we end Mussolini's grip over Italy. Today, my comrades, friends, and family, we put a permanent end to Fascism."

The faint purr of an engine echoed throughout the hills.

"Get down!" Ezio waved for everyone to remain in place.

Peeking his head out from cover, Ezio watched the road, but no vehicle had come into view yet. Glancing at the opposite side of the road, Ezio spotted Carla and Lorenzo waiting anxiously for his orders.

Lorenzo offered a nod of encouragement to his son, reminding him to keep his resolve.

Eventually, a black vehicle rounded the corner, followed by another, and another, and another. It was a convoy, just as Ezio had feared. If their enemy had the security of numbers, they would likely retaliate.

Yet Ezio found it curious that it was a Nazi convoy and not one of Mussolini's. Still, he was certain that this was the road the dictator would use and was confident he had made the right decision.

"Now?" Nora asked as Ezio watched the vehicles approaching.

"Too soon," Ezio whispered as he shook his head.

With his hand raised, Ezio looked back at some partisans ready to enact their plan by blockading the road.

"Now!" Ezio shouted.

Father Alexander blew his whistle, the partisans threw trees, rocks, bushes, logs, and other debris onto the road, blocking the path of the convoy, and Ezio, Nora, Lorenzo, Carla, along with the remaining partisans, charged with weapons trained on the vehicles.

"Out!" Ezio shouted in German at the driver, who had his hands raised.

With fearful eyes, the occupants of the vehicles exited swiftly, hands held high in the air and terrified.

"On the ground!" other partisans shouted in German, and the Nazis swiftly obeyed as they lay prone before the ambush, and Ezio was thankful that they were utterly demoralized and not of the opinion to retaliate.

"Where is he?!" Palmiro called out as he looked through the men on the ground.

"It's not his convoy!" Alessandro yelled. "None of these men are Italian."

"He's not here!" Carla threw her rifle over her shoulder. "This was a decoy."

"Line them up." Ezio waved for those surrendering to be organized. "We'll inspect them to make sure he's not disguised."

"Il Duce is not among them!" Carla grew frustrated. "We're wasting time! He likely took another route to escape."

"Look at these men!" Ezio grew annoyed with her as the Nazis stood and formed a line. "They're all officers; men of rank. Even if Mussolini is not among them, this should make every Italian proud."

With the Nazis, about thirty in all, lined up, Ezio began studying their faces, looking for anyone who would resemble Mussolini. He was certain the dictator was in disguise, and Ezio was determined to find him.

Yet as Ezio looked at the men, he was reminded of Captain Cacioppo, and how, when he advised that he was going blind, was able to truly look at a person's face. Examining the faces passing in front of him, Ezio saw men who were scared, and rightfully so. They weren't afraid simply because they were losing the war, or because they were surrounded by angry partisans, but Ezio saw the fear of guilt etched into their wide eyes and clenched jaws.

"Lieutenant!" Alessandro called from further down the line. "He's here. He's among them."

"What makes you so certain?" Ezio called back.

"Because this is his mistress." Alessandro roughly pulled a woman away from the group, and Ezio was surprised that he hadn't noticed her before.

"Keep looking!" Ezio called to the rest of the partisans as they began inspecting each and every man. "He's here! Mussolini is here!"

Continuing with his inspection, Ezio began searching for any markers or identifiers. Before, Mussolini had stood out in the crowd due to his confident stature, commanding presence, and charisma. Yet all of these men were downcast and defeated. Not one among them appeared as a dictator or one who had ruled Italy for over twenty years.

Eventually, Ezio arrived at a man wearing a Luftwaffe coat and helmet. He found it odd that the man would be wearing this designation, and his rank seemed too lowly compared to the rest that had been captured.

What Ezio found most concerning about the man was how wretched he appeared. There was an emptiness in his eyes that Ezio recognized within his own soul. He had known that look for nearly ten years, and staring back at the man, Ezio knew that this was none other than Benito Mussolini.

"Papers?" Ezio held his hand out to the man for his documentation.

Yet the man didn't move. He simply stood, staring passed Ezio at the Swiss Alps, his safety and security so far away yet so close.

"Papers?!" Ezio demanded.

The man turned his gaze slowly to Ezio and looked him in the eye. It was the same man in the painting that had hung on his office wall, the same man who had promised to foster in another Roman Empire, and the same man who had terrorized his own people for decades.

"Search him." Ezio nodded to another partisan who he realized was Luigi.

"Take them all." Walter made a circle in the air with his finger to indicate the surrendering officials were to be rounded up.

"Here!" Luigi handed the documentation to Ezio.

"Grazie," Ezio spoke to Luigi, still feeling somewhat contrite for his dismissal of the man as nothing more than a drunk, recalling the painting that the captain had purchased from him.

"It's fake." Luigi pointed to the passport.

"This is Il Duce." Walter pulled Mussolini closer to him and grabbed him roughly by the jaw. "He's shorter than I remember, but this is the man."

"You're certain?" Ezio asked as he studied the man. It was true that he resembled Mussolini in features, but in spirit, he was nothing like the charismatic dictator.

"There's no mistaking him." Walter narrowed his gaze at the tyrant.

"What do you intend with him?" Ezio asked as he remained studying Mussolini, still surprised by how dejected and demoralized he appeared.

"We'll discuss that back in Giulino." Walter pointed back toward town.

"We should kill him where he stands!" Luigi shoved Mussolini, who, Ezio noticed, still didn't offer any response or emotion.

"Stay your hand!" Palmiro barked at Luigi.

"My family went hungry for years because of him!" Luigi again attempted to push the dictator, but Walter pulled him out of the way.

"Kill him now!" Carla also shouted, and others echoed her enthusiasm for Mussolini's death.

"He needs to stand trial!" Ezio countered, encouraged that some agreed with him.

"How many trials did he permit us?" Alessandro pointed at Mussolini. "Why shouldn't he be offered the same courtesy? Hang him by the neck, as he did to so many of our own people!"

A shout arose from those in agreement with Palmiro.

"Because we're not like them!" Ezio held his hand high, and the crowd calmed a little. "We cannot become the terror we want to eradicate. We need the liberties of order and proper judgment. Give him the trial that you would expect for yourself. Show the world how to properly deal with these monsters! List his sins, one after another, in a public court. Heap shame upon his head if you must, but don't stoop to his level. I've seen what resentment can do to a person's heart, and I see that hatred in your eyes. I understand that better than most.

But I beg of you, for the sake of Italy, deal justly with him."

A murmur went through the crowd, some agreeing while others disagreed.

"He's right." Carla nodded to Ezio.

"Take them into custody. We'll deal with them in Giulino," Walter called out, and at once the partisans rounded up the officials and began clearing the road.

"Where would be a good place to hold him in town?" Father Alexander asked Ezio.

"That decision will rest on your shoulders." Ezio handed his rifle to the priest. "We're not returning with you."

"What do you mean?" Father Alexander frowned as he reluctantly took the rifle from Ezio.

"Italy is no longer our home." Ezio looked back in the direction of Giulino with anguish and yearning.

"Ezio, ragazzo mio, running from your sorrows is no solution." Father Alexander looked at Ezio with sympathy. "I'll hear your confession. I'll help shepherd you where I can. You know my story; I also lost my family. I understand the pain you're enduring."

"Someday, Father, I might." Ezio studied the priest's eyes for any insincerity. "It's not that I'm trying to forget them. I don't believe that's possible. I'm not sure if this is the right thing to do, but I have to try something."

"I can empathize with that." The priest looked back at Ezio with a measure of defeat.

"Don't let them kill him." Ezio stuck his hand out to the priest as he nodded to Mussolini, who was being roughly shoved into a vehicle.

"They'll listen to you long before they listen to me." Father Alexander took Ezio's hand, realizing there was no use in arguing. "I'm just a silly priest. You, on the other hand, are one of them. Your voice carries weight."

"Arrivederci." Ezio squeezed Father Alexander's hand.

"Best of luck, Lieutenant." Father Alexander drew a deep breath. "If you're ever in Milan again, I'd love to offer you a proper tour of the cathedral."

With that, the priest, along with the partisans, commandeered the caravan's vehicles and began taking the prisoners back toward town as Ezio, Lorenzo, and Nora watched.

"I hope they kill him," Nora spoke coldly as the vehicles rounded the bend and out of sight. "I know that's improper of me to wish, but it's true."

"I pity him." Ezio recalled how dispirited Mussolini appeared. "I thought to find him a great man; intimidating and commanding, but in the end, he is just as inconsequential as the rest of us."

"I kept his hat." Lorenzo dug out a black cap from his pocket.

"His hat?" Ezio chuckled as he inspected it. "When did you take this from him?"

"When we were searching him for documents." Lorenzo shrugged. "I found it tucked inside his helmet."

"But why keep it?" Nora also chuckled.

"Might be worth something someday." Lorenzo sniffled. "You never know."

"I'm glad you're coming with us." Ezio examined his father with a measure of pride.

"You're my home." Lorenzo offered a hard pat on Ezio's back to veil his vulnerability. "Give me grandbabies. And soon, per favore."

Ezio chuckled slightly as he glanced at Nora, who rolled her eyes yet failed to contain a grin of her own.

With the three standing on the road, Ezio reflected on how his life had changed since he met Nora. Existence had become static, boring, and dull as Ezio wasted away behind his desk as a lieutenant. If he had followed through with Signor Lehner's arrest order when it had first come through, he would've never met Nora.

431

Thankfully, his conscience had stayed his hand and led him down a path he could've never imagined for himself.

Taking Nora's hand, Ezio looked at his wife as he pondered how fortunate he was to have met her.

"I don't promise this will be easy." Ezio looked at Nora and then at his father. "I'm not naïve enough to believe that moving to Switzerland will somehow erase our heartache. I imagine our sorrows will likely follow us wherever we go. Still, if we suffer together, then maybe we can lessen the burden."

Another purr of an engine emanated throughout the hills, and Ezio glanced in the direction of Switzerland to find that a car was approaching them.

"Should we be concerned?" Lorenzo asked as he held his rifle down low.

"No." Ezio shook his head before smiling at Nora. "It's been arranged."

"What's been arranged?" Nora frowned as she watched the vehicle approaching.

Ezio didn't reply as he looked back at her with a grin.

"Ezio?" Nora held her conclusion in reserve. "What's been arranged?"

"You'll see." Ezio turned his attention to the approaching vehicle.

"Ezio?" Lorenzo gripped his rifle tightly as the vehicle came to a stop about twenty yards away from them.

"It's alright, Papa." Ezio held his hand out to console his father.

With the vehicle stopped, the back passenger door popped open as Ezio turned to watch his wife's reaction, which she did not disappoint.

Throwing her hands over her mouth as tears fell down her cheeks, Nora watched as Signor Lehner gingerly left the vehicle and walked over to them.

"Faustina?" Signor Lehner asked with a trembling lip as he stood at a distance while removing his hat.

"Papa?" Nora's eyes welled in disbelief. Then, abandoning decorum, Nora sprinted to her father with open arms and embraced him as the two wept at their reunion.

Glancing at Lorenzo, Ezio was surprised to find him in a sullen state at the happy meeting, and he knew that his father wished that he could have such a reunion with Vittoria.

Suddenly, a gust of wind wrapped around Ezio and Lorenzo, through their clothes, hair, fingers, and faces, before it departed again as quickly as it had arrived.

With wide eyes, Lorenzo looked at Ezio, who understood that his father also sensed this was supernatural.

"They're not gone, Papa." Ezio looked at his father with tearful eyes of sorrow mixed with joy. "They're not gone."

Leonarda Cianciulli was found guilty of her crimes and sentenced to thirty years in prison and three years in an asylum. She died on October 15, 1970.

Giuseppe survived the war.

Sources differ on what happened to Mussolini after his capture by the partisans, but the accepted version of history is that Walter was responsible for executing the deposed dictator, and his mistress, in Giulino. After his execution, Mussolini's body was taken to Milan, where he was strung up as a spectacle. The public took their revenge on Mussolini's body and disfigured it almost beyond recognition.

The Italian Resistance, which included about 35,000 women, was instrumental in fighting the occupying Nazis. Nearly 50,000 partisans died fighting to free Italy from Fascism.

The End